Best wishes
K. Lewis

THE WINDMILL

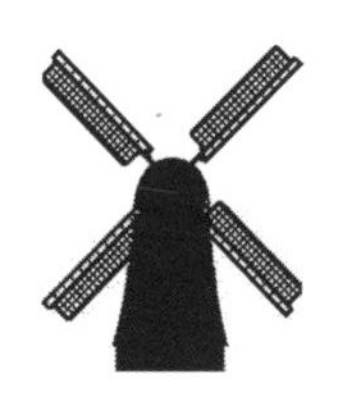

THE WINDMILL

K. LEWIS ADAIR

This is a work of fiction. Names, characters, businesses, places, events and incidents are either the products of the author's imagination or used in a fictitious manner. Any resemblance to actual persons, living or dead, or actual events is purely coincidental.

Matador
9 Priory Business Park,
Wistow Road, Kibworth Beauchamp,
Leicestershire. LE8 0RX
Tel: 0116 279 2299
Email: books@troubador.co.uk
Web: www.troubador.co.uk/matador
Twitter: @matadorbooks

ISBN 978 180046 008 9

British Library Cataloguing in Publication Data.
A catalogue record for this book is available from the British Library.

Printed and bound in Great Britain by 4edge Limited
Typeset in 11pt Adobe Jensen Pro by Troubador Publishing Ltd, Leicester, UK

Matador is an imprint of Troubador Publishing Ltd

For Jane,
My dear friend 'Burns'.
Always remembered.

ACKNOWLEDGEMENTS

With love and thanks to my husband, family and friends for their continued encouragement and support.

I would like to acknowledge The Rijksmuseum, Amsterdam, for permission to use the wonderful painting *Windmill of Wijk bij Duurstede* by Jacob van Ruisdael, circa 1670.

PART ONE

CONNECTIONS I

A pungent smell of wet earth pervaded as the dampness reached deep inside to scrape at their bones. An unbearable coldness numbed their legs as they crouched low in the shallow, mucky, water-filled ditch. Their eyes strained, searching in the darkness for shadows and silhouettes. Farther down the trackway, balls of light emanated from torches, arching from one side to the other, scanning intently for something or someone who must be found. All her senses were alert as she concentrated on every movement. Her chest pounded, and she experienced such anxiety, never felt in her life before, knowing she must keep control, not for herself but for the sake of those beside her. She tenderly squeezed the arm of the child beside her, sensing his heart quicken.

'Be strong,' she whispered as she listened to the faint voices gather around the light on the track. The whimper of the child next to her told her it was time to move on. These conditions would not allow them to stay here much longer and the danger was imminent. She bent forward, feeling for the hand of Freya, and fumbled until she touched her face, drawing her near.

'Comfort the children. Keep them quiet, no matter how cold or uncomfortable they become; this is imperative for their safety.' She took a deep breath to evade any signs of nervousness. 'I'm going further up the ditch on my own.'

'But...'

'No argument, Freya! For the sake of the children. I know what I must do. Stay here whatever happens and at dawn creep back into the coppice. Follow the treeline and do not come out. Do not go on the trackway. Move quietly and quickly. Do not stop until you reach the edge of the forest. There, seek cover but remain alert and wait, no matter how long... until you are safe. Do you hear me?'

Her breath shallow, she nodded in compliance.

'I will see you again... someday, I promise.'

With those final words, she reached over once more, this time to kiss her on the forehead, whilst letting go of her clenched hand.

The young boy next to her had attached himself to her, his hand encircling her arm as if in an iron vice. He only relinquished his grip as she prised open his fingers and placed his hand in Freya's and patted his shoulder to comfort him. Aware of his tears and the fear he exuded, she kissed him softly. The emotion rising inside her was becoming overwhelming, and she turned and thrust her hand into the bitter cold water of the ditch before any of the other children would notice; the striking pain tore away at any sentiments of weakness that would have broken her only a moment ago. Not only for their sake, she did this, but for her own sanity.

Numbed by the gelid conditions, her legs and feet, almost paralysed, would not respond. One after the other, slowly she moved each limb, trying to be quiet; she needed to cause a distraction, but not here... further away.

At last, her limbs, although still leaden, were able to function without her dragging them and she grabbed the edge of the bank, digging her nails into the drenched grass, and cautiously pulled herself up. From here she could again see the light from the torches in the distance. The mud-sodden trackway appeared empty. With all her might, she heaved her listless body out of the ditch and scrambled to her feet. Still awkward and clumsy, she managed to cross the track.

On the other side, the ditch wasn't as deep or wet and she manoeuvred herself into it, aware that behind her was a steep climb up through the trees. The view from here gave a better vantage on what was materialising, and she became alarmed at the proximity of the torchbearers to the location of the children and Freya.

A sudden commotion started amongst the searchers, and the shadows appeared to advance up the track. With no time for hesitancy, there was only one thing to do, and her body surged into action, pumping adrenaline through her, forcing her to launch herself without care onto the trackway and stand in the darkness. Through the mist she viewed the silhouettes congregate near the ditch, opened her mouth to scream... nothing.

Desperate and with no control of her panic, she took another breath and let forth a soul-terrifying shriek born of true frustration.

And it worked.

Surprised at the cry exploding from her, soaring down the track to catch the attention of the intent searchers. Frozen to the spot now, unafraid; defiant, she refused to move. The swathes of light stabbed in the darkness as bursts of sound reverberated up the track... within seconds the pursuers converged around her.

Relief came to her in this moment, knowing she'd drawn them away from the ditch. For the sake of the children, she remained standing exactly where she was, determined. Not seeing anything... but the lucent, blinding light.

ONE

SATURDAY, 13TH AUGUST 2005

Panic rose within, her heart quickened; motionless she was aware of the lights that travelled towards her, bringing with them an impending sense of danger…

~

A loud noise awoke her as she stirred, alert to a physical sensation of fear that remained in her body; trying to focus, she listened. The knocking emanated from the hallway.

'Hold on… coming.' Today was a day off and, happy in a sound sleep, Ginny pushed back the quilt reluctantly and draped her listless body on the edge of the bed. The rapping on the door continued.

'Wait a minute.' In desperation, she shuffled around the bedroom on one leg, trying to co-ordinate the other into her grey jogging bottoms. She pulled on her blue T-shirt with the shimmering motif of 'Sexy Babe' broadcast across the front of it, clipped up her hair and shouted, 'On my way,' as the knocking persisted.

Plodding up the hallway, she saw the silhouette of a person through the frosted glass of the door. Letters lay halfway along the hall floor. Ginny opened the door to reveal a grumpy, bearded postman, pointing to a brown envelope.

'Sorry,' she said.

He glanced at her T-shirt and Ginny felt a little embarrassed by her ridiculous nightwear.

'Sign here for this,' the postman snorted in a disgruntled manner.

Rather bemused, she peered at the mail as well as him.

'Pen, please?'

After a few moments fumbling in his sack, he presented her with a half-mauled biro to scribble a signature.

'Gee, thanks.' She handed the sad implement back to the disinterested face, bid a hasty retreat and slammed the door.

The remainder of the projectile post she picked up and headed to the front room.

A warm, gentle breeze agitated the living-room curtains as it ebbed through the open window caressing Ginny's face. The summer air smelt sweet to her as it teased loose a curl from the rest of her shoulder-length blonde hair. Still holding the other post, she now dropped them on the table, as she was in no rush to open these; she knew what they would reveal: the bank statement telling her she did not have enough money and the electricity bill needing to be paid. Predictable! But then she paused, noting the postmark on the brown envelope. *Curious,* she thought, then yawned. Before dealing with this one she sensed her faculties needed to be recharged; she required a stimulating drink.

The previous evening Ginny had been excited to catch up with her friends Megan and Alistair, having not seen them for ages, not since her grandmother's funeral. Both of them worked and lived in Glasgow, where she had met them at university.

At her suggestion they arranged to meet at The Hogs Head pub in town. Whilst sat waiting she remembered an old chap – said he went to school here in the 1940s. *How strange,* Ginny thought, *you could buy a pint in it now.* The memories for him were different to hers, but the building still endured.

Each enjoyed the time catching up. Meg and Al were like a brother and sister to her. With no siblings of her own, this greatly comforted her. What a trio they were. Although, sometimes Ginny admitted being a little envious of their relationship; it was clear they were so in love. So far lasting romantic partnerships had eluded her.

As the evening came to a close, they promised they must do this again. It had been such fun. On arriving home, she had switched on the television in search of a good old black-and-white film, which she loved, and it was three o'clock in the morning before she got to bed.

The lid plunged down on the cafetière, exuding such an aroma of coffee to her senses, her taste buds tingled with anticipation. This was one pleasure in her life and her mother often commented on her insatiable thirst for the 'awakening fluid'. Now content, she turned her attention again to the curious letter as she sauntered into the living room.

The franking mark on the letter showed it came from London, Cartwright, Appleby & Sons. Perplexed, Ginny could not think of anyone who would be sending her mail from London. She ripped open the envelope. Inside, she could see a formal letter, carefully folded into three. Opening it, the address revealed a solicitor in Amsterdam: Stelling, Olly and van Horst, Rembrandt House, Westerdoksdjik. It stated that Miss Virginia Faulkner had been bequeathed a property in Hampshire:

'Redivivus,
Pound Green Lane,
Silchester,
Hampshire.'

'What? Never heard of the place!' Also, the letter added, the person bestowing the property was a Miss Florence van Hassel. Ginny gazed at it in astonishment, muttering to herself in complete disbelief.

'Who the hell is Florence van Hassel?'

Further down, she recognised her grandmother's name: Edith Bartlett! What was she doing here? And, her maiden name: née van Hassell.

Ginny hadn't known her grannie's maiden name. Was it really van Hassell? If so, she must be related to this Florence?

On reading further, the property had been left to her on the death of her grandma. Ginny stopped as her memories flooded back to the sad day.

In May that year, on her eightieth birthday, Grandma Edith had looked and felt great, a strong, fit woman, who always said the women in this family were 'tough old girls!' Her sudden and unexpected death a few weeks later came as a surprise to everyone. Edith's condition had deteriorated; she relapsed, suffered from another heart attack and slipped into a coma, one from which she would not recover. That evening, as the rain splashed against the hospital window, she'd passed away.

To stop the rising emotion, Ginny swallowed hard and carried on reading. Edith Bartlett had been a trustee for the property. She was still unable to comprehend this; nobody ever mentioned any house in Hampshire. What did Grandma have to do with this?

It was all so bewildering. The name van Hassel she considered with curiosity whilst re-reading the letter.

'What is Grandma's connection to this name, to this Florence?'

As she sat with these thoughts mulling around in her head, she recollected an unusual conversation at the crematorium. Although, at the time it made no sense, she overheard an elderly relative saying to someone, 'What a shame Edith never put the past to rest, and "you know who" just vanished that spring all those years ago.' Of course, this had sounded like complete nonsense to Ginny, who thought nothing of it, but now, on further thought, could it have something to do with this Florence? What did they mean by not putting the past to rest? There were more questions than answers at the moment.

'I've been given a property by someone I've never heard of. This can't be happening.'

Struck by something not yet absorbed, she looked again at the information. Part of the inheritance was dependent on her birthdate. Not the year, but the actual date 7th March 1975. And it stated, the estate should only go to the beneficiary *if their date of birth matched this criterion. How very odd,* she thought; it would appear her birthdate had more to do with her receiving the property than an actual preference for her.

The rest of the letter explained, in legal jargon, she had only fourteen days from the receipt of the letter to notify the London solicitors of her intentions. If she did not contact them or collect the keys to the property, the house would go back into a trust until the Dutch solicitors received additional instructions. In signing for the registered mail this morning, Ginny, without realising it, started the clock ticking.

Stunned, Ginny stared over at her lamp as a myriad of colours caught her eye as the sun's rays refracted through the Tiffany-styled lampshade. She remembered it was a special purchase. In fact, the first item she bought on moving in to the red sandstone tenement apartment in Glasgow.

Three years ago, she decided to put down roots. Now she was secure in her job as assistant archivist in the Hunterian Museum at the University of Glasgow, a job she had been fortunate to get. Her many voluntary hours working as an undergraduate, and an excellent first-class degree in Anthropology and Ancient Studies, had assisted her in acquiring the post.

She adored what she did but had to admit it may have put a strain on her relationships. Although she was fond of her partners and cared for them, they never worked out. Something deep down was always missing. So, at twenty-seven, she'd purchased the flat. Now thirty, it was her pride and joy.

On moving in, the place had been run down, but with careful planning and hard work, Ginny decorated her home the way she wanted: in contemporary art deco style. The period was so inspirational to her, but she did not know why; so, she returned the apartment tastefully to how she thought it wanted to be. Ginny believed in a synergy with things in life. Such thoughts brought back happy memories for her.

However, this morning's post required her mother Annie's input to help explain things, so she decided to call her.

After a period, the phone transferred to voicemail. The monotone voice sounded in her ear. '*The person is not available now; please leave a message after the tone.*'

'Hi, Mum, only me… just calling for a bit of a catch-up. How are you? I'll ring again later. Oh, and one thing I need to talk to you about, is that I received a rather unusual letter today, which I don't really understand… Chat to you soon. Bye.'

Confused by this morning's events, Ginny walked through to the kitchen. To work something out, the apartment usually got a good clean, and thrashing around scrubbing, polishing, washing, bleaching and vacuuming helped her to organise her head.

After an hour, it would be fair to say her home shone. However, she had still not arrived at any conclusion – none whatsoever. This day had proven so far to be perplexing. Nothing about the correspondence made any sense at all. Her confusion was now intermingled with the smell of cleaning products. Odours of bleach and polish followed her, and she elected she needed a shower.

A little while later, refreshed and smelling far more fragrant, she pulled on her skinny jeans. Comfortable, her long slim legs suited them. She threw on a black T-shirt and a little make-up – usually a small streak of black eyeliner which highlighted her green eyes. Before putting on her sandals, she brushed her blonde hair, then slung her bag over her shoulder, checking for her mobile phone and keys. She pulled closed the front door and headed down the stairs, through the tenement Close and emerged into the sunshine of the street.

TWO

SATURDAY, 13TH AUGUST 2005

Annie threw her keys on the kitchen worktop and placed her shopping on the floor. She slipped off her shoes as she made her way to the fridge.

'Yes,' she said, reaching in with anticipation, and grabbed the cold bottle of Bombay Sapphire. She poured it into a tall glass, then added the tonic. With crushed ice and a chunk of lime, the job was done. So refreshing after a long day shopping; she looked at an array of many-coloured bags sat on the floor.

'Crikey, what have I bought?'

Earlier that morning, Annie caught the train into London from Hemel Hempstead. She had arranged to meet her dear friend Heather outside Selfridges in Oxford Street. Thank goodness, as Heather always knew what to wear and for all the right occasions.

First stop had been Oddono's café for that essential cup of tea.

'Why are we shopping today, Annie?' Heather asked. 'What's the occasion?'

'Well, after this stint away with his business, Ben promised to take me on holiday to the South of France. "Let your bohemian heart run free," he said, "but remember you might need a few more conventional outfits to eat out."'

Heather gasped. 'In all the years I've known you, Annie Bartlett-Faulkner, I can't believe my ears... conventional, you!' And thus, the shopping spree had begun.

Annie strolled into the dining room, opened the French doors to the garden, and placed her drink and crisps on the patio table. Sitting down, she swung her bare feet onto the table. The sweetness of the juniper berry was inviting as she sipped her drink. Ben was away and she rarely drank, but tonight she thought, *Why not?* He wouldn't mind. No one could have cared for her and Ginny like he did; he was the best husband ever. Conservative at times, but nobody ever loved her as much as he did – she knew this. The love they shared came from deep within.

Satisfied, she eased back and wriggled her toes as she thought of her friend's words this morning. 'Conventional, you?'

When did she get that reputation? At university, people would have considered her quite boring. But she set herself free. Somebody a long time ago saw a fiery soul within her and offered to liberate her from the entrenched social expectations she would be lured into. It had been back, over thirty years ago, in 1974 and a bookshop in Kingston-upon-Thames, and... Jack.

~

'No, not this one.' A young man stood at the counter talking to the assistant, who was trying not to become frustrated with him. Annie hadn't meant to overhear the conversation, but it was a small shop.

'Do you keep his other works?' The guy's accent sounded different… 'continental', perhaps?

'No, sir, we don't.' The sarcasm in the assistant's voice was quite evident. 'Sorry, I don't think I can offer you any extra assistance.' And with that the guy was politely dismissed.

He stood with his back to Annie. She assessed he was about six foot tall, slim, with blond, wavy hair. Whilst viewing him with curiosity, he made an abrupt turn, clearly exasperated with the assistant, and caught a glimpse of her. Annie shot back, pressing her nose up against the bookshelf.

The shop sold many types of books, from new published literature to old papers and even antiquary journals. *What book did he want?* she wondered, as the tinkle of the shop doorbell announced his leaving. With a sigh of relief, she stepped forward to the front of the premises. Then came to a startled halt, because, staring blatantly through the window directly at her, was the same guy. Frozen to the spot, the blush on her face displayed her awkwardness.

'Oh God, why now?' she muttered to herself.

Almost enjoying her embarrassment, he smiled at her and after a moment walked away. With that one smile, Jack won Annie's heart.

Annie had not been at Kingston long. Only managing to scrape through her A levels, she resolved rural Shropshire, beautiful as it was, no longer held her attention anymore. She needed a change, an adventure, and being offered a place at university, she seized the opportunity and declared to her mother that she 'wanted to live life to the full'.

'You'll soon find out what life is all about,' her mother said. 'You're a dreamer and they usually wake up with a stern shock.'

A little pessimistic, Annie had thought, but she now understood her mother's concern for a child who was about to flee the nest. She reflected sadly at the thought of her mother; only gone a month, and she ached with the emptiness left by her passing. It was the same when her father George Bartlett had died when she was only fifteen. That too was unexpected. She had only a few memories of him, but they were fond ones.

She was the youngest of the three children. Their squabbling would drive her mother to distraction, and she used to say to Annie if she was fighting with Tom or Margaret that she was lucky to have her brother and sister. 'You never know what might happen in life, Annie,' Edith had said. 'One day you might just find that both could just disappear and then how would you feel? Not ever knowing what happened to them.'

It always struck Annie as an unusual thing to say... but most mothers were a bit peculiar sometimes, including herself. *Poor Mum,* she thought, standing up. Edith never showed she was ever disappointed with her, even though Annie tested her on more than one occasion.

'Stop all this morose thinking,' she uttered, deliberating on whether to have another gin and tonic – she didn't deliberate for long.

~

The night needed music and she pulled out her old Pink Floyd LP, *Meddle.*

'Wow, this has been well used over the years.' She inspected the many scratches the record had received on its journey through life with her. The label read '1971' and, laying the vinyl on the deck, she remembered buying the album on release. The intervening years had flown by.

Outside she waited for her favourite song, 'One of These Days.' The evening was humid and smelt sweet. Annie observed the sky change with the onset of dusk. A beautiful sunset was evident as the golden, red-hazed sphere ebbed slowly behind the hawthorn hedgerow at the bottom of the garden. There, the hammock caught her attention.

Still holding her G&T, she sat in it, which was easier said than done as she had to throw herself backwards. Not the most elegant of launches and her legs swayed in all directions, but she managed to settle without spilling a single drop of her drink. Regaining control of her limbs, she puffed up the cushions behind her head and gazed up into the night sky as the melodic tones of her music reached her across the air. It reminded Annie of another time. On an evening not unlike tonight lying on the grass in Regent's Park, London.

~

Transfixed that night by the palette of colours produced as the sun began to set, her view was broken only occasionally by the gentle breeze blowing the leaves of the oak tree across this photogenic image. A boy named Alex, who was on her course, asked her to a party in the park. Both of them studied Art History and only spoke in passing, but most people from the class were invited. A fair way from Kingston, but students from

University College London had arranged the event. Annie took her new friend Heather. She wasn't on the same course, as she was studying Fashion, but from the same university.

The city that evening was lively, bustling away in its own cacophony of noises, but the tranquillity of the gardens in Regent's Park was a stark contrast. Music, quiet at first, drifted in their direction, as did a shallow wave of voices. Not knowing many people, Annie and Heather felt awkward to start with, but glasses of wine were thrust at them and the evening mellowed. Students were milling around, either chatting, smoking or dancing. They both stretched out on the grass under a tree and a guy from UCL sat down beside them and offered them a smoke. It smelt quite different: a pleasant smell with a heavy odour. Heather instantly refused, but Annie accepted as she found the aroma enticing.

'Sure,' the guy said, and lit up a joint for her. 'Go on, you will be free as a bird, babe.' And passed her the spliff. 'Chill, lie back and enjoy the sky.'

Curious, she drew on it, spluttered and coughed.

'Don't worry, go steady and the vibe will be cool.'

'Nothing, I don't feel anything,' Annie answered, puffing once more.

'Just relax and gaze at the stars, you'll be fine.'

'OK, I will.'

A little while later, Annie lay down, chilled and gazing. 'Wow! Hey, Heather, you should try this stuff, the sky is beautiful, like... like a kaleidoscope!'

Then her vision was obscured by an upside-down face that appeared above her. 'Did you choose your book?' a voice questioned.

'What book?' asked Annie. 'Who are you?'

'So many questions, Ms Sky.'

The young man sat down beside her. Nice, wavy blond hair which seemed familiar; two bright green eyes stared back at her. *Not bad*, she thought, and then he smiled.

Bingo! The penny dropped.

'Jack,' he said, continuing to stare at her. 'You recognise me, now, don't you, Ms Sky?'

'Annie,' she introduced herself. 'Long way from home?'

'Visiting my mate Alex,' he said. 'I believe he is on your course?'

'Yes, he invited me here, but I don't really know him.'

'Best to keep it that way,' the guy said with a grin. 'He's an awful stinker.'

They both laughed and that was how Annie met Jack.

~

Annie fell for him so quickly; something about him intrigued her. So clever, knowledgeable and ahead of his twenty-one years in wisdom, appealing not only in looks but in personality.

'Tea is all you drink?' said Jack.

'So? You have coffee all the time, I prefer my tea.'

'It doesn't wake you up like coffee… or stimulate the senses.'

'Yours don't need any more stimulating; you're always on the go. I prefer being more relaxed.'

'OK, Ms Sky.' Jack had taken to calling her this since that evening in the park.

This evening, she sensed, he appeared a little agitated. With his studies finalised at UCL, this left Annie requiring another year to complete, and Jack was contemplating where his future might take him. Always searching for something. In the couple of months she knew him, she was passionate about him. But as much as he cared for her, something in Jack's life was missing; she knew so little about him, as he was a private person.

'Annie?'

'What's on your mind, Jack?'

'Always plenty going on in my crazy mind, but I need to tell you I've been offered a place for post-graduate research at a university at the end of September.'

'Great news—'

Jack cut her off mid-sentence. 'Might not be... not for you. It's not nearby.'

'Where is it then?'

'New York.'

The waitress interrupted, bringing them their tea and coffee.

'Thank you,' he said, and stared into the hot black liquid.

For certain, Annie knew what bothered him and what this all meant, so she raised the cup to her mouth and sipped.

~

'This is enough for tonight,' decreed Annie, and finished the last of her gin. It was now approaching ten o'clock and almost dark. She hung her legs off the edge of the hammock. *At this point,* she thought, *perhaps I shouldn't have drunk two gins or even entertained using the hammock*. Bent forward, she almost catapulted off the contraption. The cushions bounced off, flying in all directions as she landed awkwardly on her feet.

'Death trap!' she cursed, and strolled into the house shutting the doors behind her. The record was still going around on the deck, the stylus replaying the same old scratch over and over again.

'All right, stop protesting, I'll put you out of your misery.' For a moment she stopped, thinking she could make out a faint vibrating noise coming from the kitchen. Was the mobile ringing? Where was it? As fast as she was able, she hobbled into the kitchen to look for her handbag. A healthy fifty-two-year-old, she was fit, but tonight she swore at the hammock – either that or the shopping trip – for making her body ache.

She recognised Heather's number as she pressed the button on the phone.

'Hey, Annie. Got back all right then? Was only checking, knowing what you are like.'

'Delighted to hear you're concerned; I take it you got back to Oxford OK?'

'Yep, no worries. But at our age, a snooze on the train is almost expected.' Heather laughed.

'Listen, thanks for all your help today, I wouldn't have managed without you.'

'Always a pleasure. Don't be a stranger, stay in touch and catch you soon. Bye, old girl.' With that, Heather was gone.

Annie smiled. 'The abuse she gives me! Wouldn't have it any other way!'

And then she noticed that she had a voicemail message waiting.

THREE

FRIDAY, 28TH FEBRUARY 1975

The warmth in the room rushed out to greet him. A bitterly cold day, he shook his feet one after the other to rid the slush from his boots. Jack smiled at the waitress, who greeted him in her broad New York accent.

'Just one, sir?' she asked, curious to know if he indeed was on his own.

With a wry smile, he replied, 'Yes please, one will be sufficient.'

She led the way to a table positioned at the front of the café and motioned to Jack to be seated. 'I will come back to take your order in a moment.'

On the wall to the left of him Jack noticed lots of sodden, heavy coats all draped on top of each other on coat hooks and added his to the pile before sitting down on the chair nearest the window. Blood pulsed again as he rubbed at his reddened nose. The place was full, which was no doubt due to the weather. People huddled, chatting around the small square tables. The waitresses hustled up and down the narrow avenues between the rows of tables, adeptly stepping over bags and shopping which lay in their path on the floor as they skilfully delivered a variety of much-appreciated warm snacks and beverages. Jack glanced at the varied selection of knitwear people chose to wear and smiled to himself. The colours and styles were... unique. *Each to their own,* he thought as he studied his black-and-grey flecked knitted jumper. It was functional at the very least.

Seeing the waitress on her way back to his table, he picked up the menu from its holder on the table in front of him.

'What will you have?'

'I'll have a strong black coffee with a toasted rye bread, ham and cheese, thanks.' Jack flashed a smile at the young woman.

'No problem, sir.' She flicked her long dark hair away from her face and walked off to the counter to talk to the other waitresses, who looked back at Jack. He turned away from their attention to look out the steamed-up window, rubbing a small circle on the glass acting as a peephole to the busy street.

Lights outside were accentuated now as the evening and darkness drew nearer, the neon glow highlighting the names of the many shops, cafés and restaurants hung in the air. Red flashes, white flashes, sequential patterns of red, amber and green light controlling the flow of the traffic, as the view was interspersed by the movement of cars, taxis and buses.

People bustling around, all going somewhere, and all heading in different directions. Jack had been part of the city bustle. Until, on his way back from the Metropolitan Museum where he had been working with Professor Flackman, he selected to detour into the welcoming little coffee shop.

Jack accepted his post-graduate place with the New York university researching ancient artefacts. With this love of the subject, he often got lost in the mystic of the past. Always happy to indulge himself in learning something new, he never understood where this love of antiquities came from. It just did!

The pretty dark-haired waitress was beside him again. 'Here you go, sir.'

'Thank you.'

'Enjoy your food. Just shout if you need me.'

He held his gaze on her, watching as she walked off to attend to her other orders.

The steam rose upwards, carrying a rich, full coffee aroma, scintillating to his senses. He left both hands clasped around the cup for a moment, warming them to rid him of the cold day as he peeked once again from his little spyhole on the window. Fortunately, his flat was not too far away, located on the Upper East Side of Central Park, meaning a short, generally pleasant, stroll home. He had found private accommodation after two months living on campus. He knew how lucky he was, not only in getting the apartment but also in his posting. He was grateful to his tutor at UCL. Impressed by Jack's natural aptitude for his studies, Dr Pindle believed in Jack's sixth sense about the subject.

Jack finished his snack and realised he wasn't in too much of a hurry to go home, knowing the flat would be empty. He didn't seem to be lucky with relationships; they never lasted any length of time. This was strange, as Jack was never short of admirers. The question as to whether he would ever meet the right girl, he admitted to himself, he simply did not know. He thought of Annie Bartlett and wondered what she might be doing. She saw the restlessness in him, and there was no denying he had been drawn to her, but he knew his unsettled nature had forced them apart.

He stood, putting a tip on the plate – the pleasant service, friendly smile and pretty face demanded some form of just reward – and headed for the coat rack, where his damp old duffel lay under several coats. Retrieving it, he shivered as he wrapped it around him – wearing sodden clothing was a horrid experience – and tightened the toggles. Then he slipped out of the café into the darkened and freezing street, heading for home.

A couple of blocks along the way Jack stopped at a newspaper kiosk and bought *The New York Times*. The headline stared him in the face:

U.S. PERFORMS NUCLEAR TEST AT THE NEVADA TEST SITE.

Again, he glanced at the paper and read a small section. The key word that triggered his attention was 'London'.

43 KILLED IN LONDON UNDERGROUND AS TRAIN SPEEDS PAST FINAL STOP.

Jack hoped that nobody he knew was involved in the incident. London was the city he considered his second home. At the age of ten his mother deemed his education would be better served at boarding school in England and packed him off to Dulwich College in Greater London, where he met his best friend Alex.

Jack tucked the newspaper under his arm and resumed his journey home. On approaching his apartment, he greeted an older man who was throwing salt down on the steps. 'Evening, Walter, a cold one today?'

'Certainly is, the ice is setting in already. You'll have to mind your step, son.'

Walter Kowalewski was the janitor and Jack spoke to him most days – an old chap who lived in the bottom apartment by himself, always with a tale to tell. Polish, he arrived in New York before the Second World War broke out. Often he would chat to him about his home and his experience in the US marines. When he arrived, he signed up straight away, wanting to do his bit to help. Jack mentioned once his father survived the German occupation, but he said his family never spoke of anything related to the war.

'Don't to be too long outside or you might just become a new feature at the front of the building.'

Walter laughed and threw down another handful of salt. 'Almost done, you won't be catching me out here for much longer. I'll finish the job and go inside for a tot of rum.'

Jack climbed the steps cautiously and was opening the door when he turned back. 'Nearly forgot, old-timer, I got you the *Times*.'

'Thank you, son, much appreciated.' Walter waved as the door closed behind Jack.

With trepidation Jack looked at the old lift; he was never that enamoured with the old iron box – a rather rickety construction that appeared unstable, although plenty used it. More for his own peace of mind, he climbed the eight flights of stairs to go to his floor, as he usually did. If nothing else, he remained fit. The many apartment doors he passed en route made him think of all the divergent lives in one place, how on the odd occasion you bumped into someone you made polite conversation, never really knowing them.

Entering the apartment, Jack flicked on the light switch and stood in this one large expanse that accounted for both his living and dining area. He strolled over – past the dining table covered in books, papers and archaeological journals with a random cup squeezed into the free space remaining – to close the blinds on the sash windows to shut out the dark, cold night.

Extricated from his damp coat, he next kicked off his shoes, leaving them underneath the table alongside an array of other discarded footwear, and sat down on the red leather sofa. He stretched out his long legs, feeling tired, and yawned. His attention was drawn to the letters that still lay on the coffee table from yesterday – it wasn't unusual for him to rush out and forget the mail. He reached across for the post, sifting through the dull envelopes until he seized the one whose handwriting he recognised. This came from England, and, in particular, his good friend Alex.

He began eagerly to open the envelope and rushed to read the letter. Alex wanted to visit in the summer. This pleased him. Since leaving London late last year, Jack was beginning to miss all those familiar faces at home. Fair to say he liked New York, but to see Alex would be amazing. In particular, sharing thoughts with Alex on scholarly issues would be fantastic. At work, Professor Flackman had him delve into records not researched before. Strange how he felt about his new studies – as though they were distantly familiar, like wearing old slippers, in some small way helping to appease his restlessness.

He stopped for a moment to absorb the last piece of information in the letter. Lots had been happening and Alex wanted to tell him something important, apologising for not telling him in writing, but said he wanted to meet his old friend face to face.

'What exactly could be so important that he couldn't tell me in a letter?' It made Jack a little uneasy. What could it be that he needed to tell him?

FOUR

'No, not a problem at all, Ginny, you come down to us whenever you want, darling. Are you able to take time off then?'

'Sure, work said all was fine; I have so many days owing to me and we are in a quiet period at the moment.'

'It will be lovely to catch up with you; we won't be here for long before we go off to the South of France.'

'Oh, of course, I forgot about that. Are you looking forward to going?'

'Can't wait, darling – pretty much bought a new wardrobe. Heather dressed me, you know how adept she is at picking the right outfits… and what I'm like. Such a good day out, though.'

'Blimey, I hate to think what you both got up to, having been let loose in London.'

'Why you make us sound like a couple of misfits, for goodness' sake? I'm only your mother.'

'Funnily enough, I'm kind of aware of that fact.'

'So why the visit then, darling?'

~

Ginny slammed the tailgate of her VW Polo shut, watching

as a shard of rusty metal landed on the road at the side of her foot.

'Can't do that each time or there will be none of you left to drive,' she commented, strolling round to the driver's door. Her bottle of water and a pack of sweets lay on the passenger seat ready for the long journey ahead. The VW was her pride and joy – an old thing, in fact an early model going back aeons, but she loved it for all its faults.

With Glasgow in her rear-view mirror, the weather was cloudy but dry. On joining the motorway, Ginny sang along with the radio, listening at the news breaks for any traffic problems that might occur. It didn't take long to travel away from the hectic city, the sprawling conurbations and the intertwining road systems. And the view before her was so stunning, even resplendent, as the rounded hills of southern Scotland topped with lilac and pink heathers merged into the bright skyline, sitting majestically as they had done for all time, warming Ginny's heart.

On approaching the next service station, she took the slip road off the motorway and tucked the car into a neat little parking space, only a stone's throw away from the main building. Across the rear seat lay her denim jacket, and she stretched her legs before reaching over for it. The sun broke through the clouds, but the air was cool and, grabbing her bag, she hurried her way inside the complex.

Already knowing she wanted a latte, she located the café, but was spoilt for choice on finding the Danish pastries. These were her mother's favourites. As she queued to pay, she thought back to her conversation with her mother.

FOUR

~

'So why the visit then, darling?'

'Yesterday, when I left the message, I said I received an extraordinary letter.'

'Oh... what about?'

'Well, that's why I'm coming down, to explain when I see you, but apparently... I've been bequeathed a property in Hampshire!'

'Did I hear you right, Ginny?'

'Yes, Mum... someone has left me a house.'

There was a pause. 'What are you saying?'

'Like I said, it's bizarre. Can't understand why someone would want to leave me a property.'

'A house in Hampshire...' Annie repeated, perplexed and unable to absorb what Ginny told her.

'There's loads to talk about and I have to claim it in the next fourteen days – in fact only got thirteen now as today is Sunday.'

'Where have you got to go to sign for the property?'

'A solicitor in Cavendish Square in London.'

'London?'

'Yes... the correspondence didn't initially come from Cartwright, Appleby & Sons but from a solicitor in Amsterdam.'

'Amsterdam?' said Annie in astonishment.

'Yes... It is all very peculiar.'

'You can say that again. What the heck is this all about, Ginny?'

'I have no idea! The other thing that was peculiar, Mum... was Grandma's name was mentioned.'

'Your Grandma Edith?'

'Yes.'

'What was she doing in the letter?' Annie was now more than confused.

'Well, she was the keeper, or rather the trustee, for the property, apparently.'

'My goodness… my mother connected to a house in Hampshire? I'm at a loss as to what to say… dumbfounded. I know absolutely nothing about this.' Annie was starting to understand how confused Ginny must be. They say there are always plenty of skeletons inside a family's cupboard, but where did all these bones come from?

'Mum, you still there?'

'Yes, darling, I'm still here. A little shocked.'

'I understand… it is all rather strange. Listen, what was Grandma's maiden name?'

'Stanley, I think, before she became Bartlett on marrying Grandpa George after he came back from the war.'

'Thought you mentioned that before. The information quite clearly states that Grandma's name was Edith van Hassel.'

Annie reached for the kitchen chair and sat down. 'Say that again, Ginny, what was her name?'

~

Armed with wine gums and chocolate eclairs, Ginny made her way to the car. Comfortable, she followed the exit signs back to the motorway as melodic tones of southern boogie in the form of Lynyrd Skynyrd filled the interior. Her head nodded to the beat. Ginny loved this; it was what drives were made for.

The humdrum roar of the car was now a pattern of noise as the weather changed and the road became much busier. Orange and white cones to the right of her directed the traffic, merging into one slow-moving line of never-ending roadworks. She was astounded at how much of the road was shut down before you even reached the actual construction or repair. Stuck in the slow-moving queue for over forty minutes, Ginny chose the toll part of the motorway and checked her purse for money. In the zipped pouch, she came across her lucky coin. A gift from her mother when she started university, Annie relinquished it to her daughter as a token of protection for her long journeys in life. She placed her lucky keepsake on the dashboard and wondered why her mother held on to a Dutch guilder. She must have thought a great deal of it to pass it on to her.

~

'Why do you think the property has been left to you? Don't get me wrong, darling, but...'

Ginny interrupted her mother, pre-empting what she was going to say, as she herself already pondered this. 'Yep, I know,' she said. 'Why not go to either you, Uncle Thomas or Aunt Margaret? Don't have a clue. Can you tell me the dates of birth of both of them?'

'Their birthdays?' Annie reiterated.

'Yes.'

'What's that got to do with anything?'

'Not sure, just an idea. Yours is 8th April, what are the others?'

For a moment Annie thought. 'Thomas is the oldest, born on 11th June 1947 and Margaret was on 29th January 1951. You know mine; the year was 1953.'

'Thought that might be the case.'

'What do you mean?'

'The letter I received stated the bequeathing of the property was dependent on my birthdate, my birthday being 7th March.' Even as Ginny spoke to her mother, it still sounded so extraordinary.

'Hang on, are you telling me the inheritance is not to do with you, as a relative, but more to do with your birthdate?'

'That's what it said.'

'Crikey, I suppose this would fit. No one in the family that I'm aware of has the same birthday as you. How bizarre. All so inexplicable, isn't it? What do you think the significance of your birthdate is?'

'No idea… it meant a lot to whoever decided on this course of action. One other thing, who is Florence van Hassel?'

The stunned silence at the other end of the phone was indicative in itself.

~

'At last!' Ginny stretched up in relief, flexing her shoulders as she exited the M1 and proceeded to follow the road into Hemel Hempstead. Later she pulled up on the gravel driveway of her family home. Parked, she patted the dashboard of the car, collected her coin and ceremoniously thanked her little VW for a safe journey. Despite being August, the weather turned nasty and the sky was dark, heavy with rain; large spots were now splattering on the bonnet as confirmation. One landed on Ginny's forehead as she took her bag from the boot and checked the time: five minutes past six. As she straightened her aching back, the front door opened and there stood Annie. Her long auburn hair was loose, and she flicked it off her face as she smiled excitedly at her daughter. Then she proceeded out of the doorway in her fluffy pink slippers to embrace Ginny, the way any mother would who had not seen their offspring for some time.

'My you look tired, but well, darling. How was your journey?'

'Long,' Ginny said, smiling. 'I'm pleased to see you, Mum.'

'Come on, let's go inside, the weather is turning nasty. 'We can have a long chat and attempt to work out this extraordinary situation.'

As they entered the house, Ginny sensed the comfort of home surround her as her mother took her luggage from her and then stepped back to push the door shut, blocking out the miserable, wet evening.

FIVE

FRIDAY, 18TH JULY 1975

In the office at the base of the Metropolitan Museum, Professor Flackman pulled the angle-poise lamp closer to attain a clearer view of the artefact he was studying. The shelves above him were full of books. Cabinets behind were packed with archaeological journals, scientific publications and papers. Posters on the wall displayed copies of many beautiful paintings and sites of historical interest from around the world. A typical academic's office!

From behind him, the tranquillity of his studies was interrupted by noise and chaos as Jack burst into the room, struggling with the weight of several boxes. His hair was matted with dust, as was his torn T-shirt, faded from blue to a dirty beige. The professor swung round in his chair, disturbed by the whirlwind. Jack launched forward, slamming the boxes down on the worktop, and let out a sigh of relief. He ran his hand through his hair, clearing his eyes, adding a streak of dirt to his face.

'Goodness, what have you got?'

Jack turned and apologised for his dramatic entrance.

The professor stared, mesmerised by his dishevelled appearance. 'Where on earth have you been? You're filthy.'

'I'm not surprised. Have you ever been down to the sub-storage levels? Because the light of day has not been down there in a long, long time.' He shivered. 'What an eerie place. Caked in dust and most probably full of primordial creepy-crawlies lurking around. I could hardly see anything.' Jack continued brushing at his shirt. 'These boxes...' he said, tapping them, 'I found by chance trying to locate the first-century fragments of Samian ware you were after. They must have been placed in storage ages ago. Just about to leave, and I had a feeling other items were further back when I uncovered these. It was so dimly lit I couldn't make out any markings on them, but we might have a better chance at identifying them up here.'

The professor got up, now intrigued with the boxes. 'The sub-storage levels, you say?'

Jack nodded as the professor retrieved the lamp; realigning it on the books, he angled the beam of light on the top of the first box.

'Behind you on the third shelf – in a tin mug – is a small, soft-bristled brush,' the professor said. 'We can remove some of this dirt with it.'

Jack handed the brush to him and watched as the professor stroked it across the surface of the box. Plumes of dust rose into the air, captured in the light. Some faded markings became more visible. The professor stopped, coughing as he did so, and nudged up his spectacles.

'Seems to read... "The British Museum". Then another word, and I think... numbers, maybe a date. Can't quite make them out.'

Moving aside, he picked up the magnifying glass sat on his desk as Jack pulled the lamp lower to concentrate the lamplight on the wording they just revealed.

'Yes... yes, that does look like "the British Museum", stamped on the box. The other word is harder to determine.'

The magnifying glass he now handed to Jack, who began scrutinising the markings.

'Yes, much better, the letters are an N, D, O, and another N. Must be London? Which would make sense. Can you pass me the brush, please?'

Dust particles filtered into the air, irritating Jack's nose as he brushed, then sneezed loudly.

'Bless you.'

'Wretched stuff.' He resumed his examination. 'Beside the word London is A, N.' He brushed some more. 'No... hang on, there are letters in front of it. L... O... Yes! LOAN!'

'What are we doing with these?' Jack asked. 'Do we have any records of loan artefacts from the British Museum?'

'Well, it is common practice for museums to loan different objects to one another, especially for an exhibition. In theory we should have documentation of transfer for these artefacts, but the reference would be assisted by the date. Also, it seems unusual. These items would in normal circumstance be recalled by the British Museum. Under the terms of institutional loans most are subject to annual review. Can you make out the numbers?'

'Mm... they're not clear, but I'll try,' he said, using the magnifying glass again, rubbing with his finger. 'Think this is one, nine, and I believe the other digits are a... three and a nine. So dated... 1939. Can that be right?'

'Are you sure it reads 1939?'

Jack nodded, certain of the date.

'OK. Are all the boxes the same?'

'I'll check.'

Careful as he un-stacked them, Jack brushed the top of the next lid. The name and date he recognised quicker – same as the previous one. The last box was different.

'First five boxes are identical, and all marked to correspond to the initial box. I can't make out any markings yet on this final box.'

'Right,' said the professor, walking toward the door. 'Have a look at the last one and I'll go to the sub-storage levels to see if I can locate any transfer documents from that period. Can't think why we might have them, but I'll go and dig up what I can.'

To alleviate the tension in his shoulders, Jack stretched for a moment and lifted up the sixth box with the expectation of a similar weight to that of the others. It rose so lightly; catching him by surprise, he almost dropped it. Something inside slid to and fro.

There were no markings whatsoever: only two fastening clips located at either side. With growing curiosity, he scanned the office for something to open the box with. On the desk behind him was an empty glass jar with small screwdrivers.

That should do it, he thought. The screw was aged and fixed with rust; it made it difficult to loosen and the screwdriver slipped out of position, making Jack lurch forward, banging his hand.

'Shit.'

Again, slowly this time, he started to turn the screw,

twisting until the pace of the turn quickened and the screw dropped on the worktop. Aware his hand was sweaty, he wiped it down the leg of his now-filthy jeans before undoing the others.

Jack sighed as the last one fell, and he threw the screwdriver down on the bench. With both hands gripping the lid of the box, he began to lift. It creaked and writhed its way upward and with one final pull, he stepped backwards as the cover gave way, rising into the air. Still holding the lid, he moved to look into the box. As suspected, nothing. No artefact – just what appeared to be a blank sheet.

To check if there was anything on the other side, he lifted up the paper. When he turned it over, he could see it looked like a docket. This was different. Written by hand, declaring the British Museum was recalling artefact 198463 from the Rijksmuseum, giving the year 1939 and the loan reference. Nothing specified what the item was. Jack looked at the curious handwriting. There was something he couldn't put his finger on.

Muddled, his head now woozy, he leant on the desk; his mind drifted, the writing went in and out of focus and his heart began to race, giving him palpitations.

The professor marched back into the office to see Jack stagger back a couple of paces. 'Are you all right? You don't look well.'

Jack turned, hearing a muffled voice – not belonging to the professor – and tried to focus, but his vision was so blurred. A vague outline emerged. What seemed to be a woman stood in front of him. Unable to clearly see her features, he thought she was talking to him, but Jack couldn't decipher the words. In a split second the vision began to fade, and the room began to spin round. He could feel his head falling, falling weightlessly. His body slumped down until he landed, drained and motionless.

'Jack... can you hear me? Can you see me?'

Aware of the light before him, his eyes refocused, drawing him back into the familiar surroundings of the office. The words resonating in his ears now becoming recognisable.

Professor Flackman was knelt on the floor, holding a glass of water. 'Are you OK?'

Confused, Jack stared at the professor.

'Here, drink this; take a moment to gather yourself. You fainted.'

'Sorry, what happened to me? Never passed out before.'

'Think you are overdoing it: you never stop working – probably worn out. Relax for a minute, then we will go outside for some fresh air.'

Sat upon the fire exit stairs at the back of the museum, Jack took a deep breath of the early summer's evening. The gentle breeze soothed his pulsating head as he sipped another mouthful of cool water. Behind him, with the door propped open, he listened to the footsteps of the professor returning.

'How are you now?'

'Better, thanks, a dull headache; guess I'm tired.'

'Not surprised, you have been in here before me each morning and you're the last to leave. Take a couple of days off and relax. You seem like a man on a mission – there is plenty of time.'

'Feel a bit of an idiot.'

Professor Flackman caught him by the arm. 'Don't be silly, it could happen to anyone. Besides, it was only me, so you have nothing to worry about.'

Jack stared quizzically. 'Were you the only one in the room?'

'Yes... why?'

'Oh, nothing; just something I thought I saw, must have been you.'

'Come on, time you went home.'

Professor Flackman patted him on the back and both men started to walk in the direction of the office.

'I wondered if you managed to find out any information regards the boxes?'

'Oh yes,' he said. 'Granted, not much, but apparently the artefacts were sent over to us by the British Museum early on in 1940, due to fears of expected bombing raids by the Nazis. Rather a fortunate decision, as in May 1941 an incendiary raid destroyed galleries and parts of the museum. They were lucky not to receive more damage, as London was severely bombed in the Second World War. We're all aware of the Blitz.'

'So, they have been here all this time? I wonder why they did not get sent back?'

'Well, you yourself said it didn't look like anyone had been down to the sub-storage level in years, so it must be an oversight and they have been forgotten about. They were only minor artefacts. Did you find anything in the last one you opened?'

'No, nothing of importance; just a docket written by hand, requesting the return of a loaned item.'

SIX

FRIDAY, 18TH JULY 1975

Before leaving work, Jack went back to the office to retrieve his jacket. The box still lay open and he couldn't explain what happened to him. On the floor he spotted the handwritten docket and shoved it in his jeans pocket before dashing home. Now he needed to hurry, as this evening someone important would be waiting to meet him.

On arriving home filthy and running late, he jumped in for a quick shower and made himself more presentable before heading to JFK International. The signs hanging from the ceiling told Jack the way to Terminal Three, termed the 'Pan Am Terminal'. Their prominent blue logo he thought should make it easy to find. Out of the huge window he viewed the constant activity of the airport as he strolled along. The balmy summer's evening was becoming darker, revealing momentary glimpses of flashing lights as the aircraft manoeuvred around the taxiways when something captured Jack's attention and he backtracked a few steps to view it.

'Amazing.' Its majestic beauty caught his eye. The first supersonic jet. Concorde, as it was known, was so much larger and faster than any other aircraft sat on the apron. It was not yet set for commercial flying, but to fly on that would be an experience. *One day,* Jack thought as he stared at it, when a soft-spoken voice at the side of him interrupted his daydream. He turned to see who was addressing him and found himself peering into the eyes of an attractive Pan Am stewardess who smiled at him. She gestured at the aircraft in front of them.

'Pardon? Sorry, I didn't catch what you said.'

'I just commented on what a beautiful looking aircraft she is?'

'Yes,' he said. 'Amazing.' His attention was still drawn to the aircraft.

'Well, I must be going.' Checking the time, she turned to move away. 'Enjoy your trip.'

With a jolt, Jack snapped back to reality. 'Oh, crap, bugger, what's the time?'

The stewardess looked a little astonished and surprised by his tone – it was almost a demand.

'Sorry,' Jack said. '…I didn't mean to be so abrupt. Bloody late for the Pan Am flight from Heathrow. Could you point me in the right direction, please?'

'That came in over an hour and a half ago,' the stewardess said. 'There's a waiting area in the arrivals lounge; follow the signs to the left.'

'Bugger… no, I didn't realise; I better get a move on.'

A thought occurred to him as he turned. 'Oh, miss, is there a bar in the arrivals hall?'

'Yes, at the far right-hand corner of the building.' She smiled, watching as Jack turned and ran off. If he were that late, which he now was, Alex would only be in one place. The bar!

SEVEN

TUESDAY, 16TH AUGUST 2005

Stood in the doorway, Ginny waved as her parents reversed off the drive. The car was so laden down with bags she'd have thought they were going on holiday for a year.

The window on the passenger side slid open and Annie popped her head out. 'Would you feed the fish, darling, before you leave?'

'Yes, will do.'

'Take care, we will phone you when we arrive,' Ben said, reaching across Annie. 'Any worries with this solicitor business, give us a ring.'

'Will do, Dad. Now don't worry, go and enjoy yourselves.'

Back inside, Ginny relaxed and thought how wonderful to come home yesterday and share lovely memories with her parents.

The previous night, Annie took her straight into the kitchen for one of her infamous cocktails. This had the desired effect of washing away the arduous drive. Ben arrived a few minutes later and was delighted to see her, embracing her warmly.

Both parents hugged, and she could tell how much in love with each other they still were. The twinkle in her mother's eye spoke volumes. After all, Ben was still in good shape: tall, slim, with a full head of thick hair which made him look more distinguished as the ageing layers of the years settled upon him.

His expressive brown eyes shot a knowing look at Annie, who sent him a warm, comforted smile, one that broadens over time, nurtured with the knowledge of being part of a secure and loving relationship.

Ginny had enjoyed chatting at dinner, listening to her parents laugh, still finding humour in how they met so many years ago following Annie's abrupt exit from university. Ben never reneged on his promise to 'love and cherish' Annie throughout the intervening years.

Ginny pulled on her lightweight black raincoat over her stone-coloured linen trousersuit. The weather had taken a turn for the worst, although in the early hours of the morning it appeared promising – typically, British.

While brushing her wavy hair, she heard the toot of the taxi.

'Station, please,' she said, smiling at the driver as she got in. At least being driven meant she'd keep dry.

Fortunately, the wait for the London train took no time at all. Now sat by the window, Ginny inspected the quiet carriage. Plenty of time until her one thirty appointment with the solicitor. From behind the murky glass, she viewed the varying scenes that now began to pass by. Allowing herself to settle in to a rhythmic trance, she stared as the homes and gardens moved aside for litter-strewn hedgerows intermixed with leafy trees, embankment walls, random workshops, car parks and back again to rows of houses. Intermittent were rectangular areas of green lawn, some manicured, others littered with children's toys. Glimpses of people's lives flashed before her, mixed with bursts of sunshine stabbing through the rain-laden clouds.

The announcement – stating the stations left until arrival at Euston – jolted Ginny back into the present. Somebody sat down beside her. She was so absorbed in her thoughts she had not even noticed the elderly gentleman arrive.

'London?' he enquired.

'Yes,' she said.

'Not long now. What a lovely day it's turned out to be.'

'Yes, delightful.'

London was unfamiliar to her, and the concourse bustled with commuters and tourists heading for the sights of the city. The station board confirmed her arrival was on time. Not knowing how to get to the solicitors' office, she opted to take a ride to her appointment.

Besides, she thought to herself as she approached the taxi rank, *it's not every day you ride in a traditional old hackney cab.* She opened the door and stated her destination to the round-faced, white-haired driver.

'Are you sure, love?'

'Yes, thank you.'

'OK then, but it ain't far.'

'No problem,' said Ginny. 'Not sure of the area and would rather arrive there on time. Got a dreadful sense of direction.'

'No worries, love. I'll drop you right at the door.'

The cabbie put his foot on the accelerator, and the diesel engine grumbled, pulling away from the rank. Relaxed, Ginny placed her raincoat to her side, taking in the hustle and bustle of the London streets directly outside of the station.

The cabbie engaged in telling her historic facts as they drove.

His name was Gilbert, as discerned from his name badge; he was clearly a Londoner and she listened with interest to the fast-tongued Cockney accent. It seemed strange in comparison to the Glaswegian pronunciation she was now used to.

Different in sound, but the pace of delivery was in fact much the same – fast.

It seemed no sooner had she got in the cab that it pulled up at the kerbside to let her out. Surprised, she looked at Gilbert.

'Told ya it wasn't far, love,' he said. 'Will ya want a lift back anywhere later on?'

'Thanks. No idea how long I'm going to be.'

'All right, love, enjoy your day.'

Outside, she paid the fare and Gilbert drove off.

Ginny gazed upwards at the affluent Georgian building before her. Two Doric columns stood each side of the main door, which featured an ornate brass knocker and a nameplate. Two other business names were listed, but Ginny's attention was drawn to the one she was familiar with: Cartwright, Appleby & Sons.

Anxiety rose inside her and she checked the time again.

Due to the shortness of the cab journey she realised she was over forty minutes early. At the top of the road was a small grocery store. The sun was shining, getting warmer and Ginny wanted a drink. Undoing her suit jacket, she ambled along, viewing the pleasant surroundings: an idyllic little haven.

The shop was quiet, with a chiller located at the back. After a few moments of deliberation, she proceeded to the counter to pay for her bottle of water. She also grabbed a sandwich and a newspaper. She already knew where she could have her picnic, having spotted a bench earlier. In the queue she surveyed the young man in front of her as he paid for his items. How well-groomed he appeared in a light grey suit with a pale blue shirt; the two colours together were smart and refreshing, and she liked his dark wavy hair against his tanned skin. She then homed in on all the biscuits he had bought. *A biscuit lover, indeed,* she thought to herself.

'Next, please.' A voice interrupted her thoughts and she stepped forward, placing her items down on the counter as she took a final peek at the back of the young man as he walked out.

'Are these yours as well?'

'Pardon?'

'These biscuits?'

'No… they must belong to the man who was before me. Oh, I'll catch up with him.' Ginny turned to dash out the shop.

'Madam,' said the assistant. 'You need to pay for your items.'

'Yes, of course, how much?'

'That will be £4.75, please.'

'Here you are.' She thrust a £5 note at the girl. 'Keep the change.'

She grabbed her shopping and scurried out of the door, picking up the sarcastic tone of the assistant behind her.

'How *generous*.'

In the bright afternoon sunshine, she squinted, looking left and right, trying to locate the dark-haired young man. *This might prove to be a little difficult*, she thought, having only seen his back whilst waiting in the queue. However, turning into the next street, there he was!

'Excuse me,' she shouted, but he didn't reply, so she called again.

Nothing. *Odd*, she thought, as he still didn't respond. Beside him, she touched his arm as he turned; pulling out two small earphones, he stared straight at her with a blank expression.

Ginny caught her breath: the front of him was much more appealing.

'Can I help you?' he said, looking at her.

For a second Ginny paused, aware of two piercing green eyes looking back at her. 'Sorry, I didn't mean to startle you,' she said, and flashed a smile. 'It was just you couldn't hear me.'

'Oh, the earphones,' he said. 'Is everything OK?'

'Yes… I believe you left these at the shop a moment ago.' Ginny waved the biscuits at him. 'Very tempted, as I rather like these.'

He laughed. 'Thanks, didn't realise I'd left them; it was kind of you to bother.'

'Not a problem.' She handed him the packet of chocolate digestives biscuits.

'Hey, thanks again.'

Before she crossed the road, he turned to her. 'Really, you should have given in to temptation – they are delicious.' With a glint in his eye, he smiled.

There was something about that face, Ginny thought as she walked over to the bench she had selected, nestled under a pretty maple tree. She looked back for the man, but he was nowhere to be seen. *What a shame,* thought Ginny, sitting down to take a sip of her water, and reflected on his amazing green eyes: an image she couldn't get out of her head.

Deep in thought, she absorbed the tranquillity which surrounded her as the birds drowned out the noise of traffic from the busier nearby road. After a while, she closed her newspaper, threw her rubbish into the bin, adjusted her clothing and glanced over to the solicitors' office she was now about to enter. Inside, it would appear that she would be given a set of keys to a property she'd never before heard of, from someone unknown to her, and that she had been extremely lucky to have just inherited. She pinched herself. This was all so inexplicable.

EIGHT

Ginny stepped into the light entrance hallway of the beautiful Georgian townhouse. The door to the right was labelled 'Reception'. Ahead of her, the stairs with an elegant balustrade wound upwards to the first floor and the solicitors' offices. A large, impressive chandelier hung from the ceiling in reception. It was a pleasant sitting room, tall and spacious with large sash windows. She turned to speak to the receptionist sat at her solid oak desk.

'I have an appointment to see Mr Cartwright.'

The receptionist checked on the computer, not caring much for small talk. 'Please take a seat, Miss Faulkner.'

Ginny moved over to the leather sofa and made herself comfortable, absorbing her surroundings.

A buzzing noise emanated from behind the desk. The receptionist pressed a button to cease the sound. Dressed immaculately, wearing a pale green floral dress, tailor-made to fit her slim body, she lifted a folder with her manicured nails and smooth hands.

She then disappeared through the hall door as it closed behind her.

Sat on her own, Ginny felt a little dishevelled after the vision of perfection she had just witnessed. Was there anywhere she might at least tidy herself up? The glass-framed painting in front of her made it possible to view her reflection; she took the opportunity and grabbing her clip, she twisted her hair up and tweaked at the ends.

'Much better,' she whispered, trying to reassure herself. She now focused on the scene in the painting; something about it drew her to examine it. The information she found at the bottom of the frame read: *WINDMILL OF WIJK BIJ DUURSTEDE* by JACOB VAN RUISDAEL, CIRCA 1670. A title, quite unpronounceable; a picture of gathering dark storm clouds above the windmill and the river. The landscape, so moody, caught Ginny's imagination; she felt it – like a distant memory, greater than fascination. Somehow, she was encapsulated by the view.

'Miss Faulkner.'

She drew her attention from the painting and turned to the receptionist. 'Such a lovely painting,' Ginny remarked.

The receptionist's face remained expressionless as she answered. 'Donated by a Dutch client through our partner solicitors in Amsterdam,' the woman said, quite matter-of-factly. 'Everybody has their own taste. Please come this way?'

With this, she turned and walked to the hall door. Dumbfounded, Ginny paused for a moment and took one final look at the painting. She then proceeded to follow the austere receptionist. *What could be worse?* she thought. Only attending a job interview.

Now following the 'android', she spotted a piece of fluff on her own sleeve. Not wanting to appear scruffy, she brushed it off. They climbed the stairs and stopped outside of an office as the android knocked the door twice and waited for a response. The door opened, and Ginny glanced down to see the fluff now settled firmly on the android's back. Unable to help herself, she smirked as they moved into the spacious room.

A resplendent mahogany desk with a worn red-leather top faced her: the archetypal London solicitor's office. In front of this were positioned two brown Chesterfield armchairs. *Most imposing,* thought Ginny. To the left of her were wall-to-wall shelves, crammed full of books, old and new. Above hung a sizeable Monet painting.

A plump, middle-aged man sat at his desk. He stood to greet Ginny as she entered. He too was perfectly dressed, wearing a sharply tailored blue pin-striped suit. This looked expensive. The bottom button of his waistcoat was undone. Ginny scrutinised him for clues. Laughter lines around his eyes, she noted, repressing her slight nervousness; she thought he might be all right.

Then the man introduced himself with a smile. 'Ah, Miss Faulkner, how lovely to meet you. My name is William Cartwright. How was your journey down?'

'Not too bad, thanks.' She shook his hand and felt herself begin to relax as he gestured to her to sit down, and the android left the room.

Mr Cartwright moved an open file on his desk nearer to him. 'Well, Miss Faulkner.'

'Please, call me Ginny or Virginia.'

'Of course,' he said. 'I shall read through the paperwork with you and then later you might like to have a cup of tea or coffee. Would that be agreeable with you?'

'Yes, that will be fine.'

'Hopefully you have brought the required documentation?'

'Yes, I have my birth certificate and my passport with me.'

'Good. We shall need those as proof as we proceed through the will statement.' He opened the folder and read for a moment, then lifted his head to address Ginny. 'Are you aware, Virginia, we are in fact acting on behalf of our Dutch partners, Stelling, Olly and van Horst, and although the estate is in Hampshire, the bequest comes to you from Amsterdam?'

Though a little bemused, Ginny nodded.

'The property in question is: Redivivus, Pound Green Lane, Silchester. The entitlement to the property has passed to you, Virginia Faulkner, as the first member in the family to be born on 7th March, year excluded. The property was left by Florence van Hassel and was to be bestowed on the death of the trustee, your grandmother, Edith Bartlett, née van Hassel, sadly deceased as of June this year, 2005. May I now have your documents, please?'

Ginny reached down into her handbag and pulled out an envelope. 'Do you know why the inheritance was dependent on my date of birth?'

William leant forward to take the documents from her. 'To be honest with you, Virginia, no. To prove your identity is, of course, common practice. Especially, in this case, given that the inheritance is conditional on you having the exact birthdate as stipulated in the will. This is unique, I must say, but Florence van Hassel was specific on this point.'

As he spoke, he ticked a box on another sheet of paper, putting the certificate and passport on top of the folder. 'For the moment I'll hold on to these, as we'll need photocopies to file them with all the paperwork. Is that all right?'

Happy, Ginny nodded, and he pressed the intercom button. 'Miss Aurthrop.'

Ginny grinned; she never imagined that would be her name.

'Would you come and photocopy documents for me and then return them straight away? Thank you.'

After a short pause, the android entered the office, collected what she needed and left quietly. The fluff was still on her back.

'Right then, Virginia, everything appears to be in order; we will need your signature on some documents and then we can organise some keys for you.'

'Is that all that needs to be done?'

'Yes, nothing to have worried about, really, quite painless.' After he marked a small X, he offered his Mont Blanc pen to her.

Ginny took it but hesitated. 'Nothing expected of me at all, nothing else I'm supposed to do?'

Mr Cartwright laughed. 'Perhaps you could tap dance for me,' he said. 'It's an unusual bequest and you are a lucky young lady. On signing these documents, the estate is yours. The how and why are for you to understand, but from our point of view, you sign here and we give you the keys to the property. All the remaining legals can be sorted out in time with your solicitor.'

Not sure what I'm fussing about, Ginny thought. *It's probably a caravan with a grand name.* With this, she signed the forms, still amazed.

'All done,' Mr Cartwright said. 'Not so bad after all? How about a nice cup of coffee?' He nodded towards the sofa and picked up the phone as Ginny threw one last unbelieving glance at the paperwork in front of her, then moved to sit on the sofa, her head full of many unanswered questions.

'Is she not around? Would you mind, that would be grand… Yes, two coffees, thanks again.' Mr Cartwright tidied up the forms into the folder and excused himself from the room to fetch the keys for Ginny.

Although bewildered, she was privileged, having inherited a property. Grateful as she was, she knew she would have to explore the situation behind all this in greater detail. There were many threads that needed to be tied together.

The door opened and Mr Cartwright strolled back in, jangling a set of keys in his hand.

'These are for Redivivus, Virginia, I'll sort them out with you in a moment,' he said, handing the keys to Ginny.' As he did so the phone on his desk rang. 'Will you excuse me, please?'

As Mr Cartwright chatted on the phone, Ginny noticed the door opened again. Nobody came in. *Strange*, she thought, *it's an old house… ghostly occurrences?* Then, a minute later, from further down the corridor, she heard what sounded like… rattling teacups. The coffee, she surmised, was on its way. *Whoever is carrying them*, Ginny thought to herself, *must be seriously unsteady*. How funny that unusual noises like this just made you want to laugh.

Now all she could concentrate on was the increasing sound of the jittery cups. *Must be a three-legged dog balancing the tray on its tail*, Ginny decided. The noise reached fever pitch at the door as Mr Cartwright put the phone down and drew his chair over to join her.

Much to her surprise, a young man stumbled his way forward to the coffee table. No three-legged dog. He placed a tray down, accompanied by a plate of biscuits.

'Thank you, James,' said Mr Cartwright.

As the young man straightened up, she recognised immediately who he was.

'The digestive biscuit man,' she blurted out.

Mr Cartwright looked at Ginny, as did the young man, who stared straight at her, smiled and picked up the plate of biscuits.

'Please have a chocolate one; they're very tempting.'

William Cartwright sat, looking perplexed at both of them.

NINE

FRIDAY, 18TH JULY 1975

Jack walked through the door of the bar and inspected the room for anyone that might look like Alex. Tall, slim build, black hair and big brown eyes – the girls loved him.

The room was fairly quiet and the booths to the right of him housed couples enjoying their evening. A section extending around the corner led to a small viewing area; there he saw the back of a young man wearing a T-shirt and jeans, with a full rucksack sat to the side. That was Alex all right.

Jack approached the bar.

'Can I help you?' the barman asked.

'Do you know what the English guy sat by the window is drinking?' Jack said, nodding his head in the direction of Alex.

'Yes, sir. Served him a bottle of Bud beer.'

'Can you get me two more, please?'

'Certainly.'

Jack headed over to Alex, who was sat looking out of the large window. From behind him, he tried to replicate a New York accent, albeit rather badly.

'Two bottles of Bud, sir?'

Alex began to turn. 'I didn't order any...' He stopped, realising this was not the barman at all but his very late friend.

Jack stood smiling. Alex jumped up, so pleased to see his mate.

'Peace offering,' Jack said as he extended the bottle of beer and apologised. 'Got held up at work... will you forgive me?'

Alex laughed. 'If you hadn't brought over the beer, probably not.'

They shook hands and then embraced each other.

'Really great to see you, Jack, even if you are...' – he checked his watch – 'over an hour and forty minutes late!'

'I'm a dreadful time keeper, you know what I'm like.'

'Oh yes,' said Alex as they clinked bottles together.

'Cheers. Well, old chap, how's life?' asked Jack in his best British accent. 'Forgot how to speak "proper" English with all these New Yorkers around me.'

'You're not an integrated New Yorker yet – not with the attempt you made earlier, and you kept your weird twang.'

'Now are you sure?'

'You're rubbish... as well as mad; you haven't changed,' said Alex, taking another sip of beer. 'So, Jack, how is the research work coming along? Are you enjoying it?'

'Yeah, good, keeps me busy; just so absorbed in it. There's so much stuff to organise. Only today I was re-cataloguing Roman artefacts I found boxed in the Mets sub-storage room since the Second World War. Get this – they didn't belong to the Met, but to the British Museum – sent before the bombing raids in London. Misplaced for all this time. One box even had a handwritten loan docket in it from the Rijksmuseum in Amsterdam… but no artefact! You'd be amazed.'

'Sounds intriguing.'

'It is,' said Jack. 'Now, you must be starving. Let's drop your luggage off at my flat. I know the perfect place to take you. We can talk, catch up with everything and eat. There's no rush; we've got plenty of time, old chap.'

'Sounds great, I'll drink to that.'

The yellow cab drew up at the kerb in front of Jack's building.

'Swanky place,' said Alex.

Jack patted him on the back. 'Come on, I'll take you up and show you the flat – I was lucky to get it. Have to warn you, though, it's on the fourth floor. Ready for a hike?' He raised his eyebrows enquiringly at Alex, who was looking at the steps to the front doors. 'Come on,' said Jack as he led the way in through the entrance. He ignored the old-fashioned lift in the hallway and headed towards the stairs.

Alex adjusted his rucksack on his back and shouted to Jack, 'OK, I was hoping those out front were the only steps to climb.' He groaned. 'Still hate lifts then?'

'Who, me?' Jack replied. 'This is how you keep fit round here. A couple of flights and you're there.'

'Couple of flights?' said Alex. 'You told me your apartment was on the fourth floor. Sounds to me like more than a couple.'

'Ah, stop your moaning, there's only eight,' Jack said with a grin, as he shot off out of the way, expecting something to be thrown at him any second. Sure enough, Alex's hat hurled past, narrowly missing his head. Jack laughed. 'I've missed your abuse.'

Jack was attempting to tidy up by the time Alex dragged himself and his bag up to the eighth landing.

Puffed, his friend made his way inside, dropped his rucksack and looked around. 'Nice flat. Got traces of you in it.' He gestured to the cluttered dining table.

'Well, you know what us academic types are like,' Jack replied, and pointed at the door to the left. 'Drop your stuff off in there – that's where you'll be staying for the next couple of weeks, so no complaining.'

'Right-o, sir,' said Alex, and cheekily strolled off to the bedroom.

Jack attempted to tidy up the place, thinking it was just cluttered, nothing to worry about. 'Do you want a drink here, Alex, or shall we go out? There is this amazing Italian restaurant a short walk through the park, off Fifth Avenue, and the waitresses are awfully tasty too.'

'Sounds like a cool idea, and I'm starving,' said Alex. 'By the way, the painting of the Dutch windmill, hanging up in my room – I like it.'

'Yes, that's a favourite of mine,' Jack said. 'Don't know why, just seems comforting somehow. Perhaps it reminds me of something. Now then, why don't you tell me the exciting news you couldn't tell me in writing? At least I hope it's good news?'

A great big smile lit up Alex's face and Jack laughed.

'Ah, Alex,' he said with a smirk. 'You haven't gone and got yourself ensnared by a pretty senorita? You, who was never going to be hitched to anyone, or so you said? So, this was the big surprise?'

Alex beamed again. 'Surprise to me too, Jack. But, yes,

she's pretty much the love of my life. Her name's Helena and we met...'

Jack laughed. 'Come on then,' and, with an incredulous look at Alex, 'mate – you are a lovesick puppy. Let's go and do some celebrating, and you can tell me all about her.' Jack threw his arm over Alex's shoulders, caring for him as though a younger brother, and walked out of the apartment, shutting the door behind them.

It was a beautiful, sultry summer's evening as Jack and Alex entered Central Park, passing Belvedere Lake. They stopped to look at Cleopatra's Obelisk, surrounded by the blossom trees that framed the monument with their elegant contortions, before they continued.

'Actually, I met Helena coming out of the Kingston University library,' Alex explained as they made their way through the park. 'Sat on her car by accident, her pride and joy. Thought the blooming thing was mine. Well, she arrived, ready to tell me off, when she dropped all her books on the ground. Chaos. Obviously I offered to help pick them up and got myself out of trouble. We began to chat, and one thing led to another.'

As his best friend spoke, Jack noted the contentment showing in his eyes and how his face lit up when he spoke of her. 'Wow, you really have found your perfect match,' he declared, and Alex beamed again.

They strolled on, still chatting as they went, eventually leaving the quiet park. Jack then pointed out a magnificent building. 'The Metropolitan Museum of Art,' he proudly announced above the street bustle, 'where I work.'

Alex was duly impressed.

Now late, they arrived at Mamma Cassa's restaurant. A

red canopy, stretched from the front of the building, sheltered the diners who chose to eat outside. Their radiating chatter and laughter merged into the fragrant, warm air, as most customers finished their meals.

Inside the restaurant, the place was a hive of activity. The waiters and waitresses darted from table to table, carrying drinks and beverages, exquisite puddings, bottles of wine, and many empty dishes. The sweet herb and garlic aromas percolated in wafts through the room.

'Told you it was good,' Jack said to Alex, who by now was sniffing the air.

'If the food is as good as it smells,' Alex replied, 'then hurry up and get us a table.'

'That might prove difficult.' Jack glanced around the restaurant.

Suddenly a shriek sounded out, reverberating its way to where they were standing. 'Look who is here – Jack? Where have you been these last few weeks?'

Walking towards them, with outstretched arms, was a short, rather round, elderly Italian lady with rosy cheeks, white hair pinned up in a bun on the top of her head and a well-used apron tied around her.

Alex deduced this might well be the chef, perhaps even Mamma herself. Rushing up to greet Jack, she squeezed him tightly and kissed him on each cheek before tweaking them.

'Where have you been? We no see you in a long time?' She looked at him up and down. 'You are turning into a skinny boy.'

Alex laughed at this and received an abrupt, hefty nudge in the ribs.

'Mamma Cassa, what can I say?' Jack smiled. 'You are so right; we are in dire need of your supreme food and, Alex, my dear friend, has come all the way from London. Because I told him, until you eat at Mamma's you don't know what you are missing; she's the best Italian chef in New York.'

'Oh, you make me blush.' Mamma nodded at Alex, grinning, and viewed both young men. 'For you both, I make you something really great. Make you my special pasta. To fill skinny boys up… yes?' She turned and shouted in Italian to an auburn-haired waitress, 'Rosa, you come and help here: you seat my guests on a good table and look after them, while I go and make them my *lasagne alla Bolognese* – this will fill them up.' With a huge, hearty smile, she pinched Jack's cheek one last time, then marched off in the direction of the kitchen.

'Not seen you for a while. Been working hard?' asked Rosa. From the glint in her eye, Jack knew she was probing.

'Busy with work, no time for anything or anyone else. My eyes only like the pictures of beauty in here, Rosa.'

Rosa smiled happily, enjoying the flirtatious moment, and gestured toward Alex. 'You didn't introduce me to your friend. Where are your manners?'

'This is my good friend Alex, who has come to visit me all the way from London.'

'How very nice to meet you, Rosa,' Alex said. 'Don't mind him, his manners are appalling.' He kissed her hand and she blushed, then asked them to follow her, enquiring if they wanted to sit inside or out. The evening was too good to hide indoors, and she located them a table under the canopy at the front of the restaurant. She lit the remnants of a used candle, dripping its wax down the wine bottle, and repositioned it on the red-and-white-checked tablecloth. Jack's gaze followed her as she went indoors.

'A romantic table for two, eh?' Alex sniggered. 'So, you don't come here often then?'

Jack laughed. 'Well, one has to integrate into one's surroundings, don't you think?'

'How do you do it, Jack?'

Rosa returned with a bottle of Chianti and two glasses. 'With the compliments of Mamma Cassa,' she said, placing them down on the table.

Alex smiled and thanked her as she left.

'Wouldn't be at all interested in an Italian beauty like Rosa then?' asked Jack.

Alex grinned. 'One can admire.'

'So, tell me more about Helena?' Jack said.

'You know how against getting attached to one person I was,' Alex's face was serious now, 'and how against being engaged or even married, but this is so different; it feels so right. This was why I had to tell you face to face. Does that sound silly?'

Jack shook his head. 'Not at all,' he began, 'and I can see it in you, I do believe you have found your true love. So lucky, I wish I could experience that. Though I came close to finding mine with Annie... but regrettably, not meant to be. There's a part of me still searching for something or someone; true love eludes me.'

'Talking of Annie,' said Alex, 'I didn't see her again, she dropped out of university, just left; not sure why...'

'That's a shame,' said Jack. He paused for a moment, thinking of her, before taking a sip of his Chianti. *Regrets,* he thought to himself, he had many. He changed the subject. 'So, when will you get married?'

'Nothing planned yet,' Alex said. 'Don't think we'll wait too long, and my other reason for coming is, when we set a date – I want you to be by my side, to be my best man. If you would accept the role, I would be honoured.'

There was a lump in Jack's throat as he spoke. 'Can't think of anything else I would rather do than support a dear friend who has found his true love. He beamed and raised his glass. 'To Helena, for making you so happy.'

'To Helena,' said Alex, grinning broadly.

With the time fast approaching midnight, Jack and Alex said their goodbyes to everyone – both of them light-headed after more than a few glasses of Mamma Cassa's excellent Chianti – and set off to walk back to the apartment. The street was still full of activity with people making their way to their various destinations, the lights of the shop and restaurant fronts illuminating the pathways.

'Rather bright out here,' said Alex, 'and my stomach is so full up, I don't think I can move.'

Jack sniggered. 'Mine too, there's pasta in my body going all the way to my feet – they won't work.'

'Have we got far to go? Think I might be slurring my words a little.'

Jack stared at Alex, bewildered. 'Really, I can't tell you are slurring your words, they sound good to me. Do you know what?' Jack said as they began their return through Central Park.

'Nope,' returned Alex.

'Earlier on today I couldn't hear anything.'

'What are you talking about?'

'This afternoon with Professor Flackman, something weird happened to me.'

'What do you mean?'

'Well, I opened a box... those artefacts I was telling you about before, the ones from London. The funny bit is, the docket I found in one of the boxes looked familiar.'

'How is that possible?' asked Alex. 'Wouldn't it have been written about the time of the war?'

Before Jack could answer, they were startled by a movement somewhere nearby. They stood staring into the darkness, unable to ascertain what disturbed the silence.

'Probably just a fox or something,' Jack said, unperturbed, as they staggered on. 'Anyway, as I was saying... uh, what was I saying?'

'Something about a date... no, a docket... perhaps both,' Alex said, trying hard to remember what they had in fact been chatting about. 'I *was* listening.'

'Right!' Jack remembered. 'The docket... after I viewed the writing, I recognised something about it and a bizarre moment occurred.'

'What happened?' asked Alex.

'Mmm... this will seem strange, I saw a figure of... well, of a woman. It was hazy, so difficult to tell, but I'm pretty certain it was a woman. In the room, everything went quiet, although I could see her trying to talk to me. All was muffled and distant.'

'Bizarre, as you say yourself,' said Alex, checking the bushes again. 'What did she look like? Could you make out anything?'

'The figure was not clear, but I got the definite impression the clothes were different to the fashion of today, not something we would wear now.'

'Sure you didn't drink at lunchtime?'

'No. Professor Flackman was surprised to find me lying on the floor when he returned and we both thought I'd just fainted, thinking that I was overtired – which is probably true.'

'Mustn't overdo things, mate. You do get absorbed in your work.'

'Yeah, I know I can be a workaholic, but there was something, I swear, I can't explain. Something awoke inside of me.'

Alex's attention was on something else. He nudged Jack. 'Those two guys ahead, did you notice them a minute ago?'

Jack shook his head. 'Nothing to worry about, I walk home through the park most evenings.'

'I just don't remember seeing them on the path in front of us or behind us before now?' said Alex.

They continued on as the two men passed by. Jack glanced over at them and smiled as they passed. 'See, what are you worrying about?' he said.

As he spoke, a shout from behind made them both turn around suddenly.

The two men were stopped a short distance along the path. The taller man hollered back, addressing Jack. 'Got a light, buddy?'

The tall man approached them as Jack patted his pockets. 'Not me. Afraid I don't smoke.'

The second guy had arrived, positioning himself closer to Alex. Both men were shabby, shaky and reeking of booze.

'You don't smoke either, do you?' Jack said to Alex, who nodded in agreement. He had sobered up a bit now, sensing there was something not quite right about this.

Suddenly, out of nowhere, the taller guy revealed a switchblade, thrusting it toward Alex.

Luckily, he missed, and Jack jumped in quickly to protect his friend.

'Hey, guys. Chill! We said we don't have a light!'

'Money. Give us your money. Goddamn tourist!' Again, the man threatened Alex with the blade as Jack stepped closer to him.

'Woah! Take it easy.'

Voices approaching drifted in the night air and the taller of the two checked over his shoulder furtively. Jack stalled for time, pretending he was getting his wallet out. The voices got louder. At this point Alex shoved the shorter guy. Panicked, lurching forward, both muggers pushed past them, knocking Alex over before running off through the undergrowth.

'Bastards!' said Alex, standing back up on his feet and brushing himself down. 'That was bloody lucky... could have gotten nasty.'

There was nobody else around; the voices had drifted away, taking a different path.

'That's never happened before,' said Jack.

'Bastards,' Alex shouted again. 'Can't believe the gall of them.'

'Alex.'

'Yeah.'

Jack had not moved. 'My hands are warm and sticky,' he said.

'What are you talking about?' Alex said, walking over to him. 'You're a drunken fool – we almost got mugged and all you go on about is your hands.'

Jack fell to his knees. 'Don't feel so good, Alex,' he whispered.

'Jack!'

Alex froze, unable to take in the realisation of what had just happened.

TEN

SATURDAY, 19TH JULY 1975

The unopened post lay on the coffee table; Alex stared at it, wondering what to do, when his eye caught sight of the multitude of books sat upon the dining table. Only last night he'd thrown his bag down as he entered the apartment and jokingly commented on the clutter.

Not unexpected, he thought; it acknowledged a synergy with the flat and Jack.

Sat motionless, he could not analyse how he felt, where he was, or worse... what to do next. Everything was so unreal. Mind and body drained, a part of him wrenched out, leaving a chasm of utter despondency, with his stomach churning and contorting. This couldn't be real... It didn't happen to him... did it? With his head lowered, his attention was drawn to a pair of Jack's trainers which lay underneath the table in a dishevelled state as though only just kicked off. Alex drifted back disbelievingly to the events of the morning.

~

'Oh shit... Oh shit!' Alex didn't know what to do first. Jack was lying on the ground. Shocked, kneeling down in front of him, he touched his face, watching the expanding red patch on Jack's T-shirt. The material absorbed the blood that was spilling fast from the stab wound in his chest; Alex gagged and sprang to his feet, scanning in a forlorn hope to see somebody, anybody.

'Oh shit!' Startled like a hare in a car's headlights, he looked one way and then the other. The adrenaline in his body surged; it took such effort to concentrate. Alex had never been so out of control. Taking off his shirt, he scrunched it up and knelt back down. In an effort to reassure Jack, he struggled to take a deep breath, trying to regain some composure.

'Mate, listen to me, I'm going to place this under your head.' With Jack's blood-stained hands in his own, he squeezed them tighter on the wound. 'Hold it there; keep applying the pressure. Do you understand?'

Traumatised, he groaned, vaguely recognising his friend's voice.

'Please hear me. Keep pressing on the wound.'

Jack tried hard to focus, then smiled at Alex. 'Yes, I hear you.' His words were listless.

Alex was relieved to have his friend's attention at last. 'Jack, I have to go to try to get help. I don't want to leave you,' he choked, trying not to lose hope and to keep it together. 'Just keep pressing on the wound and applying pressure, Jack... OK?'

'Sure, Alex, I'll try.'

'Stay awake for me, mate, I'll be back with help.'

Alex stroked his forehead to reassure him and leapt

up again, wiping his hands on the back of his jeans. Now resolved, the best thing to do was to retrace his way back to where they ate earlier, back to Mamma Cassa's. Slow to start, he was frantic to move faster, but his legs were like lead.

'For Christ's sake,' he shouted in frustration. 'Don't do this to me, I need speed… move!'

The park appeared darker now; as he ran, the bushes slashed at him as he undercut the corners of the pathway, desperate to return to the restaurant. On and on, he pushed himself. It struck him how eerily quiet everything became, except the thunderous roar pulsating from his chest. A light ahead told him the street was close. His legs dragging, he felt so tired. The thought of Jack on the cold, hard ground wasn't what made him push on; the thought of his best friend lying on his own did. Alex kept pushing through the pain. He was aware now of the street, brightly lit yet so quiet, all the people gone. He stopped for a moment to get his bearings, searching both ways for something familiar, a place he could recognise. Then he saw it. All the lights were off, but there was Mamma Cassa's. Outside the restaurant, the tables and chairs previously full of people, he and Jack included, were cleared away. It was a surreal moment – they were having such a marvellous time only a few hours ago. Sure he could make out a light on in the kitchen, he banged at the door over and over. Someone had to come. This couldn't be happening; a surge of panic rose inside of him. With a final, desperate knock, the main light came on and one of the waiters saw him at the door, hesitant to do anything. Behind the waiter, Alex recognised the waitress.

'Rosa, Rosa, it's me, Alex, Jack's friend. Please open the

door. I need your help.' Exhausted, he let his aching arms drop to the side of him almost in complete and utter despair as she ran to unlock the door.

'Alex,' she said, looking at the state of him and staring at his blood-soiled hands. 'My God, what has happened?'

When the paramedics arrived on the scene, Alex had been pushed out of the way. They were in charge now. All he could do was watch the activity around him. Laid on a stretcher, they moved Jack to the ambulance and Alex followed them with urgency. One of the medics prevented him from coming closer and his awareness was wrenched to the body inside the vehicle that lay listlessly, his friend Jack...

'Need to go now.' Whilst the paramedic spoke, Alex could not pull his gaze from the quiescent figure in the back of the ambulance.

'Are you a relative?' asked the medic.

'No.'

'Then move aside... please.' Not meaning to be awkward, he froze to the spot... incapable of movement. A hand forced him back away from the vehicle as the doors shut before him.

With his eyes following the brightly lit ambulance, the siren sounded as it pulled away from the entrance of the park and sped off down the road. Further and further away from him it went as he simply watched.

An arm encircled Alex, pulling him over to the side; he turned to see who was helping him, taking a moment to realise that the sympathetic brown eyes peering back belonged to Rosa.

'Come with me, Alex!'

Not understanding what was happening, he frowned.

'Let's go, Alex. Mario has a car, at the restaurant. We can go to the hospital. Quickly!'

Now she pulled at him, ushering him on. He still was not speaking, concentrating all his efforts on trying to walk. It all felt so laboured.

Rosa rushed in and came out with a jacket and a glass of brandy, insisting he take a sip as she accompanied him to the car.

'Get in, Alex,' she said, opening the back door.

Still dazed and holding his brandy, he did as he was told.

Rosa closed the door and got in. 'Quick as you can.'

Mario started the motor and headed out to the still-quiet streets of the morning.

~

Startled by the sharp whistling noise, Alex jumped as it shattered the silence of the room as might a book falling in a church. Up on his feet, he made his way to the kitchen, taking the kettle off the burner, and poured the water in a mug of coffee, watching the steam rise upward in wispy spirals. Like an automated machine, he got the milk from the refrigerator, still completely numb. What was he going do? This same question he'd posed to Rosa earlier at the hospital.

~

Rosa opened the door and pulled Alex out, abandoning the car. Both she and Mario dragged him along into the reception area of the emergency room, sitting him down in the chair before she rushed over to the desk. Mario sat down beside him, keeping out of the way. Oblivious to the activity and noises that surrounded him, Alex became transfixed on the fluorescent light above that flickered on and off. He was unaware of the people milling around, some injured, or doctors in a hurry, the nurses asking questions, doors banging to and fro, opening as patients were ushered in on stretchers, being rushed through for medical care. Then silence would descend on the waiting room before new sounds burst in, bringing with them the external aromas of outside: the early-morning air now intermingled with the antiseptic entrenched in the room, along with wafts of alcohol and cigarette. Alex watched the ceiling light continue to flicker on and off.

After what appeared an eternity, she returned. Mario stood as she approached and glanced at her before she dropped to her knees in front of Alex. The movement from the side caught his attention and he glared at Rosa. Mesmerised by her red, swollen eyes, numb, he just sat there. Rosa tried to speak. A single tear ran down her face, hanging from her chin as though held in time before dropping to expand across her hand.

Alex stared at it, uttering the few words he was able to. 'He's dead, isn't he?'

Powerless to speak, she looked at him, and her sad eyes already told the story. Unable to contain her grief, her head fell to her knees.

'What am I going to do?' Alex asked in complete and utter disbelief, again staring at the light above, which, by coincidence, darkened, having extinguished its life too.

TEN

~

Jack had drifted in and out of consciousness, shivering. Coagulated blood oozed through his fingers as he pressed on the wound. The scented flowers were not present in the air anymore, instead the metallic smell of his own blood. Somewhere in the background, Jack heard a siren and closed his eyes – tired, so very cold. With a different view now. People had gathered around, barely audible. There stood Rosa, a stunning, attractive girl... such a shame, she was so distressed. Alex leant over him. His dear friend, saying the same thing over and over: 'Please stay with me, Jack.' The words dissipated as he reached higher into the atmosphere. All noises and the commotion drifted further and further away. Streetlights in the distance grew dim and the scene of chaos below grew smaller and smaller. Scarcely able to make anything out anymore, it became darker.

Words, faint at first, repeated. They were calling him back, back to a different place. Jack realised in this instant what he had been searching for all this time. With things still to do, and someone to find, he wasn't finished – he couldn't be.

Darkness gradually came to him, like a blanket, falling over him silently.

~

Alex walked out of the kitchen with his coffee and caught a glimpse of himself in the mirror.

'Christ!' Sickened at the image projected back, he hardly

recognised himself. A sudden abhorrence and panic swept over him. He rushed to the bathroom and began running a hot bath. He frantically took his clothes off: the jacket Rosa had loaned him, his jeans, socks, shoes and underwear. Naked, he stood shaking and distraught, turned the taps off and jumped in. His urgency was desperate; he saw in the mirror he was covered in blood… Jack's blood. That was the worst feeling ever. It was imperative that Alex removed it, to detach himself from the horror of the previous hours. Submerged in the hot, steamy water, an explosion of emotions arose from within; there was nothing he could do to stop it. He sobbed uncontrollably, the fragility of his spirit broken. The tears rolled down his face as Alex scrubbed furiously at his body, especially his hands. To get clean, to be rid of all the blood… he must, to let Jack go.

A short time later Alex sat wrapped in a towel at the end of the bed, with his shoulders slumped, heavy, exhausted. It was a tiredness he'd never experienced before. He lay back on the bed, drained, lifeless, wanting to simply close his weighted eyes. He was aware that the purge of emotions from earlier had left him weary but also strangely comforted… soothed. For a moment his eyes opened as an element of clarity enveloped him. He was not scared anymore. And when he woke up, he understood what to do and, more importantly, he would now have the strength to do it. The haze gone, he didn't feel alone. All he needed was to rest, and with this, Alex closed his eyes and fell into a deep and, somehow, comforting sleep.

ELEVEN

TUESDAY, 22ND JULY 1975

'Thank you, Professor Flackman, that will be helpful – with luck I can now locate his family.'

'Please send me the final details for the funeral, I would like to try and go if I can… if I may, Alex?'

'Of course, Professor, as soon as I have everything wrapped up here, I'll be in touch, and thanks again for your help.'

'Glad I was able to be of assistance,' he said with regret. 'Sad, I liked Jack, he was a nice young man.'

'Yes, he was, thank you again… Goodbye.'

The call finished, he viewed the piece of paper on the table. A couple of days now and he'd been trying to organise arrangements for the funeral, including the return home to what would be Jack's final resting place. Not sure where that was yet; he was starting to discover there was a lot he didn't know about Jack. This surprised Alex, as he was so close to him, having met him at boarding school at the age of ten; they, in fact, were more like brothers. The revelations left him unsettled.

All the years he knew Jack, he took him under his wing, as did his parents; they all thought fondly of him. On more than one occasion, Jack had said how he loved being at home with all the Elderson family in Hampshire, feeling an affinity with the area.

There were times, Alex reflected, when Jack was so deep, introspective, like he possessed a second sight. *How bizarre,* he thought, dreading how uncomfortable it was going to be to tell his parents what happened, let alone track down Jack's mother.

With the difficulties he was having in locating Jack's family, he maintained by organising the flat it made him less anxious, keeping his thoughts from wandering. The dining table lay clear and tidy as he boxed up all the books and letters. Then he picked up a docket with a small note attached that said, 'Handwriting?'

Curious, Alex viewed it, thinking there was something familiar about it. Did Jack speak of this to him the night he was killed?

He remembered him saying something regarding a docket sent from London to New York but also that it was linked to the Rijksmuseum in Amsterdam, about the time of the Second World War. Alex frowned, certain that Jack had mentioned having a funny turn.

'Overtiredness', Jack had said caused it. What had he been going on about? For safe-keeping, Alex slipped it into his wallet.

Alex was still in a quandary about Jack's true address when an idea flashed through his mind... Dulwich!

'Yes, of course.' Why did he not think of that before?

They must have all the details of Jack's home and family – surely? The dilemma for him was, he was still stuck here in New York. He sat tapping his pen and then decided to call Helena. Thousands of miles away, she was without a doubt the rock that was supporting him; if anyone could help him it would be her. Now more than ever, he realised how much he needed her.

Later on that afternoon, Alex climbed the last flight of stairs; stumbling with the shopping, he pulled the keys free from his pocket, noticing the UCL keyring as he put the key in the lock. At the door to the apartment, he could hear the shrill ring of the telephone. Surprised, he dropped the bags where he stood and rushed in, grabbing the receiver as he shouted down the mouthpiece.

'Hello.'

'Alex?'

'Yes.'

'Funny, you sound different.'

'Out of breath, Helena. Do you realise I almost gave myself a coronary trying to reach the phone?' he said in jest. 'However, I'm a whole lot happier for hearing your voice. How are you?'

'Think I'm feeling better than you, at this minute. Darling, are you really all right?'

'Coping,' he said, pausing before continuing. 'I find it hard to come back to the flat. Been tidying up today and went to the shops – the everyday routines give me some sense of normality. Takes my mind off all the turmoil... even if only in short bursts.'

'So wish I could be with you,' Helena said, wanting to hug him. 'Each day will get easier.'

'I know it will, and I miss you terribly, but as hard as I find all this, I'm here for Jack... someone has to take care of him and I'm glad for it to be me.'

'Oh, darling, he would be pleased knowing you are there for him.'

Alex sighed and elected to change the subject. 'Did you manage to find out any information from Dulwich?'

For a moment she hesitated. 'Truly I have to say they were a bit frosty with me, typical bureaucrats. "Because you are no relation," they commented, quite stiffly, "we couldn't possibly help you, madam, so please step aside." I mean, honestly, it's not as though I was asking for the crown jewels. Even explained you were an ex-student of the school and that you were on the alumni register. Well, that didn't work – he just dismissed me, giving one of those stiff, nonchalant looks.'

'So, have we hit a brick wall then?' asked Alex, only half surprised.

Helena sensed his frustration. 'Actually, not quite, as it happens.'

'Not quite? What do you mean?'

'Bit of luck,' began Helena, appearing more optimistic now.

'Sounds intriguing, go on.'

'The clerk, who was quite unhelpful, even bolshie, left me feeling despondent. So, I sat on the bench in the entrance hall to gather my thoughts, not knowing what to do. Whilst pondering the situation, a gentleman approached me. He apologised for intruding and explained he'd overheard me asking for information on a Jack van Buren. Cautious to start with, I informed him I was trying to acquire Jack's home address and family details. Intrigued, he told me he knew him in a professional capacity quite well, being his mentor at University College London. Now at Dulwich to give talks on the Art History course, he was pleased and surprised to hear Jack's name mentioned. He then introduced himself to me, Dr Albert Pindle...'

'Can you say that again?' Alex interrupted.

'Yes, do you recognise it?'

'Does sound familiar.'

'Dr Pindle said he'd seen enormous potential in Jack and delighted in telling me how he had recommended him for the post-graduate research position in New York.'

'Thought I recognised the name! Jack always said how grateful he'd been for his help. Think he saw him as a father figure, for assisting him in his career. Makes sense, with Jack's father not being around.'

'Trouble was,' explained Helena, 'he then asked me how he was getting on—'

'Ah, difficult,' said Alex. 'What did you say?'

'Well, what could I do? I told him what happened. Saddened, he shook his head, and commented what a dreadful shame it was. I did feel pretty awful.'

'It's not your fault, darling, what else could you do?'

'Good news is, he took my telephone number, saying he would do all he could to help me and would be in touch with the necessary information. Grateful, I thanked him and told him how pleased my fiancé would be. He asked for your name, and he remembered you through conversations talking of you with Jack. Then he rushed off to deliver his lecture. There you have it.' Helena listened to the silence at the other end of the phone.

Alex had listened as she recounted her story, stood vacantly staring out of the window, when he was disturbed by a creaking noise coming from the direction of the front door.

'Are you there?' Helena shouted once more.

'Sorry, darling... Yes, I heard everything you said and that is really great. We have been incredibly fortunate – such a stroke of luck you ran into Dr Pindle.'

Alex turned to the door as another noise distracted him and was surprised to see Rosa enter the flat. He smiled at her as she gestured to him to carry on with his phone call, but his expression changed as he scrutinised the man behind her suspiciously. *How did they get in?* he wondered. Then realised he couldn't have shut the door properly when he dashed in earlier.

'That's excellent, Helena, I can't thank you enough for all you have done. Any reply from him yet?'

'No, still early days...'

Finishing her last word, Alex interrupted her. 'Look, darling, sorry to be rude, I'm going to have to go now as I just received some unexpected visitors.'

'Oh, who's that then?'

'Awkward to say at the minute.'

'OK, tell me later then... everything is all right, isn't it?'

'Yeah... look, nothing to worry about; I'll ring you back.'

Alex returned the handset, staring at Rosa and curious about the man stood beside her. She apologised for coming into the flat unannounced but was concerned on finding the groceries strewn all over the floor – she wondered what happened.

'In my haste to answer the phone,' Alex explained, 'I dropped the bags, spilling the shopping.' Again, his focus was on the man, who wore a dark suit jacket with a blue shirt and green tie. This was undone, making his attire look scruffy, as did the washed-out jeans and tatty sneakers.

Rosa, aware of Alex's enquiring look, now introduced him. 'This is Detective Dave O'Keefe.'

At this the man stepped forward and offered his hand to Alex and began to talk. Alex listened to him, aware of his broad New York accent.

'Hey, sorry to barge in like this. I'd been talking to Miss Sirellio about the details of the other night and she told me she was on her way over here to check on you. I asked if I could tag along as I needed to speak to you about the events leading up to the death of your friend Jack.'

'So how may I help you?' asked Alex.

'I've a few things I need to ask.'

Alex pointed to the seats around the table and they sat down.

Rosa put the shopping in the kitchen and shouted, 'Let me make some coffee while you both have a chat.'

Detective O'Keefe took out his notepad. 'I'm sorry to have to ask these questions after what happened, but it is, after all, a homicide.'

'No, that's fine,' he agreed. 'You're only doing your job.'

'Thank you, Alex. You gave us Jack's details the other day and a description of the two muggers. We're at present following up on a lead. From other victims' statements, we believe they are probably junkies, committing crimes to support their habit. Both of you were easily targeted, as are most tourists.' The detective rolled his eyes and continued. 'Personally,' he said, 'forget tourism, how about the victims, hey?'

Alex began to warm to him, sensing his annoyance; he genuinely wanted to catch these criminals, wanted to change what was happening in his city. Therefore, he acknowledged what he said and listened.

'The difference in your case, which is unlike any of the other incidents where there were no...' – he faltered to look at Alex – 'there were no fatalities. Jack was unlucky... wrong person, wrong place, wrong time. We want to put these guys away. So is there anything that might stick in your mind? Anything at all, however unusual it may be it might just be the clue we need, you never know. Minor details could really help us, anything?'

The detective studied Alex's face as he tried to recall the events. It seemed like such a long time ago and his perceptions were blurred now. He rubbed his face as though trying to purge the distasteful scenes from his thoughts. Still disturbed by them, he glanced down under the table and caught sight of the detective's sneakers. And something sprang into his mind.

'There was one thing,' Alex said, pausing as Rosa came in with the hot drinks. They both thanked her, and the detective urged him to continue.

'Well, it seemed silly at the time, so I never thought to mention this before.' He took a sip of coffee. 'The guy I tussled with... well, he wore different shoelaces in his sneakers. This I remembered when I noticed your shoes a moment ago.

Scruffy, tatty old things.' Alex stopped, realising what he said. 'Didn't mean...'

'Go on,' said Detective O'Keefe.

'One sneaker was tied with a red lace and the other I think was blue. Why I remember I don't know; perhaps because I'd fallen to the ground... I'm not sure, it was just different?'

Alex shrugged, watching as the detective wrote everything down.

'That's good, might seem an odd thing to note, but every detail will count, which could be useful.' He closed the small notepad and drank his coffee. After a moment he asked Alex another question. 'Have they notified you at the mortuary when Jack's body will be released?'

'Sort of,' Alex began. 'They reckon by the end of the week if all the paperwork is finished and they have permission from the family and yourselves.'

Rosa sat down beside Alex and rubbed his arm. 'Did you manage to get in touch with the family yet?'

'It's proving difficult,' he said. 'I'm awaiting a phone call from Helena. If she's been able to speak to Jack's old tutor, he will give me an address where I can contact Jack's mother or someone... really not looking forward to that.'

'Is it in London?' Rosa asked.

'Don't know. Which is why we have had so much trouble locating them. We think they are Dutch.'

'Oh?' said Rosa, inquisitive. 'Never said much to me, though he did mention London a lot.'

'Not even I knew his address. Jack rarely spoke about his family. When I met him at boarding school in London – I suppose being young, we never bothered about such details, there were other more important things to get on with. However, Jack did tell me once that his father had died when he was young. His mother had told him that his father never got over incidents to do with the war but didn't expand on what they were. Jack had said this had made him curious, but after that he never mentioned anything again. He was a part of my life… he was family.' For a moment Alex paused, reflecting on those days, and smiled.

Rosa glanced reassuringly at Alex as Detective O'Keefe placed his mug on the table and stood up. 'Must be moving on now,' he announced. 'Thank you for your time, and for the coffee.' On approaching the door, the detective turned to shake Alex's hand before leaving and asked one last favour of him. 'Before you return home to England, can you leave me a forwarding address and telephone number I can reach you at?'

'Of course.' He was hopeful to receive the consent they needed from all involved to fly Jack home… wherever home was.

Being so occupied with his own thoughts, Alex realised he had neglected Rosa, and found her washing up in the kitchen. Rather guiltily, he approached her to find her head hung low, sobbing. With the towel he dried her hands then raised her head, looking into her eyes. Those big brown eyes of hers. It distressed him to see her upset as he pulled her closer and hugged her, hoping to take away her pain and reassure her everything was fine.

'I'm so sorry. I've been so wrapped up in my own misery and gloom I selfishly never appreciated who else was hurting.'

Rosa tried to say something back, but her sobs made

it inaudible, and she gripped Alex, now glad to receive the warmth he offered.

'Should have seen it before – you cared for Jack… didn't you?'

Still upset, she nodded. 'Silly, I know, as I always liked him. My emotions were strong for him… though he likened me to a sister.' Rosa would have wished for more, but Jack was never going to let that happen.

'Charismatic,' said Alex. 'That was him and I know he regarded you with affection – he thought a lot of you.' Alex smoothed down her auburn hair. 'Now, he wouldn't want us to be sad; I'm glad and grateful you have been here. I couldn't have managed on my own. Without your friendship and your kindness, I might never have got through this.'

Rosa took in a deep breath, opening her sore eyes to look up at Alex. 'Being so emotional, I'm so sorry, I should be supporting you, not crying.'

'Nonsense. Don't be daft, these feelings creep up on us, and we're here to help each other… hey?' He pushed aside the hair from her eyes and wiped away a tear tracing down her face. In that moment she looked so fragile and very tired.

Rosa let out a sigh and shook her head. 'Felt all right until I came into the apartment. While it's empty of Jack… it's actually full of him.'

Alex nodded in agreement.

Going in the front room, she went and sat on the sofa, taking with her the pad from the dining table. Alex joined her.

'Now, what needs to be done?' she asked, lifting the pen.

TWELVE

TUESDAY, 22ND JULY 1975

Helena phoned later that evening following Alex's visit from Detective O'Keefe and Rosa.

'Darling, listen, got some fantastic news.'

'What's that?' said Alex. After the questioning that afternoon, he needed a pick-me-up, as it had brought back the events of Jack's murder.

'Dr Pindle, as he promised, came back to me with some information we needed regarding Jack's family.'

'That is fantastic, as you say.'

'It would appear that he is from Holland, as the correspondence address he gave me is in Amsterdam.'

'Blimey!'

Helena sounded out the details to Alex:

'Stelling, Olly and van Horst, Rembrandt House, Westerdoksdjik40, 1014 Amsterdam, Nederlands.'

'That doesn't sound like a home address, though. Sounds like it might be a solicitor,' Alex said.

'Yes, that's what troubled me. Do you think you'll be able to find a phone number for them?'

'Perhaps I'll have a word with the detective, see if he can pull in some favours with tracing international numbers. Got to go to the chapel tomorrow as they said they may take Jack following his release from the police mortuary. Once I speak to Holland, I can make arrangements to transfer him home.'

'OK. Good idea. If you need me to do anything, just shout.'

When Alex rang, as suspected, he got through to a solicitor. They said they were in charge of affairs to do with the van Burens. Alex explained it was imperative he got in touch with a member of the family. Curious, they asked why? In two minds whether to say or not, Alex then mentioned the bereavement. The man on the other end of the line went to fetch another colleague. This man sounded older.

'Bereavement, you say?'

'Yes.'

'A van Buren family member?'

'Yes... look, I've said all this.' A little frustrated, he waited for a response from the gentleman on the phone as he paused.

'That means it can only be Jack.'

'How did you know that?'

'Such an unlucky family,' he said. 'May I take your name, number and call you back?'

'Yes, not a problem,' said Alex. 'Unlucky, you say?'

'Very,' said the voice on the other end. 'I'll contact the mother to pass on the sad news and get back to you. Thank you, Alex.' And the line from Amsterdam went quiet.

A week later, Helena stared out of the window at Schiphol

Airport, viewing the blue colours on the Royal Dutch Airlines aircraft from New York as it taxied along the runway, approaching the apron, where it came to a standstill. Helena purposely took the earlier flight to meet Alex as she wanted to surprise him; she needed to be with him. Stood watching one head after another bob out of the aircraft doorway, she then found what she had been searching for. A tall figure with dark wavy hair stepped out, as the afternoon sun struck at his tired eyes, causing him to avert his gaze as he queued with the rest of the disembarking travellers.

Helena waved enthusiastically from above, although he did not see her. A sense of happiness rose within her and she realised how much she had missed him. The mere sight of him made her heart sing and she couldn't contain her smile. It reminded her of how she had felt the first time they met. She rushed downstairs to the arrivals hall, eager to greet him.

Sat beside Alex in the back of a city cab in Amsterdam, Helena reached over to take his hand in hers, squeezing it to offer him support. He turned to smile at her; looking into her clear blue eyes he considered the comfort she gave him. On meeting her at the airport, Alex became overwhelmed; his emotions were being torn in two directions, for he was ecstatic on seeing her, his sweet-faced Helena, but so remorseful for why he now visited Amsterdam. Both sat in contemplative silence in the taxi behind a hearse proceeding to an unknown address, to meet a family they'd never met before. A totally unreal experience.

Alex glanced out of the window and became aware of the beautiful surroundings they now travelled through. The decorative architecture of the merchants' houses that ran along the canals were just as they were seen illustrated in the old masters' paintings. The synthesis that existed in Jack for his love of the arts and the resplendent city of Amsterdam he now understood. It was in his blood. Sat quietly, Alex sighed to himself, now reassured Jack was home, allowing him to feel comforted knowing he would rest in peace.

The cab turned into Vondelstraat and came to a stop. Helena nudged Alex, commenting on the street name. 'This is the place, look?' Agreed, he nodded, then gestured to her to step out as he paid the driver. Further along the path Helena admired the park opposite. How beautiful. All this luscious greenery in a city, everything at its best as summer worked its magic. Alex walked over to stand beside her when she realised she'd lost sight of the hearse.

'Oh no. How stupid of me for not paying attention – too busy admiring the park.'

'Don't worry, I know where we are going.'

'How can you? You've not been here before.'

'No, but I know where to go.'

He took her hand and walked to where an old magnolia tree could be seen rising above a wall. Long since bloomed, its twisted boughs gave it grace and elegance, and its old age was indicative by its grand height. The entrance to a house with two large iron gates stood before them. Parked on the gravel driveway was the black hearse and to the right of this was a small lawn that housed the beautiful magnolia tree. Helena gasped, firstly at the size of the tree and then at the splendid old townhouse sheltered behind.

'Wow! One big architectural statement,' she said as she

again asked Alex how he knew this was where the hearse would be.

'Easy. The name of the house is "Oude Magnolia Huis".'

'Kind of obvious,' began Helena, 'when you have the full address... isn't it?'

'Certainly is,' said Alex as he strolled towards the steps that led to the double-fronted entrance door. Turning back to the now-empty hearse, he looked at it in an endearing way.

'You're home now, Jack... you're home, my friend.'

THIRTEEN

Helena sat down on the chaise longue positioned in the middle of the room. Alex wandered over to the window where he viewed the magnolia tree, thinking how surreal the whole situation was. The sun strained to break through the clouds as shards of light bounced off the windowpane. Content, he took a deep breath, taking in the atmosphere the house offered. It was a beautiful home. The old oak floor prompted him to ponder the many footsteps that had trodden over the creaky boards through the generations. The room itself imbued a sense of different times gone by. Opulent paintings hung on the wall, complementing elegant furnishings showing the rich patina of the various woods on the separate items. Sat on the mantel of the sizable fireplace, Alex admired the Ormulu clock. As the pendulum swayed, the rhythmic tick emitted a calming pulse that purged through their surroundings in a pleasant manner.

Both waited in silence. Then the doors opened at the far end of the room. A nurse entered, pushing an elegantly dressed elderly lady in a wheelchair. Clear to see, she was frail and appeared to be in considerable discomfort. Her attire was not only refined but immaculate. Black leather shoes shone, and she wore a black silk suit, fitting perfectly to her slim, fragile figure, giving an impression of great expense but not displayed in a vulgar way. Her grey hair was dressed up in a French roll and attached to the lapel of her jacket was a gold brooch in the shape of a windmill. Her hazel-coloured eyes were drawn and weary, worn on a woman who carried such tragedy on her narrow shoulders. This was someone who had done all this before.

The nurse brought her into the room as she smiled at Helena and looked at Alex, who stepped forward to greet her. The lady raised her hand to receive his greeting. A presence about her commanded one's attention naturally.

'Good afternoon, Alex. I'm Audrey Sophia van Buren. Thank you so much for coming and for all you have done these past few weeks. Please be seated,' she said, gesturing to the chaise longue where Helena was already sitting.

Alex moved to join Helena and introduced her to Audrey Sophia, who pre-empted this, stretching out her hand.

'Pleased to meet you too,' Audrey Sophia said, with a pleasant, quiet voice, as she spoke perfect English, carrying in it a Dutch accent. 'I only wish it was under different circumstances.' Awkward as to know what else to say, she turned to her nurse, who remained standing in the background. In her native tongue she asked the nurse to fetch some refreshments for her guests. The nurse, Anna, then left the room as Audrey Sophia returned her attention back to Alex and Helena.

'Did you both have a good journey?'

'Yes, we are just a little tired, but well, thank you,' Alex said.

'Good. Jack is resting in the drawing room until the

service tomorrow. You are welcome to pray and pay your respects later before you leave.'

Again, another stumbling silence.

At any other time, Alex would have chatted freely, but he hesitated, never having been in a situation like this before. Helena tried to break the ice asking about the exquisite house. *Less uncomfortable to talk about a than death*, she thought. Audrey Sophia seized on the opportunity, as she'd been struggling and was grateful for the lifeline thrown by Helena.

'My husband Johann loved this house; it was dear to him. Passed down from father to father over the centuries with a history of the van Burens attached to it.'

For a moment she looked around the room. 'The house is too big for me and the staff, so no point in keeping it all open. I live in a few rooms at the back of the property, as I like to have access to the walled garden – much easier for me with my disability.'

Aware of their puzzled expression, she explained, 'I was struck with multiple sclerosis – MS – a long time ago; this was why I sent Jack over to England to board at Dulwich. I was reluctant to let him go at first. A friend of mine from the British Embassy recommended the school. Isn't that where you first met him, Alex?'

With a cough he cleared his throat. 'Yes, it was; we became good friends, having similar interests, though… Jack was more abstract in his thinking and far cleverer than me.' He smiled at her.

'Jack had been angry at me for sending him away, especially after all that had happened. I used to write to him, but he replied so infrequently.' She looked hurt and dejected.

'A terrible writer...' Alex said, sensing her pain, knowing that Jack spoke so little of his family. 'But he often spoke of you.' He said averting his gaze.

Audrey Sophia smiled, so pleased at what Alex said.

'Were you aware, I was with him when it happened?'

Sad, at first, she simply nodded. Then after a moment, she spoke. 'My solicitor did say. And as tragic as all this is... I feel at peace that you were with him.'

Gratified, Alex thanked her.

'Jack, I always thought, was the lucky one,' she said, then sighed, glancing out of the window. The sun retreated behind the greying clouds, adding to the sombre mood of the day.

'He had a brother, you know.'

Before she could say any more the doors opened, and the nurse re-entered with another lady carrying a tray.

'Oh, thank you, Anna,' Audrey Sophia said. The housekeeper laid the pot of coffee and cups down on the oval table in front of the chaise longue. Anna turned to Audrey Sophia holding a glass of water and a yellow tablet, offering both to her.

'Is it that time already?' Huffing, she took them as though she were going through the motions of a reluctant duty. 'Painkillers,' she said. 'Such a bore.'

'And very necessary,' Anna said in response.

Audrey Sophia patted her kindly on the back of her hand and thanked her before she left the room. Helena sat for a moment and then offered to pour out the coffee. Audrey Sophia gratefully acknowledged her help and Alex prompted the conversation she started before the refreshments arrived.

'You said Jack had a brother? I never knew.'

'Jack never spoke much about the loss of his father or his brother.' Every painful recollection was etched on the fine features of her face. 'Jack was only young at the time. It happened before his second birthday.' She smiled to herself, reminiscing. 'Such beautiful golden curls,' she said as she reached out to receive her cup from Helena.

'Do you mind my asking what happened to Jack's father and brother? Did their deaths happen at the same time?' Alex was curious now.

Audrey Sophia gazed out of the window again. 'Johann loved the old magnolia tree... so much bigger now,' she said, saddened as the memories of yet more loss came flooding back to her. 'They were both killed in a car crash,' she began. 'Stefan was only five years old at the time. It happened on 23rd October 1954.' The facts came from her as though on an automated recall. 'They crashed trying to avoid a deer on the road as they travelled back from Wijk bij Duurstede – the other side of Utrecht. Stefan begged his father to take him and Johan, knowing it to be a short trip, agreed. Needed to collect something on behalf of the museum... didn't say what. Wretched museum! Always there. It was as though it consumed him.' At the mere thought of it she tutted and cursed.

'Which museum?' asked Alex as he put down his coffee.

'Johann worked at the Rijksmuseum,' she raised her arm, 'over to the right of you. Not far from here; up at Hobbemastraat, no distance at all. You can walk there.' Her attention returned to the magnolia tree as she fell back through the years. 'The museum is where I met Johann.'

A little twinkle in her eye was caught by Helena as

Audrey Sophia reminisced of that moment. 'All that time ago.' She sighed.

'What year was that?' Helena asked.

'Oh my,' she said. 'Must have been… 1948.' Thoughtful, she studied the two youthful faces sat to the side of her, seeing something in them she believed she had found once, but for her it was not to be, unlike them.

'After the war, I worked in the offices of the museum. Johann was a charming man… truly lovely, but he never loved me.'

Helena practically choked on her coffee at this moment, staring disbelievingly at Audrey Sophia who sat unperturbed at what she said. She was unable to grasp the emphatic way in which Audrey Sophia declared Johann did not love her… like that was normal! *How strange*, she thought as she glanced at Alex, who raised his eyebrows in a puzzled expression.

'I'm sure he must have loved you?' Helena said.

Audrey Sophia looked at her as she turned from the window. 'I don't doubt he cared for me and loved his children, but I did not have a hold of his heart. That belonged elsewhere.'

A dejected head fell forward as she took a sip of her coffee and sank back in her chair. It was obvious to both of them that she was becoming tired. All three of them sat in silence as the resonating beat of the mantel clock continued pulsing in the background. After a moment Audrey Sophia thought of something and gestured to Helena to go to the beautiful flamed mahogany sideboard at the back of the room, asking her to collect the two photographs on the top of it.

'The one on the right and the smaller frame in front. Bring them to me.'

On receiving the photos Audrey Sophia smiled. It was obvious these meant a lot to her.

'This one,' she said, pointing to the old black-and-white print, 'is of Johann – he was about twenty-four. He never liked his picture being taken… but he always admired this one.'

Helena took the photo offered to her as Audrey Sophia then glanced at the second one.

This time Helena noted how Audrey Sophia's face lit up. She was aware who the photo was of before Audrey Sophia announced it. Only a mother could view the image of her child with that amount of pride and love.

'And this…' Audrey Sophia paused to catch her breath, 'is Jack.'

'See what you mean about his curls,' Helena said. 'They are beautiful.' She regretted never meeting Jack when he was alive. All she had seen were a few pictures that Alex had taken at college.

'This photo of Jack,' Audrey Sophia began, 'was taken the day after his third birthday.' She handed it to Helena, who sat down beside Alex again. He took the picture, viewing it amusingly.

Exasperated, Audrey Sophia raised her eyes, displeased at what life had thrown at her. 'Nearly lost him on his birthday, you know – as if I could suffer any more?'

'What happened?' asked Helena, now intrigued by the unhappiness prevalent in this family.

'I wanted him to enjoy his day,' she said, almost pleading for understanding. 'That was all. We'd been through enough… all that grief. I was much more able then. My MS would not be diagnosed until a few years later.'

For a moment, she thought back to Jack's birthday.

'I invited Jack's friends, along with their mothers, to the Vondelpark opposite here. There is a boating lake in the centre – it's not deep at all and a delightful place to picnic, with the trees all around. So serene. A most resplendent day in May, warm for the time of year, and the older boys and girls with us were organising rowing races. It was a pleasant respite from all the misery in our life. I remembered watching Jack, hoping this would cheer him up. Happiness at last... just for once.'

There was a warm glow on her face as she clearly recalled the day's events and drew a breath before resuming.

'Christensen, a few years older than Jack, was a lovely, attentive boy, very thoughtful. Lost his father at the end of the war, so I think he empathised with Jack's loss, and offered to take him out on his rowing boat. I remember him teasing Jack that if he didn't help then the pirate girls would steal the ship.' Audrey Sophia looked at them both and laughed. So far, she was enjoying the memories of this day.

'Jack went along, not quite sure what to make of it all. Jack could be so serious at times.'

At this point, Alex interjected, unable to process the information that the Jack he knew could ever be serious. 'Can't imagine him in this way,' he said. 'I've seen him determined with his studies; it seems so alien – he was always playing around.' He stared at the doors that led out to the entrance hall and beyond to the drawing room where his dear friend was rested. Alex was confused as a shiver led all the way down to the bottom of his spine.

Audrey Sophia nodded. 'Yes... I know why you're

struggling with this. Up to that birthday' – she shrugged her shoulders, unable to explain – 'he was a different child. Christensen took him out on the boating lake. Content in the knowledge that he was safe, I relaxed, happily chatting away and relishing the freedom the day brought. All would have been fine until one of the boys on the other boat got cross at Christensen and began whining – spoilt brat, never liked him much. There is always one spiteful child, isn't there?'

Helena nodded in agreement.

'This child… don't recall his name, picked up the oar and swung it at Christensen, who pre-empted what he was about to do and ducked out of the way. Unfortunate for Jack, who had no idea what was happening, just sat there. Took the full blast of the oar across the back of his head and fell forward. Christensen lost his balance as he turned to check on Jack and within seconds both of them fell into the shallow water. It all happened so quickly.'

The previous joy Audrey Sophia had experienced dissipated now as she reflected on different circumstances.

'The other mothers and myself were unaware of any of this. Imagine the furore that ensued as panic set in. Christensen was standing in the lake, soaked through, unable to control himself. He stood frantically searching for something in the water… now screaming.' The thought of those piercing screams made her shake, haunted by them.

'Such screams,' she said. 'Christensen was standing up to his knees; he was fine, as I said, the water wasn't deep, it didn't impose any real threat. However, Jack did not enter the water in a conscious state. In my mind, it seemed to take forever before I got there, watching Christensen in despair, fumbling for something in the water. A man who had witnessed the commotion jumped into the lake and pulled out Jack's listless body. I stopped, frozen in time, my heart thumping – too scared to move, so very, very scared.'

Once more she looked outside, her attention steadfast on the magnolia tree, as if the view assisted in keeping her calm and spoke kindly. 'Thank God for that man.' She clasped her hands together. 'Jack was so blessed; I can tell you. That man was an ex-mariner and knew exactly what to do; dragging his body to the bank, he listened to his heart and then began resuscitating him. At this moment, I do not recall hearing a single sound, not one – isn't that strange?' She turned now to look at Alex.

'No, not strange at all,' he said.

'What he has put us through... hey?' A tear welled in her eye, but she was determined to continue.

'The relief I felt as Jack gasped for air, as life burst into his body. From that day on, I swear to you now, he was a different Jack. Grew up to be the person you knew so well. A different child, so vibrant, so happy.' She paused, thinking. 'Thought perhaps he had broken our unlucky jinx, and that all would be fine, but that was until now... my poor, poor Jack.' Audrey Sophia sighed heavily, a despondent figure full of melancholy.

Helena reached for her arm, hoping in some small way to ease her pain. 'Do you wish for me to call the nurse?' she asked, able to see Audrey Sophia looked tired, not a normal tired but tired of life. Pale, her face was drained as she turned and nodded. Helena walked and opened the doors. Sat on a seat on the other side of the marble-floored entrance hall was Anna.

Alex leant forward, holding the image of Audrey Sophia's husband Johann. 'May I ask, Audrey Sophia, is this your writing at the bottom of the photograph?' He waited as she sat, unresponsive to his question. Had she not heard what he said?

Anna came into the room with Helena, who sat back down beside Alex. Audrey Sophia's gaze was still transfixed on the old magnolia tree. Anna, realising she needed to rest, thanked them both for coming and gave them the details of the funeral for the following day. They proceeded to the door, but before leaving, Anna bowed to listen to what Audrey Sophia had to say.

'The question you asked, Alex,' Anna returned, opening the door, 'the answer is no. Hope this makes sense.' Both then disappeared out of the room.

Helena glared at him. 'What was all that about?'

'Oh, something I thought I noticed... nothing in particular.'

FOURTEEN

WEDNESDAY 30TH JULY 1975

Their flight back to London was not for a couple of hours. Helena sat in the bar at the hotel, leaning on the table with her face in her hands. There was a quiet murmur of voices all around with the occasional raised laughter and clink of glasses. A waft of smoke drifted by.

'Do you want another glass of wine?'

'No, better not, think that I drank one or two too many sherries earlier on.'

'Doesn't show... Really!' Alex laughed.

'My face is warm,' she said, and smiled.

'Going to get a beer, I didn't drink the sherry... be back in a minute.'

Alex strolled over to the bar, disturbing the plume of smoke that still hung heavy in the air. Helena leant back in the red vinyl booth, viewing Alex as he ordered his drink, so proud of him. Today he'd managed to cope with a most distressing day. For her to remain strong was essential, giving him the support he needed, as he had just buried his best friend. This would take all her extra encouragement and strength.

Jack had been laid to rest in the family plot of De Krijtberg Kerk, with his father and his elder brother, reunited in death. The van Burens had used the church for many years and the priest, an elderly gentleman, did his best to personalise the service. Helena viewed the tragic scene. Audrey Sophia fought hard to keep control of her emotions throughout the sermon. Her heart, not just broken but torn to shreds, lacerated beyond recognition; the poor woman.

Afterwards, Alex remained by the graveside for a while. Mr van Horst, the van Buren solicitor, waited and, after a respectful amount of time, approached him, careful not to intrude upon his grief. Mr van Horst thanked him for all he had done for Jack on behalf of himself and the van Burens. The solicitor added that if he were to ever need assistance any time not to hesitate to contact them; they would be only too happy to help. He'd been instructed by Audrey Sophia to make this message clear, as she wished to express how much she owed to him for his kindness. Alex thanked him and shook his hand before he left.

Stood in the churchyard, Helena noted that only herself, Alex and Audrey Sophia with Nurse Anna now remained. The inclement weather of the day worsened, and the wind picked up around them. About to leave, Audrey Sophia surprised him with an exceptional gift of the two photographs that he'd admired the day before. Both the photos she requested should stay together, father and son. The one of Jack interested Alex more, but she was keen for him to have the two.

'The picture of Johann was not taken by me, and Jack always liked this photo, as did his father. Please, take them, I think Jack would be happy if you did, Alex.'

For the first time, during the whole of the day, he was utterly choked.

Holding his hand one last time, she smiled and asked one more thing of him. 'Will you keep in touch?' He nodded. 'Give my love to Helena.'

Tired and even frailer, as though life would soon expire from her wearisome body, Anna turned to wheel her back to the car; this lady had endured enough.

Jack, home once more, was now left to rest in peace with his ancestors.

Beer in hand, Alex returned and sat down, drained. It had been a long, emotional day and Helena rested against him, placing her head on his shoulder.

'Thank goodness that's all over,' said Alex, evidently relieved. To survive he needed to move on, and today he hoped the closure of the funeral would help him.

'Yes,' she agreed. 'We could both do with a relaxing holiday, somewhere warm and sunny, what do you think?'

Alex looked at her, so lucky to have her. 'That would be a great idea.'

'Kind of Audrey Sophia to present you with the photographs, don't you think?'

'Hmm... yes,' he began. 'A funny situation.'

'What do you mean?'

'Audrey Sophia offered me the photos because of my connection to Jack, hence the picture of him as a youngster. The photo of his father, Johann, she added because she said he liked it so much. But really, she didn't want it... not *that* photo, for whatever reason.'

'Why do you think this?'

'Come on, Helena, even you were surprised yesterday when she admitted Johann, as far as she was concerned, did not love her. Why did she say this? Also, she said the handwritten note at the bottom of the photograph was not hers. Don't you think that suggests something?'

'We don't know anything for certain. What did the words say?'

'No idea. It's in Dutch and hard to read because of the style of writing.' For a moment Alex stopped; his mind flitted to something else that occurred to him. 'No, it couldn't be,' he said.

'Couldn't be what?'

'Might be nothing, but the handwriting looks similar to that on a docket Jack spoke of. It's in my wallet if I still have it.' He fumbled inside for it. 'What do you think?' he asked, passing it over to her.

'Hard to tell, this is so old.' Helena squinted at it again. 'It does seem similar. How could this be?'

'Don't know. Where did Audrey Sophia say Johann worked?'

'Not sure – some museum, I think. It had an unpronounceable name.'

'Was it the Rijksmuseum?'

'Sounds a bit like it, why?'

'Oh, no reason, just thinking, that's all.' He put the photos and the docket back in his wallet and supped his beer.

At the airport, Alex sat reflecting on all that occurred recently and realised the one thing holding him together was Helena.

'Come here.' Pulling her closer, he leant down to touch her mouth with his lips, sensing her body's closeness; smelling her fragrant scent, he kissed her passionately as he had wanted to do for ages. It was as intoxicating, as was Helena. The blood surged around his body to remind him why he was alive and why he was so lucky to be here touching and holding the one thing in his life that became more precious each day. He whispered softly to her, thinking everything about her was so perfect; he knew what he wanted.

'I love you with all my heart, Helena.' A silence hung between them as they both enjoyed the moment, neither wanting to let it go. But they did have a plane to catch.

FIFTEEN

Darkness cloaked his surroundings, except for a stream of effulgent light. Its intensity was alluring and so comfortingly serene, a resplendent and enticing draw to a supreme seduction of nirvana. A place he'd sighted before and, as beautiful as it was, he did not want to investigate further. He was not ready. There were other matters he needed to sort out. There were still things he had to do – important things. There was someone he had to find, and they were not here. They were somewhere else. He did not want to wait, he did not want to remain in this state anymore and he did not want to feel the essence of the light or search amongst the black velvet skies. He wanted his opportunity, and he could sense now it would not be long. He knew the time was approaching; time to open his eyes... time to see again. It would happen, and it would happen soon. Very soon indeed!

SIXTEEN

THURSDAY, 13TH MAY 1976

'What an ungodly hour,' Alex muttered as he shut the door of their apartment in Richmond and ran down the path to where the Mini was parked. Helena sat squashed in the tiny front seat, tired and uncomfortable. Straight away he rushed around to the driver's side and got in, slamming the door shut and began fighting to start the car. Several turns later it spluttered into life and lurched forward as Helena moaned.

'Are you all right?' Alex asked as she grimaced.

'Yep... just get going.' Helena barked the words at him.

Alex manoeuvred the car down the road on this fresh early morning, still coming to terms with what was happening. Nervous, he glanced at his wife and realised at the same time he was actually feeling excited.

'Oh God, not again.' Helena stretched out as best she could in her cramped surroundings.

'Are they getting closer together?' Panic sounded in Alex's voice as he pushed down on the accelerator.

'No, but much stronger... oh!'

'Try and relax, it will help.'

'Trying,' she snapped. 'Sorry, I'm so uncomfortable.'

'Don't worry, let's get you to hospital.'

They drove along the road as she eyed the dew-laced patches of lawn, grimacing yet again as she curled her toes, another contraction creeping up on her.

'Why don't they tell you how swollen your feet get?' she asked Alex.

'They're not too bad,' he said, patting her on the leg.

To talk about her feet, he realised, took her mind off the pain and the contraction passed. A little anxious himself, he looked at her, fully aware he'd not done this before either. 'The baby's not coming… is it?'

Helena laughed as she turned to look at him. 'Your face is such a picture.'

'It's not then… no?'

'Don't panic; it is, but not as fast as you think.' She smiled, and he breathed a sigh of relief.

Helena stared out of the car window, distracting her thoughts from the recurring pain. Everything had happened so fast. They'd both returned from Amsterdam, hoping to step forward with their lives. And how they had moved. Past events were not forgotten, but they had at least settled. On their return, Alex proposed to Helena; he knew she was the one for him. Both agreed they hated the idea of a long engagement, and so, on a crisp autumnal day last September, they married. A perfect wedding, despite the weather. Helena thought how easy it was to be a part of Alex's life; she couldn't explain why, but it did feel like they had known each other for aeons. She remembered with a smile when they got the news of her pregnancy. So happy, Alex had picked her up in his arms and hugged her so close to him she could hardly even breathe; she loved how pleased he had been.

'Oh, oh, this is a big one,' she said as her grip on the edge of the seat tightened and her body arched backwards. To help her relax, she began blowing and let out a yelp just as Alex slowed, driving into the grounds of the hospital. With urgency he jumped out, dashed around to Helena's side and threw open her door. The relief of being out of the squashed confines of the car was amplified as she stretched her aching spine. For a brief moment her stomach relaxed as Alex returned with her suitcase.

'Here we go, darling. This is where the fun begins.'

'Let me get this bloody baby out first, then we can start having fun!'

Dawn broke through the clouds and the city slowly came to life as they entered the hospital.

Some fifteen hours later on the evening of Thursday 13th May, Helena and Alex had a boy. Shattered by a long yet safe and uncomplicated birth, like any new mother, her adrenaline kept her going as she now admired their baby son with excitement and pure love. Alex also looked drained. He had done all he could to support Helena. He stood feeling overjoyed with his wife and son sat in the bed before him, tired but well. Overwhelmed, he tried to hide a tear, as Helena caught sight of the moment; reaching out to him, she held his hand. They didn't need to say anything; the look they communicated to each other said everything. Both sat admiring their little bundle of joy as his yellow blanket rhythmically undulated with his breathing. His milk-spotted button-sized nose wriggled for a second as he twitched in his sleep, and his little fingers, all with perfect nails, stretched and then retracted back into a tiny fist. All manner of emotions ran through Alex's head as he viewed this amazing scene with an immense sense of love and pride. He knew there was only one debate to come.

Twenty-four hours later the debate continued, in between visits from friends and family.

'We can't call him Angus.' Alex glared at Helena.

'Why not?'

'Because… don't know… it just doesn't work.'

'Sounds better than Cuthbert,' she said quite indignantly.

'I only said that joking around,' admonished Alex.

A small whimpering noise emanated from the hospital cot at the end of her bed. Two open eyes peered up at him. Desperate, he picked up this tiny human that wriggled before him. After a cuddle, he passed the small bundle to Helena.

'We're undecided about the name, but I wanted to ask a favour about his middle name.'

'Go on,' she said.

'I wondered if we could use...'

Helena interrupted before he could finish. 'Jack.'

Alex nodded.

'Think that would be lovely,' she said, and, with a thought, turned to Alex. 'How about for his first name… James?'

Alex was quiet as he pondered what she had said. A nice name, it took him by surprise, one he actually liked.

'Well, what do you think?' Helena prompted him, a little impatient, wanting the debate to conclude.

'James is a wonderful name.'

'Do you really think so, Alex?'

'Yes.' He peered down at baby James, nodding in agreement, and began to recite his name in full.

'James Jack Elderson. JJ Elderson... sounds like a cool jazz saxophonist!'

'Oh, Alex, you are daft!' Helena looked at her beautiful baby boy. 'Wonder what he will actually do when he grows up?'

'We've got years to debate that one – in fact a whole lifetime,' said Alex.

'The way we pick names, I think it will probably take that long, don't you?' she said.

The door to the ward swung open as the nurse came to do her rounds. The smell of disinfectant and the everyday noises of a busy hospital intruded on them, but they never heard anything; they were far too occupied.

SEVENTEEN

MONDAY, 15TH AUGUST 2005

Alicia Markham was on her last day temping before she went on her holidays. This particular Monday had been a hectic day, and she didn't want to be here any longer, cursing and tutting at the pile of documents she was filing away. That was the annoying thing about working in a solicitors' office; there was always so much paperwork. They kept just about everything, or so she thought. Everything had a place; everything had a purpose, even the three sets of keys she held in her hand had to be filed in a cabinet behind her. With her feet, she pushed away from the desk, projecting the chair briskly back, and unlocked the cupboard, grumbling to herself as she searched for the numerical codes.

So many keys she'd never seen before: duplicates, triplicates, keys for this and keys for that, all stored for whatever purpose. She sighed, unimpressed, no longer wanting to be here, and the job was boring her. Only the cleaners remained in the building with her; everyone else with a life had gone home – but not Alicia Markham, who still sat in the office at past eight o'clock in the evening. All she wanted to do was to go and pack ready for her two-week vacation to Spain. It was calling to her, as she imagined herself sat watching the sun rise on the beach.

Intent in her daydream, she nearly jumped out of her skin, almost throwing the keys in the air, whilst grabbing for the drawer to balance herself. In front of her stood a man; resting on the long arm of the vacuum cleaner, he glowered at her.

'Well, will you be long?' he asked, sounding rather grumpy.

'Why?' she barked at him, a little agitated.

'Why? Isn't it obvious? I need to clean where you are. What else would I being doing standing here with this?'

'All right, all right, keep your hair on!' she snapped at him. 'I'll be done in a minute... OK?' Annoyed, she glared as he huffed off, disgruntled, down the corridor.

Quickly, she finished and slapped the last keys in the drawer, which she assumed were the correct places, locked the cabinet and pushed herself back over to the desk. The small key she placed back on its hook and then she picked up two more files. She looked at them, but on hearing the imminent return of the cleaner, she quickly returned them to the pile, tidied up the paperwork and checked the time.

'Sod it, I'm off,' she said.

So Alicia Markham grabbed her handbag and ran to the elevator.

Alicia left the building!

EIGHTEEN

THURSDAY, 18TH AUGUST 2005

'Where's the key for the storage cupboard? Has anyone seen it?'

James now regretted his decision to help tidy up some of the filing that had mounted up these past few days. The office remained in chaos, as the temporary secretary, Alicia Markham, had taken it upon herself to leave earlier than expected.

'Well, anyone?' James asked, frustrated.

Nobody knew anything. James put down the files he was carrying and grabbed the small cabinet key off the hook. Something wasn't right, and he needed to check them all, as the storage key was still missing. This, he knew, was going to be tedious and cursed.

'You'll never work here again, Alicia Markham, never!'

Several cups of coffee later, having waded his way through two thirds of the keys stored in the drawer, he let out a cry of relief.

'Aha! Got you, you little beast!' He snatched the one he had been searching for when he heard a voice behind him.

'Are you having fun there, James?'

'Hello, William. No. I'm not having fun at all – in fact, I'm cursing the temp who worked here.'

'Why? What's she done?'

'Where do I begin?' started James. 'She's made some complete balls-up of this drawer, hasn't filed away the keys correctly and it's taking forever to sort out. Christ knows what she's done with the paperwork. Useless!'

'Oh,' said William, aware James was more than just a little irritated.

James didn't like the sound of that. 'William, what does "oh" mean?'

'Ah… awkward.' He cringed as James studied him, perplexed; then, after a moment it, dawned on him.

'Did you know her?'

William stood with gritted teeth like a reluctant child who never wants to admit doing anything wrong. 'Yes,' he answered finally. 'Yes, I did.' He drew in a big breath and began. 'My niece's friend, who is studying law and wanted work experience for her course through the summer. How could I refuse?' He smiled at James awkwardly, who still appeared a bit cross.

'Now I know what "oh" means.'

'I can only apologise. I had no idea. When I spoke to her, she impressed me with her knowledge and charm. Seemed efficient.' As though requesting forgiveness, he shrugged his shoulders, looking to James, who couldn't help smiling at him.

'Well, let's hope there isn't too much she's messed up?'

'When did she last work here?' William asked.

'According to Miss Aurthrop, she never turned up on Tuesday.'

'So, any mess must be short-lived then, as today is Thursday. We haven't signed off any keys to anyone recently – have we?'

'No. Just a mess with lots of filing to do. Only she knows the whereabouts of the storage cupboard keys and somehow has created complete disorder in the drawer.'

'All will be fine. We're quiet at the moment; we'll work out her muddle. Again, I apologise, no real harm done?' William smiled at James, who was sat thinking for a moment about what he said. True, it had been quieter this week, but something was nagging at the back of his mind.

'Oh God!' The nagging doubt caught up with him.

'What's the matter?'

'We did release keys this week!' James suddenly returned his attention back to the drawer. This time, searching for a particular code, he picked up the ones that were in the space. 'Found a set,' he said.

'Terrific stuff; so, no problem then?'

'On the contrary, big problem!'

'Why?' William sounded surprised.

'Because they are *not* the storage keys.'

'Which ones are they?' William asked, perturbed.

'It appears we may have given the storage set to the Faulkner case, instead of the property keys the client would have expected.'

'Faulkner?'

'Yes, Virginia Faulkner, you remember, the attractive blonde that was here on Tuesday?'

'Obviously you do.'

'That aside, William, we have a problem. Miss Faulkner

won't get into her house and we can't get any files in or out of the storage cupboard. All thanks to Alicia Markham, whom you employed!'

'Yes, Miss Markham. Last time I'll do anyone a favour. Can you get hold of Miss Faulkner?'

'We're going to have to try. Do you still have the file on your desk?'

'If nobody has been filing for the last couple of days, then I would imagine so. I'll go and fetch it.'

William headed off down the corridor to his office. James searched the rest of the keys, replacing another set and locating the misplaced ones. Sat at the desk, he pondered what to do next and admitted to himself the thought of getting in touch with Miss Faulkner again appealed to him.

After a short time, William reappeared carrying a folder in his hand. 'Can't guess how easy this is going to be,' he said, looking at James, who started to open the file in search of a number. Her home address was listed but was in Glasgow, and it was obvious she wasn't there at the moment. William thought she was staying with her parents.

'Is there a piece of paper, perhaps a loose note? I'm sure she wrote down her mobile number as a contact for us.'

James checked all the papers. There didn't seem to be anything, but as he moved the documents back into the brown file, attached on the inside of the folder itself was a yellow post-it note.

'Got it.' He ripped off the note.

'Give her a ring and see if we can't sort this mess out,' William asked.

'Save our skins, you mean!'

'Yes, that too! I'll leave you to it then.' William snuck off back to his office.

James sighed and glanced at the number. Thanks to Alicia Markham, he was going to look foolish. *Great,* he thought. The only course of action he decided was to come clean about the whole situation. What else could he do? Hesitant, he punched the digits and waited for the connection. Nothing – except a message announcing the mobile had been turned off. *Now what to do?* He strolled to William's office.

'Any luck?' William asked as he walked in.

'Switched off,' James replied, taking a seat.

'Tricky, anything else to go on?'

'Only the address of the property she's inherited,' answered James.

William sat back in his chair a moment as a thought came to him. 'Miss Faulkner has not phoned yet, has she?' He looked inquisitively at James.

'Not that I'm aware of; we can check for certain. Why? What are you thinking?'

'Well, if she hasn't called here, it can only mean she hasn't been to the house.' William raised his eyebrows.

'OK, I'm with you – when she tries the keys and can't get in, she will connect that the mistake must lay with us. So we can only assume she has not been to the property.'

'Quite,' said William, pleased with his thinking. 'Thought she mentioned she would be going down at the end of the week… Friday?' He looked at James. 'Don't you have a day booked off tomorrow and know that part of the country? Fancy a drive out tomorrow?' William asked pointedly.

'Me? Why do we need anyone to go down there? She'll phone, won't she?'

'Yes.' William hesitated. 'But someone will still have to go to deliver the keys. This is only fair to Miss Faulkner.'

James grumbled, 'It's all Alicia Markham's fault – we should never have employed her.' He then realised what he had said. 'No disrespect meant, William.'

'None taken. Look, why don't you go and show her we've pre-empted the situation? A day out for you tomorrow and you can take Monday off in lieu as you'll be doing me an enormous favour. What do you say?'

James glanced out of the window as he mulled over the suggestion, excited at the thought of a day out in the country and curiously fond of the idea of meeting up with Virginia Faulkner. 'All right then. Remember, you owe me, William, and as far as hiring temps goes… don't bother, OK?'

'What can I say?'

'You can say, I can charge all this to the company account.' James got up. 'See you on Tuesday,' he said, shouting as he walked out of the office still holding the folder.

William called out after him. 'Enjoy yourself; give my regards to Miss Faulkner!'

James smiled to himself and checked his watch; it was now time to leave.

NINETEEN

FRIDAY, 19TH AUGUST 2005

Ginny sprinkled some flakes on to the top of the circulating water. *The fish don't look hungry*, she thought, but as the paper-like particles floated down, they brought instant attraction from the small marine life.

'Maybe I was wrong! That should do you lot for a couple of days,' she muttered as she returned the tin to the shelf.

Dismissed of her duties, she checked the house was tidy, and the doors and windows were locked. Satisfied, she got in her car, viewed the directions to 'Redivivus' and agreed to herself they were straightforward enough, even for a novice navigator such as herself. The keys to the property were still in her handbag, so she was good to go. Ginny decided to check her mobile quickly. It had been switched off to preserve the battery for emergencies, as stupidly she had left her phone charger at home in Glasgow.

All she wanted to do was to check for messages. She wasn't expecting to find much, as she'd spoken to her parents the night before and chatted to Megan on the Wednesday after her visit to the solicitors. As it flashed on, she noticed there were several missed calls, all from the same number, one she didn't recognise. Just as she began to investigate, the screen went blank. The phone had died.

'Why now?' she grumbled, knowing it was her own fault, although that did not help with her frustration. There was nothing she could do and, unable to resolve the problem at present, she decided to go on her journey.

~

James yawned, trying to prise open his eyes and hearing a quiet knock at the door. The birds chattered outside his window and cows sounded in the fields beyond.

'Come in,' he called, and propped himself up on to his elbows as his grandmother entered, carrying a mug of tea.

'Morning, James, did you sleep well?'

'Eventually, Grandma, the air was very oppressive last night, wasn't it? Kept me awake for some time.'

'Yes,' she said. 'The weather forecast, they say we might have thunder later. Do you want some brunch?'

'Brunch?'

'Well, a trifle late for breakfast.'

'Really?' said James, surprised as he leant over to the bedside table to grab his watch. 'Bugger! Oh, sorry, Grandma.'

'That's all right, darling. Now, do you fancy some food?'

James checked his wet hair in the mirror, smoothing it back, and arrived downstairs wearing a short-sleeved shirt, linen trousers and his sandals. He went straight to the kitchen, where he found his grandma cooking.

'This smell is amazing.' He happily sniffed the air on his way to stand beside her.

'Shall we fry up the leftover potatoes from last night as well?'

James laughed – Grandma often got excited about cooking leftovers. 'How can I refuse you?'

'Absolutely... you can't,' she said as the kettle began to whistle.

James glanced around the old kitchen. It hadn't changed in years. Filled with nostalgia, he moved from there into the sunroom that led out to the patio, thinking how lonely his grandmother must be since the death of his grandfather two years ago. *Difficult,* he thought, *especially if you have been married to someone for over fifty years.* To have company meant a lot, and when he'd phoned late yesterday afternoon asking to visit, she had been so pleased.

James broke from his thoughts on hearing his grandma call out. Brunch was served, waiting to be carried out to the garden. Most of the contents from the kitchen filled the tray, leaving little room for anything else.

'If I bring the coffee out, James, will you get the rest?'

'Of course,' he said, lifting up the tray and smelling the lovely aroma of the food as he went back out to the garden.

A moment later his grandma sat down opposite him. 'So,' she began, 'there was a problem?'

'Long story; all a bit of a mix-up at the office. I need to exchange some keys with a client.'

'Where do you have to go?' asked Grandma.

'Not far from here, about an hour away,' said James as he stretched over to pour out the coffee. 'Milk?' he added.

'Yes please. So where is not far?' Grandma was curious now.

'Silchester, north Hampshire. Not sure of its location, but I have a rough idea.'

'How lovely,' she said as they both tucked into a delicious, hearty breakfast.

After a while, James realised, as lovely as his late morning had been with his grandma, it was time he went. With his last sip of coffee, he returned the cup to its saucer. 'I had better get going,' he said finally.

His grandma stared up at him. 'So soon?'

'I'm afraid so. I don't know when the client will arrive at the house… if she does at all.'

Grandma's face illustrated her disappointment at him leaving.

James sympathised with her. 'Look,' he said, 'I'll be back tonight, and if this is all right with you, I'll stay until Monday, what do you think?'

A huge smile lit up her face. 'That will be great,' she said, happy at his decision, and stood up. 'Now, come on then,' she started, 'you don't want to be any later and I need to get on with the washing up now.'

James, being considerably taller than her, put his hands on her shoulders gently and directed her back into her chair. 'Now, sit and finish your coffee,' he said as he bent down to kiss her on the head, and turned to leave. On reaching the French doors, he looked back and winked at her. 'Take it easy and I'll be back later.'

'Go carefully,' Grandma called before sipping her drink as her grandson walked away.

~

Ginny pulled into a lay-by and switched off the car engine. She picked up her bottle of water and took a gulp before she studied the directions. Bemused by the map, she tried tracing the roads with her finger, desperate to work out where she went wrong; she even turned it upside-down, but it still made no more sense. Nothing!

Fed up, she sighed. *I'm completely lost.*

To find help she knew she was going to have to turn and go back to the village she had passed through previously.

The weather was overcast now, as the sunshine of the morning had vanished behind the stiffening clouds; yet it was still humid, even sticky. To execute a three-point turn she began weaving forwards and backwards across the narrow lane. On doing this she was then aware of a car that slowed at the brow of the hill. For a moment she hesitated, then its headlights flashed, hinting at her to continue. Ginny cursed; she hadn't passed a single car in ages and it was typical that now, halfway through her manoeuvres, one should appear. From her position she could not make the car out, only seeing the grid at the front and a 'H' emblem in the middle of it.

'Crap!' she exclaimed as she twisted and wriggled for a further three moves. On the final manoeuvre, the gear got stuck. Aware the other car still sat there, Ginny panicked, fighting to find the correct gear and get out of there. With one last desperate effort, she rammed the stick into first, crunching the gear. It worked – but what a noise. The car lurched forward, climbing up the lane. Embarrassed, and determined not to look at the waiting car, she stuck her hand up to offer thanks as she sped past. Relieved to be away, she headed back to the village.

~

James sat patiently at the top of the hill watching a little black Polo finish its hundred-point turn. What was this person doing? It was fair to say the road was narrow but not impossible for turning cars. Disinterested with the process before him, he waited in his Honda convertible, deliberating whether or not to put up the roof, as the weather appeared more dubious. He checked his map; this time he must be on the right track. A grinding noise from outside startled him as he looked up to see the Polo speed past.

'Thank goodness.' James was now relieved the VW had gone.

The roof of his car slotted into position as he turned up his radio and resumed his journey.

~

Ginny managed to find her way back to the village. Stepping out of the car, she shook loose her red T-shirt and peeled her patterned pink and white summer skirt off her moist, clammy legs. Although murky, it was still very humid. Across the road was the shop. On pushing the door open, a bell announced her arrival and a lady at the counter viewed Ginny. To the side of her an elderly gentleman stood at the post office, shouting to a man behind the louvered glass.

'That's right,' said the elderly gentleman.

'No, I said you need a stamp.' The postmaster raised an eyebrow.

'Yes, stamp!' repeated the elderly gentleman.

'Mr Millner, we need to add another stamp, OK?' The postmaster sounded a little frustrated now.

'Yes, yes, a stamp,' the elderly gentleman said once again, and nodded at the postmaster.

Ginny smiled at the lady by the counter as she, in return, raised her eyebrows in acknowledgement of the conversation beside them and asked Ginny a question.

'Don't tell me you're lost too?' Ginny looked at her, surprised. Why would she assume this, was it obvious? She was a little taken aback.

'Well, I am,' she said, still somewhat puzzled.

'Not to worry, lovely, where are you heading?' The woman's country accent was strong and looking at her face she couldn't help noticing the mole on her chin that stood out against her ruddy complexion. Large, rough hands unravelled a local map in anticipation of Ginny's request.

'I am searching for Pound Lane, Silchester.'

'Where have you come from, my dear?'

Hesitant, Ginny – who couldn't even remember the name of the village she stood in, let alone the road she just travelled back on – turned, raised her arm and pointed to the right.

'That way,' she said, turning back to the woman, who wrinkled up her forehead as she gazed at her.

'That way?' she reiterated, nodding to the right.

Ginny felt a smidge silly now.

'Did you see the barn down the way?'

For a minute she pondered, unable to recollect seeing a barn. This was not something you could miss. *Could you?* 'No, I don't think so.'

'Where did you travel from then?'

'North London?'

'Ah right. You're the second one from there today.' She offered a false smile, looking at her inquisitively.

'Oh!' said Ginny, unsure of what else to say and starting to regret having walked into the shop – it seemed awkward. Her thoughts wandered as she compared her situation to a bad horror film. On the woman's chin, she scrutinised the unsightly mole as it moved, synchronised with her mouth.

'Well, you gotta go back the way you just come from.'

'Really?'

'Yes, my dear, you just ain't gone far enough.'

'Oh, right.' She was a little confused. 'Well, thank you very much for your time and assistance,' she said, choosing this as the perfect time to retreat.

The bell sounded again as the old gentleman re-emerged into the post office, the postmaster behind the counter shouting out to him, 'What you forgotten this time, Mr Milner?'

'Stamps,' he said as the postmaster clutched at his forehead in disbelief.

Ginny thanked the lady at the counter and started to make her escape when another question arrived.

'What house in Pound Lane are you looking for anyways, my dear?'

Ginny stopped briefly as she answered her. 'Redivivus.' As she said the house name, she sensed the bewilderment and shock behind her, just like a bad horror movie, and the silence spoke volumes.

'Redivivus!' the lady exclaimed. 'Are you sure? There's been nobody lived there for...' she hesitated as she thought about it, 'for as long as I can remember.'

Ginny closed the door behind her as the lady watched her cross the road and get in the car. The elderly gentleman now arrived at her counter as she shook her head.

'City folk.' She tutted at him. 'Now what can we do for you, Mr Milner?'

~

James reversed the car under the shade of the oak tree. The engine purred to silence as he turned the ignition off. He sat for a moment and picked up his mobile, scrolling through his directory until he found William's direct number at the office and rang.

'Hi, William.'

'Hello there.' William was surprised yet pleased to hear from his junior colleague. 'How are you getting on?'

'Fine, just arrived.'

'Did you find it all right?'

'Yep, one small detour. Listen, the reason I phoned is to find out if there are any phone calls from the client?'

'Nothing so far, James, and I have asked Miss Aurthrop to let me know the minute we receive a call from Miss Faulkner. Do you think she'll phone?'

'When she realises she can't get into the property because she has the wrong keys, I'm confident she will. OK, I'm parked here and there is no sign of anyone. Going to stretch my legs, I'll give you a ring later… unless you call me first.'

'All right then, James.'

'Bye, William.'

Finished, he stepped out of his car, placing his phone in his trouser pocket, and went for a stroll.

TWENTY

FRIDAY, 19TH AUGUST 2005

Ginny cringed as she drove past the narrow lane where earlier she had turned the car around, hoping, this time, she was heading in the right direction. The air was stifling and oppressive as the day grew ever darker. In the distance a jagged flash of lightning momentarily illuminated the sky. Ahead of her in a field, Ginny spied the old barn. A landmark, just as the woman in the shop had described. Beside it an old oak tree stood proud, and she noted how the bow stretched across the road, forming a verdurous canopy. On either side were hawthorn hedgerows laid and pleached as the lane narrowed, and she passed over an old stone bridge built to allow for a stream that trickled over the stones beneath. The road then veered sharply as she entered into a coppiced area of woodland. Leaves rustled as a surge of wind swept around them, rushing them in one direction and then another, playing with them coyly as the impending thunderstorm drew nearer.

The coppice darkened as the tall beech standards rose upward, smothering out the few shards of light. On the left of her was a raised embankment, covered with brambles and intermingled with long skeins of ivy whose talons stretched out to devour all in their path. It offered brief glimpses of what lay hidden underneath. Parts of large flint and whitewashed wall strobed through, adding to her curiosity. It appeared to be manmade but not a recent structure – much older. Ginny passed a gate that closed off an area of cleared ground to her right and knew she was getting closer.

On exit from the thicket, ahead of her stood an old brick wall, the colour muted with time. This rose up six feet so that the building behind it could not be seen from the road; only its rooftop and chimney were exposed. An old oak gate, positioned in the centre, with a hefty wooden arch above it, allowed for access. Elaborate metal hinges adorned the panelled door; weather-stained with age, they were beautiful. Ginny stared incredulously, then she saw the identity of the property: 'Redivivus'.

Awestruck, she sat for a moment, before deciding to reverse to where she had seen the gate by the cleared land, knowing she could park there. The catch moved with ease and she drove in and switched off the engine. All was quiet as she reached over to her handbag, pulling out an envelope. She opened it. *How did this strange change in fortunes begin?* It was difficult for her to comprehend as she stared down at the set of keys in her hand.

Ginny got out of the car and looked around. Behind her was another smaller entrance to the garden delineated by an old myrtle hedge matching the height of the wall. A drop of rain bounced off her forehead as she moved to the gate to gain access. A breeze circled around her, bringing with it the sweet smell of honeysuckle as she turned the small ringed handle. Nothing happened. So, she tried it the other way; it still wouldn't budge.

'Must be locked.'

Her attention turned now to the keys; looking at them, they didn't look old enough for this type of lock. All she could do was to try all three.

A moment later and, much as expected, none would unlock this gate. Ginny gave up, as another raindrop splattered onto her arm, and started to walk to the ornate gate at the front of the property. Up close it was even more impressive, and she grasped the big, heavy, iron-cast handle and tried turning it. So heavy – it was obvious it hadn't been opened often – and over time the wood had warped, making it difficult to move, but slowly it gave way.

Motionless, she gasped in surprise at the beauty before her. Not knowing what to expect, this surpassed all expectation. At either side, attached to the garden walls were old espalier fruit trees, both impeccably looked after, pruned, shaped and tidied. Only the odd apple lay on the ground, decaying, attracting the attention of a curious wasp and various other insects happy to ingest the rotting mush on offer. The lawn before her was perfect – like a bowling green. Somebody was still attending to this garden and it was being cared for by skilled hands. Vibrant and pungent-smelling French lavender bushes lined both sides of the faded brick herringbone path that led up to the entrance of the house. A light-painted wooden door, splendidly framed by a Georgian-styled Palladian surround, housed two small Doric columns on either side. The arched window situated above the door was designed in segments splaying upward like divine rays that touched the mantel stone ledge.

A few more spots of rain splattered randomly down on the path. Still holding the keys, Ginny stared at the front door. A stirring deep in the recesses of her mind tingled. Sure, she had never seen this property before or even a house like it, but the scent of the lavender and the facade of the door now promoted a sense of something familiar. The breeze lifted up strands of hair across her eyes. Ginny experienced her senses surging... surging with anticipation. Aroused, she felt nervous and didn't know why. A loud squawk emanated from the woodland, startling her. A cold shiver ran up her spine. A sensation of a presence of someone, or something, alarmed her. She turned slowly, wanting to check behind her.

Nothing – she sighed in relief – there was nothing at all, just the sound of the rain beginning to fall in a more regular pattern. Much darker now, the wind swept around her as the crows called from the trees.

Again the hairs on the back of her neck pricked up. Ginny froze, staring at the door. A sense of foreboding coursed through her body and the perception of a presence came over her once more – this time much, much stronger. She was transfixed on the spot; the gate behind her creaked.

Her heart pounded. Why couldn't she turn around? That was all she had to do. Rigidity struck her as she listened to a footstep, then another. *Just turn around!*

On the point of turning, a warm breath caressed the back of her neck as a hand came to rest on her arm. Unable to contain the rising emotions, Ginny screamed.

'Hey, it's OK,' sounded the words from behind.

Her mind tried quickly to analyse the voice. Relieved to find movement in her limbs, Ginny turned. A waft of aftershave assailed her nostrils as she recognised the dark-haired young man before her – James!

'Oh my God!' she said, placing her hand to her chest and drawing in a deep breath.

'Christ! I'm so sorry, I didn't mean to scare you.' James smiled at Ginny in an attempt to put her at ease. 'Are you all right?'

'Just about, but you really did scare the hell out of me. What on earth are you doing here?'

James noted her embarrassment as she avoided his gaze. Absorbed in her movements, he watched as she tucked a loose curl of hair behind her ear and his eyes followed the contour of her slim neck as his attention drew downward to where she rested her hand on her quickening chest. As she spoke, he snapped away from his thoughts.

'Keys,' explained James.

'Keys?'

'Have you tried the door yet?'

'Yes… I mean, no… On the verge of trying them when you arrived. Why?'

'Don't think you'll have much luck.' Raising his eyebrows, he gestured to the door.

'Oh, is there something wrong?' Ginny asked, a little confused.

'Long story,' said James as he brought out another set from his pocket.

'My *keys?*' She looked at him; this would explain the doubts about the ones she held.

'Yes. Here, try these.'

On handing her the correct set, she knew instinctively these were the ones.

Turning to unlock the door, she was aware again of the alluring fragrance of James's aftershave and she rather liked it.

Both listened as a mechanism clicked, relinquishing its hold as the door gave way, revealing a small gap.

A loud thunderous noise whipped and cracked from overhead as the wind swirled past them, blowing the door to the house open farther. At this moment the clouds unleashed their fury, spewing down rain. The lavender bushes framing the pathway bowed down subserviently to its wrath.

James watched Ginny, who still appeared to be a little traumatised. 'Miss Faulkner, please may we step inside?' James asked with urgency for shelter from the weather.

Ginny glanced at the rain bouncing off James's head and shoulders, saturating his shirt, and moved into the hallway of the house as James quickly followed, shutting out the torrential rain as yet another thunderous rumble erupted from above.

'My God! That started with a vengeance,' he said as he wiped his wet face, noting Ginny still stood passively in the entrance.

To the right and left of the hall were imposing double wooden doors. The walls were pale in colour and the limestone floor slabs weathered over time. Ginny was frozen to the spot, having not spoken a word since they stepped inside. James, who was standing behind her, saw the red T-shirt she wore was wet through. He took a glimpse at her long, slim legs extending from her short skirt – taller than he remembered.

Curious, he moved forward to stand beside her. 'Wonder what lies beyond the doors?'

Ginny stepped to the right. 'This,' she stated, 'is the drawing room.' She squeezed down on the handles, releasing the catch as she tentatively pushed them open. At the threshold she hesitated.

James followed and spoke quietly. 'Miss Faulkner,' he said, questioning her. 'Virginia, how did you know?'

Turning, she stared into his eyes.

'I just *did*,' she said, still holding his gaze.

PART TWO

TWENTY-ONE

JANUARY 1940

Colonel Taverner stared at the details in his hand. 'Extraordinary! Is she aware of any of this?'

Lieutenant Blackthorn shook his head and waited.

'What? Not even the family name?'

'No, I don't believe so, sir.'

'Extraordinary,' he repeated before continuing. 'It beggars belief, doesn't it?'

'Yes, sir. They have been on the records for some time now and I think this is something we can use.'

'Quite! Afraid we need all the help we can muster. Difficult times, Blackthorn. Not going to get any easier, not for a long time. Wretched war! Still not over the last fiasco yet!' The colonel picked up his pipe and took out his Zippo lighter from his uniform jacket pocket. Clouds of smoke plumed into the air as he turned to Blackthorn again. 'When did the father go on our books?'

Blackthorn searched through the documents for the details the colonel wanted. After a moment or two he drew his finger across the page. 'Here we are, sir, the father's name –

Hans Reuben van Hassel. The wife's name is Henrietta Jane and they disembarked in August 1917.' Bemused, he paused to catch his breath as he read further down the report before continuing.

'What is it, Blackthorn?'

'Well, sir, seems they were signed off.'

'How strange. If they arrived as immigrants before the end of the war, for all we knew they could have been spies for the Kaiser; why were they taken off the list?'

'Apparently some clout on the wife's side.'

'Oh, I see. Who?'

'The name of Colonel Charles Glassbrook is the signatory written down on the report giving permission for their removal. This, I feel, is the connection.'

'Glassbrook, you say?'

'Yes, sir.'

'Rings a bell... something to do with the Foreign Office in the past? What's the link then?'

'Might I be right in suggesting Henrietta Jane is his only daughter?'

'Ah, I suppose, does make sense,' said the colonel. 'But if they were signed off the register, why do we have the information in front of us now?'

'Because, sir, they were put back on the list in October 1917 – evidently a more dubious connection arose.'

'Really!'

TWENTY-TWO

FEBRUARY 1940

'Florence, are you there?'

'I'm here, Geoffrey. Is everything all, right?' she asked, stepping out from behind the bookcase.

'I've been looking everywhere for you. There are two gentlemen waiting to speak with you.'

'Why do they want me?'

'Not sure. They didn't say much to me – wanted to talk to you and said it was quite important.' Geoffrey, expectant of some understanding from her, saw the vacant expression on her face.

'I will finish off the docket information on the loan items for the Met in New York,' Florence said, 'then I will go and check what they want.'

The two men sat in the waiting area of the museum. The sound of Florence's footsteps echoed in the hall as she strolled towards them. A quick glance at her watch told her it was after closing time and this explained the quietness of the building. And it was dark now. She was mindful as she approached them – something about the way they stood, their appearance and heavy overcoats suggested they came from the War Office. Perhaps there were more war-time instructions for the museum to adhere to; she wondered why they would want her on such matters. Security issues were dealt with by the curator. After all, she was only the archivist. Time to find out.

'I believe you wanted to speak to me?'

'Yes, Miss Stanley, thank you for coming. Is there somewhere we may talk… privately?'

Aware they had not yet shown her the return of courtesy by introducing themselves to her, it made her feel apprehensive.

'Of course, the office is just along the hall.' The more senior-looking man placed a pipe to his lips, lighting it as he gestured at the doors, then at Florence. Still uncomfortable with the situation, she looked at the second man, who smiled at her.

'This way,' she said, aware they followed closely behind her. On arriving, both men entered, and she closed the door as the man smoking the pipe removed his coat to reveal his army uniform. Just as she suspected. Next he took charge of the seating arrangements, placing himself at her desk. With no formal introduction as yet, Florence thought him impertinent as he commandeered her office. The second man asked her to be seated and he remained standing at the door as though on guard duty.

'Miss Stanley,' the assertive voice from the puffing gentleman in front of her began, 'I apologise for our lack of introduction, but I'm afraid what we have to talk to you about needs to stay confidential. Do you understand me?'

Florence wasn't sure she did; in fact, nothing made sense at the moment, but she nodded in accordance.

'Good.' After taking another puff, he began again. 'My name is Colonel Taverner and I work at the War Office in Whitehall.' He pointed to the man stood at the door. 'This is Lieutenant Blackthorn and he works for me.' At this point he indicated to the lieutenant to pass him the brown files he held. An uneasy feeling fell over Florence, one the colonel picked up on when she noticed the red lettering on the front of the file: 'Classified'.

'Do not look so worried, Miss Stanley, we're only going to ask you a few questions...'

'Is it to do with the security arrangements?' interrupted Florence. 'Because it's not me you need to speak to.'

The colonel raised an eyebrow in surprise. 'Security arrangements?'

'Yes, for the museum?'

'No, Miss Stanley, nothing to do with those...' He gave a brief smile and cleared his throat. 'May I ask what your father's name is?'

'His name?' Florence asked, staring at the expressionless face in front of her, and then answered, 'Henry Rueben Stanley.'

'Thank you.' Again, the colonel dithered checking inside the file. 'Would it surprise you to know his name is not what you said?'

'Yes... of course it would.' Now becoming a little exasperated, she grimaced at the colonel.

'His real name was Hans Reuben van Hassel.' On saying this he keenly checked her reaction to the information.

Florence almost laughed in complete disbelief at what the colonel said. What was this man talking about?

'You see, Miss Stanley, I'm afraid your father has been evasive with the truth.' He tapped his pipe down on the edge of the desk. 'What was your mother's name?'

Florence went to speak and then stopped herself.

'Please, go ahead,' pushed the colonel.

Apprehensive at first, fearing he might say something she didn't want to hear, she answered. 'It is Henrietta Jane Stanley.' She peered at the him in uneasy anticipation. 'Are you going to tell me, Colonel Taverner, this is incorrect?'

'Not completely, her name was Henrietta Jane – but not Stanley.'

The minute he said it, Florence was certain what he would tell her next. 'So, her name was van Hassel?'

'Yes.' For a moment, he watched as the realisation dawned on her. 'Your name is also van Hassel and not Stanley – and your sister Edith is the same.'

Florence stared down at the floor, confused. This couldn't be happening. It didn't make any sense. Her heart rate quickened, the nausea knotting inside of her. The lieutenant stepped forward, holding a glass of water he'd fetched from the far end of the office.

'Take a sip, Miss, nice and slow. Just breathe, take your time.' His reassurance put her at ease. 'Are you all right?' He asked, staring into her brown eyes as she nodded appreciatively before he withdrew his hand from hers and went back to sentry duty in front of the door. The cup of water she then rested on the desk and clasped her clammy hands. With little time to collect her thoughts, she listened to the colonel speak.

'I'm sorry, Florence, for the abruptness in telling you of these family falsehoods, but there's more information we need to impart before we can get to why we are here.'

How can this be? Why did she not know any of this – to be unsure of her own identity; she had been living a lie. Without raising her head, she found the courage to ask a question. 'You said my name is van Hassel, is this right? Is this true?'

'Yes.' The colonel simply answered her question, knowing there would be another.

'But it is Stanley,' she stubbornly persisted. 'People don't change their names?' Her shock turned to anger as she gripped the edge of the chair, leaning towards him, and raised her voice. 'Why did my father replace his name? Stop this charade and tell me.'

The colonel arched an eyebrow at this reaction but was inwardly pleased, because it was exactly what he wanted, as a knock sounded at the door. The lieutenant stood aside as Geoffrey appeared. Surprised, he glanced at Florence and then at the colonel, trying to push the door open a little further, but it was blocked and offered limited access.

'Is everything all right?' he said.

'Nothing to worry about.' Florence tried to smile. 'You get off now and I'll lock up?'

He was not convinced she was comfortable. 'If you are sure then...' He scrutinised the lieutenant standing at the side of him, wary. 'See you tomorrow... yes?'

'Thanks, Geoffrey, you have a nice evening.'

With that he withdrew, checking out the two men once more as he didn't feel happy leaving Florence on her own, but she'd assured him she was OK and he was already late for an engagement.

Colonel Taverner looked up from the file, quite unperturbed by the interruption, as though it was a mere inconvenience to him. 'What do you know of your family background, Miss Stanley?'

Hesitant, she stared at him – was this a trick question?

'Are you surprised by your Dutch surname?'

'Yes and no,' she tried to explain. 'I believe my grandmother is Dutch.' Uncertain, she appeared awkward. 'I'm not sure what the truth is now?' The cupboard door had been blown off its hinges, revealing skeletons falling down around her. It didn't make for easy viewing.

Colonel Taverner comprehended the despair that blanketed Florence, aware of her discomfort, but he needed to continue; he had a purpose. Ready, he cleared his throat. 'What I'm going to tell you,' he waited for her to raise her head; he wanted her to hear his words, 'is classified information and it must remain so.' On making eye contact, he watched her nod in agreement. 'Did you know, Florence, that your mother and father arrived in England in August 1917, before the end of the Great War?'

Florence sighed turning to stare out of the window. Dark, the tiny beads of rain ran down the windowpane; their erratic trails traversed downward like the thoughts in her head. Nothing was straightforward any more.

'No.' Curious she enquired naively, 'Why would that be a problem?'

The colonel continued, 'When did the Great War end, in what year?'

What is he up to now with these silly questions? She eyed him and realised he wanted her to answer the posed question. Confused, she frowned at the absurdity but did so. 'In 1918,' she said in a sarcastic tone, wanting him to get on with it.

'Very good, Florence.' The sarcasm was not missed by him and it was unlike her to be rude. 'Correct. Your parents fled Holland on board a Belgian fishing trawler before the end of the war, landing here in Folkestone. Your mother, pregnant, had endured an arduous journey as well as dangerous.' The colonel paused to suck on his pipe and checked Florence, who sat calmly as he delved into the brown file once more, pulling out a wad of papers tied together with a red piece of ribbon.

Then, rather unpredictably, the colonel stood and stretched his arms, moving to perch on the front of the desk. Before doing anything else, he startled her by enquiring where he and the lieutenant could make themselves a cup of tea. Taken aback, Florence wondered, *How can he be talking about tea?* Her whole life appeared in complete disarray and confusion whilst he obsessed about a hot drink. Still staring curiously at the tied bundle, she told him of the small staff room down the corridor. The lieutenant who had been patiently standing by the door opened it and waited.

Colonel Taverner placed his hand on the papers and moved them towards the edge of the desk nearer to Florence. 'These are for you to read. You may well find these documents very enlightening.'

'For me to read?' she expressed, surprised.

He stared down into her face. 'These are the signed statements from your father, explaining to the Secret Intelligence Bureau in 1917 as to why he and his wife, your mother, fled Holland at such a precarious time – and why we are here to speak to you today.'

With his final words still resonating in her ears, she sat motionless as he tapped the papers and then proceeded to join the lieutenant as they walked out of the office, closing the door behind them.

'What do you think she'll make of them?' Lieutenant Blackthorn asked.

'Remarkable, even illuminating, but she's tough and that we'll use. Now, I'm parched.'

TWENTY-THREE

A neatly tied set of papers now sat on Florence's lap. Mystified, she pulled at the red ribbon on the musty old folder. A perceived life history – given to her by her parents – appeared now to have changed. On opening the file, her father's name leapt out. A sense of sadness draped over her at the thought of their memories as she folded back the first page with caution, unsure what ghosts lay inside. Sections of the material were typeset whilst other parts were handwritten. The bold heading that caught her attention was stark, even detached, as she read:

> ***Statement of Immigrant Hans Reuben van Hassel***
> *Date: 23rd August 1917*
> *Ref: IM0884HRVK: A*

Florence shook her head in complete disbelief and turned the page to see more. The words illustrated details to her, some familiar and others she had no idea of.

> *'Born 10th August 1884 in Leeuwarden in Holland and I have a sister, Hannah, who is four years older than me.'*

Astonished, even amazed, she stared. 'My goodness, I have an aunt I never knew existed until today.' With added interest, she began to scan through the reams of information that her father had written down.

'I had started working for the bank in Amsterdam as a clerk and worked my way up to be a manager. That is where I met my wife Henrietta. Her father, Colonel Charles Glassbrook, used our depository. I'd look forward to her visits. Eventually I plucked up enough courage to ask her to marry me.'

Florence smiled at this point as she considered the details of her father and mother's wedding certificate:

The Wedding of Hans Reuben van Hassel to Henrietta Jane Glassbrook
Saturday, 18th May 1912:
Hans Reuben van Hassel: Born 10th August 1884
Profession: Bank's Assistant Financial Manager
Henrietta Jane Glassbrook: Born 13th February 1887
Profession: Spinster
Parents: Parents of Hans Reuben van Hassel
Jacob Reuben and Agnes van Hassel
Parents of Henrietta Jane Glassbrook
Colonel Charles Francis Glassbrook and Elizabeth Jane Glassbrook (Deceased)
Witness: Margaretha Geertruida MacLeod

My God. She stared at the page. Details of her grandparents she and her sister Edith had never known. How would she tell Edith about this? How could she put her through any more? With the loss of both their parents, surely Edith had endured enough. For a moment, stunned, she tried hard to understand how she was feeling. Why didn't her parents ever tell her of any of this... why?

Her head bowed to the documents once more, she kept reading, wanting to extract more! The date on the files moved to 1914, to the beginning of the First World War, with an explanation for why her parents elected to remain in Amsterdam:

> *'My father-in-law, Charles Glassbrook, had suggested to move Henrietta and myself to England to stay with him before the war broke out in 1914. On reflection, I should have done but at the time did not feel it necessary.'*

Florence paused for a moment, thinking her father could never have seen what turmoil the war would bring. Who was this grandfather of hers that understood such things? She read the next paragraph:

> *'My reasons for not travelling were due to Henrietta's health. It would have been a risk at the time as she was convalescing after the loss of our first child, sadly stillborn.'*

The faded written words were blunt. Florence traced a finger over them as if to console her mother, wanting only to take away the immense pain she must have suffered after losing a baby – she longed for her mother's touch. Such a gentle lady, always there for them, just so frail; she had not regained her good health after Edith was born.

Often, Florence thought her mother was not a strong person. But now she realised, with guilt, that to endure all that she had – to start a new life in another country, for whatever reasons – took strength.

A tear fell from her eye. 'I'm so sorry, Mother,' she apologised softly, glancing up in hope that her words might be heard. Florence took out a handkerchief from her pocket, dabbed her eye and, after a moment, read once more. This time her father mentioned the importance of a family friend:

> *'Margaretha greatly helped Henrietta through this sad time in her life. I couldn't thank her enough for all she did.'*

Florence remembered once what her mother had said to her as a child: 'True friends are the ones who share similar experiences in life with you.' *Why,* she wondered, *did she say this? Could it be in connection with 'this friend'?*

The information on the next page was as the colonel had told her – it explained her parents fleeing from Holland and arriving in Folkestone in August 1917, after her father's thirty-third birthday. They were then brought for questioning to London two days later.

On finishing the sentence, the door opened. Colonel Taverner marched back in, followed by Lieutenant Blackthorn, who resumed his position at the door. The colonel sat in his usual spot, opposite her, and cleared his throat. 'Have you found it interesting reading, Miss Stanley?'

For a moment, staring down at the tatty brown folder, she thought interesting was an understatement. There were many unanswered questions, including why her parents had not told her any of this? Why had they changed their surname? 'Yes... although,' she began, 'I'm still confused by what it all means.'

The colonel gestured to the lieutenant and he passed over yet another faded brown file. This too had the words 'Classified' stamped on the front. Worry etched across Florence's face as she wiped her forehead before averting her eyes.

The colonel noted this and checked his watch. He realised she had been sat there for over an hour and might need some refreshment. 'Miss Stanley, would you like a beverage, some tea?'

Surprised by this but thirsty, she thought this a good idea. 'Please.'

'Blackthorn, would you...' Lieutenant Blackthorn had already opened the door to the office.

The papers strewn all over her lap, she placed them in the folder and returned her attention to the new sets of documents that Taverner scanned through on the desk. What new revelations would this file reveal? Certainly, there were many unanswered questions.

Colonel Taverner smoothed the edges of his bushy moustache as he contemplated how to start the conversation. 'Florence, you are aware of some basic facts regarding your family background. Are you not?'

'Yes, I am... However, many things are still not explained. Why, for example, is my name Stanley?'

'We shall get to that point in a moment. When your parents arrived in England, we needed to ascertain where they stood politically. Do you understand what I mean by this?'

'Yes, Colonel… You wanted to assess whether or not they were spies. Am I right?'

'We needed to appraise where their allegiances lay. A precarious time with sinister dealings. Your mother, Henrietta, it appears, was well associated, as your grandfather Colonel Charles Francis Glassbrook worked for the Foreign Office and the Secret Intelligence Bureau in London.'

'How was he connected?'

'An astute man – gifted, you may say. Worked overseas, mostly. His position allowed him to analyse fragile situations, with expertise, on our behalf.'

'Do you mean he was a spy?'

'Shame you say it in such a distasteful way, Miss Stanley. Espionage is intrinsically complicated. The work your grandfather carried out for us was extremely important.'

'Did my father realise any of this?'

'No. Part of the SIB reasons for questioning your parents so thoroughly was to evaluate what they did know.'

The office door opened, and the lieutenant re-entered, carrying a cup of tea.

The colonel paused, turning over another page from the dusty file. 'This file is dated October 1917, and this,' he said, pointing at the paperwork lying within yet another old folder, 'is when the SIB decided to readmit both your parents back on our "At-Risk List".'

'What does that mean?'

'It means that SIB discovered that there were concerns raised about them.'

Stunned, she put down her cup of tea; what did the colonel mean?

'Your father was asked to visit the SIB office in Whitehall in October 1917. Information came to light when background searches were undertaken, and there were circumstances that needed further investigation.'

Frustrated, Florence frowned at what she heard, trying to understand. 'What would make you want to keep my parents under surveillance? What threat did they pose to you?'

The colonel sat back in his chair and sighed. He touched the edge of his moustache again and contorted his mouth to a stiffened pout, thinking how to present the facts to Florence. There were certain matters he needed to make her aware of, but he wanted to draw her into his web, into what he wanted from her.

'Well, it's not so much about what they knew… The SIB had ascertained from the interviews that in many ways they did not have anything to hide. Not what they knew,' he looked at her, 'but who they knew!'

Florence gawped. 'Who could they know that would result in them being placed on the "At-Risk List" to be observed by the Secret Intelligence Bureau?'

'The "List",' the colonel explained, 'is not just about surveillance on your parents' movements… as a matter of fact, the opposite.'

'The opposite… What do you mean?'

For a moment, he hesitated. 'They were monitored… for their own protection.'

Florence gasped, not expecting for one minute this was to do with their safety.

'Things aren't always what they seem… are they, Miss Stanley?' His voice was quiet as he reproached her.

Shocked, she stared at the colonel. And reluctantly, she had to admit she had not foreseen this.

'Your father told us his sister, Hannah Olga van Hassel, went to boarding school in Leiden. There she befriended an older girl, highly regarded by the family, who became good friends with your father. However, this friendship led to the situation we are in today. It was this connection, to this lady, which put your parents on our list in 1917.'

Desperate to understand, Florence shook her head. 'How can one person cause so much confusion and drama in other people's lives? How do you know all this?'

Colonel Taverner glanced at Florence again. 'Because we make it our business to know. It was also Charles Glassbrook's business to comprehend such matters.'

'My grandfather was aware of all this?'

'Yes, in fact, at his insistence, your parents were monitored by SIB.'

She was stunned. 'I can't believe that!' she said, standing up. The chair fell backwards, and all the papers, sat on her lap, spilt to the floor.

Bewildered, she moved to stare out of the darkened window, detached from the chaos she created around her. Colonel Taverner got up as Florence turned around. 'I don't understand any of this. I feel like I can't distinguish who I am, or who these people are that you are talking about.' Unable to hold back her emotions, she started to sob now.

Taverner sat her back down on the repositioned chair and offered her his starched white handkerchief. Then he returned to his seat. 'This is a shock to you. It must be so inordinately alien, but it isn't as bad as you think.'

Fraught, she dabbed at her reddened eyes; her head hung low as he decided to carry on, conscious she was listening. 'Your grandfather did not identify initially your father's friendship with his sister's friend. On duty, he first met this friend when he was introduced to a Mrs MacLeod by her new husband, an older officer called Colonel Rudolph MacLeod. Colonel Glassbrook saw then, as did others, that the marriage was ill matched and unlikely to survive. Also, he realised she was a confident lady, able to use her womanly charms, attracting great attention from the younger officers.'

Taverner checked Florence; she had relaxed a little, sitting back in her chair, still holding the hanky on her lap. From a small pouch of tobacco, he refilled his pipe, padded it down and took his lighter to the bowl, whereupon several puffs filled the room.

Florence, now interested, wanted him to hurry with what he had to say.

'Your grandfather did not meet Mrs MacLeod again until some years later, bumping into her quite by accident in Amsterdam, by now divorced and struggling to live independently with little resources. Aware of the potential he could exploit and her situation, he invited her to London, where he introduced her to a lifestyle that would suit the needs of the SIB. We made her more comfortable.'

'What do you mean?' she asked him.

Again, he puffed on his pipe, thinking about her question,

and answered her carefully. 'Shall we say that… she was employed by us?'

Florence, still a bit confused, thought she understood his implication but was not totally sure.

'You see, Mrs MacLeod mixed with high society throughout Europe, she came into contact with many… important people of the time working in the theatre, becoming an infamous demimonde in a world foreign to you but recognised by the powerful criminal fraternity of pre-war Paris.' The colonel stopped, noticing her confusion as she shook her head. 'What is the matter?' he asked.

'My father would not be acquainted with someone like this; how can he be connected to her? I don't get it,' she said.

Surprised at what she had deduced, he gave a wry smile to himself – he had her reasoning, which he wanted. 'Your father would not frequent with anyone like this… and, in fact, he didn't.'

'But you said he did.'

'No, I said he knew Mrs Macleod, who'd been introduced to the family and had become a close friend.'

He knew Florence was confused – it was illustrated on her perturbed face – but the colonel did not rush to explain everything; he wanted her to work it out.

'Are you saying,' Florence began, 'there were two sides to this person?'

'Perhaps… continue.'

He was up to his tricks again, so she decided to change tactic. 'Did my father know my grandfather was familiar with this woman… whatever her name was?'

'Your father was unaware of your grandfather's

connection to Mrs MacLeod. Apart from once – when they all briefly met at the bank in Amsterdam. Whilst on her way to Paris she decided to visit your father and by accident your grandfather was also there. Later, Colonel Glassbrook told us there had been no compromise; she acted professionally. So, to your father, the loyal friend – but your grandfather knew her in a different role.'

The colonel stopped for a second. 'However, when he returned to London in 1913, he had been concerned enough by this chance meeting to inform us of her association with his son-in-law and his own daughter... something he did not find comfortable...'

Florence interrupted the colonel. 'This wasn't his only reason?'

Taverner was pleased at her analysing the information. 'No, Miss Stanley, it was not.'

Absorbed by his answer, she continued with her thoughts. 'My grandfather grew concerned he had created a danger in Mrs MacLeod and must have established others like him were watching her.' The accusation she almost snapped at the colonel, who listened without showing any response.

'An interesting web that we weave; don't you think?' he said in such a non-committed way she grew quite angry at him.

'You are playing with people's lives, Colonel Taverner, how can you be so flippant?'

He stared straight at her. 'There is no flippancy, Florence, in what we do; I can assure you of that... everything we do in Secret Intelligence we take very seriously.'

Surprised at his reaction, she detected a note of frustration in his voice, indicating he did actually have feelings. This may just have manifested itself in those few but impassioned words. None the less, not satisfied, she still needed more. 'How connected to my family was this woman?'

'Again, you say it with such disdain, Miss Stanley.' He waited and then asked her a question she would not forget the answer to in a hurry: 'What is your middle name?'

'Margaret,' she said, wondering what on earth this had to do with anything.

'Do you know what it is in Dutch?'

Florence cringed. 'No, I'm afraid I do not.' Finishing, she waited.

Colonel Taverner focused on her. 'Your real middle name is... Margaretha.'

On recognising the name, she grabbed the file still sat on the desk and flicked through the papers. Now impatient, she scanned through her father's words, drawing her finger along the pages. Halfway down she stopped. There... the same name; only a minute ago she had been informed this was connected to her. In the passage she read her father declared in his statement when Henrietta lost the child someone helped her through this trauma, he 'couldn't thank Margaretha enough.'

'Oh my God,' she shouted, still touching the paper with her finger.

Colonel Taverner waited for a minute and then decided to fill in the rest of the details. 'Her maiden name: Margaretha Geertruida Zelle. This was the lady, the reliable family friend, who cared for your mother in her time of need. The one thing Margaretha had in common with your mother – she too had suffered when her son died.'

In the solitude of her thoughts, Florence glanced out of the window at the darkness. 'That's why she had empathy with my mother; she too had experienced the same pain. My mother thought a lot of her... didn't she?' Florence remembered her mother's words: 'True friends are the ones who share similar experiences in life with you.' 'It's obvious she referred to this lady.' Angry at the colonel, she thought him smug, knowing he had set her up. An intricate web he had spun, and she was truly stuck in it. Time to have the whole story now and to understand why he wanted her. No more games... she needed the truth!

'So,' she began, 'Margaretha Geertruida Zelle was Mrs MacLeod but seen as two different people, or she played two roles?'

'Yes, the genuine family friend who cared for your parents and even your grandfather, but Mrs MacLeod became involved in a diverse lifestyle after her divorce. The facade she developed was for her survival.'

Florence looked at him. 'Why did she become a problem? What went wrong?'

'Why do you think something went wrong?'

'Because,' she started, 'my grandfather worried enough to want my parents guarded by your organisation, or should I say protected. That would imply to me she brought a problem closer to home somehow, a danger not only to my parents...' she hesitated, convinced she was right, 'but a danger to you, to the Secret Intelligence Bureau. Am I right?'

Colonel Taverner smiled at Florence and leant on the desk. 'An interesting theory, especially from one who finds espionage such a distasteful subject.'

Florence was aware the colonel would never directly admit to this, but from the look on his face, she knew she'd drawn a small admission from him.

He continued. 'We were not the only ones who had shown interest in Mrs MacLeod. Remember, she travelled throughout Europe, living in Paris, but when war broke out in 1914, she stayed in Berlin.'

'What exactly are you saying? Are you implying she worked for the Germans and the French?'

'With many varied and interesting contacts, this placed her in a position where she could be manipulated.'

Florence responded tartly to this comment. 'You mean like my grandfather, he saw her worth… didn't he?'

Colonel Taverner said nothing; he chose to ignore her criticism and referred back to the file in front of him.

Questions were spinning around in Florence's mind. 'Did my father know of the duplicity of this lady?' She waited for his response.

Taverner recognised this point gnawed at her as she kept coming back to it. 'Apparently not. To him and his family, she was their friend. In fact, he knew nothing of it until we informed him of the situation in October 1917.'

'Why did you do this?'

'By then it was essential we did.'

'Essential? You make it sound like their lives depended on it.'

Colonel Taverner tapped his fingers on the table. 'Colonel Glassbrook did meet Mrs MacLeod one last time in 1916, when she came to England whilst travelling between The Hague and Paris. At this brief meeting she indicated to him her involvement in the service of the French intelligence organisation. This issue, your grandfather had already considered. Through his sources, he was aware of liaisons with the German High Command as well. After this meeting he reported to us a situation developing with an agent he'd been in touch with for many years. Quite clearly, he stated events were beginning to spiral out of control and it would be best to cut all links to this person.'

Florence interrupted with a question. 'Why was he so worried about the situation?'

'Because,' the colonel answered, 'he had foreseen she had been naive about whom her relationships were with. Alert to the paranoia setting in amongst the French Intelligence Service, Colonel Glassbrook was mindful of the political turmoil that would ensue should any trace of Mrs MacLeod lead back to the SIB in London.'

'Is this all he was worried about? What about Margaretha?' Florence empathised that Mrs Macleod was being used as an asset by all.

'Still you think so little of us?'

'I have no reason to trust you... do I?'

The colonel smirked and searched through the file for a single piece of paper – a letter addressed to the Secret Intelligence Bureau from Florence's grandfather. He handed it over for her to read:

'To inform you of my concerns, I write about an agent named Mrs Macleod. On my recent visit, I informed her of her naivety in having entwined relationships between French and German officers in the intelligence services.

A precarious situation. I clearly stated for her not to make contact with me again.'

Florence faltered for a moment to absorb the stark words on the page.

'Please read on, Miss Stanley,' the colonel advised.

'At this stage in my correspondence, I am requesting my son-in-law, Hans Reuben van Hassal, and his wife, my daughter, Henrietta, be diligently cared for should any unfortunate circumstance befall Mrs Macleod. I have written to him expressing, he should move from Holland to England, as the situation in Europe is volatile and unstable. To him, I gave connections for transportation, for both to leave Amsterdam at their first opportunity. Lastly,' he instructed, *'that when they arrive in the country, I want them both minded, for their own safety.'*

There the letter ended.

Florence handed back the paper with the faded written words, conscious on gathering her thoughts as the colonel spoke.

'Your grandfather sadly died before your parents arrived in England. This was the other reason they decided to travel here.'

'How did he die?' Not sure what to expect with the type of intrigue he was involved with, she found herself curious.

'Nothing sinister… coronary problems leading to heart failure. By his death in April 1917, he was fifty-five years old. Whilst living abroad for many years, he contracted malaria, leaving him with poor health. The same condition took the life of his wife when your mother was only a child. The climate never agreed with her.'

All this time had passed, and Florence hadn't even thought about her grandmother. This was indeed a revealing evening, but information from the letter was still pressing to be answered. 'You have told me my parents went on the "At-Risk List" in October 1917, which is when you re-interviewed my father.'

'That is correct.' Colonel Taverner glanced over at the lieutenant. Time now to conclude on this matter and move on to why they were there. 'Miss Stanley, when we met your father again in October 1917, he admitted to us part of his reason for leaving Amsterdam came from a visit he received by a German officer working for their intelligence corps. Frightened by this, he wouldn't state what had been said, but from the implication, he needed to get his pregnant wife and himself out of Holland to safety in England.'

Alarmed at what he said, Florence interrupted the colonel. 'It must have been something serious for my father to risk bringing my mother over on such an arduous journey, remembering the misfortunes of her first pregnancy. What could make him do that?'

'A huge risk, as you say, but when lives are at stake, the risks are worth taking.'

'Lives?' exclaimed Florence. 'Why would they be in danger? They had done nothing wrong.'

'That's just it... the threat never did lay with them – because of their connection to someone.'

'Do you mean Mrs MacLeod again?'

Colonel Taverner paused. 'Your grandfather tried to warn her… she frequented with too many different associates… of varying nationalities. The French did not like this.'

'Why should it bother them?'

'Because the head of their counter-espionage, a man named Ladoux, offered her payment for information. What Mrs MacLeod neglected to tell the French was her dealings with the Germans. They did not look kindly on fraternising with the enemy. They recognised if any of this were to get into the public domain, it would not show them in a favourable light. So, they arrested her; she had become a problem.'

The colonel sat upright, straightening his shoulders back, and coughed. 'We cannot say for certain of her involvement in German espionage, but that she frequented with many people, from different nationalities, is definite. Her salubrious work in the theatre placed her in an unfavourable light within society and therefore could be found culpable of treason against the French state without so much as the raising of an eyebrow. Presumed guilty. Exposed as a danger!' Colonel Taverner stopped for a moment to look at Florence. 'Needless to say, anyone knowing her was vulnerable.' He hoped she would comprehend his meaning.

'Why would they assume my parents were spies? They were not conscious of the other life Margaretha led?'

'No, but how could they be sure there was no association, unless they took them in for questioning? Do you think your father wanted this? Did he need this situation for your mother? Although your parents were unaware of your grandfather's involvement with the Secret Intelligence Bureau, they realised he was well established in the British

Army. Doesn't paint a good picture for your parents, which is why your father realised they had to flee Amsterdam… scared also by the visit from the German authorities.'

'So, is this why you asked him back in for a second interview?'

Colonel Taverner turned over a page in the file and Florence could see a red stamped word on the top but could not make out what it said.

'To explain the situation, we had to call your father back in and tell him of the risk. We informed him of the selected details of your grandfather's involvement, of Mrs MacLeod and her tragic situation, and how it took a turn for the worst… placing them in great danger. There is no easy way to say this…' he lingered for a moment, 'but Margaretha Geertruida MacLeod, formerly Zelle, was shot at Chateau de Vincennes in October 1917.'

Shocked, Florence sat upright. 'Don't be silly,' she said. 'They don't shoot women!'

She stared at the colonel, wanting reassurance from him, thinking he was just trying to scare her. But he sat with an expressionless face. Florence found this incredulous. Only this evening, she had discovered fragments of Mrs Macleod's life and the connection to her parents, aware she led a different existence to most, and for whatever reasons – but what was she really guilty of? Amazed, Florence refused to believe it. After all, she lived in a civilised society where you didn't go around shooting women. In disbelief, she glared at the colonel, still sat quietly. It was evident this was no lie.

'They didn't really shoot her… did they?'

Colonel Taverner saw Florence's dismay and pulled out a

newspaper cutting from the file and handed it to her. Dated 16th October 1917, she read the words:

'German Agent Pays the Penalty.'

Florence tried to comprehend how such a thing could happen. There was even a picture of the lady. A shiver ran down her spine as she looked at the photo. Margaretha had known things about her parents that Florence would never know. Sombre, she touched the photo and became quite emotional, when she heard the colonel speak.

'This is why your name is Stanley and not van Hassel. It was changed to offer you security, to protect your family.'

Some of the papers he tidied up into the faded brown file, and she realised what the red wording on the document had been – 'Deceased.' Motionless, she continued to listen.

'This is why we have kept an eye on you all, to this day.'

Florence, staring down again at the newspaper article, gasped, noticing something so obvious to her – how had she missed it the first time? 'No, it can't be... I have seen this before!' she shouted as Colonel Taverner stared at her.

'Yes, this is the other reason we tried to keep you safe. Her notoriety made this all very public.'

Flabbergasted, she stared at him. 'It can't be the same person?'

'Oh, I can assure you it is, Miss Stanley.'

'Mata Hari!'

'You recognised her theatrical name, didn't you?' said the colonel.

Dumbfounded, she nodded; although she had not even

been born when the incident occurred, the infamous name of the exotic dancer had been synonymous with mysterious spy tales – years after the event. Until this moment Florence had only ever thought her a fictional character, a myth that girls talked of.

Colonel Taverner took the article back. 'Not everything is as it seems. Margaretha Geertruida Zelle/MacLeod, alias Mata Hari, a ruthless spy shot by the French and accused of being a German agent. Do you think she deserved to die?'

Florence eyed the colonel; she didn't say anything.

'We protected you, Miss Stanley, as your grandfather advised,' he stopped and stared straight at her, 'and now we need you.' He paused to close the file in front of him. 'We need you to do something for us.'

TWENTY-FOUR

MARCH 1940

Florence pressed the paper with the ink pen, concluding her sentence. The words on the page before her she padded gently with the blotter and carefully closed the book. Next, she reached for an envelope from the tray and then opened the drawer of the desk. On taking out a letter, she lingered, caressing it, pondering once more its contents. She then put it in the envelope and sealed it as though closing a precious jewel box. The message, she hoped, would remain safe for a long time to come. Again she picked up the pen, hesitating, not sure what to write on the front. Her words now written, she placed the letter on the closed book, patting it tenderly as though comforting a trusted and dear friend. With a kiss to her fingers, she tapped the photo sat on the desk.

'Take care, Edith,' she whispered to herself, 'and I'll tell you all about our new family history when I get home.' Florence rose from her seat, straightened her skirt and glanced around the drawing room. The March mist hung low as the day dawned… a day she was fearful of. A wave of nostalgia undulated softly over her; she hoped this would not happen today. This home meant so much to her. But she needed to be strong.

Startled by a gruff-sounding horn from outside, she broke from her thoughts. A last check of the room and she walked to the hall, picking up her small, brown leather suitcase. On opening her beautiful Georgian door, a rush of cold air greeted her, stripping from her every last ounce of warmth.

The mist still lay thick and, with a shiver, she walked down the path, looking at the dormant fruit trees now beginning to disclose small signs of regeneration. Through the old wooden gate, she continued, arriving at the car – a black Austin Cambridge. A military driver stepped forward to relieve her of the suitcase and opened the back door. They exchanged a morning greeting and slipped back into silence; there was little more to say. Inside, she adjusted her hat as the car started. Florence had promised herself she would not glance back at the house... her home. Unable to resist, she turned as the house drew further away, and her eyes filled with tears as she passed the hawthorn hedgerows... not knowing when she would return.

The Austin picked up speed and Florence pulled herself together to watch the Hampshire countryside pass her by as they continued along the road towards London. Arranged weeks ago, she had an appointment at 9.30am at the War Office in Whitehall. Sat clasping her hands, she wondered how all this had begun; life had been very ordinary up until this moment – you could even say a bit dull – but since the outbreak of war last September, everything was different.

Distracted, she glanced around the car, thinking the Austin lovely; normally her journeys were by train, so this was a treat. Florence hoped all the loose ends were tied up and everything left neat and tidy. Would it help Edith one day to understand? She was hopeful she would be able to tell her all herself when she came back, but she couldn't take any chances. It was a lot for anyone to comprehend, let alone Edith.

The countryside began to infiltrate less into her view now, as tall buildings of all shapes and sizes coruscated brilliantly through the Austin's rectangular window. Further into the metropolis, she entered into London. It was vibrant as always, but signs of preparation for war were evident as they drove along the road: sandbag-constructed walls, restricted barriers and criss-cross taping on windows. Conflict had not yet reached Britain's shores, but she, unlike many, realised it would be likely. Her fears came from the very people she went to visit and if they believed in this impending danger, so now did she. Her journey would not end in London, but Florence hoped to have a few spare hours to meet with her sister before continuing on to Cambridge later that afternoon.

Florence became familiar with the structure before her as the black Austin rattled its way up to the main wrought-iron gate guarded by two soldiers. They spoke to the driver and checked his credentials; one of them strolled up to look in the back of the Austin. Feeling awkward, she stared at the back of the seat. A moment later they were driving through and parking. The door opened and she thanked the driver as she stepped out of the comfort of the car into the crisp, cold air. This was it then – no going back. With her suitcase, she headed toward the large door of the building.

It was warm inside; Florence had only just sat down on the

chair when the door behind her swung open. The lieutenant breezed into the small office and placed a folder on the desk. Flustered at the speed of his entrance, she rose to greet him as he gestured to her to sit back down. The room was quiet for a moment as he familiarised himself with the last final details. Lifting his head, he looked straight at Florence, who recoiled at the strength of his stare. Aware of her reaction, he softened his approach.

'Thank you for coming, Miss Stanley,' he said, formal yet polite, and introduced himself to her. 'Don't believe we were properly introduced the last time we met. My name is Lieutenant Richard Blackthorn. You spoke to Colonel Taverner on the last occasion.'

Florence nodded in agreement and he continued.

'This is a difficult situation, but I cannot stress enough to you, although quiet at present' – Florence knew this was why they had termed it the 'Phony War' – 'we are at war with Germany.' Lieutenant Blackthorn looked over at Florence. 'Holland is not. As a civilian, you are perfectly entitled to travel to the Netherlands. However, we want you there as quickly and safely as possible. To facilitate this, we will be using some of our connections. Colonel Taverner has asked me to express to you, that you are not a spy' – she almost laughed out loud at this comment, thinking back to her previous conversations with the colonel – 'and are therefore entering Amsterdam, not incognito. You have a job to do. These are very precarious times and we wouldn't ask for your assistance if we did not need it.'

Whilst smoothing down his tie, he read on from the file. 'Later today, you will catch the 13.36 train from Euston to

Cambridge. On arriving at the station, you will be met by one of our men who will escort you to the Royal Oak guest house. To alleviate any awkward questions from the locals or servicemen at the lodging, we have booked the room on the pretence you are taking up a position with the Women's Land Army. Here, you will stay until the same contact returns for you in the morning at exactly 04.00 hours. There you will be driven to Lowestoft, where we will discharge you to a Dutch fishing trawler called the *Zeeslang*. The captain's name is Gerrit de Witte. From here on out you know what to do and how to contact us. Is this clear?'

Lieutenant Blackthorn checked Florence, who nodded in return. It was a surreal situation in itself, but the message had definitely been received. There didn't even seem to be any rush or confusion, with her emotions numb, almost expressionless.

'Is there anything you would like to ask? Or anyone you would like us to contact,' he appeared a little awkward, 'should anything happen?'

Florence sensed the lieutenant had held this kind of meeting before. The realisation crept over her now and it was vital she kept calm. 'I would like you to contact my younger sister, Edith.' For a moment she reached in her clutch bag and pulled out an envelope with her name on it. Florence contemplated the words inside and then passed it over to him. The lieutenant took it and placed it in the brown folder. At this moment, his assistant entered the office as Florence stood, knowing it was time to go. Adjusting her hat, she thanked the lieutenant and walked to the waiting officer.

Before leaving, she heard the words of the lieutenant behind her. 'Good luck, Miss Stanley.'

Unable to say anything, she tarried but did not look back and simply nodded in acknowledgment. The assistant followed her out, shutting the door behind them. In the corridor they arrived at a rather grand staircase. A large oval window in the centre of the ceiling caught Florence's attention as the adjutant, stood beside her, saluted as an officer strolled past and then turned to Florence. 'Shall I show you to the door?'

Florence thanked him and declined his offer, watching as he strolled off up another corridor, tucking the plain brown files under his arm. Drawn to all the activity around her, she viewed with curiosity the many men and women dressed in various military uniforms who busied around the corridors leading off this impressive stairway, as the sun streamed in, now through the elliptical-shaped window from above. After a moment she took out her leather gloves from her bag and pulled them on as she strolled down the stairs. Now only a few minutes past ten, she decided there was time for one last visit. The large, heavy door she pushed open and stepped out into the London street.

TWENTY-FIVE

Florence thanked the secretary and waited. The place was unexpectedly quiet and odours of disinfectant along with boiled cabbage mingled in the air. Always an odd combination, but it brought back nostalgic memories. The door banged shut behind her, echoing around the reception hall as she noted an officious short woman strolling towards her. It was no one she recognised and she was somewhat scary on first impression.

'Miss Stanley?' she enquired in a presumptive tone.

Florence responded but was cut off as the woman began to give her a lecture. 'Well, I expect you appreciate this is not school policy to interrupt a child's education on a whim. There are procedures for these types of meetings, usually arranged in advance. Do hope you are not going to make a habit of it?'

The admonishment received from the formidable voice in front of her, Florence nodded hastily in agreement. 'Absolutely, Miss Crankshaw, an ill-thought-out idea that certainly will not be repeated. In fact, if it were not an emergency then I would not have been so inconsiderate.' Florence smiled, trying to soften the old crustacean, but there was little change of expression.

'Very well,' she said, and turned. 'Better follow me.' With this she strode off down the corridor with Florence shuffling along behind her, attempting to keep up. After a moment or two of awkward silence, a child appeared from a classroom and almost froze on the spot when she spotted the lady approaching. The trepidation on the child's face was evident as the voice beside her boomed out. 'Vera Jenkins! What are you doing out of your class?'

The girl trembled before speaking. 'Sent to fetch the pencils, Miss,' she said in a quiet, shaky voice.

'Very well.'

The girl remained on the same spot, not daring to move.

'Hurry along then,' prompted Miss Crankshaw, and she shot off at speed as this formidable lady turned her attention towards Florence. 'Your sister, Miss Stanley, is over on the playing fields. Games for two periods before lunch on a Wednesday. We shall take the shortcut through the quadrangle.'

With this she stepped forward and heaved open the door, letting the warmth of the building rush out past them to mix with the steely outside air. *The only consolation,* Florence thought as she pulled on her gloves once more, *is that at least the sun's shining.*

Miss Crankshaw quick-stepped beside her to speak again. 'Your unscheduled visit, Miss Stanley... hope it's not bad news?'

Florence looked at her, smiling, knowing she was itching to find out, but she couldn't say too much to protect Edith. 'No,' she answered politely, and said no more, sensing a flash of annoyance on Miss Crankshaw's face. This peeved her, because it interrupted her perfect, repetitive routine and all for what appeared to be just a whim by somebody.

At the playing fields she told Florence pointedly to wait whilst she strolled further on to shout for the games mistress, who stood in the centre of the pitch.

On seeing the headmistress, she blew her whistle and ran over. Florence watched as they both chatted and then turned to look at Edith, who played with the other girls on the second field. The games mistress then sped off to fetch her as Miss Crankshaw returned.

'You won't keep her long, now, will you, Miss Stanley? We don't want her missing out on anything, now, do we?' A sardonic smile beamed across her face as Florence did not give her the satisfaction of showing her irritation before she went on her way.

A young girl began running over towards Florence. Amazed, she strained to view her, not quite believing it was Edith. In the couple of months since her last visit, her young sister had blossomed into a young woman – hard to believe she would soon be fifteen years old. Her face lit up when she realised Florence stood at the side of the pitch.

'Florrie, Florrie! What are you doing here?' Puffed, exhaling warm breath into the coolness of the late morning, she flung her arms around her older sister. 'It's so good to see you – why didn't you tell me that you were coming?'

She was taken aback with her enthusiasm; Edith was so excited in seeing her, it left Florence feeling deeply touched – it was so lovely to hold her. Edith had been through so much and it didn't make it any easier for Florence to let go of her.

'In the area, passing by… How could I resist?'

'Passing by?' she questioned wryly, and then shrugged. 'I don't care, Florrie, just so great you're here.' With this, she hugged her sister's arm and led her over to a bench under an old oak tree.

Edith chatted as they strolled, still thrilled at Florence's visit. 'So, what did you think of old Crankshaw then? Bet you're glad she didn't teach when you were here?'

'A bit prickly, isn't she?'

'I'll say,' snorted Edith in dismay as Florence laughed.

'Anyway, how is everything here?'

'Nothing to grumble about, got some nice friends. In fact, I was going to ask you if Charlotte could come back with me at Easter; would you mind? Oh, Florrie, it would be so good.' Edith's exuberance spilt over and she could hardly contain herself as they sat down on the bench. 'It would be great, Florrie, you can take us both to the museum where you work so we can skulk around all those weird and wonderful artefacts. We would even help you if you wanted us to... what do you think?'

Florence found it hard not to smile at Edith, who had an ability to twist anyone around her little finger.

'Listen, Edith.' Florence began stumbling for the words; this was going to be harder than she anticipated. 'Part of the reason I called in,' she hesitated, 'is because I'm going away for a time and the thing is... at the moment, not sure when I'll be back.' For a moment she stopped, sensing the alarm on Edith's face. 'All is fine,' she reassured her. 'Work has got me to oversee the movement of certain artefacts and their paperwork for a museum in Amsterdam.'

'Amsterdam!' cried Edith. 'Why there?'

Florence reached over to hold her hand. 'It's nothing to worry about; they just want some special items moved from the Rijksmuseum to make sure they are kept safe.'

Edith gawped, confused. 'Why you, why not someone else?' Disappointed, her head dropped, and Florence didn't feel great herself.

'Listen, it's my job. They need my help, I'm good at archiving and it won't be long – back before you've even missed me.'

'Why you?' The tears fell from her eyes, splashing onto her muddy knees.

Florence lifted her head, looking into her teary eyes; tracing the contours of her face, she brushed her thumbs across her eyes. 'Don't cry, I really won't be long. We have to protect all the antiquities; they are special, aren't they?' she said, smiling to raise her spirits as Edith stared back.

'We're not in any danger from the Germans, are we?' she asked, looking puzzled.

'No, of course not, we just have to be careful, don't we? Anyway, Holland is fine; there aren't any problems there, so what are you worried about? Told you… just a work trip.' With this last statement she winked at Edith, as she didn't want her to worry about anything, but it was fair to say the storm clouds in Europe were gathering. Florence decided to change the subject. 'What's your friend's name again?'

Edith sat upright, looking a bit more encouraged. 'Charlotte,' she replied, cuffing the wetness and dirt off her face.

'How would you like her to come back with you at Easter break then? I can clear it with Mrs Lamsdale. I'm sure she won't mind; she likes the company.'

The disappointment of Florence not being there was still etched on her face.

'How about,' said Florence, 'you treat Charlotte to lunch at the Trocadero and then go to a show? Would that be good?'

For a moment Edith pondered the absence of her sister at Easter, but, excited at the thought of Charlotte coming back with her for their outing, a broad smile erupted; she stretched over, flinging her arms around her sister's neck. 'That will be great, Florrie; it will be such a treat. Can we really?'

Florence was not only pleased but also a little relieved. 'My absolute gift to you, so you can have a terrific time and think of me.' Happy to see her sister smile again, she stroked her face. 'Anyway, as I said, I'll be back before you know.'

Both sat on the bench. Edith could hear her name being called by her games mistress. Florence embraced her once more and sent her off towards the hockey pitches. When Edith arrived, she turned one last time to wave to Florence, watching as the sun behind her silhouetted her features as she remained stood under the oak tree. Edith had an odd feeling.

'Come on, we're waiting for you,' one of the girls shouted, and she picked up her hockey stick and ran to the pitch. There, she glanced back, but this time there was only an empty space – Florence had gone.

TWENTY-SIX

MARCH 1940

The train slowed into the station as Florence sat on the edge of her seat in the warm compartment and peered out of the window. The carriage lurched forward when the buffers butted against the engine. Steam hissed out from the cylinder drain cocks as the carriages drew to a halt.

The place now surged into life. Doors opened and slammed as people rushed along the corridor, darting in and out of open compartments, allowing for others to pass. Florence decided to stay put until it had quietened down, watching as young, fresh-faced servicemen mingled together in their various uniforms, indicative of the navy, the Royal Air Force and the army. Most seemed to know where they were going and what they were doing, whilst those who were less sure were chatting as they lit up their cigarettes, exhaling the smoke into the cool air.

It was late afternoon now as the sun began to set once more. Royal Mail trolleys were loaded with correspondence coming from all around the country and were carted off through the station. The large clock near the waiting room told Florence it was time she needed to get off the train. A newspaper under her arm, she lifted her suitcase and strolled along the narrow corridor to the open door. On the platform she dodged her way through the multitude of people dashing around as another announcement sounded from the tannoy. At the stairs she crossed over the bridge to the opposite side, admiring the steam engine from above, and saw a young serviceman hurriedly leap on to the train as the guard shut the door and blew his whistle. The train pulled slowly away underneath her, engulfing her in steam which started to clear as she descended the stairs, arriving on the platform. Florence walked past the ticket collector and smiled as she continued her way out to the front of the station. Lieutenant Blackthorn had told her she would be met by her contact at the entrance. Icy cold, she shivered but knew she needed to remain here.

After an hour had passed, she came to the conclusion something must be wrong and did not want to wait in the cold any longer. So she elected to make her own way to the Royal Oak. With no sign of a cab, it occurred to her to go and ask ticket collector at the entrance when one would be available.

'At the station master's house,' he explained, 'there is a van. The usual cabbie is unwell today and not around, so Albert the milk boy will help you out.'

Grateful for his help, she went to wait and, true to his word, a young lad appeared. Frozen to the bone, she was happy for the ride as he placed her luggage in the back.

'Where to, Miss?' he asked in jovial spirits.

'To the Royal Oak, please.'

He appeared a little surprised. 'Say that again, Miss?'

Florence did.

'Thought you said that. Are you sure?'

A bit concerned, she nodded. 'Why?'

'Oh, nothing.' He wavered. 'Only it's used by the servicemen. You being a lady an' all, I thought you might not have realised… might be awkward on your own. If you get what I mean?'

How kind, she thought, and smiled, but this was the least of her worries. 'Thank you for your concern, I will be fine.'

'All right then.' He revved up the old van and made his way out of the station, meandering through the country lanes.

A short time later he pulled up at the old Victorian hotel nestled at the southern end of the old market town of Upton Mucklebury. Florence thanked the lad for his assistance and watched as he drove off before entering the hotel. In front of a long, red-tiled hallway stood the reception area. The stairs ascending to the upper floor were just behind the desk. A young lady greeted Florence, who, in return, smiled.

'Hello, I have a room booked. Under the name of Stanley.'

She checked through her reservations list. 'Ah yes… the one night?'

Florence nodded.

'Sign here.' The young lady turned the reservations book towards her and fetched a set of keys from behind. 'Room number four, you go up the stairs and along the corridor on the right.' Then she advised breakfast would be between 7 and 8.30 prompt and if she wanted a meal to tell her, as they didn't have many guests this evening and could arrange food if she wanted.

Florence thanked her and remembered one more thing. 'May I book an early-morning call, please?'

'Certainly, Miss, what time would you like me to knock?'

'Afraid it will need to be around 3.30am.'

The young lady tried to hide her shock at the request and told Florence that it wouldn't be a problem.

On turning to leave, Florence realised she hadn't paid for the room. 'Terribly sorry,' she began. 'You'll naturally want me to pay?'

The young lady looked back at her, surprised. 'Already been taken care of, Miss.' She was still confused by Florence's request. 'The Ministry have paid for it,' she confirmed. 'That's only fair,' she responded, smiling, 'you are doing your bit for the war and all.'

Mortified, Florence gawked at her; how could she have guessed?

The young lady noted the panicked expression fall across her face, thinking it odd. 'You are the new Land Girl for Barley Mow Farm, aren't you?'

Of course – the lieutenant had booked her in with a fictitious background. *Stupid Florence!* She chastised herself and acted promptly to regain control. 'Yes, I am,' she answered quickly. 'That's why I need the early-morning call – got a busy day tomorrow and I want the farmer to think that I've done this type of work before; best to look keen?'

The young girl empathised with her. 'Not done this sort of thing before, Miss? Don't worry. Farmer Bowyer is nice, he's already got a couple of girls up at the farm, you'll be fine.' With this she smiled to reassure Florence and pointed to the stairs. 'At the end of the corridor… number four.'

Relieved, Florence nodded and picked up her suitcase.

'Dinner is 6.30, if you want any.'

Florence thanked her, already climbing the stairs.

Tired, Florence yawned and noticed the time was just after nine o'clock. Dressed in her flannelette pyjamas, she sat by the fireside, trying to gain a little more warmth from the dying embers as she finished reading the instructions given to her by Lieutenant Blackthorn this morning. All the information now memorised, she scrunched up the papers and threw them on the fire. The jagged paper balls uncurled before being devoured by the last flickers of flame, producing a momentary pocket of warmth before falling through the small grate, resting on the ashes below.

This charming room, Florence reflected, under different circumstances would be a lovely place to bring Edith on a short vacation. Before heading for bed, she picked up the poker and stabbed at the retiring embers. On the bedside cabinet she laid her watch, then pulled back the covers and wriggled in between the sheets. She squirmed at the frigid conditions and clasped at her knees in a desperate effort to draw some heat from them. The blankets she clawed snugly around her neck, determined not to let any draughts of cold air in. Fatigued and ready to sleep, her eyes heavy, she then realised she would have to prise her arm out of the covers to put out the light. This took an eternity, tutting to herself whilst fumbling for the switch. It clicked, and the room plunged into darkness. In this moment she lay pondering on the long day: her trip to Whitehall, meeting Lieutenant Blackthorn; then visiting her dear Edith and then arriving here. Once more she yawned and realised for the first time ever, she had no idea what lay ahead of her, but, if she were honest, she was excited. Florence snuggled down beneath the blankets and allowed her eyes to succumb to the darkness.

Three knocks sounded on the bedroom door, then a pause, followed by a whispered voice. 'Miss Stanley… Are you awake?'

There came a further knock before she opened the door and the young lady stood outside in the hallway in her dressing gown. Bleary-eyed and squinting, she was surprised to find Florence fully dressed.

'Good morning,' She tried to smile. 'It's now 3.30am. The front door is unlocked for you; will there be anything else?'

'No, thank you for all you have done.' With this the young lady turned and walked down the hall as Florence shut the door. For ages she'd been awake – probably hadn't needed the 'early call', but she had needed the front door to be unlocked. Her escort was due at four o'clock and she had plenty of time, assuming he was going to turn up. The room was tidy; even the bed was made.

Stood at the dressing table, she checked in the mirror and almost didn't recognise herself. Garbed up for her journey, she laughed at her reflection – she did look like a Land Army girl with her baggy trousers, big woollen jumper and shirt. Florence scratched at her neck; she may well be warm, but the wool was so itchy, driving her to distraction. To prevent it from irritating her, she tied her silk scarf around her neck and finally pulled on her hat, tucking in her dark curly hair, disposing of any feminine traces.

Her boots were a little on the large side and rather cumbersome, so she decided not to put them on yet in fear of waking anyone. These in hand, along with her suitcase, she crept out of her room, closing the door, making her way down the stairs, stopping at the reception desk to leave the keys, where she then proceeded out of the front door. Down on the bottom step, she pulled on her boots, pleased she had thought to put on two pairs of socks, not only for comfort but because of the bitterly cold morning.

Ready to explore, she walked the eerily quiet street as it emerged from the darkness. The buildings were silhouetted in shade as the sun began to rise. The sky was clear of cloud and the light frost on the hedges opposite glistened as Florence scanned the High Street, searching for the telephone box she had been told to rendezvous at. Nothing stirred in these early hours, except for a fox, who scurried across the road before disappearing up between two tall buildings. This, she noted, was a family butcher, and smiled to herself, thinking him wily, knowing which places to loiter around, wondering what treats were to be found in the backyard.

Alert to the sound of a car engine rumbling in the distance, she watched as it approached up the High Street. The sun in the early morning reflected and bounced off the top of the black Austin as it travelled towards her. From the entrance of the building, she stepped forward, a bit anxious as the car slowed and door swung open.

A voice called to her. 'Miss Stanley?'

Florence moved closer, surprised to recognise the face of the driver. 'Lieutenant Blackthorn, what are you doing here?'

He smiled up at Florence. 'I'm wondering what you are up to at this ridiculously early hour of the morning.' He laughed. 'Please get in.'

Happy, she threw her case in the back and closed the car door, admitting she felt quite relieved at seeing a familiar face. Lieutenant Blackthorn revved up the engine and began travelling back up the High Street. The car nice and warm, she took off her hat as the lieutenant glanced at her, watching her dark curly hair bounce out from under it.

'Bit of a cold morning,' he said, trying to make conversation with her to break the awkward silence between them.

'Cosy in here.' She appreciated his attempt to chat to her. Out of the window, she glanced at the hedgerows covered in frost and couldn't help but wonder why he met her at the telephone box. Yesterday morning, when he gave her the information, he had said nothing. 'I'm surprised to see you,' she said with a curious look. 'You made no mention of collecting me today. Does this have anything to do with your man not turning up at the station?'

Blackthorn glanced at Florence. 'Yes, I can only apologise about that. Unfortunate situation – he was unpredictably detained.'

Florence thought on his words; what had he meant? Not sure, she changed the subject to ask about the morning's events.

'We will rendezvous at approximately 5.30am with the Dutch captain of the small fishing vessel called the *Zeeslang*. From there on, you know the rest, don't you?'

Whilst staring out of the window, she nodded and then thought to ask him a question. 'Will you be coming along as well, Lieutenant?'

He knew she was probing for reasons for him being here. *Shrewd*, he thought, smiling to himself, but he wanted to tell her nothing more than she needed to know. 'No, Miss Stanley, I am to drop you off at the quay.'

With a brief turn, he looked at her. In this instance Florence spotted he was quite handsome and had a gentle expression on his face. Not much older than her, she thought, perhaps late twenties. Coy, she detected a hint of embarrassment as he sensed her watching, and quickly turned away.

For the rest of the journey they sat in silence, neither one knowing what to say to the other. Their barriers were in place, there to protect themselves. It was easier to be aloof than to reveal any emotion. Florence sat listening to the melodic rhythm of the engine as the Austin negotiated the narrow lanes, speeding past the ploughed fields that began to relinquish the early frost. A lapwing flapped into the air, disturbed by the sound of the car and, watching as it flew away, a notion came to her, reminding her when once she had been walking near her home in Hampshire. A sense of trepidation had accompanied the moment as though it reminded her of something far more perilous from further back in her past. It was not the first time these unusual sensations had come to her, but it had become more prevalent each time she had stayed at Redivivus.

A bump in the road made the car lurch forward as Florence felt an anxiousness fall over her as she wondered, *What if I never come back from Holland?* Somehow, as the bird flew away, it seemed like an omen. To free herself of her thoughts, she shook her head, relieved to be distracted by the view as the car approached the top of the hill. Over the brow, there in front of them, was the open sea. Blackthorn noted how intensely Florence viewed the scene as they drove on down.

By the quay it was much busier, as most of the small fishing trawlers were returning with their catch as the Austin pulled up behind a pile of lobster pots.

'Well, Miss Stanley, this is it – the end of the road. Shall we find your passage?'

Florence did feel a little tense now – no denying it – but she was ready; lifting her head, she took a deep breath. 'Yes, of course, Lieutenant.'

Outside in the fresh air, the lieutenant looked at Florence; for the first time he had real empathy for her, seeing her courage. To get this far, to cope with all they had thrown at her, she had achieved so much already. Now, he understood what Colonel Taverner had seen – her inner strength, and he guessed he still had a lot to learn, as did Florence.

The car locked, he strode on, taking the lead as they approached a blue fishing vessel, and Florence sighted the name, *Zeeslang* – this was it then, no going back.

Lieutenant Blackthorn turned to her. 'Won't be a moment,' he said, indicating to Florence to wait on the quayside.

Such a quintessential English fishing village, it had proven to be a lovely morning, if a bit chilly, but under different circumstances she would have liked it here. The fishermen spoke of their morning's catch as they off-loaded various fish in crates from their trawlers. Stood listening, she noticed some of the fish still clung on to life, twisting and turning amongst the other lifeless beings. Interested, she tuned into their conversations.

One elderly fisherman surprised her when chatting to the skipper of the other trawler. 'Tell you, that's what I saw,' said the elderly fisherman.

'Never realised they came in so close,' replied the skipper.

'You can never be too careful – keep your wits about you. You can't trust the Hun.'

Alarmed at what he spoke of, Florence turned to the old chap, and the skipper appeared nearly as shocked as she did. 'What exactly did you catch sight of then, Jeremiah?'

The old fisherman checked over his shoulder, almost as if he expected someone to be nearby, and dropped his voice a little; she strained to hear him. 'One of them bloody Gerry U-boats?'

Astonished at what the old fisherman said, Florence then nearly jumped out of her skin as Lieutenant Blackthorn shouted out to her from the trawler. Beside him was a tall man with a ruddy complexion.

'Come aboard, Miss Stanley, and meet Captain Gerrit de Witte.'

A quick furtive glance at the old fisherman, who still chattered on, and she made her way on board, wondering what she was actually venturing into.

TWENTY-SEVEN

Weak, she lifted her head up off her knees. The weather had changed. It had been a vibrant, sunny morning when the journey began. Florence had initially been enthralled, as the Dutch trawler, with poise, sliced through the calm waters as the land and the harbour receded behind them. A breeze pushed them further out into the vast, open expanse of water – the North Sea.

Florence moved off the small wooden crate she had been sitting on and knelt on the deck by the side of the boat. Unhappy, she groaned. What happened to the picturesque day? Why had the sun vanished? It was dark and dreary now, almost menacing.

Wary, she tried to hoist her upper body further over the side of the trawler to vomit once again. For a second, she straightened up, but the more height she gained, the worse she felt and, again, groaned. Her stomach had nothing left in it. Her head was spinning, feeling so awful that she sat back down on the crate and tried to regain some composure, if it were possible, and wiped her mouth with her handkerchief. Parched, her throat was sore. Salt remained on her lips and she cursed at the sea as the skies became ever darker as they journeyed further from the shelter of the land. The wind had picked up in strength and the waves tossed the small trawler from side to side. Drops of rain, slow at first but then more forceful, splashed down on her face.

Pained, she tried to stand, thinking it would be best to get indoors; she never envisaged her journey would be like this. Desperate, she clung on to the railing as though her life depended on it, managing to steady herself. Slow at first, she moved toward the cabin, as the wind pushed against her, its icy talons reaching across her face, seeping down the nape of her collar. At its touch she shivered and pulled tight the large yellow sou'wester which Captain de Witte had given her earlier. She was grateful for it now as it repelled the rain that thrashed down at her.

Steady, she paced along the deck and was not far from the entrance to the cabin when suddenly there was a loud, scraping, metallic noise that emanated from the other side of the vessel, followed by an abrasive screeching which reverberated throughout the ship. Florence, already unsteady, lost her balance and fell to the floor, where she watched as crew members rushed to the deck along with the captain. A huge amount of confusion ensued as they dashed around, chasing from one side of the vessel to the other. The shouting from only a moment ago ceased as the wind continued to tear through the ship. A solitary voice on the opposite side of the deck shouted out, pointing toward the rear of the trawler. Captain de Witte rushed down to where the figure stood, followed by the rest of the crew, searching intently in silence. Up on her feet, Florence stumbled to where the men were gathered to see what they were looking at.

Somewhat shorter than most of the crew, her view was

impaired. The captain shouted out to them above the wind and rain, and some men then turned and walked away, chatting amongst themselves. Whatever happened, they were certainly relieved, as they dispersed, allowing Florence to move closer to the rear of the trawler to find out what they had all been looking at.

'What is the matter?' she asked, stood beside the captain. 'What was that awful noise?'

The waves rose ever higher as he leant down to her and pointed to something in the water. 'There it is,' he yelled as Florence tried hard to focus, almost giving up when something bobbed up and down, but she couldn't make it out.

By the vacant look on her face, Captain de Witte realised she had no idea how close to death they had been. 'This, Miss Stanley,' he shouted, still competing with the weather as the icy cold rain laced his face, 'is a fisherman's biggest nightmare!'

'What is it?' she asked, trying once more to locate the object.

'A mine! We were lucky this one did not explode.'

Shocked, she stared at him.

'It could have blown us all to pieces. We were fortunate this time.' The captain stared at the wake from the vessel, as did Florence. They stood for a moment in silence as the realisation of what he said sank in. They strained to see the object through the rain. It had gone, and for the moment danger passed them by.

'Best to come inside now.' The captain patted her on the shoulder, turned and walked away.

Florence stood, mesmerised by the waves. The jagged sphere of metal, now taken by the sea, made her realise danger was a reality and ever present, but until this moment it had only been words, stories in the distance, like the fisherman's tale earlier this morning, nothing expressly affected her... until now!

The waves rose even higher as the rain lashed down and, Florence – for the first time ever in her life – was afraid.

TWENTY-EIGHT

Back on firm ground, she found it hard to re-adjust. Stood on the quay, she waited for the captain to return, having disembarked at Oosterdok, Amsterdam. The rain had finally stopped as they entered the harbour. Cold, and her clothing damp, she wanted nothing more than to slip into a soothing hot bath and then go to bed. For now, her seafaring journey was finished, and she couldn't feel any more relieved. Tired, she inspected along the dock and recognised the silhouette of the captain walking towards her, accompanied by another person.

'I have arranged for Hans here to show you to your accommodation.'

'Thank you,' she said, and smiled, appreciative, shaking the captain's hand.

'Take care, Miss Stanley, I wish you all the best.'

Florence took one last glance at the trawler. Although not her fondest experience, it had been an adventure for her. Hans picked up her case, and they walked off in silence as he spoke little English and her Dutch, at present, was basic. Colonel Taverner had assured Florence that the Dutch spoke good English in the city, and she would soon pick it up. This had been one of her main concerns, but he didn't seem worried. At the moment she felt too tired to even talk.

Amsterdam was so picturesque, bright, alive and vibrant. Despite the situation in Europe and tensions in Britain, everything here appeared relaxed. Florence was surprised at the indulgence of light; London had already begun preparing for blackout and light restrictions. This city appeared to be even less aware of any impending dangers.

Absorbed with the atmosphere, Florence happily followed Hans; she knew there would be challenges ahead of her and she was a little apprehensive but also excited, as she looked forward to her stay here. How odd; she felt a sense of belonging and thought of her parents, wishing they had shared this part of their lives with her. To think they had lived in this beautiful city; such a strange notion.

Hans led Florence up a narrow side street; the name illustrated on the wall read 'Lijnbaansgracht'.

How on earth do you pronounce this? she pondered before returning her attention to Hans, who had stopped and placed her case at the bottom of a small flight of steps leading up to a typical Dutch townhouse. He pointed to the number on the door – '42a – and went to knock. Stood by her case, she watched as he knocked again, as both waited for a response. The door eventually opened, and an elderly woman appeared and spoke to Hans. Unaware of what they were saying, he then turned and beckoned Florence.

On arriving, the elderly lady turned to Florence and spoke in clear English. 'Good evening.' And she gave her a hearty smile.

At this point Hans took his leave and disappeared up the street.

'Come on in, my dear. My name is Helga van Hoebeek

and I'm pleased to meet you. Come, come.' Helga ushered Florence in, who was met by a rush of warmth from the house. It was so nice to be out of the cold night air; as the door closed behind her, Helga led Florence into the parlour and gestured to the chair near the hearth. 'Please, take a seat.'

Florence's eyes lit up as she saw the flames course up the chimney. Eager, she strolled over and sat down to enjoy the fire as Helga offered her a coffee. Happy to accept, Helga shuffled off to make the drink as Florence inspected the room.

It was crowded, full of memorabilia and furniture. The small table opposite hosted many framed black-and-white photos of young children, babies and, standing proudly in the centre, a wedding photo. The clock chimed out as Helga came back to the parlour with a tray that held two cups, a plate of biscuits and a coffee pot. On the table by the fire, she placed it down and Florence noted how sprightly she was for her years as she poured out the steaming coffee.

At last, as Florence sipped the hot drink, the vile taste of salty water washed away. Helga offered her a biscuit, which Florence accepted enthusiastically, realising she was in fact starving. Unable to hide her pleasure, Florence tucked into her treat.

'Hungry, my dear?' Helga asked, and chuckled. 'There is some homemade broth on the stove I can fetch you later, if you like?'

Florence nodded eagerly, grateful for her kindness.

'Why not get freshened up first? Put your things in your room.' For a moment before continuing, Helga sighed. 'My husband always loved coming home to a warm fire and my homemade broth.'

Florence sensed her regret, watching as she stared into the flames and guessing she lived alone. 'How lovely this must have been for him,' she said, thinking Helga had a very kindly face and seemed happy to have some company. 'I had a bit of a rough trip over,' Florence explained. 'The weather was appalling out at sea.'

Helga acknowledged this and glanced at the wedding photo on the small table. 'My husband,' there was a softness in her eyes, 'he was in the Dutch navy, very aware of the perils of the North Sea – and the lives it claimed.' Still staring at the photo, she added, 'He is dead now.'

Florence sensed it hurt her to talk about him.

Helga changed the topic. 'Are you here to work at the Rijksmuseum?'

'Yes, I am,' replied Florence. 'I'm expected to start there on Friday. I hear it is a beautiful museum; is it far?'

Helga twisted in her seat to the bookshelves behind her. 'On the third shelf down, my dear, pull out the thin book. Bring it over here.'

Florence did as Helga requested and sat at her side on the floor. She had to admit it was nice to sit down again, as she still had her sea legs on and the floor seemed to sway. Intent on finding the information, Helga thumbed her way through the pages, then stopped and turned the book around to show her.

'There,' she said. 'This is a picture of the front of the Rijksmuseum and beside it is a plan of the city, showing you where it is situated.' Without her spectacles to hand, Helga squinted at the map to locate the street they were in. 'Here is Lijnbaansgracht.' And she pointed at the quickest route to the museum; tapping the back of Florence's hand, she pushed the book back towards her. 'You keep this; it will help you.'

'Thank you. It is so much closer than I thought.'

After they had finished their coffee, Helga went to an oak bureau in the corner of the room and took out a key. She beckoned Florence to follow her into the hallway where she handed it to her. 'Your room, my dear, is up two flights. My legs are too stiff to climb these stairs now, so forgive me if I do not show you to your room. A girl who comes in and helps me once a week has prepared the room for you. If you need anything, you must let me know.'

'Thank you, Helga.' Florence picked up her suitcase.

'Another guest, a gentleman, stays in the room on the first floor, but he is not here very often, although he pays me for the room, so I don't mind keeping it for him. The house is quiet, and you are welcome here.'

Florence was moved by her words as she climbed the stairs, thinking, although tired, she was already content, and everything was going to be fine.

TWENTY-NINE

Stood in the hallway of the Rijksmuseum, Florence marvelled at the design, as she had done nearly every day for a week now. Such a privilege to work within the confines of a resplendent building and she slotted into her job so easily. Everyone had been so helpful. Like the new girl at school, she was progressively finding her way around, assisting with the archiving; she merely continued her role from the British Museum. Each day she enjoyed her walk to work and was happy to feel a part of everything in her new life, her new experience. And today she felt good.

At her desk, she checked her diary for her work schedule for the day. There were paintings and artefacts to be sorted out on the first floor. This gallery she couldn't wait to visit. Excited, she picked up her toolbox, added her white cotton gloves, notepad and tape, and made her way upstairs. Florence pushed open the door and stopped in awe of the paintings on display, the work of 'great masters' depicting historical scenes through time. Beautiful, each and every one, and to Florence it was an honour to protect these rare works of art from a pending war with Germany.

Whilst strolling along the gallery she thought of the words Lieutenant Blackthorn had left her with that morning back in England: 'All that you do helps and supports the war effort – you are doing your bit… Be safe.' Both Colonel Taverner and Lieutenant Blackthorn insisted this new role was nothing more than the work she did, which was why they approached her in the first place. However, Florence felt they were being selective about what they wanted her to know. Then, as she'd said goodbye to the lieutenant, at the harbour, he asked her to be alert. When she questioned him, he had been vague. All he said was, 'Remain vigilant to any unusual activities, however simple they may be.' Florence thought this strange but assured him she would do all she could.

Florence stopped in front of a painting that caught her eye, transfixed by the detail. The darkened sky, with storm clouds highlighted in the foreground, brought the scene to life. The whole landscape was so meticulously painted you could have reached out and touched it. An old windmill on the hill; one could almost imagine hearing it creak and judder during another rotation as the storm approached, ready to spill its heavy rainfall.

There, lost for a moment, she jumped as a voice startled her from behind.

'Are you drawn in by the clouds?' the voice asked.

To check who asked the question, she turned around and found herself staring into the face of a young man. So absorbed in the painting, she had not heard a single footstep. Aware he had disturbed her, he smiled. *A very handsome face*, she thought, realising she had stared at him for too long; awkward, she turned her attention back to the landscape and answered him. 'Definitely… They just look so real, don't they?'

The young man stepped beside her. 'Ruisdael had such a

talent in his observations of light. You can tell he has really studied the scene.' Passionate, he leant a bit closer to her, drawing his head down towards hers. 'It's almost as though the sails on the windmill rest before the raindrops splash off their wooden structure as it starts to sway in the breeze, expectantly awaiting more rain about to erupt from the storm clouds at any moment... as though you could feel it.' He gazed at her. 'I've worked here for a while and seen many of the paintings hung in these galleries,' again he stopped to absorb the scene, 'but there is just something about this one... don't you think?'

There was nothing she could add, so she merely nodded in agreement at what he said, thinking he put it so much more eloquently than she ever could. There seemed to be more than the painting now capturing her attention. Florence gazed at his slick, wavy auburn hair and strong facial features, thinking him handsome. Whilst speaking, his face was animated and enthusiastic, and his vibrant green eyes lit up as he viewed the picture. With a presence about him, Florence felt drawn to this man but wondered why she had not seen him before. Did he work up here? Who was he? Almost as though he sensed her thoughts, which surprised her immensely, he stopped talking.

'Sorry,' he began. 'Didn't I introduce myself to you, Florence?'

'No,' she replied, confused at how he knew her name.

Yesterday, he had scrutinised her whilst she worked, curious as to who she was. Then he had made it his business to find out about her, and now he seized this opportunity to introduce himself. 'My name is Johann van Buren.'

'Nice to meet you, don't believe I've seen you before?' She was confident she wouldn't have forgotten him.

'No,' he began, 'I have been working in another department. I heard somebody arrived from London.' He looked at her in a curious way. 'I must admit,' he said, trying to extract a little more information from her, 'I wondered why they needed to send anyone from the British Museum?'

Aware he was prying, even though charmingly, she returned to the painting. Still staring at it, so as not to catch his intense gaze, she answered him. 'The Rijksmuseum requested help from us; we were only too happy to oblige.' Florence was determined not to make eye contact with him, as she was aware of being assessed as he asked another question.

'What area of expertise do you bring with you?'

Florence liked Johann but became wary of his questions. 'I am an archivist and conservationist – as you are already aware.' She said this with a wry smile. 'I worked at the British Museum in London and we have been effecting the storage and reallocation of works of art and artefacts out of the city museums.' She checked on his reaction. 'We do not want them lost or, indeed, for them to fall into the wrong hands, should the situation with Germany escalate.' Finished, she added a complacent smile.

Johann acknowledged this and they both walked toward the end of the gallery in silence. Florence hoped the topic was settled.

'It seems strange to me,' Johann then started, 'they should send someone from London when we have our own staff who are able to manage.'

Uneasy now, she remained calm and unresponsive. From

her other colleagues she had received no such treatment; why was he so curious? Why should it bother him? Enough of this. Florence decided to return his questioning with a touch of English arrogance, hoping it would squash his curiosity.

'I'm sure you are capable of doing your job, whatever that may be,' she said indignantly. 'However, the Rijksmuseum requested the assistance of an expert in this field.' She turned to him for the last time. 'I am that expert, good at what I do, and if you'll excuse me,' she smiled derisively, 'I need to get on with the morning's work.'

Johann realised, as she stepped forward, he had in fact been dismissed, so he moved out of her way. 'Of course, I apologise for having detained you.'

His words, she acknowledged, and she took her leave, not daring to look back when she heard him call out. 'Perhaps I can show you around Amsterdam some time?'

Still not looking back, she rather enjoyed the fact he wanted to see her, as she quite liked him.

'Perhaps.'

Later on that evening, when Florence got home, she decided to write to Edith. Any correspondence she had been told by Lieutenant Blackthorn had to be addressed to him or Colonel Taverner. This, they had explained, was to be done as a precautionary matter and obviously it would help if she had anything to add, no matter how irrelevant it seemed, to let them know.

On this evening, after writing to Edith, she added an extra note for Colonel Taverner informing him of her meeting with her colleague earlier that day, Johann van Buren. The letter she posted, the next day on her way to work, thinking nothing more of it.

THIRTY

Colonel Taverner marched into his office, as he did most mornings, and awaited the adjutant to follow him. Before seating himself, he checked the front page of the newspaper laid on the desk, tutted at the information and sat down. A moment later Adjutant Brown entered, carrying the colonel's morning cup of tea and the mail. He placed them down on the desk and hurried out of the office.

The colonel drank some tea before his attention was drawn to the post, noting in particular one envelope, as it was not the standard War Office brown. Curious, he wanted to open this first. Inside he found a second sealed envelope. The handwritten name read, 'For Edith Stanley', then he spotted a smaller notelet that must have fallen out. At once he realised who the note must be from and was eager to read it. His eyes widened as his face changed to alarm.

'Brown! Get in here!'

The adjutant rushed back into the colonel's office, wondering what was wrong with the old coot now.

'Brown,' he yelped again, just as agitated, 'take dictation. I need to get a telegram to Lieutenant Blackthorn... immediately!'

THIRTY-ONE

MAY 1940

A single ray of sunlight pierced through the narrow gap as Florence watched from her bed. Eager to engage with the day, she threw off the bedcovers and padded to the window, folding back the shutters. Florence flinched from the intensity of the bright sunshine that filled the room and pushed open the window as the sun's warmth, along with a gentle breeze, brushed past her, bringing in the muted sounds of the city below.

April was drawing to a close. It was hard to believe how fast the month had flown by. Excited, she turned on her heel, thinking of her day ahead; grabbing her robe from the chair, she rushed down the two flights of stairs to the kitchen, where she found Helga having her morning coffee, reading the newspaper.

'Good morning,' said Florence, grinning.

'You are in fine spirits today,' acknowledged Helga, and noted Florence seemed distracted, even excited.

'I am, it is such a lovely day!'

'Indeed.' Helga was curious now as to her mood. 'Anything I can help you with?'

Florence wanted to talk but didn't know where to begin.

Helga had seen this type of behaviour before and tried to make it easier for Florence. 'Are you meeting a young man today? Perhaps the same one you so often talk about, from the museum?'

Florence was surprised by this. 'Am I that transparent?'

Helga nodded laughing; she had grown attached to her. 'Fetch another cup. So… am I right?'

Florence gazed at the steam coming off her coffee and answered timidly. 'Yes, you are; he wants to show me around the city – just being polite, he's a work colleague, that's all. The thing is – it sounds daft, but I don't have a clue what to wear.' She heaved a sigh. 'I'm usually so organised.'

Helga sipped her coffee, thinking it funny, but tried not to show it, as she realised Florence was being honest – she really hadn't experienced this before. 'Now, you have nothing to worry about, you are a lovely girl… go and get yourself dressed in whatever takes your fancy.' Helga then ushered Florence up the stairs. 'Don't waste any more time; you can tell me about your day out with Johann when you get back.'

Florence stopped and looked back at her. 'How did you...'

'How could I not…? Hurry, get ready before you are late.'

Blind to all this, she pondered how much she had been talking about him. On their first meeting, she was unsure, as he questioned her so much, but gradually, on working together, they got to know each other much better. If she were honest, she enjoyed his company.

As she approached her room, her thoughts went back to

her initial dilemma … what was she going to wear? Florence stood in front of the mirror, tweaking at the same annoying curl that would not stay put as she heard Helga call once more.

'On my way,' she shouted back as the curl behind her ear sprung out once again. Frustrated, she growled, deciding enough. She grabbed her bag and attempted to put her cardigan on as she ran down the stairs. She was surprised to see Johann stood in the hallway with Helga, who gave her a mischievous smile. Florence stopped and tried to compose herself. Johann stared up and Florence felt her cheeks warm with embarrassment when she accidentally dropped her keys. He moved swiftly to retrieve them for her, noticing her slim legs, as she wore a dress today instead of her usual slacks, and becoming aware of how it nipped and tucked, perfectly accentuating her slight figure. With her curly hair hanging loosely, she was radiant. Mesmerised, he handed her the keys. Flattered by his attention, she glanced at Helga, who raised an eyebrow at her.

'Sorry, Johann, did I get the arrangements wrong?' asked Florence.

'No, forgive me, I changed them. Hope you don't mind. Wanted to surprise you by taking you out of the city for the day. Not too presumptive of me?'

'Not at all… will I want my tram ticket?'

'No, not today. My motor vehicle is outside.'

Florence was astonished; he never mentioned a car, but then they had never left the city before. 'I didn't expect all this; it's so kind of you.'

Johann smiled at her, thinking how lovely she appeared.

They both said goodbye to Helga and made their way to the car. Unable to believe her eyes, Florence stared at the parked sports car: striking, not a model she recognised, but she presumed it must be expensive. Johann walked round and opened the door for her. Getting in, she sat feeling surprisingly at ease, thinking there was much to learn about Johann; perhaps today she might find out who he really was.

'This is great.' Florence turned to Johann. 'What made you think of this?'

With a finger pointed at the sky, he said, 'Such a beautiful day – I thought you might like to explore further afield.'

'So where are we going?'

'This is a surprise,' he said, 'but one I think you will like.'

Content to just sit back, she glanced shyly at him before turning to the window and wondered why she had doubted him when they had first met. It was fair to say he had acted strangely, but from then on, he had been nothing but kind to her. At weekends he started to show her around the city, keen on everything she said. Helpful at work too. It was now evident: she was becoming attracted to him. It all seemed so comfortable, almost familiar.

After a while Johann pulled the car over to the side of the road and parked. Puzzled, she watched as he stepped out and came to open her door.

'Are we here?' she asked, bemused as to where 'here' was.

'All in good time – you shall see. Now, come with me, there is something I want to show you.'

He grinned whilst extending his hand to her to assist her out of the car as she stared up into his bright green eyes, transfixed by them for a moment before she stepped out on the grass verge. Johann kept hold of her hand as he led her along the hilltop; it was now midday and the sun was at its warmest. Sweet fragrances of the meadow were all around as they walked, and she noted the brightness of the yellow buttercups and the delicate uniformity of the perfectly displayed daisies embracing the sun's caress on this charming day. It had been an eternity since she had enjoyed such simple pleasures as this.

For a moment, daydreaming, Florence tripped over a tuft of grass, bumping into Johann, and grabbed his arm.

'Careful, we don't want you to fall,' he said as he caught the scent of her perfume in the air. Florence was happy to hold his hand, enjoying the security he offered her.

They walked a bit further and then stopped. Johann then took the scarf from around her neck and asked her to trust him as he pulled it around her eyes. Apprehensive, she obliged.

With care, he positioned Florence just where he wanted and then stood behind her to untie the scarf, where she felt his warm breath on her neck. As it fell away, she recoiled at the brightness of the day, blinking, and then her eyes focused. The beauty of the scene before her made her gasp, and she realised, instantly, the idyllic picture.

'Oh, Johann, it is so beautiful. My… I'm speechless as to what to say.'

Pleased at her reaction, he enjoyed the moment beside her.

'It's…' she hesitated, 'as though you have stepped back in time… the old windmill looks the same.'

At this point he interjected, reminding her of one major

difference. 'Except today, there are no clouds,' he said, 'not even a little one – the sky is a perfect blue, but no matter what the weather conditions the scene is just as magical, is it not?'

'It certainly is.' Florence stood there, overwhelmed, as it was such a nice thought; she turned towards him, gave him a kiss on his cheek and thanked him.

He was happy at her reaction at last; Florence was allowing him to observe the true her, melting her stuffy Englishness and, at this moment, she was shining.

'My pleasure, I'm glad you like your surprise.' They both stood for a moment or two longer before Johann reached for his camera. Eager to capture the moment, he gestured to her to step forward.

'Must get a photo of you, with the windmill in the distance,' he said, thinking how lovely she looked, and took the picture.

'As long as you let me take a photo of you – it is only fair after the effort you have made to bring me here. Something I can keep for when I return to England.'

Johann stepped aside, realising how much she wanted to do this. The scene composed, she clicked the button, capturing her perfect memory. On handing him back the camera, he took her hand in his, leading her back to the car, and told her they could picnic down near the stream at the bottom of the hill in a small coppiced wood. This sounded lovely, and she was only too happy to travel the short distance to where he had suggested.

Sat on the woollen blanket with her legs curled up to the side of her, Florence finished off her glass of wine and yawned.

'Am I boring you already?' said Johann.

'Not in the slightest – just so full up after all that I ate. A wonderful picnic, and such a lovely day. I'm very relaxed.' With a deep breath, she inhaled the fresh air, flicking her hair back off her face.

'The country air suits you – it puts colour back in your cheeks.'

She laughed a little. 'Think that was probably the glass of wine.'

Johann smiled at her as she handed him the glass, which he placed in the basket, and on closing the lid, he reclined on the blanket, propping himself up on his elbow, watching her.

'Tell me more about the Florence I don't know,' he asked, patting the space beside him.

Florence lay on her side next to him. 'There's not a lot to tell, really. All a bit dull.'

'You're not dull.' He thought on what to ask her. 'Have you always worked in London?'

'Yes, I have. My father said I'd never leave the city, as I loved it too much; he would be amazed to see me now. Although...' For a moment she stopped and thought there would be no harm in telling him of her Dutch ancestry. Besides, she didn't want to lie to him. 'My parents were from Holland!'

His expression changed to surprise, and he sat up. Not moving, she only followed him with her eyes as he turned and gazed down at her. 'You don't sound – and your surname isn't – Dutch?' Still surprised, he lay down again, looking into her gentle brown eyes as she continued to speak.

'There are reasons why my name is Stanley – I cannot tell you, it's just a bit complicated, but my family name is actually van Hassel. My parents lived in Amsterdam before I was born.'

Johann looked at her, astonished. 'Really?'

Florence nodded and then a thought sprang to mind as she leant nearer to him, excited with the idea. 'Johann?'

'Yes.'

She smiled at him. 'Would you help me find where they used to live? I'd love to know.'

Intrigued, he watched her animated face as her nose wrinkled up, and his attention was drawn to her full lips. Compelled, he moved towards her; he couldn't stop himself and his lips made contact with hers.

'So, you are a little Dutch beauty.'

Before she could say anything, he pressed his mouth against hers, kissing her. Florence responded, aware of an awakening, a soaring passion that raged through her body, leaving her with a sense of familiarity... almost as though he had kissed her before.

Johann leant back, looking into her eyes. Knowing she didn't mind, he had to stop himself from rushing forward to do it again. Instead, he swept a loose curl of her brown hair behind her ear before laying down with her, as she rested on his chest, his arm enclosed around her narrow shoulders. They spoke no words, content in each other's embrace.

CONNECTIONS II

The mud-sodden trackway appeared empty. From here, the light of the torches could be seen further away. Her legs and feet were cold, almost numb. Using all her strength, she heaved herself out of the ditch and scrambled across the track.

On lying down, aware behind her of the steep climb through the trees, the higher view gave her a better vantage point to see what was going on. Panic rose within as she watched the searchers move closer to where Freya and the children were hiding.

What could she do? No time to hesitate; she needed to lure them away.

Stood on the track in the darkness as the silhouettes congregated nearer the ditch, she opened her mouth to scream... nothing.

Her body, rigid, petrified at the silence as she tried to contain her anxiety. Determined, she took a big breath and let out a soul-terrifying shriek born of true frustration. Eyes wide open as sweat dripped from her forehead, the lights of the torches changed direction, moving toward her.

'Thank the gods.'

A huge sense of relief came to her in this moment, knowing

she'd drawn them away from Freya and the children. It wasn't fear that froze her to the spot; defiant, she refused to move. Within seconds the searchers converged around her. Unable to see anything but the lucent blinding light, bodies pushed at the side of her. Cognisant of her arms being pulled behind her back, she flinched at the strength of the grip. In front of her the lights parted as someone strolled toward her. Slow at first, her eyes adjusted, and she stared at the face she recognised – she was reluctant to show any emotion as he came closer.

'Maertha.' The low timbre of his voice was calm yet sardonic as he spoke. 'Where have you been?'

With a look of loathing, she said nothing. Next, the strike to her face took her by surprise and her cheek felt as though it had burst into flames on impact; as she winced, the hands holding her arms tightened. Again, he raised his hand and she braced herself for the inevitable contact when suddenly he stopped. In this moment, as he stared down at her, deeply into her eyes, she sensed his regret at hurting her. He turned swiftly, signalling to his men to take her away. With one last glance at him, she was sure of her intuition – but far more scared of what or who lay ahead of her.

'Wake up, Florence.' Johann shook her gently. 'Are you all right?'

With bleary eyes, she woke to find Johann leaning over her.

'Yes, yes,' she said. 'I think so – why?' Florence was puzzled. *What did he mean?*

'In your sleep – you shouted out.'

'Really? How long was I asleep?'

'Not very long. What were you dreaming about?'

'I'm not sure… It all seemed so muddled. It doesn't make any sense now – but dreams never do when you wake up.' Still confused, she half smiled at Johann.

'Sorry if I gave you a scare,' he said. 'I didn't want you to be distressed. Do you often have nightmares?'

For a moment she thought. 'No, but sometimes I have vivid dreams.'

Johann leant forward and kissed her on the cheek. 'Probably nothing to worry about.'

'Strange,' Florence began, 'I can only remember an intense bright light.'

'Doesn't sound so scary.' Johann winked at her.

'No,' she said. 'I couldn't perceive anything behind it – but it was fearsome. Got a real sense of danger.' Troubled, she stared into the distance, trying hard to recall. 'Seems I was protecting something, or someone, which is probably why I shouted. All so bizarre – like you said, nothing to worry about.'

'Come on then, let's put the basket in the car and perhaps we can go for a stroll before we have to drive back to the city.'

They walked together out of the glade and down the lane, chatting. On approaching the car, Florence noted a church further along the lane. 'Do you mind if I have a quick look? Love old buildings.'

'No, you go ahead. I'll put these bits away and catch up with you there.'

Finished looking around the inside of the whitewashed building, Florence wanted to stroll through the grounds of the old churchyard. The sun was still shining but a breeze swept around the graves, dancing with the blades of grass. Chiselled into the gravestones were the snippets of past lives – portals in history. These barely visible details, either eroded or hidden by nature, she read, wondering what they had done in life. Through the grounds, set further back near the boundary wall, sat a small tombstone and she became curious about it. At first she was unable to make out any of the words as they were badly worn by weathering. Indents of carved letters only became clear when Florence ran her finger over them.

She was unsure if it spelt Anneke or close to this, with a date declaring her death in 1754, but as she read these to herself it seemed to rouse something deep within her. Inside, senses pushed to resurrect themselves. Lightheaded, she knelt on the grass, staring at the grave. Florence sensed the details of this person, a connection, a predilection – how could this be?

It was as though her subconscious memory transmitted abstracts of a life… a life she did not recall, but it somehow was familiar to her. Amidst these erratic moments came visions of another period in time; a face came before her, blurred and not easy to recognise, and then some sort of symbol.

From further down the lane, Johann called to her. Startled, she clasped her hand to her chest and turned to wave to him. Still feeling strange, she sighed deeply and shook her head, trying to understand all that had happened, not knowing what to think. At the gate she met Johann waiting, and as they strolled away, Florence turned back one last time to view the gravestone. On first inspection it was an unremarkable monument but revealed to her a profound sense of connection. Mystified, she also knew this was not the first time this had happened to her; she was uncertain what any of it meant – but somewhere there was a meaning for her to unlock.

THIRTY-TWO

Back in Lijnbaansgracht Street, Johann watched as Florence closed the door to the house and drove off. His day out had been enjoyable; he smiled to himself, knowing how he felt about Florence. The first time he'd met her, there had been an attraction, and today confirmed this.

Johann yawned and checked his watch; he still had one more stop to make before he went home and knew he was later than had been arranged. However, the person he was meeting wouldn't mind.

The car came to a slow as he deliberately parked down the side street away from his friend's apartment and office. Johann didn't want to be seen entering the premises, even if it was late and nobody was about. A couple of months ago, Frederick Obermaier, had visited him at the museum, asking for help. Being an old friend, Johann agreed, but he was wary. Frederick was involved with the Nationaal-Socialistische Beweging, or NSB, a fascist party better known as the 'Black Shirts.' He was responsible for local youth recruitment, changing young minds. He had tried to recruit Johann, but he was not comfortable with it and remained careful of him.

'The city,' Frederick had explained, 'is changing.' He blamed it on a surge of Jewish immigrants flooding into

Holland 'taking away national identity', he explained. But Johann, who was patriotic and believed strongly in keeping a Dutch identity, felt his friend's opinions were too extreme a view for him.

The street was dark as he walked along. A noise from behind startled him and he turned to investigate but saw nothing in the blackness. A rat scampered out from underneath a bush and scurried across the road. In the office below the apartment, a light shone. Johann went to the window and knocked. Moments later, Frederick opened the door and invited him in. Before Johann entered, he checked over his shoulder once more – he couldn't shake off the sensation someone was there – but nothing was in the darkness. So, he shrugged his shoulders, and went inside, walked past the office and arrived at the parlour, where he was handed a glass.

'You're lucky I'm still working,' Frederick commented as he took a sip of his drink. 'You missed the meeting.'

Johann considered his words as the brandy warmed him. 'You know I wouldn't have attended anyway… besides, I visited the countryside for the day.'

Frederick shot a glance at him, surprised by what he had said. 'Out of the city – out of your museum? What brought this about?'

'Why must there be a reason? Just a beautiful day,' said Johann.

Frederick gave a wry smile and sat down, his eyes set on Johann, watching as though he were analysing him. 'Of course – but you never stop working.' He waited for a moment, still trying to assess this change in Johann. 'It's this girl you've been talking about, isn't it?'

Johann said nothing but grinned as Frederick took out his cigarettes from his brown shirt pocket. He tapped it and lit it, blowing out a puff of smoke, then casually continued the conversation. 'Do you know any more about this girl?' Once more he exhaled. 'Why is she here? English, isn't she?'

Johann finished his drink and placed his glass on the small wooden table. 'So many questions.'

'I'm only curious,' Frederick said, leaning forward to flick his ash, 'as to who could make you look so relaxed and so happy. Tell me, who makes you smile?'

Johann, so full of the excitement after his day out with Florence, couldn't contain himself and related most of the details of their enjoyable excursion.

'But she's English,' said Frederick whilst extinguishing the last source of life from his cigarette. 'What's wrong with a nice, home-grown Dutch girl?'

'Actually,' he started, remembering what Florence had told him that afternoon, 'she's not.'

'But didn't you just tell me she was English? Working with you… sent over from the British Museum in London. That's correct, isn't it?' Frederick stared at Johann, who tried to explain.

'Yes, this is all true – but she told me today she is from Holland. Her parents came from Amsterdam… so I have fallen for a home-grown girl after all.'

Frederick got up and went to fetch the bottle of brandy, but before he could pour more into Johann's glass, he covered over the top. Frederick gave him a questioning look, then refilled his own glass and continued to chat.

'What is her name?'

'Her name is Florence Stanley.'

'Doesn't sound like a Dutch name to me,' said Frederick.

'No, she doesn't use her Dutch family surname.'

'Why not?'

For a moment Johann thought. He was not sure why, but he recalled Florence saying she couldn't tell him, thinking nothing of it – but he didn't want Frederick to get the wrong idea. 'Don't know, not important.'

Frederick stared at him, puzzled. 'What is her proper family name?'

Before Johann could continue, a knock sounded at the door. 'Were you expecting anyone at this time?'

Surprised, Frederick looked over at him, then placed his glass down on the table and went to answer the door.

Johann turned, trying to get a peek of the unexpected visitor. He could only see so far and heard a male voice, distinctly deep, but couldn't make out what they were saying. Frederick showed the gentleman into his front office, pulling shut the door. From down the hallway, he returned to the parlour.

'Sorry, old friend, but this is a spot of business I'm afraid I must attend to; would you mind showing yourself out?'

They both said their farewells. Johann thought it odd but didn't question what Frederick did. There was a part of his life he had no interest in and not knowing was the better option. Tired he strolled back to the car, content with his day and thinking of Florence he headed for home.

The visitor who arrived at Frederick's apartment had been watching Johann. But what 'the visitor' didn't realise was, somewhere in the darkness of the night… someone else had been watching him too.

THIRTY-THREE

WEDNESDAY, 8TH MAY 1940

In the museum, Florence walked back to the office with the remnants of sticky tape attached to her sleeve, along with her workbox. On opening the door, she found Johann stood near the window, and immediately her face lit up. Pleased to see him, she quickly dropped her stuff off on the desk, but then realised he had picked up his coat.

'You're not going already, are you?' she said, disappointed.

He moved towards her, pulling the tape from her arm, and leant down to kiss her. 'I was about to come and look for you... to explain.'

'Explain what?' asked Florence, a little bemused.

Johann felt awkward, as he was cancelling all their arrangements for this evening. 'An old friend of mine called; I need to go and meet with him.' He was drawn in to those warm, brown eyes of hers. 'If it wasn't important, I would not go,' he said as he touched her face.

Disheartened, she could sense his regret, knowing it genuine, and smiled at him to make him feel better. 'Don't worry; it doesn't matter. These things happen. We can organise another evening.'

'To wait another day will be hard,' he said, pulling her towards him, kissing her with such desire he felt he was drowning in her.

For a moment longer, she clung on, wishing to have stayed in his warm embrace forever. 'We can catch up through the week,' she said, glancing up as he hugged her.

If he were honest, it was becoming difficult for him to let go of her. From her hair, he removed a piece of loose string and laughed. 'Please don't change.' He turned and walked to the door, pulling it open. 'You mean a lot to me.'

Within a second, he had gone. Touched by his words, Florence felt a flutter in her tummy and was confused by her emotions – how could someone have such an impact on her so quickly? But it was nice to be wanted, even loved.

Florence decided to stay a bit later and catch up with some unfinished work in one of the main galleries. It gave her an opportunity, whilst there, to view the paintings. Content as she absorbed the beauty of them, a noise at the bottom of the gallery distracted her. Watchful, she turned, thinking she saw movement in the far corner, but as she stared there was only stillness and darkness. Florence thought how these old halls could so easily influence one's vivid imagination, thinking you'd witnessed apparitions from times gone by – easy to do with all the history that hung from the walls.

Further along the gallery, she stopped to admire her favourite painting once more. There was just something about this windmill, and it was more amazing now having actually seen it in the countryside. It had a definite presence for her. Disturbed again by a faint noise, she turned. For a second, she tried to focus, and then walked towards the large double doors at the end of the gallery as they slowly closed.

The hairs on the back of her neck stood proud – she was sure this was no figment of her imagination and she could not explain why – but this time, she was not on her own. From the darkness there came a voice that chilled her to the bone.

'Hello, Florence. Are you alone?'

Frozen to the spot, in this split second, she tried to work out how she knew the voice. At least it was real and not an apparition. However, this may have been a less daunting proposition. The pale light from the hallway beyond cast a silhouette of an emerging figure. The voice sounded again as it questioned her with more urgency. Florence recognised the voice but couldn't believe she was hearing it, and finally…

'…Lieutenant Blackthorn!'

'Are you alone?' he pressed.

Stunned at the lieutenant's arrival, Florence tried hard to concentrate, still staring in disbelief. 'Yes… yes. I was about to lock up – why are you here?'

'Sorry I have startled you, but I had to speak to you, and it is imperative nobody knows of our connection, hence the need for secrecy.' He was able to sense her confusion, knowing he had disturbed her with his unexpected visit. The information he was to give to her needed to be handled with the upmost tact, something generally they didn't always teach you in the army.

'Well, you are very good at creeping.' She grinned at him. 'Scared the living daylights out of me. Why are you here?'

Blackthorn scanned the gallery as he composed all the information in his head before attempting to answer her.

On spotting a bench in the dimness, he ushered her towards it, sitting her down beside him as he cleared his throat and began to talk.

'I need to take you back to England with me.'

Shocked, she stared at him; everything was going so well for her here. Why? Florence began to panic, and the lieutenant held her hand, trying to reassure her as he continued to speak.

'It's getting too dangerous for you now... events are about to change.'

'What events? What do you mean? You need to tell me? Why do I have to go back to England?' Irritated, she withdrew her hand, crossing her arms defensively.

'Florence, I'm limited to what I can tell you – but the situation, here in Holland, is likely to change.' In the faded light, he checked her again – so pretty. Aware of the wayward curl in her hair, she was just as he remembered when stood at the harbour only two months earlier. 'We need to get you out of here before any changes are implemented. This may well be our last chance.'

Still not comprehending his words – perhaps not wanting to – she shook her head. 'There is nothing wrong here in Amsterdam. I'm getting on with the job and everyone is being so kind.'

The lieutenant stiffened up at this point. 'Including Johann?'

Florence noticed the difference in his voice. 'Why do you utter your words with such disdain? What is it, Lieutenant? Do you know something about him?'

It being clear there was no point in being tactful anymore, the lieutenant decided to speak plainly. 'Part of the reason you need to leave is because of him. You have placed yourself in a very precarious situation because of his associates.'

Confused, Florence stared at the floor so the lieutenant could not read her thoughts, trying to assimilate what he told her. Almost shaking her head in disbelief, she was so perplexed by it all. 'What are you talking about...? He has been so supportive... so helpful.'

'Where is he tonight?' Suspicious, she looked at him. 'Do you know?' he asked.

'Yes!' she snapped. 'Gone to meet a friend... surely that's not a crime?'

The lieutenant laughed, almost sneered, as she in return glowered back at him; she didn't like the way he behaved. Blackthorn decided it was time she knew what she was dealing with. 'Did you meet his friend, Florence? Did you?' He raised his voice at her and became quite insistent, which shocked her, as she had not seen the lieutenant animated like this.

'No,' she answered, sullen. 'Why would this matter? Keeper of his own friends – we don't need to know everything about everyone!'

Blackthorn gave her a surprised look and decided not to say anything; after all, it was actually his business to know everything. Agitated, he moved the conversation on. 'Ever heard of the name Frederick Obermaier?'

'No,' she said again. 'Why should I have?'

'Hope you never do. A particularly nasty piece of work.' The lieutenant sighed.

'Well, I'm sure you will enlighten me!'

Lieutenant Blackthorn was aware of her sarcasm, but

it was this part of Florence he needed to draw out, the one which showed her to be astute; she would need to use her strength.

'Frederick Obermaier has unhealthy connections,' the lieutenant began, choosing his words carefully. 'His family were involved in – how shall I put it? – unfortunate situations during the previous war. He is a fascist, and a person... if you can refer to him as this, which under no circumstances can be trusted. Anyone associated with him is bad news; he is poison!'

Shaken by his words, she hesitated. 'What has all this got to do with Johann?'

The lieutenant got up at this juncture and stared down at her. 'Johann is with Frederick – even as we speak. Did he tell you he was visiting this dear old friend of his tonight? Did he?'

Florence stood up beside Blackthorn, trying desperately to think about all that had happened between her and Johann. Was any of it real? It was true that when she first arrived, she had been wary of him, but all this had passed. Here at the museum, she remembered once seeing Johann talk to a tall man, but he had ignored her. It was true that Johann had changed the arrangements tonight and, like the lieutenant implied, he did leave in a hurry. Had she been naive because she thought nothing of it? The words circulated around in her head when she suddenly wondered how the lieutenant knew he'd left in a hurry.

'How do you know Johann rushed off tonight?'

'I have been watching him,' the lieutenant replied as she turned sharply towards him.

'Spying, you mean!'

'Doing my job. These fascist groups are becoming very active, and Johann's friend is receiving visits from German officers known to us. This makes us highly suspicious of anyone in connection with these factions.'

Florence thought for a moment. 'How long have you been over here?'

The lieutenant ignored her question, aware of what she wanted to know. 'Did you enjoy your day out in the country?' he simply asked.

'A lovely day, thank you.' Florence blushed; he'd been watching.

'Do you know where Johann went after your day out?'

'Home, of course, it was late.' The moment she answered, she knew the lieutenant would relate a different version.

'Oh, Florence, come now, you know who he went to visit without me pointing it out. Let's hope you haven't told him anything you shouldn't have.'

Frustrated with him, she tried to hide her shock and sat back down on the bench. Was the lieutenant testing her? She was aware how these intelligence sorts worked, but there was no way he could know – all she had spoken of was her Dutch name. What harm could a name do? Other than this there was absolutely nothing else. This was all wrong, anyway; none of this could be right.

'You've got Johann all wrong, Lieutenant.'

'Have I? Still doesn't change anything. Like I said earlier, you are in danger from more than one angle, and we need to get you out of Holland as soon as possible before you become trapped.'

He joined her on the bench to give her instructions, wanting to make sure she had understood him. 'A passage to England has been arranged for you with Captain de Witte in three days. You will meet me on the east harbour for an evening departure at 22.00 hours. You are to act as though nothing has changed, bring only a few hidden possessions, leave the suitcase; having this will draw attention to you. You must tell no one!' He stopped and reiterated the point to make sure she understood him. 'Absolutely no one, Florence!' The lieutenant looked at her; he felt bad so softened his approach as he rubbed her arm lightly and then stood to go.

'I'm sorry, Florence, but in war-time there are truths, half-truths and multiple missions. Colonel Taverner requested you come over to Holland in your professional capacity to purely assist in saving important artworks. I am doing my job – to protect our country, and you. Since you have been here, people of dubious character have come to my attention. This has put you at peril and now I am telling you that you must leave.'

Seated on the bench, her head hung low; only the quiet creak of the gallery door closing made her realise Lieutenant Blackthorn had slipped away as quietly as he had arrived. She was dismayed, not knowing what to do or what to think. Tired, she placed her head in her hands and sobbed, feeling empty inside.

THIRTY-FOUR

FRIDAY, 10TH MAY 1940

Florence woke to a droning sound emanating from outside. Curious, she threw back the blankets as her senses became alarmed; the din was getting louder. It sounded like the roar of engines. With haste, she ran downstairs and opened the front door to see what it was.

Troubled, staring to the sky, she stepped back in amazement as a man ran up the street and pointed whilst shouting, 'They're bombers – German Luftwaffe.'

There were too many of them to even count as they soared over Amsterdam; Florence had never seen anything like this in her life before. And such a noise – a constant throaty vibration that pulsed from the engines. Helga arrived behind her as they continued to stare upwards and she reached for Florence's hand.

'There are so many of them. Where are they flying to?' Helga asked, scared.

'Not sure,' Florence knew this was not good, 'they appear to be going south.' Anxious, she turned to look into the worried face of an elderly lady who still remembered the previous war, petrified to think history could repeat itself.

'Do you think they are heading for Rotterdam?' said Helga.

Florence took Helga's arm and led her back into the house, closing the door and shutting out the incredible drone. Inside she led her to the parlour and sat her down by the fire. 'Stay here today.' Florence spoke softly, trying to reassure her. 'I think it will be safer until I can find out what is going on.'

Helga nodded, relieved to be indoors, knowing she did not want to leave her home; for the moment, at least she felt safe.

'I will go to work and see what is happening in the city,' said Florence.

'You will come back and tell me…won't you?'

Aware of how scared Helga was, Florence crouched down beside her and stroked her face. 'Of course I will.' And she gave her a smile. 'Now, before I go, would you like a hot drink?'

Stood in the kitchen, out of sight of Helga, Florence expelled a huge sigh and clasped her trembling hands whilst thinking back to the words of Lieutenant Blackthorn; it was all beginning to make sense. The kettle whistled and as Florence poured the hot water into the cups, she knew she had some unfinished business to attend to with Johann.

A short time later, Florence made her way to the Rijksmuseum. The narrow streets she'd walked along so many times before remained unchanged, until she turned the corner. Rooted to the spot, she stared in disbelief at vehicles parked at the front of the museum building, along with a blockade at the bottom of the street guarded by police and NSB members. Two black shirt officers were on sentry duty at the door and staff workers were being searched as they entered.

Uneasy with this situation, she wanted to turn and walk away, but she needed to get into the museum to find Johann. With all this change, she understood deep down that she needed to keep the rendezvous with Lieutenant Blackthorn – fair to him, he had tried to warn her.

On arriving at the entrance, she joined the queue trying to get in past the guards and thought of her parents. How could this happen to one family yet again? A guard came forward to search her, dabbing at her coat, her pockets and finally, opening the buttons, he felt his way up and down the side of her body, lingering a tad too long as he stroked the side of her blouse, brushing against her breast. Florence pulled away as he gave her a sly smile, directing her through the entrance into the great hallway.

Inside, she realised there was yet another control point. This time, sat at a desk in front of her was an officious-looking man dressed in a black uniform who searched through his notes. Behind him another, dressed the same, was chatting to a gentleman in a dark brown suit, who was vaguely familiar but she couldn't think why. The officer at the desk asked the names and job titles of the staff members as they approached, then checked if they were on his list. Unsure what this was about, she started to get an odd feeling. Her instinct was to turn and run, but she must carry on. Closer, she could feel her heart begin to race, but she needed to remain calm. The man in front moved on and she stood looking down at the officious face that showed no emotion.

'Name!' he barked out, his pen poised without looking up from his list.

Florence gave hers as he searched up and down, not finding it. Then he turned over to the next page. Why couldn't he find it? Her heart raced, and she clenched her hands and shivered at his coldness as he asked her to repeat her name. The question went around in her head: *Why is it not there? Oh God.* Aware the queue had come to a stop, the gentleman in the brown suit looked over to the confused officer, who now asked for her job title. Again, nothing. Then the officer checked behind.

'Can't find this one on the list,' he said as the man came over.

Florence stared at him; there was something uncannily calm about him that worried her more than the officer. The doors to the side of the gallery suddenly swung open, causing a distraction. In strolled Johann, walking towards them, and she felt relieved on seeing him. He quickly glanced at Florence stood at the desk and averted his gaze to the man in the suit and greeted him, smiling, shaking his hand in a gesture of friendship.

'Good to see you again, Frederick. What seems to be the problem?'

'We are a bit confused as to why this woman's name is not on your list.'

Florence swallowed hard. Had he said Frederick? Her heart nearly missed a beat. The very man Blackthorn warned her about.

Bloody hell. She had walked into the spider's web. *He must know about me,* she thought, but why was he carrying on with this charade? Then another thought struck at her like a cold blade entering slowly into her flesh. Had she heard him right? The 'list' Johann had *given them*? It had taken him no time at all to collaborate – what was she going to do?

'Florence works with me in archiving,' Johann explained. 'An honest mistake, Frederick.' And he moved to place his arm around Florence's shoulders, ushering her to follow him as he led her off towards the doors he'd entered through only a moment a go.

They heard Frederick shout behind them, 'We will speak later, Johann. Where will I find you?' The chill in his voice frightened her, like the viper he was, a calculated man who was dangerous.

Without looking back, Johann replied, 'In my office on the top floor.'

On hearing the words, Florence was confused, as Johann never used this office. As they approached the doors, he pushed her through into the hallway and pointed to the gallery at the side. Not speaking a word, she looked in, noticing the movement. There were black shirts all around, lifting crates. Florence turned to stare at Johann, who caught the look of confusion and distrust on her face. With haste, he ushered her to the stairs and led her down to the basement. Florence was reluctant to follow – it could be a trap. But what option did she have?

At the bottom, he stopped, then turned to speak to her in a hushed voice. 'I'm sorry,' Johann said, feeling very uneasy. 'I've made a terrible mistake and may have endangered you. We need to get you out of here.'

Stunned, she stared at him, hoping for an explanation.

'I purposely took your name off the list to avoid any attention being drawn to you.'

'Why, Johann?'

It was a simple question, but he could not look her in the eye.

'We will talk later – I've been such an ignorant fool, Florence.' He checked their exit was clear and Florence stepped outside, saying nothing.

Johann realised it was essential to get Florence away from Frederick and decided to get her to a place of safety: his family home. This would be all right for now, but he knew he would have to get her out of Amsterdam – it was not safe anymore.

Florence followed him as they hurried down the back roads so as not to draw any attention to themselves. Out of breath, they eventually turned in to a side street and stopped at a big wrought-iron gate. Behind this stood a beautiful old merchant's townhouse. Johann reached over the top of the gate and undid the bolt.

'Is this yours?' Florence stared at Johann in surprise as he pushed the gate forward, and both walked into the courtyard, where a small magnolia tree grew at the centre, its spent petals lying on the ground. Florence stopped, amazed, to look at her surroundings, noticing the name of the house on the wall: 'Oude Magnolia Huis'. This was not what she expected – she was totally unaware of the wealth he was accustomed to.

Johann climbed the steps to open the front door and called for her to follow. For a moment, she stood, astonished at the splendour of the hall. A large crystal chandelier that hung from the ceiling glistened as she walked across the black-and-white-tiled floor to Johann, who led her through the double wooden doors to the right. Florence gasped at the exquisiteness of the room unveiled to her, illuminated in bright, natural light. The original oak floorboards, worn by many footsteps over the years, were partially covered by Turkish Oushak rugs. Opulent paintings hung on the walls alongside elegant furnishings. And on the mantel sat the most decorative ormolu French clock, ticking succinctly in time with the pendulum as it swung to and fro. On either side of the open fireplace were hung small, enamel family portraitures.

Florence stepped forward to view the paintings, thinking how lovely they were, when one in particular caught her eye – the portrait of a woman painted in the seventeenth or eighteenth century, and written underneath was her name: Anneke. *Strange*, she thought for a moment, sure she had seen the name somewhere before, but she couldn't recall where. She was intrigued; the eyes seemed so familiar... but she didn't know why.

The silence of the room was disturbed as a servant entered, who glanced at Florence briefly, then addressed Johann.

'My guest and I will take tea in here,' Johann directed. 'And is Mother at home?'

'No, sir. Out with a friend for lunch; she is expected home later this evening.' He then awaited a reply from Johann, who seemed distracted. 'Will there be anything else?'

'No, thank you.' The servant then left the room as Johann went to stand beside Florence, who gazed out of the window at the magnolia tree.

'What's going on, Johann?' Florence turned to look at him. 'Can I even trust you?

After a moment, he tried to answer her but stumbled; he looked so distressed.

Florence saw the anguish in him. 'What's going on?' she repeated.

'I have placed you in such terrible danger, but I didn't mean to… I'm not proud of myself.'

He walked over to the fireplace, and she followed him with her eyes but at the same time was thinking about the issues Lieutenant Blackthorn had mentioned. To believe him or not – he needed to explain; she had to be cautious.

Johann frowned, cross at the thought of Frederick. 'That weasel!' he snapped. 'You are at risk because of this putrid man.'

Florence went to him to give him an opportunity to explain and was aware of the sandalwood aftershave he wore. It was proving difficult for her to remove her feelings from this situation, but she must to gain the truth. To get his attention, she touched his arm and asked in a softer voice, 'What's going on?'

Ashamed with himself, he dared not look at her. 'Firstly, I need to get you out of Amsterdam, out of the country; you are now in danger, as Frederick will be searching for you. The Germans will soon be arriving, and they will not be leaving in a hurry. This is just the beginning, Florence. At the moment, it may seem calm,' he paused, 'but this is not good – like a plague, slowly spreading, and it will get worse. You have a chance… you need to get back to England, and soon – but I don't know where to begin. We must arrange a passage for you; it will not be easy, as the ports will be guarded. I have money...'

Florence interrupted him before he had a chance to say any more.

'You don't need to do that.'

'I must!' He eyed her anxiously. 'Don't you understand? I have placed you in great danger!'

'How could you? I'm no threat to anybody. Frederick and his black shirts can't penalise me just for being English?'

Johann stared at her in disbelief. 'No, Florence. Not for this – but because you are a spy!'

Aghast, she stepped back; her whole body shivered with the words spoken. Stunned, she glanced at the ceiling as though searching for an explanation that may account for what he had said. 'Do you really think I'm a spy?' Her eyes were fixed on him; she wanted to see his face as he answered, to ascertain what he truly believed.

'Don't care,' he began. 'All I want is to protect you Florence – you mean so much to me.'

Perplexed, she started to get angry with him; he'd hurt her enough, 'How have you placed me in danger?' The words, she spat at him venomously.

Johann looked at her, alarmed. 'I didn't mean to, and I have been deceived.'

'Is it Frederick?' she asked as he rubbed his face, trying to get clarity on the situation.

'He has a way of finding things out... Too well connected – as was his father. Will use everything against you for his own gain.'

'What could he hold against me? Apart from the obvious: I am British, I work as an archivist in a museum... how dangerous could I be?'

Johann spoke slowly. 'Frederick knows your name!'

'So, what's so amazing about my name – Florence Stanley – how can this be of any importance?'

'No, your real name... van Hassel.' Johann looked at her. 'I didn't tell Frederick; I only mentioned to him you were Dutch. I'm sorry – never thought anything of it, until earlier on today.'

'Why today?'

'Because when he asked me for your name on the staff list, I never said your name and he asked for you by your Dutch name – van Hassel. In this moment I realised, he knew information about you.'

Now it all dawned on her, as the blood drained from her face. This was different. The Germans had threatened her father all those years ago as a spy. No way she would be able to talk herself out of this situation, and if Frederick knew her name, he would know everything about her past. Trapped again. Why, when she met with Lieutenant Blackthorn the other night, had he not just been honest and told her she was in such danger? Perhaps he had tried? Florence knew she was foolish not to have listened. Then, she remembered what he said: he had arranged a passage for her with Captain de Witte.

'What's the date today, Johann?'

Confused, he stared at her. 'The 10th of May, why?'

'Good, that gives me just over twenty-four hours. Can you hide me?'

'Yes, of course. But what does all this mean... are you really a spy?'

Florence looked back out of the window, thinking about

all she had been through these last four or five months. 'No – I have been manipulated and used exactly as you have, Johann, and now we are both in danger.'

THIRTY-FIVE

The city grew distant behind them; Johann and Florence sat silently in the car as it travelled along the narrow country lanes. They had been careful to slip out discreetly, keeping to the back roads and out of sight. For most of the journey, Florence was deep in thought, mulling many things over. Johann cursed at himself as he glanced at her; she was having trouble trusting him and he had only himself to blame for this. How could he have been so stupid, so gullible? Frederick was now a big threat to both of them.

The car slowed down and Johann turned off the main road to proceed along a dirt track that lead to an old barn that was surrounded by a small coppice of beech trees. Parked at the side of it and under the shelter of a large tree, he switched the engine off as the area fell silent.

Florence turned to Johann. 'What is this place?' she asked, her tone frosty towards him; she had not forgiven him yet for believing her capable of being a spy.

'Come and I'll show you.'

They both walked round to the front of the old barn. It stood, weathered by time, with narrow slits in its walls and two hefty great doors that appeared to be well secured. Johann grimaced as he lifted off the beam that rested on an iron plinth and took a key from his pocket to open the large padlock that hung from the handles. The door creaked as it relinquished its grip, allowing them both to enter. The last rays from the setting sun refracted off objects laid on the ground. Johann picked up a lantern cloaked in dirt from a small crate and beckoned Florence to step further in as he closed the doors and struck a match. Dust and hay swirled in the dim shards of light. A bat, accustomed to the darkness, disturbed by the intruders, flapped around the beams, settling eventually in the eaves.

Bales of hay, probably sat there since last harvest, took up most of the space, but Florence became curious about an area to the right that was covered over by tarpaulin. 'What's under that?' she said, and pointed.

Johann walked over, placed the light down and pulled back the protective sheet. The corner became entangled on the edge of a box and Florence stepped over to assist him.

The cover removed revealed many flat wooden packages, each with dockets attached on the front. Intrigued, Florence moved closer, sensing something familiar… her own handwriting! Confused, she frowned, thinking for a moment, when it suddenly dawned on her and she turned on her heel to Johann. 'Are these what I think they are?' Florence glowered at him in disbelief.

'Yes. They are paintings.'

'What paintings? Where are these from?'

He hesitated. 'This is not as it seems…' he began, aware she was going to find it hard to understand the situation when she cut him off.

'Are these from the galleries of the museum?' Florence

demanded to know, exasperated with him; he could sense her disappointment once again. Florence knelt down and snapped off the thin wood casing. Beneath this she saw the sails of a windmill and recognised it in an instant.

'These are the originals, aren't they?' She turned to look up at Johann.

'Yes, but it's not—' He felt ashamed.

'What it seems?' Florence interjected, cross with him, her patience running out.

Amazed, she stood up and stepped back in shock. What on earth was happening?! Only a day ago she had been so content in her new life, but now she sat down on a bale of straw, tired and disillusioned.

'Did Frederick ask you to put these here – to take these from the museum?'

'Yes and no.' He replied without looking at her. 'He wants to hide them under the pretext they are being removed for their preservation because of the war – but I don't trust him. I don't trust who he is connected to with his sinister late meetings. My plan was to replace the original paintings, which you have been attending to, with replicas, and over time keep the originals here – safely. If the bloody war hadn't started so quickly, I would have been able to complete this. Now the museums are over-run with Frederick's black shirts.'

'Why this entire charade? Why put yourself at risk like this?'

'I know you won't believe me after all that's happened, but you have to trust me when I tell you Frederick is a ruthless man. Knowledge of you – or your family – he uses for his own purpose or gain... he's manipulative.' Beside her on the bale now, he continued. 'I may not have turned out to be the man you were hoping for, but there are things I care about,' he moved closer, 'and you are one of them.'

He leant forward in an attempt to kiss her, but she turned away, confused as to whether she should trust him or not. Disappointed, he saw in her eyes the lack of trust, and he couldn't blame her. Saddened, he moved over to the half-opened painting and replaced the cover back over its edge.

'My love for these paintings is the second thing I hold most dear to me and knowing Frederick wanted these for his own ill-gotten gain was too much. I had to fight back; he cannot have them… and he cannot have you!'

Florence sat deep in thought, realising all this had been taking place right under her nose. *What a useless spy I would make.* More importantly, Lieutenant Blackthorn and Colonel Taverner were right about this type of corruption happening. A small part of why they sent her to prepare the paintings and artefacts was to protect them… All of high value, not just monetarily but culturally. In the wrong hands they'd be lost forever. But she didn't expect it to happen on her watch by someone she had trusted. Could she trust him now?

All these thoughts danced around in her head, and a notion kept jumping to the fore as she remembered all the artwork she had seen in Johann's family home. Was it all his? The attractive portraitures she had been drawn to, did they belong to the museum? 'Tell me honestly, Johann. Are the paintings in your home really yours?'

Wounded, he glanced over at her. How could their relationship have broken down to this level? 'I'm no thief,' he said, looking at the ground. 'These were inherited by my family.'

Florence had been annoyed with him but now regretted asking – deep down she knew. To amend this, she asked about the portraitures. 'Can you tell me anything about them?'

'Why?'

'I'm not trying to trick you. Just interested. There's just something about them I like. Truly, I'm a bit envious… you have all that family history to relate to.' She stopped. 'Must be very reassuring.'

Johann looked over at her and saw she was genuine in her question. 'I'm not sure of the history of them, but the portrait you liked is of the Lady Anneke, I believe, painted for her suitor. We do not have all the details, but I do remember my grandmother once told me the lady had not wanted to get married. Well, not to the gentleman they chose for her, so she ran away.'

Interested, she nodded for him to go on.

'This, you have to remember, is going back to the eighteenth century and you were not expected to do such things. A bit headstrong – not dissimilar to you.'

Florence laughed at this.

'Anyway,' he continued, 'they thought at the time she must have had a lover. Someone, somewhere else, but they did not know who. They thought she ran off to the country, to Wijk bij Duursted, out where we went to visit the old windmill.'

'Have you ever tried to find out anything about her?' Florence asked, curious.

'No, my father always discouraged any of us from talking about the past – never one for talking of our family lineage – so we just accepted it.'

Johann looked at Florence and could tell she was miles

away in her own thoughts, thinking on something. He reached over for her hand. 'Do you believe me, Florence?'

Bemused, she sighed.

Impatient to know, he prompted, 'About the paintings… do you think I am trying to protect them?'

'Yes,' she said, 'you love them too much. I'm so confused with all that is happening; everything has become so complex.'

Hungry for her kiss, he drew her towards him. Florence had to admit to herself that her feelings were strong for Johann as he kissed her, holding her in his arms for what seemed to be ages. She was happy for this.

After a moment, beside herself with worry, she jumped to her feet. 'Oh my God, Helga!'

'What about her?' Johann was surprised at her outburst.

'I promised her I would return; she will be worried sick about me. I need to get back to her before I go tonight.'

Johann shook his head. 'Not possible. Too dangerous, you must stay away. They will watch her whilst searching for you. Frederick won't let you go.'

'Can't leave without saying goodbye to her.' Florence began to sob uncontrollably as Johann approached. 'Helga has been so good to me, she will worry; I just can't.'

'But it's not safe – Helga would understand and would be more upset if anything were to happen to you,' Johann said as the tears ran down her face.

'It's not just that,' she sobbed. 'My belongings are back there in my suitcase, things I need.'

'What things? Your life is more important.'

'They are of sentimental value to me; they give me strength. My picture of Edith, I can't leave it there.' Distraught, she rested her head against his chest as the tears ebbed down her face, dampening his shirt.

To console her… there was only one thing to do. 'Would it make you happy if I were to go back to Helga, to tell her you are safe and collect your belongings at the same time?'

Florence sniffed and looked at the man in front of her, knowing she loved him even when she had tried to push that love aside – how could she ever have doubted him? 'Would you do this for me?'

He simply nodded.

'Oh, Johann. Thank you so much.' She flung her arms around his neck as he squeezed her, glad to have her embrace.

'But,' he began, 'you must promise me you will stay here and not open the door to anyone. On my return I will knock three times – understand?'

Clear, she nodded and promised whilst following him to the door, as he lifted the bar and tentatively pushed it open, checking before stepping out of the barn.

Reluctant for him to go, she tugged on his arm. 'Be careful, won't you?'

Johann kissed her and gently pressed her back. 'I would do anything for you. Don't want to lose you… ever! Now, secure the door and remember what I said.'

Touched by his words, she kissed him again.

Outside, he waited to make sure she had done this, listening to the lock, and then made his way to the car.

Inside, Florence ran to the side of the barn, trying to find a loose slat to peep through, viewing Johann drive off before the car vanished in a plume of dust. With nothing else to see, her attention returned to the paintings and, in particular, the windmill.

Transfixed by the beauty of it, she was suddenly aware of a whole new range of thoughts that flooded into her head, giving her a sense of something familiar: a belonging to the past, reintroduced with a simple look at a scene in a painting, and a connection to a portrait, a gravestone, a moment in time, a place, or an intense feeling for something or someone. All these different concepts, she sensed, were coming together – not that she understood why – but she recognised the trigger to these was in front of her: the painting of the windmill.

Frantic, she scanned the barn for something to write on and found what she needed over on the crate where the lantern sat. Florence grabbed the few sheets of dusty paper and took out a pencil from her pocket. Sure in her knowledge, beliefs and now a clear understanding, she began to write.

In a side street not far from Helga's home, Johann switched off the engine, deciding he needed to be as discreet as possible. Not knowing who might be watching, he took no chances, not for his own safety but for Florence's. Along the quiet lane he searched, making sure he was not followed; he had good reason to be paranoid, as he knew what Frederick was like. From the small alleyway opposite, he checked Helga's house and, when convinced all was clear, he crossed the road.

He took out the key Florence had given him and let himself in. The old floorboards creaked and groaned in the hallway, alarming Helga. From the parlour she shouted out in hope it would be Florence but was more than surprised when the door opened to reveal Johann.

Initially she was pleased to see him but realised he was on his own – the worry grew on her face.

'Where is Florence?' she asked, a slight tremble in her voice as she stared at Johann.

He decided to sit down beside her to explain what was happening and why he had hidden Florence until they identified she was safe. To protect Helga, he gave her limited information and did not tell her that Florence would abscond the country but stressed that Florence was well.

'So, you are sure she is all right?'

'Yes, she is fine.'

Helga was still troubled, but she was at least relieved she was safe and protected by Johann.

'I need to retrieve some belongings from her room.'

Helga was happy for him to do this but asked that he would let her know when he was leaving. Johann agreed and left Helga in the parlour.

Florence's room was at the top of the house, and as he climbed, he thought he saw a light shining from under the door of the room on the first floor. When he arrived on the landing, he checked the doorway – only darkness. Once before, Florence told him a lodger kept the room, but she'd never met anyone; they were never there. Johann thought he must have mistaken it for the reflection of the hall light.

At the top, Johann pushed open the door to Florence's room and entered, fumbling for the light switch. He was surprised, as he glanced around, at how untidy it appeared – perhaps she had left in a hurry. It just struck him as unusual. Florence was always so particular.

Johann went and sat down on the unmade bed and

smoothed his hand across the indent on her pillow; he could smell the scent of her perfume as he tried to imagine her lying there. The covers were pulled back with her nightgown thrown on top. On the bedside cabinet a picture frame lay face down. The glass was broken, and the photo was half hanging out of it. He turned it over to see it was the photo of himself, the one Florence had taken on their day out to see the windmill; underneath she had added some words at the bottom of it in Dutch: '*Onze Ineengestrengelde Zielen*.'

This he smiled at, but he was suddenly interrupted on hearing Helga shout for him.

Out on the landing, he leant over the banister to find her standing in the hallway below and ran down a flight of stairs to check what she wanted.

'What's wrong?'

'Oh, Johann, I thought you had gone.'

'No, Helga, I said I would come to you before leaving. What made you think I'd gone?'

'Oh, I'm just a silly old woman… sorry to alarm you, but I thought I had heard the front door close. Must have been my imagination.'

'Probably the wind,' Johann said, 'don't worry. Promise I will not leave here without coming to see you first.'

For a moment, he waited to see her walk off, mumbling something to herself and then turned to go back upstairs, thinking Helga was fretting too much, when he noticed the door to the bedroom on the first-floor landing was now ajar. How could this have been the wind?

Johann went to it and pushed it open, reaching in along the wall for the light switch. The room – empty. The bed had not been slept in, and a thin layer of dust lay settled on top of the furniture; no one had been near this place in a long time. Satisfied, he stepped out of the door and at the same time trod on something that crunched underneath his shoe. Curious, he put the light back on. There on the floor – a shard of crushed glass. For a moment he scanned the room for any broken items: nothing out of place, spotless. Then it dawned on him – the photo frame in Florence's room.

Quick as he could, he rushed back up the flight of stairs and dashed over to the bed and checked underneath it to where the brown case would be... Nothing! Everything started to make perfect sense; it had vanished. Of course, she had not left her room in this mess. Why would they want her case?

'Oh my God.' Johann jumped up as the realisation struck; somebody had been in the house at the same time as him. Helga didn't imagine the front door closing; she had actually heard it. Someone had ransacked her room and then casually walked straight out with Florence's case.

Quickly he snatched at the photo and checked the room once more, but now he had to hurry, to get back to Florence. He ran down the stairs. In front of Helga he remained calm, enquiring if there had been anyone else staying in the house, but she had given him the answer he had expected: 'No.'

Johann said goodbye to Helga and hurried for the door. Cautious, he scanned the street, knowing full well whoever had been in the house was now long gone, but he had no idea who might be watching. Fast as he could, he ran to get back to the car, back to Florence.

THIRTY-SIX

Florence finished writing her notes when she heard the quiet reverberations of an engine coming up the old track. It appeared to have stopped further down, as the noise vanished before reaching the barn. Suspicious she decided to check and snuck back to the loose slat. It was much darker now, but the silhouette of the trees could be traced on the skyline. The light restriction made it very difficult, but she could hear shuffling and movement outside. Florence became apprehensive; something wasn't right.

Now starting to panic, she thought that she needed to conceal her notes in case anything happened and folded them up, trying to think rationally, where to hide them – when it came to her.

Silent, she crept over to the painting of Ruisdael's windmill and searched down the back of the canvas for what took an eternity, but there it was... the slight tear she had discovered earlier. Florence squeezed the papers inside – she took out a small piece of gum from her pocket and chewed at it as fast as she was able, then tore a piece and stuck it on the back of the canvas, closing the tear. With more activity to be heard outside, she dashed over to the lantern and extinguished the flame. Then she lowered herself down and sat on the ground, resigned to what was about to happen.

In the dark, her eyes adjusted slowly as the moonlight strobed through the uneven lapping, momentarily interrupted by movement as someone crossed through the course of its trajectory. Florence knew who had found her, but she just sat and waited.

Then, sure enough, cold and as calm as a demon, her worst fears had become reality.

'Hello, Florence.' The chill from Frederick's voice sent shivers down her spine. 'Are you going to come out and join us?'

Florence, aware she was about to be captured, knew Johann would return for her and wonder what had happened. How could she warn him? Her thoughts in her head were frantic when she suddenly stopped, remembering what Johann had said: 'He does not know where I have stored them or where this place is.'

How had Frederick found her? A sweat bead dropped from her brow; her hands clammy, Florence was terrified and didn't want to believe this. Had Johann betrayed her?

From a distance, someone stirred in the ditch behind the hedgerow. In the moonlight, they watched with intent at the scene unfolding at the barn. A light shone at the door and slowly it opened.

Florence stepped out, lit by the beam of light from Frederick's torch as men wearing black shirts and guns moved in to encircle her. One of the men raised Florence's arms above her head, searched her then tied her hands behind her back. Frederick motioned to his car and she was led away as he followed, closing the door as though he'd just finished spinning the last silk yarn around his cocoon… trapped!

Lieutenant Blackthorn discerned all this before him from the hedgerow, completely helpless to assist Florence. There was nothing he could do for her. There were just too many of them. Both vehicles returned down the track as the dust rose upward in the pale moonlight.

Stunned, he sat quiet and motionless, trying to absorb all that had happened. Where would Frederick take her? Quick as he could, the lieutenant decided to get to the barn in case Florence had left a lead, a hint – anything!

After a period of time, a vehicle came up the track again. Its headlights were turned off. The lieutenant heard only the distant sound of the engine. Time to go.

With haste, he left the barn, keeping low and heading back towards the hedgerow. Careful to hide, he checked behind him, watching as a man jumped out of the car and went into the barn. The lieutenant could see light flit around the inside as someone searched for something or someone. Then the image came running back out. With the torch lightening the figure, the lieutenant got a clear view of who was down there.

'Johann!'

The lieutenant thought for a moment, then crept back through the hedgerow and up the lane to where his car was parked. Without putting on his lights, he drove away.

Lieutenant Blackthorn vowed he would not forget the betrayal of Florence; in his eyes, Johann was a marked man. He'd never trusted Johann, not from the first letter he had received from Florence. And from the unexpected arrival of

Frederick at the barn – who else could have known? It must have been Johann… But why had he come back?

Johann went back inside the barn and sat down in the dirt, not knowing what to do next. He was sick with worry and distraught with guilt; he promised he'd look after her! In despair, he stared at the ground, aware of some markings in front of him. Florence must have made them. In the dirt, a sketch of a windmill. For a time, he pondered, and then it dawned on him; getting up he went over to her favourite painting – but it had gone! All that was there was an empty case. Johann began searching for further clues but found nothing obvious. What happened to the painting? If Frederick had taken it… why not take all of them?

Johann knew in order to protect the others. he would need to move them, and soon.

'Christ… what the hell should I do?' Distraught, he thought of Florence and knew he needed to get back to the city.

Outside, Johann shut the door behind him, trying to clear his mind; he needed to get Frederick. He had done this – but how did he get the location of the barn? Johann was puzzled… how did he find her? A sense of panic surged through him; it was imperative he stopped Frederick – and save Florence.

THIRTY-SEVEN

In the shadows of a darkened alley, beside a storage warehouse on the docks, stood Lieutenant Blackthorn. The trawler, the *Zeeslang,* docked in the distance as he kept watch sat on a wooden box where he'd remained for over an hour. It was a cool evening and the dockside was lit by the waning moon intermittently passing through clouds. He was expecting trouble, but he didn't know when. He had an appointment at 22.00 hours and this he needed to keep. It was his only chance to get away. Yet, there had been no signs of anything, nothing at all, which made him more suspicious. Again, he checked his watch: 21.46. He drew himself up and adjusted his woolly hat, pulling the collar of his jacket in close to evade the evening coolness.

Aware of the time, he needed to make his move. Before stepping out of the shadows, he looked around once more and reached down to pick up a small brown suitcase. Almost at the exact same time, a screeching noise of a vehicle could be heard as it came to a sudden halt that stopped him on the spot. Cautious, he retreated into his refuge to observe.

The lieutenant moved back up to the edge of the building and carefully took out a mirror he had in his pocket. Positioned in several places, he then found what he wanted.

Further down the harbour stood a tall man, his silhouette cast in the shadows. Unable to recognise him, Blackthorn checked his watch again – it was now 21.51. Time was running out. To the right of him he could hear the crew of the *Zeeslang* making their way along the harbour to the ship. At his last check in his mirror, a tiny detail caught his eye. Back behind the tall figure, tucked in at the side of the warehouse, he detected something, faint at first so that he wasn't sure he had seen it, and then it came again. A small, reddish glow emanating from the darkness, hidden from view by a pile of old crates on the dock side. The lieutenant knew instinctively who stood smoking in the dimness, waiting to crawl out. It could only be Frederick. How the hell did he know about the rendezvous? Had he broken Florence? The crew drew ever closer; he checked his watch once more: 21.56. He had to act, and that one moment was upon him. Calmly, he picked up the case and seized his chance, stepping out towards the eight men walking past.

Those in the shadows knew about the rendezvous but did not know who they were looking for or what ship, as there was more than one ready to sail – exactly why the lieutenant chose this evening.

Merged in with the other men, unperturbed by his presence, he strode along, keeping his head down to start with. When he eventually looked up, he was stunned. Further down, standing on the dock, was Florence. Blackthorn could hardly believe his eyes; he was close enough to have run and grabbed her, taking her with him on board the ship, but he was aware who skulked in the darkness. It was a trap!

Desperate not to look at her, he continued, but he had to

know if she was all right; if only he could catch her attention – for her to acknowledge him. Closer now, he glanced at her furtively, but she sat looking at the ground. The lieutenant had nearly given up trying to get her attention when suddenly Florence caught sight of a familiar item... her old brown suitcase. Her eyes drew up to be met by Lieutenant Blackthorn staring at her – he thought how beautiful she looked, such an air of supreme calmness about her. In this brief moment of recognition, enough was expressed between them without ever uttering a single word. Florence stood up; she knew what she must do. With courage, she averted her gaze from the lieutenant, ignoring him, and began walking to where the tall figure stood by a car on the dockside, in the dark.

At the trawler, Blackthorn followed the other crew members up the gangway and turned to watch Florence approach the dark silhouette as men from all directions ran out towards them both – surrounding them. The tall figure stepped forward, taking off his hat, but Florence already knew who stood before her. Just by his physique and stature, she recognised that it was indeed... Johann.

The men parted and a plume of smoke meandered from the shadows into the space they created to reveal Frederick. He glowered at Florence, aware she had done this on purpose, trifling with matters she would regret. Johann, confused, checked Florence and then Frederick. Florence, smug, smiled to herself. To release Lieutenant Blackthorn, she had seized her moment – falsely exposing Johann as the agent Frederick hoped she would lead them to. It felt good and knowing it pissed off Frederick made it even better.

Blackthorn watched from the deck of the ship as the two figures on the harbour were ushered away. Florence didn't look back... not once! She had given nothing away, therefore protecting him. Black shirts rushed around the dock, searching in vain like perambulating ants as the *Zeeslang*, under the expert guidance of Captain de Witte, slipped slowly away, heading out for the dark, cold waters of the North Sea that would hopefully lead them back to the shores of England... and safety.

Stood alone, listening to the resonating rhythmic sound of the ship's engines, the lieutenant thought about everything, playing back over bits of information in his head. It became apparent to him Frederick had turned up at each event, every time. Florence had revealed nothing; he had given her very little intelligence to try to protect her from any situation that might occur, like this evening. The lieutenant knew why she was in Amsterdam, but what he did not account for was the unexpected invasion of Holland by Germany; it all happened so quickly.

Sombre as he viewed the dark waters undulate at the wake of the ship, he now realised what else this situation had revealed. The Secret Intelligence Service were dealing with a double agent! For a fact... he knew this, but he did not yet know who! There was unquestionably a spy in their midst. But unfortunately, there had been a consequence of finding this out... Florence!

The innocent victim, sacrificed to reveal more. He had not meant for her to get caught; he tried to warn her, to keep her away, not to get involved, but she was the forfeit to expose a traitor! A ruthless traitor that he now sailed back to; all he had to do was find out who it was.

In the cold night air, he rubbed his hands, looking back to the distant lights of Amsterdam, and made himself a promise. To come back one day to find Florence and to avenge her. Also, he would need to have a chat with Johann, whom he was convinced had betrayed her on more than one occasion.

THIRTY-EIGHT

Florence sat in silence, her head facing down as her eyes tried to avoid the brightness shining towards her from the lamp on the desk. The room smelt of stale tobacco. There was an ache she still carried in her jaw from where she had been slapped previously. From behind the light, the door opened, and she could hear the footsteps of someone entering before it slammed shut. Nothing was clear, just the disjointed movement in the shadows until the lamp turned away. There was such immense relief as her vision slowly returned, allowing her to view her surroundings. The office seemed vaguely familiar and, although brought here blindfolded, she felt sure she was back at the museum. Her attention stirred at a flint spark that proceeded to ignite a cigarette, revealing the odious creature drawing breath from it, the same creature who had left her face tender and bruised. Florence tried hard to ignore the unpleasant silence as the air filled with smoke. Frederick sat and scrutinised her, but she was resolute not to show any emotion; none at all. It was necessary to be strong and to be wise to Frederick's devious scheming.

As he leant on the desk, smoke exhaling from him, Florence viewed his oiled hair as it reflected the light, illuminating him for the eel he was.

'Don't be alarmed,' he said, and gave her a wry smile. 'You do not have to be afraid of me.' Florence heard his words and remained quiet.

'You can assist me,' he began again, 'and all will be fine.' He stood, then walked around the desk to crouch down in front of her and stroked at her injured cheek. Sat with her tied hands resting on her lap, she stared back into his empty black eyes with nothing but defiance rendered across her face. This man would not win; he was utterly loathsome to her and she delighted in the knowledge that Lieutenant Blackthorn had eluded him, this being the annoyance burning inside of him.

'Easy to see your defiance – but you need not be like this. We can assist each other, can't we?'

Determined to ignore him, she wondered what nonsense he would utter now.

Then he returned to his seat and took out a sheet of paper from the drawer. 'This is very interesting, Florence… Or may I address you as Miss van Hassel?' He glanced at her as she kept her head down, wracking her brain to work out, how he knew her real name, as Johann had said to her that he never told Frederick.

'You were born on 7th March 1918; your father is Hans Reuben van Hassel and your mother is Henrietta Jane Van Hassel, née Glassbrook.' Smug, he raised his eyebrows in satisfaction at the knowledge he had acquired about her, enjoying every moment. 'I believe your grandfather, Colonel Charles Glassbrook, worked for the British Army.' From over the paper he tried to absorb her reaction, but she remained staring at the floor, apparently disinterested.

Inside she was amazed. Why were they as a family so

notorious? It wasn't long ago she'd heard some of these names for the first time from the Secret Intelligence in London; it started to feel like a curse.

Frederick noted her lack of response and, irritated, he continued. 'We know of your connections.' His voice softened a little. 'We know how the British have used you... this you must realise yourself? You sit here in a precarious situation, you owe them no loyalty.' He took a moment to re-light his cigarette. 'You do know your father worked for us... as a double agent?'

Florence turned to him, viewing him with a suspicious look, and he seized upon this. 'Yes, true; you must not resist us. We are here to help you. This is why you can assist us and we, in return, can protect you.'

She heard his words but didn't believe them, although she was confused enough to be misled. Frederick and his Nazi allies were trying to use her; who could she trust?

'Your father worked with another agent of ours, one whom you are named after.'

She frowned at him; what did he mean by that?

'Your middle name is Margaretha?' He glanced over at her, but she just stared back at him nonchalantly and listened.

'Your father was close to her... you know who I mean, don't you? Or do you know her best by her stage name, Mata Hari?'

Where did he get this information from? Confused with all these mind games, she shook her head, becoming tired; she was aware she had to be careful, but it was getting harder.

'We did not chase your father to England or assassinate your family friend, Margaretha. No – not us who did this!'

His cigarette extinguished, he carried on, enjoying himself. 'Your father needn't have gone but was happy to do so. Do you know why?'

She said nothing.

'Retaliation! That is why; he was angry at what happened to his dear friend and blamed the English for not doing more to save her. So, you are on our side; we don't want any harm to come to you… you're one of us!'

To get her attention, he strolled to the front of the desk again, but she would not look at him, as she could feel the tears; the words he had spoken actually frightened her – to think she could be connected to such a monster left her feeling vulnerable.

'You understand, we can help you.' He sighed, and then said what Florence had been waiting to hear. 'Who did you meet here in Amsterdam? Who is the agent?'

Florence absorbed the words and then started to laugh; she couldn't stop herself. To think she very nearly believed him; releasing all her emotion, she laughed, knowing he did not have the correct facts. The retaliation story – a lie, as her parents arrived in England before their friend had been shot.

Frederick tensed his hand, stepped forward and, with his full might, he slapped her once more across the face. Startled, as the pain swept through her whole head and her cheek throbbed, she stretched her jaw and she began to laugh again, watching as his face contorted, incensed with rage. For a moment she stopped to catch her breath to speak.

'All that elaborate charade… for what!' She almost spat the words at him and, although in agony, she sat upright, staring straight back into his loathsome dark eyes, exuding sheer defiance.

Frederick huffed as he walked over to the door and opened it. He called to the two guards stood outside. 'Take her away!' They entered the office and grabbed Florence's arms, then dragged her out of the room as she continued to laugh. Angered, Frederick turned and slammed his fist down on the desk – she was an annoyance to him. But he needed to know whom she'd met here in Amsterdam before they got back to England. Frederick knew it was imperative he found out… to inform a colleague in the Secret Intelligence Service; they might be in danger.

THIRTY-NINE

A while later, the door to the office opened again and this time Johann was escorted in.

'Seat him over there,' Frederick instructed, 'and untie his hands.' The guard turned to him quizzically – he jerked a nod at him and then waited until they both left the office.

Johann perched uncomfortably on the edge of his chair, desperate for answers. 'Where is Florence?'

Frederick, seeing him uneasy, went to the tall cabinet to fetch two glasses and a half-empty bottle of brandy. Then he poured some and handed one to Johann, who accepted it, aware it would be wise to fit in with him until he found out what was going on.

'What am I going to do with you, Johann? You walk from one mess straight into another.' Frederick let out a long, frustrated sigh and took a drink of his brandy as he shook his head in dismay. 'She's a spy; didn't you know?' he exclaimed.

Johann, angry at what he had said, shot Frederick a look but realised instantly he shouldn't have done so and softened his own expression, conscious he needed to tread with care. 'But how can she be? Johann asked. 'She knows nothing, not even about the paintings; what harm can she do to us?'

Frederick pulled a chair over beside Johann, straddled

it and took another sip of his drink. 'Why did you turn up at the dock?' He stared at Johann, his dark eyes monitoring everything.

'Whilst at the barn, Florence mentioned a rendezvous she had to keep with a ship at the dock. So, when I came back and she wasn't there, I wondered where she had gone. All I knew was the sailing time, so I headed for the docks. I arrived there to find nothing. I stayed in the dark to see what was happening when suddenly she appeared, walking straight to me, and then... well, you know what happened after that – you appeared with half an army of black shirts.'

Frederick grimaced. 'Smart girl!' He narrowed his eyes and continued. 'She hoped you'd turn up – used you as bait to protect the real agent.' He took his last swig of brandy and sat back. 'That's why she told us of the rendezvous, knowing you'd appear.' He smiled and then sneered. 'She must have known the British operative had a chance; why, he probably walked straight past us, with her knowing... smart girl!' He got up and paced for a moment as Johann stood with him, wary of his mood changes.

'He cannot have gained anything from her – she knows nothing,' Johann said.

Like a viper pouncing on its prey, Frederick spun round and pushed Johann back down in his seat. 'Fool!' he bellowed. 'You have no idea, do you? Playing in your museum... You do not appreciate the consequence of this.' Demeaned, he shook his head as Frederick lowered his voice. 'You are probably right; she doesn't know anything, but she wasn't meant to.'

Confused, Johann stared at him.

'She was used by the Secret Intelligence Service to draw

out our mole.' Frederick saw the perplexed look on his face. 'Yes, our agent, who is now in danger back in London as another British operative has eluded us and is returning to SIS to expose the double agent… ours!'

They both remained silent for a moment and then Johann asked another question, trying to work things out. 'Why use Florence?'

'Because,' he was frustrated with him now, 'she was a sacrifice to find out what they needed to know; they wanted to catch bigger and better fish. They used her father's previous association with a double agent in the First World War to blackmail her.'

'What are you talking about?' Johann viewed him, surprised. 'You can't know anything of her; I didn't even give you her real name.'

'Oh my, you are so naive! You think I know nothing of her background because you did not give me her real name? Were you trying to protect her? Have you got too close? Is this the problem?'

Not wanting to look at Frederick, Johann gazed down at his empty glass as Frederick strolled back to pick up his cigarettes off the desk.

'I know all there is to know about Florence van Hassel,' he said, and threw his match in the ashtray. 'I make it my business to know. Although,' he paused, 'her father really wasn't a double agent like I told her… unlike yours, Johann!'

Johann sat and listened, ashamed at what Frederick had said. He was aware of being dictated to by a monster that kept him shackled to his side for his own enjoyment because of his family's deceit and treachery – used by his own supposed friend. His thoughts were of Florence now; he had tried to get her away, but with a ferocious predator like Frederick she had no chance. Then Frederick said something that gave Johann a glimmer of hope.

'You must to do better this time, Johann – you will have to use your charms, as we still need the name of the agent. You wouldn't want details of your father's background being released to the community… now, would you? Think what this would do to your family name.'

Frederick sat down again near to him, ready to give him further instruction. 'We will need to set up an escape attempt led by you; get her to where she feels it is safe and gain her trust. Then get that agent's name. Do you think you can do this?'

Frederick spoke with such condescension towards him, but Johann knew not to rise to it. Frustrated, he squeezed the glass in his hands as he sat there, thinking how he'd love to have smashed it in his face – but he had this one last chance to save Florence.

'Leave it to me!'

FORTY

The dust settled on the floorboards around them; all that could be heard was the repetitive creak of the windmill's sail turning in the wind.

'How can I ever trust you?' Florence said as Johann looked at her, hurt, but he understood why she asked the question.

'I'm being completely honest with you. Frederick has allowed us to escape, but even though I have changed our destination, no doubt in time he will track us down. There is one way which may save us.' He hesitated. 'If you told him the name of the agent you met in Amsterdam.'

'So that's it,' she retorted, angered and losing patience with him, 'you are just the same as Frederick. You say you are trying to protect me, but all you want is the information, just like him.' Florence knelt before him, looking directly into his eyes. 'I will not tell you… ever!'

The defiance was more than evident in those beautiful brown eyes of hers. He touched her hair; he loved those loose curls framing her pretty face. 'That is fine, Florence, I gave you the last opportunity, but I don't care about the name; I just wanted you to be clear this was an option.'

'Was it, Johann? How can either of us trust that creature? You can't believe anything he says.'

'You are right, this isn't a trustworthy choice, so we need to work on another solution to get you to safety, because we both know Frederick will hunt us down when he realises what I have done. You must believe me when I say this.'

Florence nodded; she wanted to trust Johann, as she genuinely cared for him, but she knew deep down she could not – both had been used in a game of espionage. But to survive, they needed to use each other.

Florence walked over to the central beam that stretched up to the roof of the windmill and leant against it to loosen her silk scarf from around her neck. The intermittent motion of the sails caused a shadow as the sun set. The constant sound of the rotation of the sail was oddly calming and Johann stepped up behind Florence. His breath, she sensed, as he pulled her hair to one side and kissed her neck; she wanted to allow herself to enjoy this, as she had done once before when they first visited this quaint little village, but she must not. Before she could pull away there came a knock on the door. They both froze – Johann drew his finger to his lips to silence her as another knock sounded. Then they heard what they feared.

'Johann. Come out!'

Florence cringed at the sound of the deleterious voice that burst its way into the quietness of the mill. So, it hadn't taken him long at all to track them down. No doubt, he had them followed… he'd set Johann up right from the beginning.

Johann fumbled in his pocket and brought out an old pistol.

'Where the hell did you get that?' Horrified, Florence eyed him as he handed it to her.

'Be careful,' he whispered. 'It was my father's. Let me go out and talk to him. We need to stall for time; just go along with me and keep hold of this.'

In complete disbelief, she stared at the handgun and nodded, watching as Johann opened the door. He paused to glance back at her before he moved out to meet Frederick, leaving the door ajar. Florence appreciated in that brief moment how much she still loved him and recognised an ethereal bond that ran deep between them.

The same odious voice now called her name, interrupting her thoughts. Still holding the pistol, she tried to push it into her coat pocket – but it wouldn't fit. With trepidation, as something didn't feel right about this, she pushed the door open further and stepped down the wooden steps. Johann stood there with a gun pointing at him. Frederick beckoned her to move beside him. With her hands behind her, she carried the gun. Close at Johann's side, almost touching, she gave him a tenuous glance. Frederick ushered her to step away, pointing the weapon at them both.

'Johann says that at last you have come to your senses.'

Florence watched as a hideous fake smile spread across his face in a condescending manner. *Hateful*. She shuddered – he really did give her the creeps.

'You have complied with my request to give me the name of the agent from the English Secret Intelligence Service.'

Florence glared at Frederick and smiled for a moment before looking away, disinterested; she wasn't listening anymore. An unexpected gust of wind hustled around her, lifting her hair gently and taking her scarf as it escaped into the evening sky. Distracted by its sudden departure, she turned, watching as the colours were highlighted by the last rays of the setting sun – she heard a shot.

Frederick realised instantly she would never give him the agent's name. It put him in a precarious position, as his German colleagues wanted to use this mole in Secret Intelligence to their advantage, but she had endangered all this with her defiance. His anger soared at her – she annoyed him – and before he grasped what he was doing, he had squeezed the trigger.

Lissom, the scarf blew upward; Florence, aware of an odd sensation, fell to the ground, her chest on fire. Voices sounded around her, but her gaze remained fixed, watching as the scarf meandered in the fading apricot sky. The burning she felt on her body only a moment ago began to feel cold as she continued to follow the trail of the scarf. Another shot rang out in the air, followed by a garbled noise from behind her.

Johann, stunned as Frederick fired his gun, watched as Florence fell to the ground. In complete disbelief, he then noticed the pistol lying at her side as Frederick moved toward her. Enraged, Johann seized his moment, pushing Frederick away from her – then picked up the pistol and shot. Frederick stumbled backwards, clutching at his body before falling down. Johann, desperate and confused, dropped the gun and turned to rush to Florence.

On the ground, Florence stared at the scarf; it had become attached to one of the sails of the windmill… flowing gracefully with the breeze, circulating in a never-ending cycle. The muted sounds of Johann panicking were now barely audible as he knelt next to her on the ground, his hands covered in blood. Florence relaxed knowing he was beside her

– he was safe. All was quiet and her vision began to blur as she looked into his eyes and spoke softly.

'Another time, Johann!' They were her last words as she passed into darkness.

FORTY-ONE

A short time after the shooting, a Dutch police officer, accompanied by a few black shirts, arrived at the scene. Devoid of emotion or speech, Johann watched as two men lifted up Florence's cold, lifeless body and placed it on the back of their truck beside Frederick's.

A solitary curl fell on her pale face before they raised the tailgate of the vehicle.

Johann stared, numb, only to be disturbed by a senior officer, who shoved at his arm to get his attention. 'Let me get this straight,' the officer began, 'you say the girl turned to shoot Herr Obermaier at the same time he shot at her. Is this correct?'

The words... Johann heard them but remained transfixed on the small silk scarf flailing in the wind, only partially visible in the moonlight against an obsidian darkness reaching out into the wide universe. Without looking, he answered, 'Yes.'

The officer straightened up, surprised at the lack of further information. Shuffling from one foot to the other, he pondered the situation, striving to find answers.

'There is just one thing that bothers me...'

Johann listened but remained watching the sails of the windmill; he was disinterested in the questioning, but he had to be careful.

The officer deliberated and then carried on. '…Things don't quite make sense to me. You said you arrived with Herr Obermaier, just the two of you?'

'No,' Johann snapped back. 'I arranged to meet him here – we arrived separately.'

'So why were Herr Obermaier's men not with you?'

'I told you, I had a hunch where she would hide and explained to Frederick I'd get her to talk.'

Johann swallowed – he'd never been any good at lying. Unable to meet the officer's gaze, he continued. 'I was not aware he would not bring the black shirts with him; he must have considered she was not a threat. However, when he got here, he found me being held at gunpoint. We had both underestimated her.'

For a minute he lingered, disbelieving his own words, his own lies. It all sounded so surreal, and it was. The reality… he had pulled the trigger and shot Frederick. He continued. 'The girl panicked as Frederick approached. With the pistol pointed at me, he feared she would shoot. In an instant, he fired, shooting the girl in the chest – who then dropped to her knees, but her last action was to fire the weapon. Frederick collapsed, fatally wounded; he died shortly after. That is all there is to it. Suppose I'm lucky.'

'I see,' said the young officer, not entirely convinced; he realised there was little more he could ascertain from Johann and started to walk away but turned with another question. 'One last thing. I'm curious as to the weapon the girl had?'

Johann shrugged his shoulders as the officer carried on, determined to press this point. 'Unusual, as it was a

Borschardt C93.' The sarcasm was now evident in his voice. 'It probably means nothing to you.'

Again, Johann just shrugged.

'It is an old German pistol dating back to the turn of the century. They're not common. Strange how she could have had this – don't you think?'

Johann knew what he meant and kept calm, this time returning his gaze, surprising himself at his newly found stoicism.

'Spies have access to all manner of items,' Johann answered, then the officer half smiled unbelievingly and turned away to walk down to the truck waiting for him as Johann remained sat on the ground, still in shock from all that had occurred and all so quickly. This was the hardest thing in his life he had ever done, to show no physical feeling whatsoever for someone who lay dead in front of him... the person he had idealised and greatly loved... his precious Florence.

When the police officer arrived at the truck, he spoke to one of the waiting men. 'I want him kept under observation when we get back to town.'

From the base of the windmill Johann witnessed the lorry drive off up the track, whipping up the dust, as his Florence disappeared, vanishing into the distance... nothing would ever be the same again.

FORTY-TWO

Lieutenant Blackthorn pushed open the door to the Officers' Club in the Strand and stepped out of the wet, dark night. His tired eyes were slow to respond to the light and the lateness of the hour. He cursed the rain whilst removing his sodden coat, but this was no distraction for him; he had returned here for a reason.

The lieutenant strolled through to the bar in the Marlborough room and ordered two brandies. 'I have a guest arriving shortly; can you show him through, please?'

The steward nodded in response as the lieutenant took the brandies and found a seat in one of the quiet corners near to the fire.

Comfortable, the lieutenant checked out the surroundings, thinking them pleasant; the only evidence of war in here was the blackout blinds on the windows. He took a sip of the brandy, as it warmed him, and savoured the taste, reminding him of a luxury not had for a long time; he allowed himself a moment to reflect on all that had happened. Cosy by the fire and lost in his thoughts, he was startled by the voice of Colonel Taverner as he turned to see him walking towards him. Blackthorn stood to shake his hand.

'Good God, man. You look shattered! When did you get

back?' The colonel took the brandy offered by the lieutenant and both officers sat down.

'The small hours of this morning,' Blackthorn replied, watching the colonel take out a pouch of tobacco and a pipe, which he filled and then lit. His actions appeared awkward. 'Is everything all right, sir?'

Colonel Taverner, surprised with his question, cleared his throat. 'Yes, yes, I'm fine, had one meeting after the other this past week. I even had trouble getting time to meet you tonight – cancelled arrangements to be here. With the situation in Europe escalating, all is hectic. I'm just tired, that's all. Anyway, never mind me – how did you get on, anything to report?'

Blackthorn sat forward in his seat. 'You were right, sir.' The lieutenant glanced around the room to reassure himself no one else was listening. 'There is an infiltration within the department. We have a double agent, as suspected.'

The colonel blew out more smoke and leant closer. 'Does anyone know of this?'

'No, sir. Not yet, I wanted you to hear it from me first, so we can work out what to do next.'

Taverner nodded, pensive, and eased back in his chair, sipping at his brandy. 'Do you know who it is?'

Blackthorn stared at him and shook his head. 'No.'

For a moment Colonel Taverner wavered, and the lieutenant could tell he was thinking, then spoke in a hushed voice. 'This could be very bad for morale at this time; I suggest we are careful how we handle this. How did you find out?'

Blackthorn, quiet, started to explain. 'There were places and times he could not have known. This proved to me he had insider information prior to each event. Somebody had told him what was going on.'

The colonel looked over at the lieutenant. 'By "him", you mean?'

'Obermaier.'

Colonel Taverner turned to him, surprised. 'But I thought you were in Belgium – doing reconnaissance work. When were your orders changed?'

'Two days prior to me going out. I thought you had approved them, sir?'

Colonel Taverner glanced at the lieutenant and shook his head. 'No. I realised there was an agent in Amsterdam, but I didn't know it was you. Who gave you these new orders?'

'They were signed off by General Erskine.'

Colonel Taverner, perplexed by what Blackthorn had said, brushed it aside, wanting him to continue. 'What did Frederick Obermaier know, exactly?' he asked.

'He knew of my rendezvous with the ship. He didn't know the name, only the time.'

'But you got away?' Colonel Taverner said, puzzled.

Blackthorn took a sip of his brandy as he thought back to the night on the docks in Amsterdam, remorseful he had indeed survived at the expense of another. 'Yes, I did. Might not have done if it had not been for Miss Stanley.'

'What was she doing there?'

'Obermaier used her as bait to draw me out – but as you said, Colonel, I got away. He knew there was a British agent there but not who it was. Miss Stanley realised what had happened when she saw me, and then seized the opportunity to mislead Obermaier.'

'Good God,' exclaimed the colonel. 'This was never meant to happen.'

The lieutenant threw the colonel a confused look.

'Miss Stanley had been sent out there as bait but was never supposed to be in peril,' Colonel Taverner said, and sighed.

Blackthorn took a large sip of his brandy. 'I tried to protect her, sir.' He gritted his teeth. 'But there was interference from another.'

'What do you mean?'

'One of Obermaier's men who worked at the museum.'

The colonel thought for a moment. 'The one she wrote to us about?'

'Yes,' replied Blackthorn. 'Johann van Buren.' Careful, he thought on his choice of words. 'Florence became involved with him.'

The colonel raised his eyebrows in disbelief. 'How do you know she didn't talk?'

'Because,' Blackthorn began, 'I am here before you now. Besides, what did she know? We gave her little information and sent her to Amsterdam under the pretence of looking after the paintings and artefacts at the museum. Florence never knew we had used her as bait to draw out a double agent. Then unexpected events occurred – the Germans began an invasion. I tried to warn her, to get her out of Holland.'

Lieutenant Blackthorn finished his brandy and sat the glass down on the table, then continued his report. 'Van Buren led her into the countryside where Obermaier apprehended her. I viewed from the distance all that happened but was in no position to assist her without putting myself or the mission in danger. I had been following van Buren previously, but it was clear to me I wasn't the only one interested in his whereabouts.'

The colonel, cognisant of the pain on the lieutenant's face, tried to empathise with him. 'These things happen in wartime, Blackthorn. You were not to know she'd get captured at the barn. You did all that you could.'

Colonel Taverner tapped out his now-extinguished pipe, preparing to leave, as Lieutenant Blackthorn moved to rise, but the colonel eased him back down into his seat, realising he was exhausted.

'Stay there, I have other engagements to attend to. You sit for a moment. We will continue our chat tomorrow at the office.' He called to the steward, asking him to retrieve his coat and ordered the lieutenant another brandy. Colonel Taverner then took his leave.

Tired, his body heavy, Blackthorn stared into the fire, allowing the brandy to relax him. It was nice to be warm. His thoughts drifted back to the conversations he had with Colonel Taverner, reviewing in his mind all the questions that arose. Why did the colonel seem to be in such a hurry – hadn't he said his meetings were cancelled? Blackthorn sat for a moment.

'*No!*' Speechless, he jumped to his feet with the condemning words of the colonel going around in his head; his hand slapped across his mouth in complete and utter disbelief.

'How the hell did the colonel know Obermaier's first name? How had he known Florence had been captured at the barn?' For a fact, he had not spoken of the place. How could he know this unless someone else had told him?

The steward returned. 'Everything all right, sir?'

Blackthorn felt sick, flustered with his revelations; incensed, he pushed the steward aside and dashed for the door.

Now everything started to make sense; only Colonel Taverner knew of Florence's mission. Obermaier had turned up at every event because someone had told him what was going on. Florence had written to Colonel Taverner explaining her initial concerns about Johann van Buren, so Obermaier had used him to find out what Florence knew – but she knew nothing. Colonel Taverner's mistake was not knowing that SIS had sent Blackthorn out to Amsterdam – therefore, not able to warn Frederick who the lieutenant was. This explained why Colonel Taverner was not party to the change of arrangements by Erskine. It also illustrated the Secret Intelligence Service had suspected the colonel but had no proof. They'd used Blackthorn to draw Colonel Taverner out as the double agent – but who would believe this of the colonel? There was no evidence. Angry, Blackthorn thought how the colonel had brought Florence into the equation, using her family background against her. He'd manipulated it all. Then he reflected on the colonel's words only a moment ago: 'This was never meant to happen.'

'Such a fool… I've been so blind.'

He stepped outside into the dark and rain and rushed around the corner to get his car. With urgency he started up the engine, still thinking… how cunning the colonel had been, sending him on a reconnaissance mission to Belgium, thinking him out of the way, but not knowing the arrangements had been changed.

Very clever, but not clever enough! He drove off in the darkness of the blackout, wondering how many other treacheries he had committed, being active in the first Great War – had he been responsible for more treason? Who would ever believe he had done anything wrong?

The lieutenant scanned the dark streets for him; he needed to be stopped. Then, by chance, he saw him walking toward the bus stop on the other side of the road. The bus was slowly approaching.

The lieutenant recognised no one would believe him; he kept repeating it to himself, frustrated. The colonel was entrenched in Secret Intelligence and there was no real way he could prove any of this – he knew he remained untouchable. The rage inside him was too much – he had got away with everything; he'd destroyed Florence's life and duped him.

In this moment, clarity came to him and he knew what to do. He revved the engine and with haste drove on the other side of the road, putting his headlights on full beam. The bus driver suddenly caught sight of the car in front of him ablaze with lights; blinded, he swerved to avoid the oncoming vehicle and crossed over onto the path, hitting something and crashing to a halt on the pavement.

Blackthorn casually dimmed his lights and sped off, watching the carnage unfold behind him in the car mirror. Numb, he continued to drive and kept driving until he was miles and miles away. He was unable to stop thinking, his head such a mess; he became very tired, his whole body so very heavy. He pulled over and switched off the car engine. He didn't want to think anymore; not at the moment.

The next morning Lieutenant Blackthorn arrived at the War Office smartly dressed in his uniform and cleanshaven. His colleagues greeted him, pleased for him to be back. No one in the War Office asked where you had been, as they appreciated it was top secret. However, this morning, after greeting the lieutenant, they were also keen to express to him the sad news of the unexpected death of his colleague Colonel Taverner. They said that there had been rumours of another vehicle – but nobody had seen much due to the lateness of the hour.

Empty inside, the lieutenant swallowed hard, but not out of regret or guilt for what had happened but because it was going to be hard to listen to the compliments that would be bestowed upon a dead colleague, a war hero – someone whom he loathed!

Lieutenant Blackthorn had things to do; this war had now, for him, become personal. He had to try to right these wrongs on behalf of a corrupt associate of his who had destroyed people's lives. Now, he had an agenda. And he promised Florence he would fight for her... his dear, innocent Florence.

FORTY-THREE

Darkness cloaked her surroundings, except for a stream of radiant, effulgent light. Its intensity was alluring and so comfortingly serene, a resplendent and enticing draw to a supreme seduction of nirvana, a place she had sighted before, and as beautiful as it was, she did not want to investigate it any further. She was not ready. There were still things she had to do, important things. There was someone she had to find, and they were not here. She did not want to wait, she did not want to remain in this state anymore and she did not want to feel the essence of the light or search amongst the black velvet skies. She wanted her opportunity, and she could sense now that it would not be long. The time was approaching; time to open her eyes... time to see again. It would happen, and it would happen soon. Very soon indeed.

PART THREE

FORTY-FOUR

FRIDAY, 19TH AUGUST 2005

An explosion of thunder burst into the room as the light above forked in rebellious turmoil. The room was barely visible as the lightning strobed intermittently, revealing glimpses of covered items sat preserved in situ, long forgotten through time.

Ginny stepped further into the room as another eruption powered overhead, unsettling her for a moment. James scanned the room, looking for a lamp, and noticed one on the desk. He tried the switch; it clicked on and off – nothing happened. Ginny stood motionless and realised James was speaking to her, but another loud outburst drowned out his voice. Next he turned and made his way out of the house to fetch a torch from the car.

Outside, the rain lashed against the window as the thunder rumbled on in the distance. Ginny, alone now, drew in a deep breath, struck by a sense of familiarisation and nostalgia as she tugged at the dust cover on the desk and dropped it to the floor, staring at the preserved scene before her. All perfectly placed, as if left only yesterday. For years it had remained like this. The dust tickled at her throat as yet another flash of lightning illuminated the empty ink well sat on the desk alongside a pen and old blotter. Thoughts were triggered in her mind, but she was disturbed when she heard the door slam shut as James returned.

'You wouldn't believe this was summer,' he mumbled as he walked back into the room, dripping but with a torch in his hand.

Ginny was unable to stop herself from laughing, as he was truly soaked through; his dark hair had gone so curly.

'Not funny,' he said, aware of her amusement. 'All this wet misery is so you can see.'

'I'm sorry,' she said. 'I do appreciate...' Ginny suddenly stopped, turned back to the desk and pointed to the top drawer. '...think there may be some candles in there.'

James moved to open the drawer and to his surprise found three. 'How did you know?'

Ginny shrugged her shoulders. 'I'm not sure.' She had no explanation and realised how odd this must appear. 'Most old places have some tucked away... don't they?' she said, trying to appear convincing.

James, who was still bemused by her knowledge of the location of the candles, proceeded to light them. 'You will need to phone the electric company in the morning to arrange to get the power reconnected.'

Ginny nodded, but she felt muddled, trying to comprehend how she had got to this day; it was so much to absorb.

James thought all this a bit of a shock for her and, with no amenities, realised she couldn't remain here. 'Where will you stay tonight?' he asked, handing her a lit candle.

'I'm afraid I didn't think that far ahead.'

'Well,' began James, 'my grandmother lives a short distance from here. Let me give her a call and you can stay with us this evening.'

Ginny felt a bit awkward. 'No, I couldn't. Wouldn't want to impose on you.'

'Don't be silly,' James said, aware of her bashfulness, and grinned at Ginny, who thought his smile nice. 'My grandmother loves the company. Besides, you would be doing me a favour as well.'

'Oh, how's that?'

He peered at her with a cheeky glint in his eye. 'There is only so much I can talk about; she might prefer some female companionship for a change. So, you would be helping me out. You will be no imposition… I promise.' Again, he smiled to put her at ease, sensing her hesitancy.

With someone trying so hard to assist her, Ginny realised how fortunate a position she was in and how kind his offer was. 'Thank you, James, that would be great.'

'No problem, I will need to go outside for a minute. Can't get a signal for the mobile here.'

The flame from the candle flickered as he opened the door once more to step out into the rain – less intense now as the storm was quietening.

Ginny returned her attention to the desk, drawn to a brown envelope that lay in the centre. Written by hand, it was addressed '*To Edith*'. This she thought a little strange and discovered on turning it over that it was, in fact, empty.

Why leave this in pride of place on a desk, with nothing inside? As she pondered this, she reached across to a wooden picture frame with a black-and-white photo of a young girl that caught her attention; she believed it to be her grandmother. It was hard for her to imagine, only remembering her as an elderly grey-haired lady, but the picture was lovely, so vibrant and she appeared so happy.

Still holding the photo when James arrived back in the room, Ginny flinched from the bright torch, having become accustomed to the candlelight.

'Sorry,' he said, realising the light shone in her face, and he spotted the photograph she held.

'Nice old picture, anyone you know?'

'Yes, I think, perhaps it's my grandmother? She is so young.' For a second, Ginny mused. 'Any idea of the location?'

James took a look. 'This is the Lyons tea room at the Trocadero in London. Really old, is there a date?'

Ginny turned the frame over – there was nothing visible, so she began carefully to take the back off. The photo slipped out, along with a piece of folded paper. On seeing the inscription on the back of the photo, she initially ignored the other item, more interested in the writing, which was by the same hand as on the front of the envelope, and read:

'Dear Edith, All my love, Florence, 1939.'

This now confirmed the delightful picture of her grandmother. And, more importantly, it proved the existence of a woman that nobody in the family knew anything about. There was so much mystique about this person, and it left Ginny wanting to find out more.

James, in the meantime, had picked up the discoloured piece of paper, curious as to why it had been tucked away in such a place. 'Must have been put in the frame at the same time as the photo – probably over seventy years ago.' He passed the note to Ginny. 'What does it say?'

Ginny unfolded the paper with care. 'There are just two names written down.'

'Is that all?'

'Yes.'

'How very strange,' said James. 'Who are they?'

'A Colonel Godfrey Taverner and Lieutenant Richard Blackthorn.'

On reading out the information, something struck hard in the recesses of Ginny's mind, but she had no idea why.

Even James appeared just as confused as Ginny so decided to update her on the evening's events. 'I've spoken with Grandma and she wanted to cook us dinner tonight. How could I refuse?' he said as Ginny shivered, feeling the cold, stood in her damp T-shirt. 'Come on, we need to get you some dry clothes.'

'You are sure she doesn't mind?'

'Like I said before, she loves the company.'

At this point Ginny noticed his darkened, wet shirt. 'You are soaked too. I'm sorry to have dragged you into this.'

James acknowledged her kindness and shone the torch towards the desk for her.

A moment later she collected the envelope, along with the piece of paper, photo and a large book, not yet examined; she blew out the candle and walked with James to the hallway.

'Haven't even check around the rest of the house,' she said, dismayed.

'You can search tomorrow in the daylight; apparently the

weather is going to improve. Do you have the house keys to lock up?'

Ginny patted her skirt pocket and they both stepped out together, closing the door firmly behind them.

James asked if she wanted to leave her car as they strolled along the path. 'I am happy to drop you off tomorrow, and no point in taking two cars back.'

'Well, if you are sure, I don't want to keep you from any plans at the weekend.'

'Nothing planned anyway, Virginia.'

'Please… call me Ginny.' She smiled at him as they walked on. 'I need to get my bag from the car.'

At the side of the house, Ginny opened the gate, and James saw the vehicle parked at the back. 'Is that your Polo?'

She gazed at him enquiringly – there was no other car. 'Yes?' she responded quizzically.

'Oh,' he said, glancing at her.

'Why do you ask?' said Ginny, confused.

James laughed.

'Why?' she asked once more, ever curious.

After a moment, he managed to stop laughing. 'I happened to watch a little black Polo, just like yours, earlier today. It proceeded to do a "hundred-point turn" on a country lane – severely crunched the gears – before it sped off.'

'Really,' said Ginny, remembering the moment, trying to keep a straight face. 'These country lanes are very narrow.'

'Obviously!' James replied as Ginny opened the car door and leant in to get her bag. James watched as she bent down, noticing her long, slender legs, thinking them very nice when he quickly diverted his gaze as she stood up and locked the car. Ginny turned to him, her hair curly with the rain, and James thought to himself how pretty she was as they strolled off together along the lane to his car.

FORTY-FIVE

After their evening meal, James washed up the last few dishes as Ginny dried them. His grandmother Elspeth had surpassed herself with a delicious homemade dinner, greatly appreciated by both on such a dreadful, wet night. Ginny thoroughly enjoyed her time with Elspeth, thinking her an absolute delight. It made her reminisce on the times spent with her own grandma and she was impressed with how comfortable James and Elspeth were together. It was obvious they got on very well.

James fetched a cup and took the milk off the boil. He placed it on a small tray and took it up to Elspeth, who had drunk a hot chocolate every night for as long as he could remember. Ginny finished wiping the worktops and, on his return, James grabbed the two glasses of wine from the table.

'Come on, we will finish these in the lounge.' He gestured to her and walked out of the kitchen as Ginny followed along behind. On entering the light, cosy lounge, James put the glasses of wine down on the coffee table in front of the fire and went to switch the lamp on.

Immediately, a history of a family – illustrated in an array of many different photographs hung on the wall and others placed on a half-crescent table – shone out brightly. Ginny thought it a beautiful room filled with love. Curious, she moved nearer to the photos and James watched as she studied them in turn.

'You cannot be interested in that collection of "most wanted"?' He laughed.

'They are lovely,' she began. 'Your grandmother clearly cherishes them.'

'Some can be embarrassing.'

Ginny picked up on an unsuspected coyness in James, as he appeared so confident. 'OK, which one are you?' she asked.

'Oh no. You can work that one out for yourself.' James sat back in the chair and took a sip of wine whilst Ginny deliberated before pointing to a photo. To save him from his youthful embarrassment, she instead picked out another gentleman.

'Who is this?' she asked, smiling.

'This, as you probably have a sneaking suspicion, is not me.'

'Needless to say, I was being polite.' She paused, catching the look in his eye as he glanced at her. 'But there is a definite likeness – your father, perhaps?' She spotted the long robes and the mortar board he wore. 'Which university did he go to?'

For a moment James thought as she made her way over to the sofa. 'A lucky guess.' He grinned. 'And I believe my father – Alexander William Elderson – graduated from Kingston in about 1974. A long time ago; hence the rather groovy photo.'

'Oh, really.' Ginny was astonished. 'What a coincidence... my mum studied there.'

'No way!' said James. 'Wonder if they knew of each other?'

They both laughed as James stretched his feet out on the footstool and Ginny focused dreamily on the fire.

James looked over at Ginny, who sat wearing his jogging bottoms and sweatshirt, which were oversized for her, but somehow, she managed to make even them appear stylish. 'Are you warm enough?'

'Yes, thank you, I'm fine.'

'You seemed lost in your thoughts?'

'I was thinking about today and what we found at Redivivus. So much of this doesn't make any sense to me. It's difficult to understand why someone would leave an empty envelope on the desk, why two men's names were written on a piece of paper hidden in a photo frame. It's just bizarre!'

James agreed and had to admit he was none the wiser. 'What was in the black book you brought with you?'

'I've not had a chance to look at it yet.'

James leant forward in his chair. 'Is it nearby?'

'Yes, in the hall—'

Before she could say anything else, he placed his glass on the table and rushed out of the room.

'...by my handbag,' Ginny finished.

A moment later James returned with the book in hand and sat down enthusiastically beside her. 'Come on,' he said, passing it to her. 'Let's see if we can start to find out.'

Ginny looked at him, a little hesitant, then smoothed her hand across the top of the hard cover and took a deep breath. Slowly she opened her Pandora's Box, fearful, as there was no way of knowing if these secrets of her family were going to be good or bad. On the first page, she at once recognised the handwritten script, which matched Florence's hand. The title simply read: *'This book belongs to Florence Stanley. The van Hassel Family Tree. 1939.'*

James turned to Ginny. 'Is this the lady who bequeathed you the house?'

She nodded. 'Until I received the letter, no one had heard of her and none of us were aware of the name van Hassel... strange, isn't it?'

Unable to disagree, he thought for a moment of the picture sat on the desk at Redivivus. 'But you must have known your grandmother's maiden name?' said James.

Ginny took another sip of wine. 'No. Neither my mother nor grandma were aware of this. Grandma's name was Stanley until she married, then she became Bartlett. A secret such as this would be too immense for anyone to keep. They genuinely did not know of their real name – van Hassal!'

James pondered for a moment. 'Something funny about all this.'

Ginny nodded in total agreement and proceeded to turn the next page. Both stared in amazement. Laid out in perfect detail was the beginnings of a family tree, starting with two names: Edith and Florence.

Dumbfounded, Ginny stared at the ancestral history of her family plainly written down before her, the words revealing life stories never yet brought to light, and, if she were honest... it was exciting.

Details of her great-grandparents emerged: Hans Reuben and Henrietta Jane van Hassel. The Dutch connection appeared to be on her great-grandfather's side and her great-grandmother's maiden name – Glassbrook – was British.

'Look,' she said, pointing to the page, 'even the details of my great-great-grandparents. A Colonel Charles Glassbrook and his wife Elizabeth Jane Glassbrook, with her family name of Stoddart. This is a real treasure trove; I'm astounded! To view all this ancestry which no one knows anything about... Why?'

James glanced at her, then at all the written information on the page. 'Don't know, Ginny. Perhaps even Florence struggled to capture all the details; there are question marks on her father's lineage, on dates of birth and deaths. Check here?'

Ginny looked at where James was pointing. 'The seventh of March – this is my birthday!'

'It appears to have been Florence's too... how odd. Why do you think your grandmother never told you anything?'

'No idea.' Ginny shook her head. 'If you asked about the family, she always changed the subject, reluctant to talk. So, over time you stopped asking; even my mother knows nothing of this. What could drive a family to keep such secrets?' Flabbergasted, Ginny finished off the last of her wine.

'Perhaps these are the sort of questions you are meant to find the answers to,' said James.

'I'm on a quest to find out more.' Ginny grinned at him. 'Need to start with Florence. Somehow, she is the catalyst to this. I want to understand more about her. Evidently, she existed, but what happened to her? I feel an affinity to her, but I don't know why.' Ginny raised her empty glass. 'To the quest!'

'I'll drink to that,' said James, '...except I've finished mine as well.'

Ginny closed the book and yawned.

'Perhaps in the morning?' James added.

'I don't want to impose...'

James interrupted her. 'I may be able to help. You are aware, I work in a solicitors' office and on occasion we need to verify documents and records, so I can access a few websites, check a few databases, that sort of thing.'

Enthusiastic at the idea of this, Ginny nodded eagerly at James whilst touching his arm, grateful for his kindness and help. 'Thank you. I'm going to need all the assistance I can get.'

'You are welcome,' said James, pleased at her reaction. He stood up and stretched out his hand. At first, she hesitated before putting hers in his as he gently pulled her up. A little sleepy, she stumbled, and he caught her, putting his arm around her waist to steady her, aware of her slight figure.

'Didn't realise how tired I was,' Ginny said. 'Guess it's been a long and rather odd day.'

Still holding her hand, he led her out of the room. 'Oh,' he said as they continued towards the stairs. 'So you think I'm odd, do you?'

'Well, I didn't like to mention – but come to think of it.' She stopped as they reached the top of the stairs and he turned to her, noting the mischievous twinkle in her eye as he opened the guest bedroom door. He leant in very close to her, and she was aware of the warmth of his breath as he slid his hand along the wall toward the light switch. Ginny grimaced at the harsh brightness and James raised an eyebrow.

'That will teach you to be cheeky.' He gave a wry smile, turned away and whispered, 'Goodnight.'

Ginny grinned and returned the sentiment as he listened to the click of the door. Before going downstairs, he glanced back. James shook his head and sighed, pleased the door was shut and, therefore, so was temptation.

FORTY-SIX

The next morning Ginny awoke to the sunshine streaming in from underneath the heavily patterned curtains. She had no idea of the time but was aware she had slept comfortably. A knock at the door sounded as she sat up in bed.

'Are you awake, dear?'

'Yes, I am. Please come in.'

Elspeth arrived with a big cup of hot tea. 'Hope you don't mind.' She smiled at Ginny. 'I always do this for James when he's here.' She passed the drink over and walked over to the window. 'Such a beautiful day,' she said, and she opened the curtains and pushed up the sash window.

The room immediately filled with the warm glow of a perfect summer's day as the sound of the garden flowed in along with the sweet bouquet of the flowers.

'James is cooking breakfast as a treat for us. Your clothes are dry, hanging over the back of the chair.'

In amazement, Ginny stared, unaware of them being there when she came to bed last night, and, grateful, she thanked Elspeth before watching her leave. Content holding her cup, feeling totally spoilt, she thought of her grandma, so similar in nature, and it was easy to see that Elspeth enjoyed having the company. Happy, Ginny indulged herself in a quiet morning moment snuggling up in the covers, sipping her tea.

A short time later she arrived downstairs to the aroma of cooked breakfast and fresh coffee… her favourite. It made her feel hungry.

James looked over as she stepped in the kitchen. 'Morning. Did you sleep well?'

'Like a log,' she replied as he motioned towards the open door leading to the garden.

'Please, grab a seat, I'm just bringing the food. Grandma is already outside. Hope you're hungry?'

Ginny patted her stomach. 'Starving. Anything I can do?'

'You can bring the drinks if you don't mind, and don't drop them; the coffee is my favourite,' said James as he winked at her.

'Mine too.' She smiled, pleasantly surprised.

With the tray in hand, she followed him to find Elspeth sat under the pergola draped in honeysuckle. The table, all set, faced out to the flower-filled garden. In the warmth of the morning sunshine, they tucked in to a hearty breakfast.

'So, what are you planning to do today?' Elspeth asked whilst curiously looking at both of them.

James glanced at Ginny as he placed his coffee cup down. 'Well, I need to take Ginny back to the house to sort some bits out and collect her car,' he deliberated. 'But if she wants some assistance with anything,' he checked her again, hopeful, 'I'm only too happy to help.'

'That's very kind of you.'

Elspeth considered them, thinking how unusually relaxed they were with one another, as they had only recently met. 'Well,' she said, 'sounds to me like a plan, and I expect, Ginny, you will need a hand. How exciting – you can explore your new house today. James told me a little about the situation this morning.' She then asked who owned the house.

'I believe,' Ginny began, 'although Florence bequeathed it to me, originally it may have belonged to her grandfather, which would be my great-great-grandfather?'

'Ah,' said Elspeth. 'Yes, he would be. What's his name?'

Ginny pondered for a moment, trying to remember the bits of information she had collected so far. 'His name is Charles Glassbrook.'

Elspeth sat upright and stared at her. 'Colonel Charles Glassbrook?'

Both her and James looked at Elspeth, surprised.

'Do you know of him, Grandma?'

'Your grandfather certainly did.'

'How?' James was ever curious.

'Mainly by reputation.'

Ginny grimaced, a little unsure what to expect. 'Good or bad?' she asked cautiously.

'Quite a mysterious character.' Elspeth hesitated. 'But apparently infamous in the Foreign Office.'

'Gosh!' Ginny was shocked. 'This could perhaps explain why none of us in the family have any knowledge of him.'

'You're not likely to either... everything around him was very hush-hush.'

James jumped in at this point, having been sat quietly listening. 'How did Grandfather know him?'

'By name and reputation, when in service in the Second World War.'

James stared at his grandma, perplexed. 'Thought he served in the navy? How would he know someone in the Foreign Office?'

'He also spent a lot of time in the War Office in Whitehall.'

'I didn't realise.'

'To be honest, James, I never understood much of what he did either, and he never spoke of such things; he always said better not to ask, so I took him at his word.'

'What did he tell you about Charles Glassbrook?'

'Some incident that happened about the time of the Great War – not sure what exactly, but I recall your grandfather mentioning his name.' She paused for a moment then continued. 'This was why I remember, because he said so little about anything... unusual.'

Ginny eyed James, astounded. 'Families... how weird is this?'

Elspeth checked them. 'Right, time you two were going; get the most out of this beautiful day.'

'You're not usually so quick to get rid of me, Grandma.' He laughed.

'Today is different. You have Ginny to help.'

FORTY-SEVEN

When they arrived at Silchester, James parked next to Ginny's VW Polo in the recessed area to the left side of the house and smiled. Ginny stepped out, aware he still mocked her for her manoeuvres yesterday.

'Hopefully,' she began, choosing to ignore James's amusement, 'this brute of a key should open up the garden gate.' She pointed over to the wall delineating the end of the parking area of the property, where the gate was positioned to the right.

The latch was old and rusty, and had not been used in a long time. Ginny struggled as James pulled the door tight; she pushed the key in and twisted with force. The gate, stiff at first, creaked and then opened.

Today, the sun shone down and illuminated a most resplendent scene; both Ginny and James gasped as they pushed through and stopped on the path in front of them to absorb this picture of beauty.

A white Jasmine flower in full bloom, its scent so fragrant, trailed up the brick wall to the right-hand side. To the left side of the path, the border was lined with French lavender, alive with the humming of the bees. Behind this sat a broad herbaceous bed full of many different types of flowers, agapanthus, delphiniums, alliums and hollyhocks, all bursting with colour. Behind these on the wall were more espalier fruit trees splayed outward, stretching across the breadth of it. All had been so meticulously kept. It was clear someone attended to this garden with care and love.

Along the path ahead of them an arch covered with climbing pink roses led out to the main terrace. But prior to the end of the path there was an archway on the left-hand side. This led to a porch and what appeared to be the door to the kitchen.

Ginny and James walked ahead through the rose-covered archway onto the terrace that stretched the whole width of the property; its only interruption was an elegant orangery sat central on the terrace leaning out from the back of the house. In front of this were three steps that descended to the perfectly striped lawn, split by a path through the centre. And over to the far right was a small orchard, full of apple trees.

Beyond the garden, on either side was a coppice of trees that joined to a thicket at the very back of the garden, more natural in appearance and delineated by the old flint wall – the same old wall Ginny had noticed as she travelled down the country lane yesterday. Overgrown with vegetation and crumbling in parts, the flint sparkled from the sun's rays, making it quite magical.

'Somebody is maintaining this to perfection,' said James as they both stood in awe, wondering who the elusive gardener might be.

After a moment, James suggested that they go back and try the door to the house; he passed through the arch. Ginny, still staring at the garden in amazement, then turned on her heels to follow.

Access this time was no problem at all. They walked through a dated but pristine kitchen. Ginny looked at the old range as they passed through the doors to stand in the stone-floored hallway. To her left were the two steps that led up to the front hall and the front door that she had entered in through yesterday. Beside her as she strolled along were the stairs to the left, and she stopped in front of them to touch the elegant mahogany Georgian-styled balustrade that rose up to the first floor.

The double doors to the study, only half disturbed from last night, were still open. A quick check inside, and Ginny then decided to see what was beyond the unopened doors opposite. 'Time to explore.' In expectation, she pulled down the handles, and the doors opened. Stunned, she could scarcely believe her eyes.

'Wow. This truly is a time capsule,' said James behind her.

They both moved into the room, astonished, looking around, trying to grasp all they were seeing. An old fireplace stood proud in the centre of the room to the right, and in front of it an old Chesterfield sat upon a large Persian rug. Above the fireplace, catching Ginny's attention, was a hefty framed painting of a middle-aged gentleman in full military uniform.

His proud, bronzed face sported a thick moustache and strong, bearded jaw. Two piercing blue eyes glared down at them.

'My, such an imposing face.' Ginny shuddered. 'You can't help but think we are perhaps intruding in his room. Do you think this may be my great-great-grandfather, Colonel Charles Glassbrook? Check out the background… Where do you think this was painted?'

'Well, certainly not in Britain,' James suggested. 'It appears to be somewhere hot. If we search around, we might find some information. This is a place lost in time.'

Dust sheets covered most items, and they started to pull them off as beautiful pieces of art deco furniture began to emerge. They pulled away another to reveal an old radio in an oak cabinet and, sitting beside this, so beautiful, an old gramophone.

Stood by the old turntable, blowing off the dust from the top, James pulled an old record out of its sleeve and gave an impish smile. 'Shall we give it a go?' He cranked up the arm at the side and listened to the sounds crackling into the air. Such an odd sensation, the rhythmic tones reverberated as though breathing life back into the house.

Ginny shivered as the melodies burst through.

'You can't be cold today,' James said.

'I'm not...' She stopped, realising she couldn't explain, sensing a moment of familiarity in the room, all warm and cosy with the faint smell of tobacco filling the air. '…It's nothing,' Ginny finished and turned away, leaving James to enjoy the music as he walked over to the bookcases that were full of varied topics, some quite old, but most editions appeared to finish at the time of the Great war and were collected from many different countries.

'Ginny, these are amazing.'

Intrigued as to what James had found, she moved beside him.

'So many different genres here – the colonel must have loved his books. Quite a range, from Greek classics, geography, anthropology, military histories to even languages, and so many maps – what do you think he was up to?'

Ginny glanced over at the painting. 'Knowing he worked for the Foreign Office, if he had an interest in all those topics… goodness only knows.' She shrugged her shoulders and decided to continue her explorations elsewhere, moving toward the door. 'I'm going upstairs,' she called to James, who was happy listening to the old 78 of 'Tea for Two'.

The scratchy melody wafted out from the sitting room as she arrived on the landing. Not sure what to expect, she opened the first door and walked in. There before her was an old-fashioned bedroom with a small fireplace. It was quite plain but still had charm and seemed unused. After a quick glance, she closed the door behind her, moving along the hallway.

This time, straight away, as she pushed the door open, she could tell it had been used, but not for a long time. Old fashioned, with its walnut veneer bedroom furniture, it was tidy. Ginny glanced around the room and walked over to the dressing table to look at the misted glass ornaments, comb set and a small perfume jar with faint residue inside. Beside this was a hairbrush. Ginny picked it up, knowing instantly who this room belonged to. A dark strand of hair twisted outward from the bristles. This, something tangible, was evidence of a presence, of somebody who once lived here. She was confident it must be Florence. This made her real.

Ginny carefully placed it back down and turned to look behind her. On the bedside cabinet stood a wooden frame with a black-and-white photo. There were two people, one she recognised as her grandmother and the other one... must be Florence. Ginny sat down on the bed to look at the photo, tracing over the figure of Florence with her finger. She felt sad that nobody ever spoke of her; as a tear fell to her cheek, she was sure in her gut that something bad had occurred – otherwise, why not return? Somehow, she sensed a connection to Florence and needed to find out what happened to her.

After a moment sat quietly on the bed, Ginny noticed the drawer of the cabinet was not flush. When she pushed, it wouldn't go back in. On checking, she was surprised to find the drawer empty. *Perhaps,* she thought, *the problem lies underneath.* And she knelt on the floor to see if anything obstructed the runners. Nothing. Ginny leant forward to feel along the back of the structure when her hand knocked against an item. On closer inspection, there was a brown package stuck to the back – not jammed, but taped there. Why on earth had Florence done this? She tugged at it and it fell, allowing the drawer to close. Ginny turned the dusty old envelope over. It was sealed and addressed '*To Me*'.

Curious, she squeezed the package, believing it must be a small book or a diary, but before she got a chance to peek inside, James called.

With a last look around the room, Ginny took the envelope and rushed downstairs.

As she arrived back in the drawing room, James was sat on the sofa with a pile of hardbacks on his lap. 'Check these out,' James said as Ginny sat down beside him, and he pointed up at the portrait. 'Your great-great-grandfather,' he said, pausing as he patted the books, 'wrote and collected all kinds of different information about India and Afghanistan.'

'What sort of things?' Ginny asked, surprised.

'All sorts – and I only checked a couple of journals. He has collected detailed intelligence on the terrain of the countries he visited – what was he up to?'

Ginny reflected, trying at last to pull together all the bits of information collected over a short period of time. 'OK,' she began. 'Out of the blue, I am bequeathed this property... Redivivus. The solicitors I originally received the details from are situated in Amsterdam. Last evening, we started viewing an ancestral lineage I was not aware of. My ancestors came from Amsterdam and were Dutch, or certainly my great-grandfather was. Now, to add further confusion, we discover my great-great-grandfather, who is English, not Dutch, appeared to work for the Foreign Office... and visited Amsterdam. I think I'm starting to wonder if there is a connection – to Amsterdam?'

James turned. 'Well, I might just be able to help you start.'

Bemused, she considered him.

'The solicitors! We need to get to London.'

'London? Why?' Ginny asked.

'To my office. Come on.'

FORTY-EIGHT

At the steps to the solicitors' office, Ginny glanced up the street to the shop where she first encountered James buying many biscuits.

He turned to beckon her in but realised she lingered, lost in her daydream. 'Penny for them?' he called, distracting her from her thoughts as they walked in the entrance.

'Just thinking of you.'

'All good stuff, I hope?'

'I remember you have a big craving for biscuits.'

James laughed. 'Ah, yes, and I recall you shouted this out at our meeting?'

All was quiet, with it being Saturday, as James led Ginny up the stairs to the first floor and along to his office. At his desk, he switched on the computer, and Ginny put her bag on the chair and strolled over to peer out of the window, glancing down at the small garden opposite, where on her previous visit she'd sat having lunch.

'This will take a moment or two to load up,' he announced as he jumped up. 'Do you want a cold drink?'

Ginny nodded as James headed off down the hallway to a small kitchen. There he opened the fridge and grabbed the only two options – sparkling water and cola – then headed back.

Ginny sat at the desk with her folder in front of her and began to sift through some information.

'Pinched my seat?' James said as he entered, holding both drinks in the air, and Ginny indicated to the water as he pulled the other chair over to sit beside her.

'Right, where do we start?' Ginny turned to James, who was logging in to the computer.

'Your initial contact came from our partners in Amsterdam – Stelling, Olly and van Horst – so let's begin there.'

'Sounds like a plan.' Ginny picked through some of the paperwork from the book as James began by talking of the facts in order to use these to search the database.

'So, Florence, your great-aunt, at some time registered this letter with our company in Amsterdam. After the death of Edith, it got sent over to our London office, and we were to locate and track down the client,' he rested, 'that is, you, as they discovered because of the very specific criteria – which was?' James looked at Ginny in anticipation.

'My date of birth: 7th March.'

'How odd,' said James. 'Why would Florence bequeath the property to someone by their birthdate?'

Ginny looked at him. 'I have absolutely no idea. When I received the letter, I thought this strange and I'm still no clearer.'

They both sat back for a moment. Then James had a thought and began typing once again. 'We can try and work out where she had been before.'

'What do you mean?' Ginny asked, interested.

'Well, bit of a long shot – may not lead to anything, but worth a go.'

'You've lost me.'

'I'm going to do an internet search on van Hassel – see what comes up.'

'Ah, got you, good idea.'

After a short time searching, it was apparent they were not having much luck, and a little despondent, James got up to open the window and stretch his arms as the mid-afternoon sun shone in.

Ginny, with a new thought, quickly beckoned him back. 'We are not thinking about this correctly,' she said getting more excited as he sat back down to listen. 'We're searching under the wrong name!' she explained. 'Remember, she didn't use the name van Hassel.'

James quickly realised what Ginny was saying. 'Of course; we should be looking under Stanley. Let's try again.'

With the correct details entered this time, James hit the button. They both waited, looking intently at the screen. Before long, many names appeared before them.

As they scrolled down, one jumped out at Ginny. 'James… there! Stanley. They are connected to the British Museum.'

Excited, indicating again towards the monitor, he clicked on the relevant title as it brought up another page with the new information. Amazed, they hurriedly began reading. 'Can't believe this,' said Ginny, 'she worked as an archivist. Incredible! I had no idea.' For a moment, Ginny sat back, trying to absorb all the new information.

James continued to read and, without taking his eyes off the screen, patted her arm to get her attention to a sentence at the bottom of the page. 'Read this.'

Ginny looked to where he pointed.

'Florence Stanley later assisted with the movement of artefacts and works of art from the Rijksmuseum in Amsterdam at the beginning of the war. Sadly, reported missing, she never returned.'

'Oh my God,' exclaimed Ginny, unable to believe what was written. 'This is so sad... but is making sense with the few snippets of information we have.' She turned to James. 'Why didn't she come back? What happened to her?'

James watched as her green eyes filled up, and he rubbed her arm. 'You OK?'

'Yes, I'm fine, being silly.' She hesitated. 'Somehow, I feel a connection to Florence – it sounds daft, but I want to find out what happened to her.'

James nodded – he understood – wondering if she needed a moment, and thought she might like a coffee. He walked off to put the kettle on, thinking about all they had discovered, not only today, but when they were at the house. Whilst placing two mugs on the worktop, something struck him, and he left them to return to Ginny.

'Do you have the note which fell out of the picture frame?'

Ginny grabbed the folder and rummaged through it until she found what she was looking for. 'Yes, here.'

'What are the two names?'

With care unfolding the faded brown paper, she read them out. 'Colonel Godfrey Taverner and Lieutenant Richard Blackthorn.'

In the background, the kettle boiled as James told

Ginny to do a search for both and strolled back to make the coffee. So, starting with Colonel Taverner, the search began. A moment later, the drinks arrived as many of the same surnames appeared on the monitor. The list was endless, when she caught sight of a 'Taverner' followed by the initial 'G' rank, 'Colonel'.

'Any luck?' James asked as he passed her coffee.

'This must be the one, surely.' She highlighted the name and clicked. 'My, such a lot of information.'

He looked over as she sipped her drink. They both read down the list of the colonel's life story and military history with all his commendations, awards and medals from his obituary.

'Goodness, a busy man,' commented James.

'Been all over the place, even before the First World War. Look here, at this bit.' Ginny pointed and nearly choked on her coffee as she read the literature underneath this.

'Are you all right?' asked James, patting her on the back as she coughed and spluttered. Then he realised what had caused this.

> *'Colonel Godfrey Taverner worked alongside the late Colonel Charles Glassbrook in counter espionage, prior to the First World War.'*

'Good God! He worked with your great-great-grandfather!'

They could hardly believe what they were reading.

'Unbelievable! Such a small world,' Ginny said, now recovered.

'What on earth was Charles doing with Colonel Taverner?' remarked James.

'The plot thickens?' Ginny stared at James as he read further down.

'This appears to be his obituary from *The Times*. You'll never believe this.' Ginny leant over. 'It's mainly military jargon, as expected,' said James, 'but see who wrote the quote?'

Again, Ginny checked, and was awestruck. 'Lieutenant Blackthorn! They must have worked together.' Amazed, she stood and walked over to the window, feeling the light breeze drift in. 'What was Florence doing with these guys?'

James shook his head and began typing.

'Do you think Florence was aware this Taverner may have been connected to Charles?' Ginny gazed out the window as James began another new search. Within seconds, more lines of information appeared.

'Guess what, Ginny...'

Hesitating, she stared at him. 'What?

'Lieutenant Blackthorn... is alive! Discharged from the army with the rank of major.'

'Crikey, how old must he be?'

'Not sure, but you'll be amazed at this.'

'Oh no, I can't bear it. What?'

'He only lives a short distance from here.'

'No way!'

FORTY-NINE

James checked the postcode as he punched the information into the satellite navigation system in the car; a moment later, the route was planned. Ginny read through all the paperwork they printed off on Major Richard Blackthorn, and his home address, as they drove.

'I can't believe this guy is still alive – born on 10th January 1918.'

'Blimey, how old does that make him?' He turned right into Wimpole Street as she did some calculating.

'Must mean he is eighty-seven years old.'

'Gosh, a good age. Do you think he will be lucid to talk to us?'

'We won't know until we get there.'

'What time is he expecting us?'

'When I spoke to his housekeeper, she told us to arrive at about four o'clock. Don't think he would have seen us if I had not mentioned this was in connection with information we were searching for on Florence van Hassel. Must have recognised the name… as I didn't say Stanley.'

'Well, his memory obviously isn't too bad then.'

They drove through London, past Marble Arch and entered Hyde Park, going along South Carriage Drive. The gardens were beautiful in the sunshine, busy with people enjoying the space. At this point Ginny reflected on what they might find out about Florence and what happened to her all those years ago. It was ironic that it could be someone from outside of the family who might be the person to tell her all about her ancestor – how strange.

James asked for the major's address.

'Flat 4, Kensington Crescent.'

'Very nice,' he commented. 'He's done all right for himself.'

They turned in to the road, trying to find a parking place when Ginny pointed to a Victorian redbrick building. 'There it is.'

'OK, I will turn around.' He decided it would be rude to be late for their appointment, so he went back and dropped Ginny off.

'You go on in and I will park the car somewhere and walk back – at least you will be on time.'

Ginny hated not to be punctual for anything, so she jumped out of the car and stood at the steps in front of the building. 'Here goes,' she muttered to herself, tightening her grip on the folder, and she proceeded to climb the few steps to the entrance. There was a list of names beside the flat numbers. On seeing Blackthorn, she pressed the intercom button and waited. There was silence, then a crackling noise, followed by a lady's voice requesting her name.

'Virginia Faulkner,' she spoke clearly. 'I have an appointment at four o'clock with the major.'

There was a pause. 'You are expected. We are on the second floor, door on the right as you arrive or, if you take the elevator, straight ahead as you exit.'

Another sound crackled out before the door buzzed open. Ginny walked through to the entrance hall and decided to take the stairs, arriving at the second-floor landing. In front of her was a heavy oak door with the nameplate for Blackthorn – Flat 4. A little nervous, she hesitated, then knocked.

After a moment, a short, middle-aged woman, dressed in a pale blue tunic, greeted her at the door and ushered her in to the hall. At the end of the hallway were double doors, of which one was open, allowing her a glimpse of a bright, sunny room. The housekeeper showed Ginny through.

Stood ahead of her was a large central window with two high-backed chairs at either side of a cherry wood crescent table. Above this hung a painting of a windmill. In the alcoves, on either side of the window, were bookshelves, full to the top. To the right sat a beautiful mahogany desk with a few small objects, when she caught sight of a rather dilapidated box file, which appeared out of place, as everything else was so spotless. Ginny looked once more to the painting with its stormy rainclouds, trying to think where she had seen it before, when, unexpectedly, the door behind her opened.

An elderly gentleman walked into the room, impeccably dressed, slim and very well presented. Still with a full head of white hair, combed to the side and tidy, he wore a short-sleeved shirt and light-coloured trousers, and his Loake shoes shone. Ginny didn't mean to gawk at him, amazed; he appeared so much younger than his eighty-seven years.

His bright blue eyes observed her for a moment, transfixed by her image. Then he spoke quietly. 'I'm sorry, my dear, to stare so… you remind me of someone from a long time ago.' With a tenderness, he smiled at her. 'So similar – except for your fair hair.'

He approached Ginny and shook her hand; holding on to it, he looked straight into her eyes, almost as though he searched for some familiarity within her, and she shivered with the intensity of the look. Then he released her hand and motioned for her to have a seat as he moved to the desk, drawing his finger along the top of the old file, aware it may unleash long-forgotten memories. 'So, my dear, I believe Florence brings you to my door.'

For a moment they waited as a tray with two glasses and a jug of iced water arrived with the housekeeper. Placed on the small table near Ginny, the housekeeper then walked out, and Major Blackthorn sat down on the opposite chair. 'Please.' He gestured.

'Would you like some?' Ginny asked, picking up the crystal jug.

He nodded, thinking how similar her movements were to Florence's, even her mannerisms. 'How do you know of Florence?' the major asked.

It seemed odd to Ginny, but she couldn't help thinking the major – somehow, in some way – had been expecting her.

'Well,' she began, 'all a bit unusual.' And she lifted the file from her bag. Ginny opened the file, took out an old black-and-white photo and offered it to him.

Surprised at seeing the picture, checking it, he stroked his finger lightly over the faded image. 'This is her,' he pointed, 'and the other young girl is Edith. I never met her.'

'She is – or rather, was – my grandmother.'

'Was?'

'Yes... she passed away in June.'

'I'm sorry to hear that.' His hands clasped together, he sighed, thoughtful.

'May I ask how you knew them both?' Ginny said, aware the major's eyes stared back at her with kindness, emotional, before he turned to look out of the window beside him.

'Such a long time ago now.' He glanced out, remembering Florence sat in the car the morning they went down to the harbour. The sun had been shining and she seemed so relaxed as they drove along, the light reflecting on her auburn hair. The memory of her on this morning, he had never forgotten. To compose himself from his thoughts, he swallowed before the guilt he carried rose to consume him once more.

'I met Florence Stanley in February 1940 not long after war had broken out. An archivist working at the British Museum. Another gentleman and I visited her at the museum for a specific reason.'

Ginny considered him curiously as he got up and went to his desk, opened a drawer, took out a photo, which he glanced at, and then passed it to her.

'This was taken at the front of the museum.' He hesitated. 'I had her under surveillance.'

Surprised, Ginny stared up at him. 'Surveillance? Why? Had she done something wrong?'

'No – she did nothing wrong!' His eyes cast down, he sighed, remorseful, and took a sip of his water. 'It was us... we did wrong by her.'

Sad, he reflected on the evening in 1940, and the inquisition which he and Colonel Taverner had put her through. Oh, how they had used her. Agitated, he rubbed his forehead.

Ginny realised this was bringing back a lot of uncomfortable memories for the major, but at the same time her curiosity was growing. What had happened to Florence? 'How did you do wrong by her?'

For a moment he thought. 'Because we dared to ask her to help us, that's why.'

Ginny was perplexed at his answer as he stared at her.

'You are so like her in so many ways. Your eyes.' For a moment he lingered. 'We needed her; you have to remember, this was at the beginning of the Second World War – hostilities were high and spies everywhere. Our job in Secret Intelligence was to make sure the country was safe and secure.'

Ginny took a sip of water, absorbing all the major said. 'What on earth did you make Florence do?'

FIFTY

The major stood at his desk, opened the dilapidated box file, the one Ginny had spotted earlier, and took out a faded old file, which he then handed to her.

'What is this?' Ginny asked curiously as she read the faint red lettering stamped on the front: 'Classified'.

'A dossier I kept.' The major sat down in his chair. 'We showed this to Florence on…' He saw Ginny had already opened the file. 'You don't have to read it now.' She looked at him. 'There is information I'm sure will help to answer a lot of questions you may have,' he hesitated, 'but it is for you to keep.'

Ginny was overwhelmed. 'Are you sure?'

'I was minding it for Florence, but it's not mine to care for anymore.' He smiled. 'Your job now.' The major nodded to the file on her lap. 'All very complicated. You shall see this when you read through those notes, and parts are still classified – some of the truth is not known to this day.'

Ginny considered what he had said, but one burning question came to her mind: *Why did Florence go to Amsterdam?* However eager she was to ask this of him, she was also aware of a melancholy that hung over him with regard to Florence, making it difficult to ask, so she rephrased her question. 'Did you know her very well?'

He glanced at her. 'Not as well as I would have liked to. We met through the job. Part of my duties was to watch over and protect her.' He reflected sadly, then gazed candidly at Ginny. 'But I couldn't save her.'

Aware this was hurting him, Ginny softened her voice. 'What happened? We can only appreciate that she never returned?'

The major cleared his throat and stiffened up. 'Johann van Buren! That's what happened to her.'

Ginny duly noted the major nearly spat the words out and she shivered on hearing this name with a sense of knowing, but how could this be? 'Who is Johann van Buren?'

Major Blackthorn was just about to answer when the housekeeper came back into the room to inform him a young man was asking after him. Ginny explained that James was helping with her research. Blackthorn nodded at the housekeeper, who then showed James in, and he strode towards the major, introduced himself and shook his hand.

The major sat down again. It was quiet for a moment, and the major observed Ginny, experiencing a sense of connection with her to Florence, and allowed his mind to drift back in time, thinking he could once again see Florence sitting in the chair in the office of the British Museum. He remembered how drained she had looked after the colonel had told her all about her unknown family history. The major had watched her, seeing the determined look in her eyes as she agreed to Colonel Taverner's polite but near-insistent request to go to Amsterdam. Her gentle, dark eyes, the innocence he saw in them, along with her grace and beauty, made him sad. His thoughts were disrupted as Ginny then asked the one question she really wanted an answer to.

'Why did she go to Amsterdam?' Ginny looked straight at the major as she asked.

'We arranged for her to go over to Amsterdam on the pretext of Florence actually doing her job as an archivist. She was to continue with the work she did over here at the British museum but at the Rijksmuseum: collecting paintings and artefacts to be moved to safety for their protection against the impending war.'

'Did you send her over there?'

'Not me, per se – Colonel Taverner, my commanding officer at the time, arranged it.'

'So, all she was supposed to do was her job?'

The major thought about his words. 'Yes... and no.'

Ginny peered at him, confused. 'If you and this Colonel Taverner sent her to Amsterdam to continue working, was this a pretence or not?'

'No. It was important she continued her work. The paintings and artefacts needed to be protected; all museums were warned of the destruction and theft that could occur in conflict. We were aware she had been preparing many items in the British Museum to be moved out of London, sent to New York to the Metropolitan Museum for protection.' He delayed, taking a sip of water. 'We also wanted Florence for another purpose.'

'What other purpose?' Ginny was almost fearful of asking.

The major looked awkward at this point and shifted a little in his chair. 'We had reason to believe within the Secret Intelligence... we had a double agent!'

Ginny stopped to absorb what he had said; she was shocked. 'What did this suspicion have to do with Florence?'

'It didn't. This was the point... she knew nothing. We were using her as bait, hoping to attract interest as to why a British national had been sent to Amsterdam. The Dutch had their suspicions of an infiltrator working for the Germans but could not determine who. When Florence arrived to work at the Rijksmuseum, they would think she was an English spy.'

Ginny leant back in her chair in disbelief. Major Blackthorn saw the disappointment on her face.

'So, you used her?'

Saddened by her words, the major recognised they were true. 'In a time of war, we did what we needed to.' Again he turned to look directly at Ginny; she reminded him so much of Florence. 'I did everything I could to keep her safe.' He hesitated. 'It's just there were other elements.'

Ginny thought on all he had been telling her, thinking of his disdain for one name he mentioned previously. 'Did it have something to do with the man you mentioned earlier?'

The major frowned and then answered, 'Johann van Buren?'

At this point, James, who was sat quietly listening, interrupted. 'Did you say van Buren?'

Quick as a flash, Major Blackthorn turned to James and studied him with his piercing blue eyes, wary as to why he asked. It made him feel very uneasy. 'Yes.'

James recoiled at the coldness of his reply, not sure whether the name or his asking had brought this change in the major. James smiled to allay any concerns. 'It's nothing,' he said, 'thought I recognised the name, probably just work-related, or something similar.'

Ginny too discerned the major's attitude towards James but did not want him to stop talking; they were making so much progress. However, Blackthorn seemed distracted and called to his housekeeper, requesting she bring him a glass of brandy.

'The bottle is empty,' she said.

Not too alarmed on hearing this, the major then checked James, knowing what he was doing. 'Do you think you be so good as to fetch me another bottle from the shop at the end of the road?'

James stood up. 'Of course, Major, I will go now.' He was only too happy to oblige.

Blackthorn appeared pleased with this and as James left the room the major relaxed a little before returning his attention to Ginny.

'How are you connected to this man?' He spoke in reference to James, which took her by surprise.

'Well, essentially, he is the solicitor assisting me with the inheritance I received.' She wondered if the major would be aware of anything regarding this. 'The house which belonged to Florence that was bequeathed to me after the death of my grandmother, Edith, in June.'

The major rose from his chair and headed to his desk to open a drawer. There he took out a folded piece of paper and handed it to Ginny. 'I took this from Redivivus.'

Ginny took it from him, knowing he did recognise the property, as she had been careful not to say the name of the house.

'I didn't take it for any other reason than to protect Edith,' he said. 'Think I left the envelope. Not sure why.' He shook his head.

Ginny understood. This would explain why she had found the opened envelope on the desk with nothing inside yesterday, but now she held the letter in her hand. Before reading it, she simply asked him why.

'Because,' he sighed, 'Florence, as you will read, left her information on why she had gone to Amsterdam. I didn't want this knowledge to put Edith in danger... she had suffered enough with having lost Florence.' Sad, he moved closer to Ginny. 'Edith never stepped a foot inside of the house – she knew nothing of it.'

In this moment Ginny realised the major was the only other person with knowledge of the house. 'Is it you, Major, who has been looking after Redivivus?'

'Yes, it was the very least I could do, but it is your job now.' He stopped. 'You remind me so much of her,' he said, 'in so many ways.' He smiled, viewing her as though once more seeing Florence.

Flustered on hearing the door shut as James arrived, the major stepped away from her, putting his guard up again; the softness in his eyes changed as he put on his militarily trained exterior. Without doubt, he was cautious of James. 'You need to be careful with this man,' he warned quickly, 'especially if he is acquainted with a van Buren!'

Before he could say any more, James entered the room with a bottle of brandy which he gave to Blackthorn. At this point, Ginny wondered if the major recognised he had no brandy left and had manipulated the situation to remove James.

Blackthorn poured himself a glass of brandy and sat down. A distant expression veiled over his face. Ginny realised it was time to go. And time to reflect on all the new information received. Before leaving, she asked if it would be possible to speak to him again, and the major was happy to agree. Ginny leant forward to shake his hand, seeing the softness in his eyes, knowing somehow Florence had melted his heart all those years ago, something he still felt to this day. *Strange*, Ginny thought; she felt so at ease with him, and it didn't feel like an unfamiliar visit. She was comfortable when kissing his cheek, like visiting an old friend. But what had bothered her was his warning about James.

FIFTY-ONE

As they both stepped outside, James pointed up to the end of the long street to where he had eventually managed to find a parking space. The early-evening air was balmy as they strolled along. When they arrived at the car, James spotted a wine bar on the corner.

'Come on,' he said, 'I'm thirsty, and so must you be.' He grabbed Ginny's hand and crossed over the road. Tables and chairs were set up outside on the path under a large parasol with a few people chatting and drinking. The bar inside was rustic, vibrant, and music played out above the voices of the many. James squeezed his way to the bar, still holding Ginny's hand.

'What would you like to drink?'

'White wine, please – with lots of ice.'

James ordered, and a moment later they collected their drinks and checked for a seat outside. Both were happy; it was nice just to sit and enjoy the moment. James rolled his shirt sleeves up and took another gulp of his beer, then asked Ginny about Major Blackthorn.

'Did you notice at one point his attitude towards me changed?'

'Yes... yes, I did. When I asked about somebody called van Buren.'

'And I said at the time – it was in connection with work.' James paused. 'But actually... it was nothing to do with work.'

Startled at what he said, Ginny glanced over at him and reflected on the major's warning, but as she looked into his soft green eyes, there was no sense of fear, so she had to be honest with him. Something told her honesty was everything. 'The major,' Ginny began to feel a little awkward, 'actually warned me about being careful of you.'

James shook his head in disbelief, taken aback at what she had said. He stared at her, perplexed. 'Why?' James said, confused. 'The major only just met me today! Such an old sceptic, he mistrusts everyone. It was his job, after all – and he's still living it.'

Ginny took a sip of her wine, her face flushed, having caught a bit of sunshine, and James thought she looked even prettier. 'You don't need to be wary of me... I would never harm you.'

Ginny knew instantly, aware of the softness in him as he spoke those words to her, that this was true. Touched by his sentiment, knowing deep down she could trust him, she liked how he regarded her in that moment.

'I know,' she said, and smiled at him. 'But how do you know this van Buren?'

'Well, I only know the name... more to do with my father.'

'Oh, really,' she said as James continued.

'I believe my father met a Jack van Buren at university. I know nothing more; it's just an unusual name so easy to remember – but my dad may be able to tell us something. Could be interesting?' James finished his pint, placed the glass on the table and then gestured to Ginny. 'Come on, let's go.'

'Where to?' she asked.

'Drink up and you will find out.'

After a short drive across London, the car pulled onto a gravelled driveway in front of a light brick Victorian house at an address in Richmond. Ginny looked across at James as he switched off the engine.

'This is where my parents live... in fact, where I once lived.'

Ginny stared at him, a little shocked. 'Are we going to meet your parents?'

'Funny when you say that – but I guess, yes.' James grinned.

'Crikey,' exclaimed Ginny.

James was startled at her reaction.

'I'm sorry,' said Ginny, realising how it must have sounded. 'Didn't mean that quite as it came out.' She grimaced, trying to explain. 'I don't mind in the slightest meeting your parents; I'm more concerned as to how I look – what they might think of me, as I have never met them before.' With haste, she grappled in her handbag, pulled out her comb to tidy up her hair, then squirted herself with perfume.

James coughed and laughed. 'Stop! You don't need to panic about anything – my parents are really easy-going... and you are fantastic anyway.'

Ginny blushed. 'Sorry, I didn't expect this.'

James patted her arm. 'Come on, and don't be silly – besides, how could anyone not like you?'

Ginny followed James as he opened the front door and

stepped into a lovely spacious hallway with black-and-white diamond floor tiles. A soft breeze blew through the hall, bringing with it the sound of music and laughter.

James took her hand, sensing her anxiety. 'They must be out back.'

Walking to the end of the hall, it led them into a light, spacious kitchen with glass doors wide open, giving access to the garden. Sat at a table outside were his parents, absorbed in what they were doing, not even noticing them at first.

'You should have been paying attention, Helena,' admonished Alex.

'Not fair, you owe me money for Old Kent Road.'

On hearing a noise, Alex turned, surprised, then was excited to see them. Ginny noted his broadening smile on acknowledging James as Helena looked up from the chaos of the board game.

'Darling!' she shouted, and stood up. 'How lovely, when did you creep in?' She bustled in to receive a kiss and a hug as Alex got up to pat his son on the back.

Ginny viewed it all, feeling a little awkward, but James pulled her beside him, introducing her to both. With no hesitation, Helena grabbed Ginny, almost hugging the life out of her, then sat her down at the table beside her. Ginny caught her breath as she sat there, thinking how welcoming they were. Next Helena picked up the empty jug on the table and indicated to Alex to refill and get extra glasses.

'You'll have a Pimm's, won't you?' Helena said as she turned to talk to Ginny, who simply couldn't refuse.

Alex ushered James back to the kitchen with the empty vessel. 'So, what brings you home?' said Alex.

James waited, knowing there would be another question as his father grinned mischievously, looking in the direction of the garden. 'And who is that charming young lady? Tell me all.'

James couldn't help but laugh. 'I've only just met Ginny, and it's not quite as it may appear.'

'Oh, indeed.' Alex raised his brow. 'How does it seem then?' he asked as he mixed up a fresh pitcher of Pimm's.

'I know Ginny through work,' said James.

'Does she work with you?'

'No, Dad, she is a client. We messed up her keys for her property in Hampshire, gave her the wrong ones. I knew she was going down to the house and wouldn't get in, so I went to deliver them to her... and the next thing was the awful weather!'

'Ah yes, the storm, some amazing flashes of lightning. Mum and I watched from the bedroom window before the downpours of torrential rain.'

'True, it was spectacular, lasting for most of the evening. And without a doubt, it added an atmosphere to a house just opened for the first time in years. Lit only by candles, with no electricity! It's a time capsule, for sure. However, we were lucky; Ginny's house isn't far from Grandma's.'

'Did you stay with Grandma?' Alex asked.

James glared at his father. 'You already know this, don't you?'

Alex laughed. 'Of course I do. Your grandma was straight on the phone to your mother after you'd left this morning – although we were not expecting to see you. This is a lovely surprise.'

A tray of glasses was passed to James and they both walked back into the garden.

'Actually, Dad,' James began as he sat down, 'we were hoping you might be able to help us with research we're doing into Ginny's family background.'

Alex put the jug on the table, intrigued. 'Me? How can I help with that?'

'Wow, this sounds far more exciting than a game of Monopoly,' added Helena.

'Only because you're losing,' interjected Alex as he passed her a drink stuffed full of fruit and mint.

Helena peered at Alex, then the glass. 'Did you do that on purpose?'

'What!' he said, and laughed.

'Don't do it to Ginny's, she'll never come back.'

Ginny laughed, thinking how at ease she was sat there in their garden. As she turned to James, she was aware he had been watching her; feeling protected, even cared for, she smiled at him.

Then Alex spoke. 'What could I possibly know to assist you two?'

So, briefly James explained the information they had discovered over the last couple of days, tracing a genealogy that, until lately, nobody thought existed. Both Helena and Alex listened attentively to what they had to say.

'The strange thing is,' James continued, 'prior to coming here we went to meet this old guy, Major Blackthorn, who worked with Ginny's Great-Aunt Florence. So incredible when you think about it.'

'Crikey,' said Alex. 'What age must he be?'

Ginny then explained, 'We couldn't believe it when we searched his information on the computer and discovered he was still alive, living in London! He's eighty-seven, but, having met him earlier, he is sharp for his age.' She wavered. 'It sounds silly to say, but I couldn't help but feel he was, in some small way, expecting me.' She glanced at James, who nodded in agreement.

Alex noted the look between them.

'Why would you think that?' asked Helena.

For a moment Ginny thought back to her meeting with the major. 'The information he gave me was sat ready and waiting on his desk. He never seemed surprised at what I had to say or to ask.'

'Oh,' Helena remarked, 'that does sound a bit odd considering you only phoned and arranged to meet him today.'

Ginny nodded. 'We also discovered he has been caring for Redivivus all this time.'

James turned to Ginny in surprise, as Alex and Helena appeared confused. 'Redivivus,' clarified James, 'is the house Ginny has inherited from her Great-Aunt Florence.'

Both nodded. 'But what has the major got to do with this house?' Alex asked.

Ginny shrugged her shoulders. 'I don't know. Not even my grandmother knew anything about the house. The major had kept it a secret from her when Florence never returned. He told me it was all done to protect her.'

'I think Major Blackthorn is more than capable of hiding and manipulating situations,' remarked James.

Ginny agreed. 'Part of who he is and what he was trained for – although I believe Florence touched him in some way, as he softened whenever he spoke of her.'

James grunted. 'Well, he didn't when he spoke to me – not that he said much, and he appeared wary of me!' He laughed.

Ginny acknowledged there had been a change in the major toward James. 'True – Blackthorn's attitude towards you differed after he revealed a name, one that you recognised.'

Alex was interested at this. 'But who could you be acquainted with in connection to him?'

'So odd,' said James, 'but I don't actually know the person, and maybe there is no link at all,' he added, looking at his father. 'But you, Dad, might have an idea... a name you know but speak little of.'

Alex stared back at James, confused but at the same time intrigued. 'Don't keep me in suspense... what's the name?'

'The major mentioned a Johann van Buren.'

On hearing this, Ginny shivered and caught the shocked expression on Alex's face – frozen, as though someone walked over his grave. Even Helena stopped short. James was only too aware of the reaction of his parents when he presented the name to them.

FIFTY-TWO

Alex turned to Helena, who placed her glass on the table and watched as he stood up and then paced up the garden, reflecting back over the many years. It was obvious those recollections were hard to recall.

James eyed him, a bit surprised. 'Is everything all right, Dad?'

'Yes.' For a second, he faltered. 'I've not recalled that name in a long time. To be honest with you, it was not Johann van Buren – but Jack.'

Helena glanced at him as he swallowed, trying to suppress the memory of his friend and the terrible consequences of the evening, and his death. Ginny was taken aback and realised something dreadful must have happened.

'I'm so sorry to have mentioned this name,' Ginny said, '... especially as it brings back sad memories for you.'

Alex looked over. 'Please don't apologise; it's not your fault, but there is a connection to my friend Jack. You see, Johann was his father, but what he has to do with your Great-Aunt Florence... I have no idea.'

Perplexed, Ginny agreed. 'Neither do I. In fact, until today I'd never even heard of Johann van Buren. Whatever his connection was to Florence, it was clear Major Blackthorn held him responsible for something – perhaps the reason she never returned home?'

After a moment Alex got up and went into the house. Helena, who had been sat quietly, spoke. 'Well,' she started, 'this is for you two to find out about.' She stretched over and topped up their glasses. 'Let's drink to new beginnings.' They raised their glasses as Helena began extracting more information about how Ginny and James met.

A short time later, Alex came back into the garden holding a small box, which he placed on the table. The lid was tight as he pushed it off and took out an old colour photograph of his dear friend Jack and passed it over to James, who in turn showed this to Ginny. Then he began to tell them how he had first met Jack whilst at Dulwich College in London, a long time ago. Whilst speaking he noted how Ginny stared at the photo; strangely, he thought in some way she reminded him of Jack. *Probably her blonde hair,* he thought. Staring more intently, he noticed her green eyes, but he was disturbed suddenly as James shivered.

'What's the matter?'

'Not sure, I just get an odd feeling,' James said. '...did he die in a bad way?'

'What makes you ask that?'

James shrugged his shoulders. 'No idea.'

'As it happens,' Alex hesitated, 'yes, he did.'

James stared over. 'Was he murdered?'

Helena, startled by what James had asked, knocked over a glass, breaking the silence, and watched as it shattered into many pieces. 'Oh, how clumsy of me.' She rushed off to get something to clear it up.

Ginny and Alex both stared at James, bewildered.

Alex decided to continue to explain where he met Jack. 'After Dulwich and our days at boarding school, our friendship grew stronger as he went off to University College London and I went off to Kingston University.'

Ginny smiled as he said this, as she recognised the name and informed Alex her mother went there.

'Really! Such a small world… what did she study?'

'Believe it was Art History.'

In disbelief he stared at her. 'Crikey! Same as me… what was your mum's name?'

'Faulkner,' she gave in expectation as he tried to recall the name.

'No, sorry, I don't recognise it – such a long time ago now.' Alex carried on, recalling their friendship and the details leading up to Jack's death. It brought back memories for him that were hard to deal with.

James sensed his father's pain at the loss of his friend and thought it tragic. It made him feel cold, even scared him a little, that he could empathise so easily with the event. To relieve the tension, he offered to make some coffee and headed off to put the kettle on.

Alex began to root through the years of memorabilia stored in such a simple cardboard box as Ginny turned, realising all this had affected James, and followed him into the house.

Helena watched her go as Alex caught sight of the look on her face.

'Don't go interfering, now, will you?'

'What? Didn't say a word, but they do appear so good together, don't they?'

Alex looked back at them. 'Yes, they do!'

Ginny stepped in the kitchen and James turned, smiling at her. Conscious, peering into his eyes, she sensed some pain. 'Are you OK? The story appeared to affect you?'

'Yes, I'm fine.' He then continued making the coffee and, for a moment, looked back at her. 'When Dad explained about Jack' – she moved closer to gently rub his arm – 'I went cold, as though I was there.'

He shook his head, but strangely enough Ginny didn't think it odd; although she'd never said, the affinity she sensed on discovering Florence was as real to her, perhaps, as this moment was for James to Jack…

'Sometimes,' she said, 'these emotions can't be explained.' She said this in the hope it might reassure him as they finished making the coffee together.

Helena switched on the garden lights as they approached, placing the drinks on the table as Alex pulled another photo out of the box.

'This is the one,' he said, and offered the black-and-white picture of a smartly dressed gentleman to James.

'Who is this?'

'I believe this is Jack's father, Johann van Buren?'

'How on earth do you have this?' James said, amazed.

Alex remembered back to the funeral of Jack in 1975. Audrey Sophia had given him the photo, telling him she didn't much care for it. She explained it had been Johann's favourite, but she wanted nothing to do with it. This he thought a strange thing to say but forgot, putting it out of his mind – all those years ago. 'Jack's mother gave this to me. But how did Major Blackthorn connect to Johann?'

Ginny sipped her coffee. 'I'm not sure. When I asked about Florence somehow Johann came into the conversation; with no understanding of what happened, both of us got the distinct impression the major blamed him for something.'

'Do you think this may have been to do with Florence?'

'Could be.'

'Crikey, the plot thickens – so maybe they knew each other!'

Ginny stared at Alex. 'That is just too weird...'

'You're not kidding,' said James, who was still looking at the photo when he flipped it over to see the writing on the back. It wasn't in English.

Without saying a word, Ginny checked it, but at once recognised the handwriting. How could this be? A message written by Florence on a photo of Johann van Buren, held in James's hand – whom she had only just met.

And a family story barely discovered, but she had met the major today, who identified with both Florence and Johann... could this be any stranger? Stupefied and tired, she leant back in her chair as James spoke.

'This message is in Dutch. I'm curious, but we need to translate.' Ginny stifled a yawn and he glanced at his watch. 'Perhaps we can do this tomorrow, as it's getting late.'

Happy to comply, she nodded. 'Been a long day.'

Helena quickly asked if they both wanted to stay the night, but James explained they would stay at his flat. In the morning they would probably do more research and take Ginny back to Hampshire, to Redivivus, to get her car. His flat was only a short distance away.

Ginny turned. 'Are you sure you don't mind me staying this evening?'

He smiled. 'Not at all.'

After waving goodbye to Alex and Helena, they drove off to Twickenham. Ginny decided to check her recently charged mobile, which had been on silent in her handbag. There was a message from her mum waffling on about their holiday and another from a number she did not recognise. On listening to the message, she realised it was from Major Blackthorn asking to meet again in the morning; this was a complete surprise to her, but she was pleased he wanted to meet. However, what he said next alarmed her, as he made it quite clear he did not want to see James.

After all he had done for her... how could she tell him?

FIFTY-THREE

Back at the apartment, James showed Ginny through into the living room. Although it was an older building, he had painted the inside with light colours, and the furnishings were contemporary in style. It was comfortable and tidy, apart from a pile of case notes strewn across the desk in the corner.

'Rather stuffy in here,' he said as he went to open the French doors leading to a narrow balcony with a small table, two chairs and a few plants in pots. The warm evening air drifted into the front room as he ushered Ginny to take a seat, taking the pile of information from her and placing it down on the coffee table. 'Fancy a night cap?'

She nodded, and he left her to get two glasses, some Bailey's and ice. On his return he found her sat out on the balcony enjoying the night air.

He placed the drinks down on the bistro table and nipped back into the living room. Ginny listened as soft jazz flowed out of the room as he then returned to sit opposite her.

'Thank you so much, James, I'm beholden to you for all your kindness.' They clinked glasses and sipped their drinks whilst she thought to herself how lovely all this was.

'Can't help but think what an amazing story all this is

transpiring to be. Intriguing, isn't it?' James said as Ginny totally agreed.

'Certainly the strangest thing I've ever come across. I thought primarily being left a property was a little unusual, but it keeps getting more and more bizarre.'

'Surreal,' said James. 'Even to the extent that old Major Blackthorn is connected with the van Burens, or definitely Johann, but, amazingly, my dad's best mate, Jack, was his son. And this was nothing to do with me; I was only helping you out! All I did was bring down the keys.' He grinned.

'When you say it like that, it sounds so crazy!'

James watched as she laughed and thought her stunning when she smiled – such an ease about her, and he found himself so relaxed in her company, reflecting once more on the familiarisation between them. As he drank, he thought how glad he was that his silly secretary had mixed up the keys; if she hadn't, then Ginny wouldn't be sat with him now.

They took in the fragrant smell of the fading summer's evening whilst she deliberated for a moment and decided she did not want to hide anything from James. 'I received a message on my phone from the major.'

'Oh, really, that was quick – thought he would be in touch but that was sooner than I anticipated.'

'Yes, well, he wants to meet up with me tomorrow morning.'

'Blimey, he isn't hanging around – this is good.' He noticed she looked a little uncertain as she didn't appear so happy. 'Is it good?'

Ginny sat upright and leant nearer to him, clearing her throat. 'Well, it is, but I feel bad.'

'Why?'

'The major stipulated he doesn't want you to visit again. Must only be me.'

James took her hand in his. 'Ginny, don't worry; this is something you need to do.'

'It feels wrong,' she said. 'You have been so kind and helpful; how could he think like this of you?'

'More than likely it's not me he is threatened by, but he is suspicious of the fact I recognised the van Buren name. What you need to do tomorrow is to try and find out why.'

Ginny looked up at James into his soft green eyes. 'You're so right.'

They both relaxed, happy in each other's company, and chatted on about the connections and the day's events, trying to work out a strategy to research more information, but this led to more questions than answers. They still had not found out what happened to Florence, but somehow they believed Major Blackthorn thought Johann van Buren had been involved. They agreed James would drop her off at the major's apartment and keep out of the way. Both were aware they would get more from a meeting between just Ginny and the major.

As it stood, the major did not comprehend the direct connection to James and the van Buren family. If he did, he may not have seen Ginny either. James agreed to go to his office to search for more material for her and later she would catch up with him. With their plan of action complete, they both sat back and finished their drinks, listening to the sultry tones of jazz.

FIFTY-FOUR

Dropped off in front of the major's flat, as arranged, James left Ginny and headed for the office. The housekeeper showed her straight in and this time the major was sat waiting. On her way to take a seat, she noted a gap on the wall where the painting had been only the day before.

'Glad you were able to come back, I appreciate you doing so at such short notice.' The major paused. 'And alone.'

'My pleasure, Major. I'm very grateful to you for seeing me; after all, I have intruded upon you.'

'Nonsense, been a long time coming.' He coughed as he got up to go over to his desk. 'You must have many questions you want to ask of me.'

Ginny thought of all the details spinning around in her head. 'Please understand, I am only just beginning to find out about all of this and didn't hear of Florence until recently.' She sighed as she thought about what she wanted to ask. 'I know so little of her and I am fortunate to meet you. To be honest, I'm wondering what she was like and if you can tell me... what happened to her.'

Blackthorn opened a drawer at his desk and took out a sealed envelope. 'Florence saved my life.' He spoke with regret. 'For this I will be eternally grateful. It makes me sad, sad because I was unable to save her.'

'Why were you unable to?'

'I discovered everything too late.'

'Was it something to do with this Johann van Buren? Did he have something to do with her disappearance?'

The major stared over at Ginny; she could see the disdain in his eyes, and she was sure what his answer would be, when the next words he spoke were a surprise.

'Not entirely. But someone I held in high regard was the main cause of her disappearance. It was to do with my superior, Colonel Godfrey Taverner.'

Ginny frowned as she tried to understand. 'But wasn't he working with you? He sent her out to Amsterdam, didn't he?'

'Yes, and I let him, and for that I will never forgive myself.'

'What do you mean, Major?'

Back in his chair, he poured himself a brandy, as though it was medicinal, and offered one to Ginny, who politely refused.

'As I said to you yesterday, one of the reasons we sent her to Amsterdam was to draw out a double agent – remember, she understood nothing of this. Well, the two-faced traitor was Taverner... How I loathe the thought of him and what he did.'

Ginny stared in amazement trying to understand what he said – she was speechless.

The major then passed her the envelope he held. 'Do not open this now, but keep it for another time.'

She looked at him and nodded in agreement.

'That will tell you how the traitors died. I should have guessed when I first read the case notes on Florence, or rather, her family's background. You have this information in the file I entrusted to you yesterday. Is it safe?'

Ginny nodded; she was starting to realise she was holding the key to the door of a cupboard full of very bony skeletons.

'Something I read,' the major began again, 'when Florence's – your – family landed in England and were taken into military intelligence to be vetted on arrival from Amsterdam during the First World War. There was a report I discovered written by a Colonel Charles Glassbrook.

Ginny stared over at the major. 'What did you just say?'

'Do you recognise the name, Ginny?'

'Yes.'

'Well, your great-great-grandfather was suspicious of an officer who worked with him, that he believed to be a double agent. As your parents had arrived from Amsterdam and had been threatened by a visit from a German officer, Charles wanted them protected. I later discovered, Charles worked in the field, in counter espionage, with Taverner before and during the Great War... but I did not find this out until I was asked to write the colonel's obituary after he died in,' he paused, ' in an accident back in 1940. This confirmed to me the "officer" Charles mentioned must have been Taverner.' After another sip of brandy, he glanced over, trying to empathise with all she was learning – such a shock and he could read this on her face. 'It was Taverner who was keen to send Florence out to Amsterdam and the reason for her to go was real – she was to help the museum prepare to hide its treasures.' Again, he looked at her. 'Even I believed that!'

Ginny was confused. 'What has this to do with Johann if it was Colonel Taverner who betrayed her and his country?'

The major sighed, thinking back. 'I had to go back out to Amsterdam to warn Florence, as I had been told there was a double agent operating out there, but we didn't know who, and that she may be in danger.'

'Can't imagine you would have wanted to have heard this.'

The major smiled at her. 'No, it did not sit well with me, so I followed Florence without her knowing, enabling me to witness who was sniffing around her...'

'Johann?' Ginny guessed.

'Exactly. Wasn't even him who alarmed me to start with, but it became clear he was connected with a far more dangerous person, a Nazi sympathiser... a nasty piece of work called Frederick Obermaier.'

'Oh my God,' exclaimed Ginny. 'This sounds like a nightmare, poor Florence.'

'I'm convinced he was involved in her disappearance, and the last time I saw her...' He stopped for a moment to catch his breath.

'Please take your time, Major.'

'I need to tell you of all this. I'm so sorry to impart all these details, but this story has waited too long... it needs to be told. The last time I saw Florence was the same time she saved my life.'

'How did she do this?'

'She deliberately stepped towards another person defiantly to make Frederick's black shirt officers think she had arranged to meet them at the dock and not me. They believed she was meeting the agent from London. All this happened as I slipped past them and got on the ship, heading for home and safety.' He struggled, overwhelmed with emotion. 'That was how she saved my life... by offering her own, and the guilt of that evening has never left me.'

Ginny began to cry. She got up to go to the window to compose herself. Wiping her eyes, she turned back to the major and moved to kneel down in front of him, suddenly aware that she knew what to say. 'Florence did everything to save you. Please do not be sad or feel guilty about this, because she understood you'd have done the same for her had you been able.' He nodded; tears filled in his eyes. 'Whatever happened to Florence, I tell you, Major, she would not want you to blame yourself.'

With strength and true conviction in her sentiments, Ginny did not want this elderly man to suffer any more, knowing if Florence could speak to him, this is what she would have said.

The major stared at her. 'You are so like her,' he said as she encouraged him to have a little more brandy, then she sat back down in the chair with another question.

'What made you realise Colonel Taverner was the double agent?'

The major took a deep breath and sniffed, then continued. 'On my journey back, I started to put all the pieces together: Every move I made, someone had been two steps ahead of me. When I arrived home, it was imperative I got to headquarters to try to sort all this mess out, but I decided to call the colonel first to explain my thoughts. So, he met me at his club in the Strand.'

For a moment he stopped, and Ginny could see the major thinking on his words.

'I can remember it now so clearly, and the first question he asked I now know was so significant, but initially I missed it. He asked me if I had told anyone else of my suspicions.

Of course, I said no. But it wasn't this that gave him away. Taverner did not realise I had been re-deployed to Amsterdam. Thought I was on a mission in Belgium. Florence had been doing her job at the museum. Unaware I had been following her, somehow, she became involved, inadvertently – because of Johann van Buren – in the movement of artefacts and paintings to a barn just outside of the city. He was part of it and was doing just what Frederick told him to do. Florence got caught in Obermaier's sticky web. This is why I hated van Buren.'

Ginny, sat listening, swiftly became agitated. 'Did Johann put her in danger?'

The major remembered watching Johann from the hedgerow as he drove off, leaving Florence behind. 'I was making my way over when I saw a truck and a car coming up the dirt track, so to avoid them I leapt in the ditch. I viewed Obermaier step out of the car as black shirts surrounded the area. The barn door opened slowly. All I could do was watch as they dragged Florence out, tying her hands behind her, finally pushing her in his car.'

The major stopped for a moment; he felt sick at the thought of it.

'In reply to your question... Yes, it was Johann. I'm sure he was the reason she never came back, as he led that vile creature to her. Guess we will never truly know what happened, but it's clear to me van Buren set her up, making sure he was out the way when they arrived.'

He reached for his brandy and took a sip before glancing at Ginny. 'When I got back to England, on meeting Taverner, he made a fatal mistake which confirmed my suspicions...

he was the double agent. You see, when I relayed all the information to him the night at the club back in 1940, I never revealed where I'd last seen her, only that Obermaier had caught up with her. This was when the colonel turned to me and said, "You were not to know she'd get captured at the barn." As I sat after he had left, suddenly it dawned on me that I hadn't mentioned where she had been captured. Taverner had known; this was the proof I'd needed – it had been him all along.'

Hesitant, he turned to Ginny. 'Who would have believed me? A decorated first-class officer held in the highest esteem, yet he had betrayed me, our country and, what was worse, led Florence to her death… that I couldn't forgive.'

Ginny listened, thinking hard on every word the major told her, but before she could ask anything, he stood up and called for his housekeeper to come in. 'I have something for you.' He signalled to the housekeeper to place the wrapped gift beside Ginny. 'This is for you from Florence.'

Confused she glanced at him.

'After all the mayhem of that evening when Obermaier rushed her away, I had still been in the ditch, watching. So, I went to the barn to check if there were any clues, just something for me to follow, but there was nothing, except for a windmill drawn in the dust on the floor.'

'A windmill?'

'Yes, I must admit I nearly missed it, but it led me to collect this.' He pointed at the gift. 'To this day, I still do not understand why she gave it as a clue, if, indeed, she did. I found nothing. But as it was the last thing I had known her do, it meant something to me. Now I want you to have it.'

Ginny glanced down at the gift beside her, cognisant of what it was as she had briefly sighted it on the wall yesterday.

'Anyway,' he said, 'take it away with you and if you find out anything, you can tell me.'

'Thank you, and if I do, you will be the first to know.' She paused, still shocked with all that had been said. Wanting to know what had happened, she asked another question. 'What happened to Frederick or Johann after the war?'

'Obermaier disappeared. I tried to find him, as he had not been arrested by the British or the Americans – simply no trace of him. I hope he died badly!'

Ginny stared at him astonished at his honesty; he was nothing but true to his convictions. 'What about Johann?'

The major appeared pensive. 'I understood he was still in Amsterdam after the war; somehow he survived through all his treachery! Though I never met him, but I later discovered in the 1950s, he had been killed in a car accident... tragic!'

There was something about the way in which he delivered the details that made Ginny a little suspicious. Most of what he said or did was usually well thought out. 'Tragic indeed. I suppose there was nothing of Florence?'

'I tried to find out what had happened to her, searched through the POW lists and used all my connections, but she had vanished, disappeared. An unwanted KIA was stamped on her file.'

'KIA?'

'Killed in action – it went on too many a record.' Major Blackthorn sighed as though he was now tired of life, remembering all the people who had passed before him. 'Was it worth all those lives?'

Ginny moved over to him and hugged him. 'Everything you have done in your life has been worthwhile; yes, many died, but you also saved many too. Florence would not want you to be sad; you need to let it go now.'

The major gazed at her with a great sense of relief. A huge weight that had sat for far too long on his shoulders was now, at last, lifted. Having been able to tell his side of the events, he merely felt drained and tired. Yawning, he apologised to Ginny, who thought it time to go. He'd given her an insight into a story long since passed but with so much more to find out about. After giving him another hug, empathising with his emotions, she thanked him, picked up the package and left the flat.

FIFTY-FIVE

With her meeting concluded, Ginny made her way to the office in Cavendish Square to meet James. On arriving, she pressed the buzzer and waited for a moment before he appeared, smiling. 'How did you get on?'

'Very well,' she answered, walking into the reception area.

James spotted the parcel she carried. 'What do you have there?'

'The major gave me a painting.'

'A painting!'

'Yes. A long story, but he managed to retrieve this from a barn after Florence left a clue drawn on the ground leading to it.'

'Sounds intriguing; what was she doing in a barn?'

'Oh my, James, so much to tell you. I'm not sure where to begin.'

'Take it you had a good meeting with the major?'

'Yes. He has been waiting to tell his story for such a long time.'

'Did he know what happened to Florence?'

'Not entirely, but he was adamant she saved his life.' She deliberated for a second. 'He also felt quite strongly that

Johann van Buren was involved in her capture and subsequent disappearance.'

'Really!' He said this thinking back to all he had heard of the van Burens. 'Makes you wonder, how could he do such a thing?'

'What do you mean?'

'Well, when you heard how my father spoke of how lovely the van Buren family were and how good a friend Jack had been, seems odd Johann should be considered ruthless, doesn't it?'

'Yes, you are right, but Blackthorn categorically holds him responsible and we still don't know what actually happened to Florence. The major is certainly very remorseful for not bringing her home.'

Ginny turned to James. 'Also, he told me, because of the situation with Florence, and all that occurred, he was able to determine who the double agent was in the War Office.' She paused, leaning towards him. 'You'll never believe this... It was the colonel. The one who had sent her to Amsterdam.'

James gasped in astonishment. 'But how could this be?'

'Taverner was working with the Dutch fascists who in turn worked with the Nazis.' Catching her breath, she tried to relay all the information, hoping not to forget a single detail. 'If that wasn't crazy enough, Blackthorn knew of our Colonel Glassbrook!'

'No way! How?'

'He said my great-great-grandfather suspected Taverner as a double agent from dealings with him in the First World War, and the major found a note in the files belonging to Charles where he had written of his suspicions. He never trusted Taverner after some incident, apparently. Anyway, this is,' she paused, 'unbelievable, isn't it?'

James, motionless, deep in thought, tried to digest all she was telling him. 'This truly is incredible. Have you realised the more we find out, the connection to Charles gets ever closer? Even my grandfather was aware of him. We need to investigate further about him and find out what he was up to... he's everywhere.'

Ginny moved to the sofa, placing the painting to the side of her and peered outside, conscious that the clouds grew heavy as it began to rain. Heaving a sigh, she felt content, just for a moment, to simply sit down, allowing her to put all this new information into place. There was so much to comprehend. A feeling inside of her told her this knowledge awakened something within her.

James could see her trying to make sense of it all and sat beside her. After a moment, he told her what he had been doing. 'When I got here this morning, I decided to search for the translation of the phrase written in Dutch on the back of the photo of Johann.'

'Did you know the handwriting was Florence's hand?' Ginny asked.

'No, I didn't. But this phrase – "*Onze Ineengestrengelde zielen*",' he stared at her, sensing her desire to know, 'translates "Our souls entwined".'

Ginny's green eyes opened wide. 'My goodness.' Not knowing what else to say, she watched James as he again continued.

'The other bit of information I wanted to check up was the house name.'

'My house? Redivivus?' she said, perplexed. 'I never thought of a meaning, just accepted that was its name.'

James looked at her. 'It has a meaning all right; you will be amazed.'

'What does it mean?' she asked with a wary curiosity.

'Reborn – recycle!'

Both sat in stunned silence, trying to absorb everything, wondering what this all meant.

'Are these coincidences?' Ginny questioned.

James shook his head, unsure, when Ginny remembered something else. 'Interesting you mention this. At the house yesterday, I went upstairs whilst you were in the front room. In a room I believed was Florence's, I found a book taped to the underside of the bedside cabinet.'

'Hidden there?' he asked in amazement.

'I believe so. I didn't get time to check it until last night. Written inside was an old Irish tale named *Liadan and Kurithir,* which dates back to the ninth century. I have not had a chance to finish it, but it's about two lovers who fall in love, lose each other but then find one another again. Florence had underlined a piece of text.' From memory she read aloud: '"We have found the way to each other at last, and both of us knowing it!"'

Ginny stopped then, and James sat silent.

After a moment, he turned to her. 'That is so beautiful.' He looked away and repeated the words to himself before asking, 'Why do you think Florence hid this secretly under her bedside cabinet?'

'I have no idea, but she was obviously trying to puzzle something out.'

'Well, it is certainly a puzzle with a lot of pieces.' James looked to the package that Ginny had brought back with her. 'What is the gift you received from the major?'

'I'm already aware what it is,' Ginny said.

'Why don't you open it?'

Ginny began to tear at the paper until proudly displayed was the painting of the windmill.

James viewed it, then looked to the wall behind her. 'Strange – it's the same.'

Ginny twisted around to where he was pointing. 'So this was where I saw it before. Is it a print?'

James glanced down at the picture she held. 'Actually, I thought we had the original. It was donated to us by a client from our partner company in Amsterdam.'

'Oh,' said Ginny.

'Are you thinking what I am thinking?'

Her attention drew back again to the painting from the major, she sensed something about it. James considered it too, staring at it, then at Ginny. In this moment, with all that had come to him, he took a deep breath, knowing. Slowly he got up as if in a trance and walked to the door. 'I need some air.' He pushed it open and turned back to her. 'This is everything to do with the windmill… isn't it? I keep seeing the sails in motion, perpetually turning, going around and around… it's what they do.'

The door closed, almost lingering, behind him. His words circulating in her head, she understood. Ginny sat staring at the windmill when a thought came to her, and she turned the painting over to check the back. It was incredible to think she was now touching something tangible to do with Florence, knowing this meant something to her; it gave her a sensation in the pit of her stomach.

Stroking down the back of the canvas, she felt a rough edge near the bottom of the frame. Reaching for her hair grip, she peeled off the rubberised end and cut a tiny tear, then cautiously poked a finger inside to lightly touch the edge of a small folded piece of paper and gently pulled it out. How on earth anybody managed to get this inside, amazed her. A hint of wax or gum on Ginny's finger suggested someone had deliberately sealed it afterwards. Now, slowly, she unfolded the note and instantly recognised the handwriting as Florence's. The words were faint, but she read them to herself. Ginny was beginning to understand.

'My name is Florence van Hassel.
I have lived before.
My name was Anneke van Buren.
I have loved before.
Today that love is with me again.
He is Johann van Buren.'

With these words resonating in her head, she viewed the painting once again, but this time with more urgency. Her attention was drawn to the sails of the windmill. She thought on what James had said earlier; it wasn't just the action of them. Quite clearly now in her mind she saw a scarf, slow at first, meander and float higher up into the sky, drifting on the breeze.

Shocked, knowing, she jumped up, placing the painting on the chair. With the opened note, she rushed out of the office.

It had begun to rain harder now and standing on the top step she looked as James turned to her. They both stepped towards each other.

Gently, he reached forward and placed his hand behind her neck, drawing her softly towards him, dropping the other hand to her waist, his face brushing against hers as the rain splashed off them. Intent on finding her lips, sensing the fullness of them as they merely touched, the anticipation tingled inside of him, and he could wait no longer. His grip tightened tenderly on her neck; he embraced her touch and kissed her passionately. They were oblivious to the weather as he pulled her closer, their bodies pressed together. To both of them, the kiss felt so familiar and one that had taken their life story back centuries. Releasing his hold, his heart raced as he waited for her to open her eyes, staring into them, knowing for certain this explained all he sensed. With his finger touching her lips, he kissed her tenderly once more.

The rain continued to fall; Ginny sat down on the step and James followed. They never spoke a word to each other... they didn't have to. He stroked the wet hair from her eyes; holding her small hand in his, he raised it to his mouth and kissed it as he placed his arm around her. Then, his hand upon her forehead, he drew her head to his shoulder; the emotions overtaking her, she wept. But these were not tears of sadness which trickled down her face; they were of complete happiness. They sat still as the rain washed down over them, as though in this moment it cleansed them of all that had happened in their pasts, over centuries and through time.

Florence looked at Johann as Ginny looked at James. They realised this was just the beginning; there were more questions than answers, and fate had reunited them for a reason, although what this reason was... they still had to find out!

CONNECTIONS III

Stood looking into the darkness, he rubbed his arms, as it was icy cold this evening. The droveway before him was dark and muddy, when suddenly he thought he heard movement to the right of him. He turned to check, raising his hand to stop the approaching searchers, who lit the track abstractly with their torches. Without saying a word, he signalled to his men to search near the ditch. They moved slowly. The darkness he stood in only a moment ago gradually filled with light. From further up the droveway, something moved. He scanned intently, when he thought he could make out a silhouette of someone. At this moment there came a soul-terrifying shriek, which pulsed through their cold, shivering bones. All stopped momentarily. He remained still as his men now rushed forward past him to where the noise emanated from, their torches quickly gathering around a figure slowly emerging from the darkness. Nonchalantly, he strolled up the track towards them, and they all moved aside to allow him to view the solitary person before him. He stepped forward, smiling irreverently, aware how cold and muddy she looked, struggling to see through the lucent blinding lights, refusing to move – she stood defiant.

'Maertha,' the low timbre of his voice was calm yet sardonic as he spoke, 'where have you been?'

In the darkness of his room, he sat upright in in his bed, aware of his disturbing dream. The same damn recurring dream. He wiped the sweat from his forehead and grappled for his glass of water, hoping it would quench his thirst. *This damned place*, he thought to himself as he got up to go open the glass doors and stepped onto a small balcony, where the stifling night air hit him. It was as hot a night as it was in the daytime. Blasted place was always so hot. He drew on a cigarette and reflected on the dream which woke him. It had been so vivid, as though he stood there – he could even smell the mud and feel the coldness of the evening – something he couldn't say about this wretched place. Once more, inhaling deeply, he thought about the name. Why did it seem familiar to him and how could this be… who was Maertha?

A loud knock at the door disturbed his thoughts as he heard his adjutant calling for him. 'Captain Glassbrook… Captain Glassbrook?'

'Yes, what is it, Walsh?'

'Captain Glassbrook, you have been requested to go to headquarters immediately; there is new intelligence they need you to look at.'

'Tell them I will be right there.'

'Yes, sir.' Walsh went on his way.

Charlie finished his cigarette, staring out into the night-time starry sky, relatively un-phased by the message the adjutant had delivered.

Matador